INTO THE REALM OF ECSTASY

Tess knew getting any closer to Revan was simply asking for trouble and heartbreak. None of that mattered. It might be only passion on his part, but instinct told her she would find none to equal it. She would worry later and follow her heart now.

Sitting on his lap, Tess rubbed her bottom against him. He grasped her by her slim hips to halt her tormenting movements. Her breathing was as erratic as his, her passion was running as hot and mindless as his.

"Tess," he murmured, "I want to touch you. I want to taste every soft sweet inch of you. I want to bury myself deep inside you." Cupping the back of her head in his hands and burying his fingers deep in her soft hair, he held her mouth against his. When he moved, pressing her down onto the bedding so that she was sprawled on her back beneath him, she offered no resistance. . . .

HIGHLAND HEARTS

SANDRA DUSTIN

DIAMOND BOOKS, NEW YORK

HIGHLAND HEARTS

A Diamond Book / published by arrangement with
the author

PRINTING HISTORY
Diamond edition / June 1992

ISBN: 1-55773-719-3

Diamond Books are published by The Berkley Publishing Group,
200 Madison Avenue, New York, New York 10016.
The name ''DIAMOND'' and its logo are trademarks
belonging to Charter Communications, Inc.

PRINTED IN THE UNITED STATES OF AMERICA

10 9 8 7 6 5 4 3 2 1

Chapter

◆ 1 ◆

Scotland, 1455

"COME TO GLOAT, HAVE YE?"

"I beg your pardon?" Tess asked, surprised. It took a moment for her to still the alarmed beating of her heart. The man's deep rich voice had scared her half to death. She had passed through her uncle's dungeons earlier and it had been empty. Cautiously, she edged closer to the cell, thrusting her candle forward to shed some light into the shadowy recesses of the prison.

She gasped. Chained spread-eagle to the wall was the most beautiful man she had ever seen. Even his bruises, blood, and dirt did not dim his handsomeness. Then she frowned. There was something familiar about the blond giant there, glaring back at her.

"When did you get here?" she asked.

Revan frowned. The piquant little face pressed to the bars was not the face he had expected to see. Neither were the big dark eyes, wide with surprise. He wondered if Fergus Thurkettle was playing some kind of game. For the moment he would play along. "Oh, I just strolled by near to two hours ago."

"And decided to nap amongst the iron chains, hmmm?"

1

"'Tis cleaner than that bed o'er there."

Glancing at the rat-gnawed cot in the corner, she silently agreed. What was her uncle up to now? Uncle Fergus, she mused, carried his pretensions to being lord and master of all he surveyed a little too far. It was no longer just a slight eccentricity; it had become an obsession and it was chilling.

"Ye would not say so if ye kenned what was hanging there just last week," she said lightly.

"Aye? Who was it?"

"Oh, some skinny man who hadna discovered the benefit of a wee bit of soap and water."

"What happened to him?"

"There is a funny thing. I dinna ken." She had some dark theories but decided to keep them to herself. "I saw him here, weeping like a bairn. From what little I could learn he hadna committed a crime. I decided I would let him out, but I had to get the keys. By the time I got back—he was gone."

"So swiftly?"

"W-well, it wasna quite so swiftly. It took two days. I couldna just take the keys, for that would be noticed. So I talked to Iain, the blacksmith. He wasna easy to persuade, but I finally got him to make me a set. By the time I got the keys, the wee man was gone."

"Where do ye think he went?"

"I dinna ken. Dinna ken why he was here or why he suddenly wasna here. And, now, just why are ye here?"

"Ah, it seems I tried to reach beyond my station."

She noticed the bitterness tainting his fine voice, but she did not really understand what he was referring to. Her uncle, while an unreasonable man, had never locked someone up before. Then Tess slowly grasped the thread of an idea, one she did not like much at all.

"Oh, were ye sniffing round Brenda, then?"

"Sniffing round? I was courting her." More or less, he mused but was not about to confess to this chit. Hand in hand with cuddling up to the voluptuous Brenda Thurkettle had been his spying.

"And that is why ye are hanging up in there?" There were a few times when she had contemplated similar punishments for the men who had courted Brenda.

"Aye." He felt only a small twinge of guilt over that half-truth, then wondered why he even felt that. Some madman had chained him to a wall, and now some curious girl was watching him. There was little doubt in his mind that Thurkettle meant to murder him. He should feel no guilt at all over lying through his teeth if it got him out of this mess. Yet, something about those huge dark eyes made him feel guilty. He told himself not to be such a fool.

"Well, that is a sad and foolish reason to hang a man up like a gutted deer," Tess said, deciding her uncle had finally lost what tenuous grip he might have had on sanity. "He shouldna shackle a man for having the poor taste and judgment to pursue a woman like Brenda," she murmured, reaching into a pocket in her doublet to fiddle with her keys.

Revan almost laughed. Brenda Thurkettle was blue-eyed, auburn haired, and had a form to make any man alive ache with lust. No one would accuse a man of poor taste for pursuing a woman like that. Except, he mused with an inner chuckle, another woman. Or, he thought an instant later, someone who knew the person beneath the beauty. Revan began to wonder about the woman he was talking to.

"Are ye meaning to free me?"

"Well . . . are ye sure 'tis *all* ye did? Court the regal Brenda?"

"'Tis all and naught more. Did ye expect some heinous crime like robbery or murder or something?"

She shrugged, slowly tugging her keys out of her pocket. "It can grow rather tedious hereabouts."

His gaze fixed upon the keys. "Ye live here?"

It did not really surprise her that he did not know her, but she was growing weary of being consistently unnoticed. "Aye, I am Tess, the niece. I have lived here nearly five years." She stared at him, contemplating. "I remember you now. I saw ye strolling about with our Mistress Brenda, taking her for a wee ride upon those matched horses. Verra nice. Was that a new doublet?''

"Aye, it was. Well?" He gently shook the chains attached to his wrists and ankles.

"Dinna rush me, I am thinking." She rubbed her chin with one hand. "Ye are the manservant to that fat laird, Angus MacLairn. Aye, that wouldna please Uncle. Howbeit, if ye *owned* MacLairn's keep—"

"Are ye intending to let me out of here or not?"

"Oh, dinna fash yourself." She set her candle down and unlocked the cell door. "Here now." She brought her candle into the cell and set it down on a small wobbly table by the cot. "Ye werena caught *in flagrante delicto* with Her Highness Brenda or the like, were ye?" She was not sure she ought to free a man awaiting a forced wedding even if Brenda cast her favors to nearly every man for miles about.

"In what?"

"Ye ken what I mean—mucking about, tussling, rolling in the heather. I dinna care to set myself into the midst of that sort of trouble."

"'Tis nothing like that, I swear it. Why would ye even think that?" He had the sinking feeling he had been thoroughly fooled by Brenda, had missed a perfect opportunity.

"Well, the thrice-cursed fool is certain to be caught soon. Ye canna do something as often as she does that and not get caught. Do ye want your legs freed first or your arms?"

"My legs," he grumbled, then scowled as she knelt by his feet to unlock the shackles. "Ye are dressed like a lad."

"My, ye do have a keen eye, Sir Halyard," she murmured as she freed his legs, then stood up to unlock the shackles at his wrists. "Hell's fire, wrong key." She moved back to the light to clearly study them.

"Here, hold but a moment. How the devil did ye get in here? I just realized I didna hear ye come down the stairs. Ye were just there."

"Well, there is a secret way out. Uncle had it made to allow the family to slip away if the need arose. Aha! Here is the key." She returned to unlock the manacles at his wrists.

Once free, Revan slowly sat down, rubbing his wrists to start the blood flowing again. As he did he covertly studied his rescuer. She was a tiny little thing, and the somewhat ill-fitted doublet and hose accentuated her slenderness. At a glance he would guess her to be very young, but something about her husky voice told him that guess would be wrong.

"They hung my sword, hat, and cape over there upon the wall."

Even as Tess went to fetch his things, she asked, "Ye always wear your sword when ye go courting?"

"I was planning to take Brenda riding. I thought I might need it." He grabbed his boots from where they had been set by the damp stone wall and yanked them on.

She held his things out to him, watching as he slowly stood up. He was big: tall, broad-shouldered, and lean. The perfect male. Inwardly she sighed. He was every lass's ideal lover but definitely a man only the Brendas of the world could hope to win. As she watched him buckle on his sword, fixing the leather belt around his slim hips, she wondered why Brenda had not defended him to her father. This one had to be the best of her crowd of admirers. By far.

She considered asking what he had done to get on the wrong side of her uncle, then she stopped in horror. Someone was coming. She heard a door creak open and saw a glowing light on the stairs that led to the dungeon. Someone was coming to see the prisoner she had just released. She turned to warn Revan only to be grabbed by him, his sinewy arm wrapped around her upper body. Since the cold steel of his dirk was pressed against her throat, she made no attempt to fight as he dragged her out of the cell.

"Where is the way out?" he hissed in her ear as they edged away from the approaching men.

"Keep backing up," she whispered fiercely. "Ye will

come to the wall. What looks to be a large rack of shelves is, in truth, a door.''

"How do I open it?"

"A loop of rope hangs down on the left side. Ye pull it open.'' She tensed as much from the cold blade as from her uncle and his two closest men-at-arms, Thomas and Donald, as they reached the bottom of the stairs, turned, and saw them.

"God's beard, what goes on here?'' Fergus Thurkettle bellowed even as he drew his sword and pointed it at Revan.

"Ye best not try anything, Thurkettle,'' Revan warned in an icy voice, "or I will cut your niece's throat from ear to ear.''

"Your method of showing gratitude could use a wee bit of refinement,'' Tess murmured, wondering how she could have so misjudged the man now dragging her toward her uncle's private escape route.

"Curse you, Tess, how did the man get free?''

"Well, now, Uncle, 'tis a question worth pondering,'' she managed to reply.

"Ye stupid bitch, ye set him free. Didna ye ken he is a murderer? He murdered Leith MacNeill.''

"Who?''

Revan cursed as he realized Thurkettle had not only planned his death but a way to blame him for a cold-blooded murder as well. "That wee man who didna like soap,'' he hissed in Tess's ear. "Ye will have to find another fool to blame that on, Thurkettle,'' Revan said as he reached the door, "because this fool is leaving.'' They were both pressed up against the wall. "Pull the door open,'' he ordered Tess.

It was hard to move since his grip had all but pinned her arms to her sides. Grabbing the small loop of rope in her hand, she tugged several times before she opened the heavy door enough for them to slip into the small stairway behind it. She could see her uncle and his men edging after them. She grabbed the large iron handle on the back of the door.

Without waiting for his order, she yanked it shut after she and Revan were inside. Then she shot the heavy bolt to lock it. A sudden thumping told her her uncle and his men took at least a brief chance at following them.

"Where does this come out?" Revan demanded as he hefted her up slightly so that her feet were off of the ground and made his way cautiously along the dark, slowly rising passage.

"In the stables. What looks to be a large rack for hanging bits and tools upon is a door. Ye willna be able to saddle your mount and ride out of here dragging me about like this."

"Ye would be surprised."

"They will be waiting for you."

"Of that I have no doubt."

"This is the last time I will do anyone a favor."

"Shut your mouth."

Since she could not think of a reply that could prevent him from using her as a shield, Tess decided to obey his curt order.

Revan cursed as he tried to hurry without losing his footing. He was the lowest of scoundrels. There were times, he mused, when being on the right side did not feel all that right. Just before Thurkettle had appeared, he had nearly talked himself out of taking the girl to pry information out of her. Thurkettle had turned that decision around. Although Revan hated hiding behind the girl, she was his only means of escape from Thurkettle's keep.

When they finally reached the door he ordered her to unbolt it, then kicked it open. At first the sudden light blinded him. Squinting tightly, then slowly opening his eyes, he looked out. He smiled grimly when he saw Thurkettle waiting, five armed men now flanking him. He edged into the stable, moving away from the open door.

"Toss aside your weapons." He smiled coldly when they hesitated. "Dinna push me, Thurkettle. I have naught to lose in this venture." Slowly the men tossed aside their weapons. "Now, ye"—he nodded toward a lanky, gray-haired stable hand—"saddle my horse and dinna forget all my belongings—including my bow and shield." He waited tensely as the man obeyed.

"Ye willna get away with this," Thurkettle hissed.

"I'm not doing too badly thus far."

"We wiil hunt ye down."

"Will ye now? Dinna nip too close at my heels. I will have this fair niece of yours."

"You canna hold the lass forever."

"Long enough." Seeing that his horse was ready, Revan signaled the man, with a jerk of his head, to return to his companions. "Now, get in there." He nodded toward the tunnel he had just exited. Hissing curses, Thurkettle led his men inside. Revan kicked the door shut, then pushed Tess toward it. "Bolt it."

Doing as he said, she told him, "If ye move swiftly, ye ought to be clear of the walls ere they can get out."

"Not clear enough." He grasped her by the arm and pushed her toward his horse. "Mount."

"Ye are taking me with you?"

"Mount."

She mounted. There had to be a dozen ways she could break free, but not one came to mind. He swung up in front of her, reaching back and grabbing her wrists firmly. He then quickly tied them so that she was bound to him. When he spurred his horse to a gallop, she hung on, praying the fool did not kill them by riding like some madman in the dark.

Charging out the door of his keep, Fergus Thurkettle saw his prisoner riding off. "Cut that bastard down," he ordered his archers.

"But, sir," protested Thomas, "we could kill your niece."

Fergus cursed viciously, then abruptly halted. "What day is this?"

"What?" Thomas asked in total confusion.

"What day is this?"

"Tuesday, the fifteenth day of March."

"Aye, so it is, and yesterday was her birth day, her eighteenth birthday," Thurkettle murmured. Suddenly he was smiling.

"What are ye muttering about?"

Ignoring Thomas, Thurkettle stood watching the pair ride away as he hastily mulled his choices. Tess was eighteen. The fortune he had held in trust now belonged to her. If she died, he was the only heir. For five long years he had longed for that fortune. Now he began to see a way, a way to kill two birds with one stone.

"Go after him," he ordered his men.

"But, sir," Thomas asked, "what about Tess?"

"Dinna fret over her. Look, that craven dog kens too much about my business with the Black Douglases. Soon Tess will too. So that makes her dangerous, no? Now—ride."

Once his men had raced off, Thurkettle strolled back into his keep, whistling a merry tune. He went inside, poured himself a tankard of fine French wine from a richly carved silver jug, then silently toasted himself.

"I suppose there is little chance of Sir Revan being brought back alive," a voice said behind him.

Glancing over his shoulder, Thurkettle frowned at his daughter as she moved to sit at the table. "Very little."

"Ah, what a shame." Brenda studied the jeweled rings on her fingers with an air of boredom.

"Nay, a necessity. I canna risk allowing him to reach the king and tell what he has learned just so ye can get your claws into him. Ye should have played your virtuous game a little less ardently."

"I did that for you, so ye could find out if your suspicions were correct. I have seen little sign of gratitude."

"Ye *willna* see any. Ye were protecting yourself as well. If the man is dragged back here and is still breathing, I will let ye have him for a few hours ere I kill him."

"How kind." Brenda frowned. "Ye had best be very careful of how ye handle this in front of Tess. She isna quite as dumb as she looks."

"There is no need to fret over Tess." Thurkettle curled his thin, bloodless lips into a faint smile.

"Nay? She is the one who set the man free, is she not?"

"Aye, the stupid bitch. She also showed him how to escape. He now uses her to try and protect himself. Well, he will soon discover that willna work."

Very slowly, Brenda's eyes widened as she realized what her father was saying. "Ye mean to murder Tess."

Scowling at his daughter, Thurkettle snapped, "Aye, what of it? Dinna tell me ye will miss her."

"Most of the time I barely notice her. 'Tis not me ye will have to explain it to but that horde of kinsmen Aunt was mad enough to wed into."

Fergus Thurkettle shuddered as he recalled his sister's marriage. "I willna have to explain a thing. 'Twill be a sad case of kidnapping and murder."

"Which we swiftly avenged."

"Exactly."

"Isna killing her a wee bit harsh? 'Tis true, she released Revan but—"

"Ye *can* think beyond what gown to wear, can ye not? She has to ken something about our activities. That bastard will soon get it out of her. Together they can hang us all. Aye, and hanging would be the most merciful death we could pray for."

"Oh—aye, I suppose she would have *had* to have noticed something in the five years she has been here."

"Just so. There is more to it than that, however. She was eighteen yesterday. Her fortune and land are now all hers."

"Fortune? Land? Tess has money?"

"Aye, Tess has money. Half the gowns ye wear were bought with her money. I had the expense of rearing her and all," he murmured. "I was allowed to extract funds for all that. For five long years I have tried to think of a way to get that money yet not bring the Comyns or Delgados clamoring at my gates. I have it now. She gave it to me herself."

"Are ye saying ye get all that is hers if she dies?"

"Every last ha'penny. Aye, and there is a cursed large pile of them."

"Just how big a purse? Are ye sure 'tis worth the risk?"

"Does thirty thousand gold riders appeal to you as worth a wee gamble?" He nodded when she simply gaped at him. "There is also a fine, rich keep south of Edinburgh, as well as some land in Spain. The girl is wealthy. Very, very wealthy."

"I canna believe it. Where would that . . . that mincing portrait painter, Delgado, get that kind of money? Or the Comyns?"

"Most of it comes from neither. 'Twas my sister's. Our father wished to be sure she had something to live on when she came to her senses and left that mongrel she married. It grew over the years."

"So neither the Comyns nor the Delgados can lay claim to it?"

"Nay. 'Twas Eileen's, thus Tess's."

"Are ye sure, 'tis a perfect plan? Very, very sure? Near half those Delgados and Comyns are in the military or the service of the king. Aye, and the law or the church. We certainly dinna wish them to look too closely."

"She was kidnapped and murdered. What can there be to question?"

Brenda still frowned. "I will hold my celebrating until ye have the money in your hands and none of that mongrel, lowborn family of hers clamoring at your gates."

She watched her father shrug, and she silently called him a fool. The man was celebrating before the deed was done, and Brenda considered that the height of folly. Sir Revan Halyard was a clever man, and little Tess was not without some wit. The pair of them could prove far more difficult to catch than her father anticipated. It might be a good time to supplement her private funds, she mused. If her father stumbled and fell, she did not intend to join him.

"Ye worry too much, Brenda."

"Aye? I think ye shouldna be quite so free of concern. I will keep mine, thank ye very much, until I see Sir Revan Halyard and Tess buried."

"Then ye had best see to the airing of your mourning gown, dearling, for ye will soon be standing over their graves."

Chapter

◈ 2 ◈

TESS GROANED AS REVAN PULLED HER OUT OF the saddle. She did not even want to think about how long she had been on the back of that horse. For hours they had ridden in a tortuous, circuitous route in order to shake off their pursuers. There did not seem to be a part of her that did not ache.

Revan roughly pulled her toward him and neatly tied her hands to the pommel of his saddle. She cursed him viciously under her breath. He was cruel and inhumane. The rope was so short she had to stand on tiptoe, pressed close to the sweaty horse. At the very first opportunity she was going to stick her dirk into the man. A stomach wound, agonizing, slow to heal but not fatal, she mused with a viciousness born of her discomfort and fear.

"Your language could do with some refinement," Revan murmured as he moved to push aside a large rock from the low banking.

"Aye? Well, your ideas on how to treat someone who helped you could use some improvement."

"Sorry, lass, but if I hadna used you to get out of there, I would have been dead ere I'd gone two feet."

"Well, then, I am even more sorry I wandered by." She

13

watched him drag some brush aside. "Curse ye to hell and back, what *are* ye doing?"

"Readying a place to hide."

"Oh, ye mean we aren't going to gallop through the moonless night like some cloaked reiver any longer? I am devastated."

"My, ye are a bitter-tongued wee thing." He glanced up at the quarter moon, then at her. "And 'tis not a moonless night. There's enough light to see what I was doing."

"Ah"—she glanced up at the sky—"of course. That moon. Its radiance was such that I was blinded to its presence."

It was certainly hard for her to see what he was doing, she thought crossly. The horse badly obscured her view. But she could hear Revan shifting a great deal of rock and bracken. Every time she tried to nudge the horse a little in an attempt to move the beast around, the animal nudged her right back. His horse was as ill-begotten as he was, she thought angrily.

"Come along, then," Revan murmured as he untied her from the horse, and rebound her wrists.

"Where?" She tried to resist his tug on her bound wrists. It looked as if he was dragging her and his stubborn horse straight toward the wall of rock that banked the hills. Then she espied the fault in the shadows, the hint that the wall was not as flat as she had thought. When he pushed her in front of him, she saw the opening.

"A cave," she drawled, as she stumbled inside. "How suitable."

Urging his horse into the roomy cave, Revan ignored her remarks. He grabbed the end of the rope that was around her wrists and looped it back around the pommel of his saddle. While he readied a campsite for them, he did not want to risk her fleeing. He couldn't risk her drawing Thurkettle's men to his hiding place. After what they had been through, he doubted she would want to see those men, either, although he dared not trust in that.

Once he had prepared the campsite, he untied her again,

instructing her to sit in the back of the cave. Keeping a close eye on her, he then quickly covered the opening as best he could from the inside.

Tess walked over to the campsite and wearily sat down on the bedding he had spread out. She knew she ought to try to flee into the waning night, but at the moment she was simply too tired, and he was too on-guard. Also, she wasn't fond of being out alone in the dark.

She had some difficulty believing the tangle she had gotten herself involved in. Much of it made no sense. She glared at Revan as he crouched by the fire and began to make some porridge.

"Ye murdered someone, didna ye?" Even as she accused him, she could not believe him guilty of such a crime.

"Nay. I didna even draw my sword ere I was seized by Thurkettle."

"Then ye stole something."

"Nay. Not a farthing."

"Now, see here, ye had to have done something more than gawk at Brenda—"

"I did *not* gawk."

She ignored his remark. "My uncle isna one to act like this for something as trivial or common as courting. Curse it, if he tried to kill every man who trotted after his daughter, there would be corpses piled knee-high all over Scotland."

"Do I detect a note of jealousy?"

"Nay, ye do not. Are ye prepared to answer my questions or not?"

"I have answered them." He looked at her, studying her closely. "Now ye can answer a few questions of mine."

"Oh, I can, can I?"

"Are ye truly Thurkettle's niece? I dinna see much of a resemblance." He snatched the battered hat she wore off of her head, then half-wished he had let it be. That action had loosened what few hairpins she had used to keep her hair up. A thick glossy mass of wavy, raven-colored hair tumbled past her shoulders almost to her waist. The way the light of the fire touched it only increased its beauty. He now understood how the floppy, wide-crowned hat had stayed on her head during their wild ride. The thick hair filling the crown had held it in place.

"If ye kenned the family well, ye would see one or two similar traits," she said scornfully. "Will ye free my hands now?" She held her bound wrists out toward him.

He gently pushed them back into her lap. "I will think about it. What is your name—Tess Thurkettle?"

"Contessa Comyn Delgado." She found some satisfaction—but no surprise—at his stunned look. Her full name surprised everyone.

"Ye are Spanish?" he mumbled when he collected himself. "I didna think Thurkettle had such a connection."

"He doesna. My father did. Thurkettle's my mother's brother. When my parents died, I was sent to live with him." She inwardly grimaced, thinking of how she had gone from the wrenching tragedy of losing her parents to the continuous tragedy of living with uncaring relatives. "My father's mother was a Scot, a Comyn, and his father was Spanish. My father wasna considered good enough for a Thurkettle, as he was only a painter at the royal court."

Revan had little doubt that Tess spoke the truth. Thurkettle was well known for his pretensions. He had discovered some tenuous connection to Robert the Bruce and often boasted about the fragile bond. If the senior Thurkettle had held even half the self-importance the younger did, it must have required a lot of courage for Tess's mother to wed Delgado. Life could not have been too pleasant for Tess, either, since she was a walking reminder of her mother's choice of husband. The Thurkettles would certainly have had other more profitable arrangements in mind.

"But," he spoke his thoughts aloud, "that doesna seem cause enough to kill you."

"*Kill me?*" she said, astonished. "No one was trying to *kill* me. They were after you."

"And you. They were firing arrows thick and fast, not to miss."

She did not want to talk about it. Until now she had managed to push aside her own suspicions. Although Revan had taken her as a shield, not one of her uncle's men had taken any care not to hurt her. Deny it as she would, the truth in all its chilling ugliness refused to go away. They *had* been aiming for her with as much intensity as they had been aiming for Revan. It was the final rejection of her mother's family.

Yet, to kill her? That was so drastic. Her uncle had had five years to do it. *And he had tried,* a voice whispered in her mind. He had tried three times.

Furiously she tried to shake away the insidious suspicion, but it refused to be ignored. The fact that three specific incidents came immediately to mind told her she had never fully believed them accidents; she had fooled herself into turning away from the clues.

"Ye are wrong," she snapped, turning her hurt into anger against him.

Smiling wryly, Revan shook his head. At first he had thought Thurkettle's men were merely stupid. They were indeed stupid; however, they would never do anything without exact instructions from Thurkettle. If they were shooting to kill with no thought to Tess's safety, it was because Thurkettle had ordered it. What he needed to know was—why?

And she knew, he thought as he poured them each a cup of wine. He could read the knowledge in her wide, beautiful eyes. He could also read her struggle to deny it. It gave her a touch of innocence he decided was wise to ignore. He did not want to assume she was not part of Thurkettle's treasonous plots and intrigues. Not yet. Trusting her too quickly could get him killed.

"Nay, I am *not* wrong, and ye ken it," he said, "I can see it in your eyes."

She gave him a contemptuous look as she accepted the

cup of wine he held out. "Read it in my eyes? How foolish. They are eyes, not a letter."

"Your eyes are as readable as any letter, the script clear and precise. Ye are trying to deny what ye ken is the truth."

"Of course I deny it. 'Tis a heinous accusation. Why would my uncle wish me dead?"

"I was hoping ye could tell me."

"Well, I canna for he doesna." She sipped the wine, annoyed to find it tasted good.

"I canna believe 'tis because he disapproves of your bloodline," he murmured, watching her closely.

"Disapproval can be easily accomplished through ignoring me. He doesna have to bloody his hands to disassociate himself from me. Ye have been trotting after Brenda for a while, and ye didna ken I was about, did ye?"

"Nay. Ye came as quite a surprise."

"Aha! So, he didna have to commit murder to cut me off from the family."

"True. So, what is the next possibility? Murder can have many motives. Jealousy? Nay. Unless there is some lover's triangle I am unaware of."

"Dinna be such an idiot."

"Nay, in truth, I think love doesna enter into this family quandary at all."

The truth of that hurt, but she tried to hide it behind a look of disgusted annoyance.

Revan saw the brief flash of pain in her look and felt a twinge of sympathy. He had kept a close eye on the Thurkettles for weeks, yet had never known about Tess. She had been thoroughly ignored by her own kin, tucked out of sight like a shameful secret. The time she had spent with her uncle could not have been pleasant. He quelled his sympathy, however. He was still not sure he could trust her, still did not know if she was an intricate part of her uncle's intrigues.

"Money, then. Greed. Do ye have some money?"

Considering her rough, unsuitable attire, he doubted it but then saw a look of realization widen her beautiful eyes.

Money, Tess thought, and shock rippled through her. It was the one thing her uncle loved more than himself. And she had some—a great deal by most people's standards—now that she had turned eighteen. The painful fact that her birthday had passed unnoticed again faded into insignificance. Her lands and money were all hers now. Her uncle was supposed to relinquish all control to her. The doubts she had struggled to hold on to faded. For wealth her uncle would most certainly try to kill her.

Those "accidents" had been attempts to remove the only heir that stood between her uncle and her fortune—herself. He wanted her dead and had wanted it for years. What he had needed was a way to point the finger of suspicion away from himself. An even-tempered mount suddenly gone wild and a fall that could have broken her neck was one way. A simple errand that sent her trotting back and forth over a flood-weakened bridge was another. Then there was that loosened masonry that chose to fall just as she stood beneath it.

And now, she thought as she looked at Revan, there was a kidnapper.

It was perfect. She had been abducted and, it could be claimed, murdered by her abductor. Even if it was guessed that she had died in the heavy pursuit by Thurkettle's men, her uncle would look innocent. What choice had he?

"Well?" Revan pressed after letting her think it over for a moment. He was rather bemused by how clearly her changing thoughts reflected in her heart-shaped face. "Ye do have some wealth?"

"A bit." She was not sure why, but she was reluctant to tell him just how much she was worth.

"Now, lass, Thurkettle wouldna trouble himself this much for only 'a bit.'"

"A few thousand gold riders, a wee bit of land." To

some people thirty could be a few, she told herself, defending her lie.

"Well, 'tisna as much as I had expected but enough to rouse Thurkettle's greed."

He sensed she had not told him the whole truth but decided not to press. The exact amount did not really matter as long as she accepted the truth. Although still not sure he could fully trust her, he did think she would now be less likely to try and run off. He took out his knife and neatly cut the bonds at her wrists, then resheathed his knife.

"I am free?" She eyed him with mistrust, wondering if he planned some trick.

"I think ye will gain little by running away."

"Aye, I believe ye may be right." She stared at her wrists as she gently rubbed them to ease the slight chafing of her bonds. "I seem to have an excess of people trying to end my life." She glanced at him. "I assume I had best not exclude you just yet."

"Ye assume correctly."

"Isna it a wee bit stupid to threaten me now that I am free?"

Shrugging, he tested the porridge. It was ready to eat. "I dinna gain a thing by killing you." He spooned some of the hearty if plain fare into a wooden bowl, then handed it to her, tossing a spoon on top. "Ye do exactly as I say, and ye will be fine. Thurkettle willna give ye the same chance."

Reluctantly admitting to herself that he was right, she tested the food. It was not her favorite fare, but as hungry as she was, it tasted good. However, she silently prayed that if they were going to hide out together for a while, there would be some variety in their menu. If she had to suffer porridge on a day-by-day basis, she was sure she would soon decide her murderous uncle was not so bad after all.

Her life, she mused as she ate, had gone from bad to wretched in the blink of an eye. The only hope of improvement she had was to reach her father's family. They would take care of Uncle Thurkettle. And—she glared at Revan—

the kidnapping Sir Halyard as well. The problem was, they were many days' ride away, and there was only Revan's mount. Worse, she was not certain she could find her way to them unaided. The Comyns were not renowned travelers. It was said that her uncle Silvio Comyn could get lost climbing out of bed. It was an exaggeration, of course, but the truth was, she and her relatives did have a tendency to go the wrong way.

She had only one real choice. Somehow she had to convince Revan that it was in his best interest to take her to them. Inwardly she sighed. Moses probably had an easier time parting the Red Sea. Revan had kidnapped her and threatened to cut her throat. He would not be eager to meet her kinsmen after that. Still, she decided it never hurt to try. She certainly could not get into any worse trouble.

"Ye can cease all that plotting," Revan murmured as he took her empty bowl.

Startled from her thoughts, she frowned at him. "And who says I am plotting anything?"

"That sly look that came over your face." He casually sipped at his wine.

"Sly look?" she muttered as she helped herself to another drink of his wine.

"Now that ye are comfortable—"

"As cozy as a rat in the meal."

"We shall talk about your uncle."

"What now? I should think we ken all we need to. He wants us dead. Now we ken why he is trying to put me to rest in the cold clay, and I dinna believe ye have yet explained why he wants to kill you. Shall we discuss *that*?"

"I ken a few truths about him he would like to keep secret."

"Those could fill a book."

"Aye? Such as what?"

"Well, there are a few wives who must pray nightly that he keeps a discreet tongue in his head. He flaunts that weak drop of royal Bruce blood, and the fools believe it. They think it makes him special." She shook her head in disgust. "That wasna the sort of secret I was thinking of."

"Nay? Well, mayhaps ye should tell me exactly what ye are interested in. Ye tell me what ye think ye have, and I will tell you if I ken aught that will confirm or deny it."

"Will you?" He watched her closely as he added another stick to the fire. "Why should I believe that? Ye would be betraying kinsmen."

"True. Most of the time ye would have to torture me to madness to make me do such a thing. But this collection of kinsmen is determined to murder me. I believe that cuts all bonds. Only a fool offers blind loyalty to a man who wants to kill her."

"And ye are no fool."

"Not all the time. So, what do ye think ye ken that could make Uncle so determined to put you in the ground?"

Revan thought over his answer. There seemed little reason to keep secrets. She was in as much danger as he was, and he did not think her so stupid as to believe she could make some bargain with Thurkettle. He just hoped he was not acting in response to a huge pair of rich brown eyes, eyes that pulled at the truth, demanding his honesty. Silently he promised himself that in future he would be very careful about looking into those eyes of hers.

"I believe he is dabbling in many illegal activities," he finally answered.

"Hell's fire, I thought ye were meaning to tell me something I didna ken for myself."

"Ye ken he is doing something illegal?" He decided her skill with sarcasm was not only good but could grow very irritating.

"My uncle? I should be very surprised if he wasna. Exactly what do ye think he is dabbling in?"

"Treason. He plots with the Black Douglases against James the Second." He found the shock that transformed her face somewhat reassuring.

Tess nearly choked on her wine. She had guessed at her

uncle's criminal nature a long time ago, but she had never thought her uncle into any serious treachery. Treason against their king? She shook her head. Surely her uncle could not be such a fool, would not taint their family with such a black crime. But then, she thought as she struggled to subdue her shock, Fergus Thurkettle was clearly trying to kill her and Revan. He was also, suddenly and inexplicably, closely entangled with the Black Douglases, who had openly defied the king.

"Are ye certain about that?" she found herself forced to ask.

"Aye, very certain. I but needed some more proof, a few facts."

"Proof and facts?" She looked at him in slight surprise. "Ah, so that is why ye were slathering over the regal Brenda."

"I wasna slathering," he snapped, then sighed, ruefully admitting to himself that he had come close a time or two. "I did think I could gain a little information from her, something that might lead me to the proof I sought."

"Well, ye didna ken the queen Brenda very well, then."

"She was a bit duller of wit than I had expected."

"Nay. A lot sharper. Whate'er old Fergus is doing, his royal daughter kens all about it."

He sighed as he set his wineskin aside. "I wondered about that whilst I was dangling from the wall in the dungeons." He had been taken for a fool, and it annoyed him.

"Brenda is a sly one," Tess said. "One too many questions from you, and she would grow suspicious."

"And probably kept Thurkettle informed of every step I took," he muttered.

"There is no 'probably' about it."

"Ye dinna need to rub salt in my wounds."

"No need to be so thrice-cursed ill-tempered over the matter. Men," she grumbled, shaking her head. "Show them auburn curls, big blue eyes, and a couple of other very big things, and their brains turn to warm gruel and leak right out their ears.''

There was some painful truth in that, Revan thought, but he fought to ignore it. ''Are ye planning to tell me more about your uncle?''

''I canna be certain I have much to tell. I always kenned he wasna a good man, but I canna say I was witness to anything that carried the taint of treason.'' She rubbed her forehead with one hand as she tried to think, but exhaustion was gaining on her, clouding her thoughts. ''Mayhaps ye should have asked me earlier. I begin to have difficulty recalling my own name.''

She did look tired, he thought and reined in his suspicions. He was feeling rather weary himself. There would be time enough after they had both rested to press her for information.

''Ye can lie down where ye are,'' he said as he started to bank the fire. ''We can talk in the morning.''

Nodding, she yanked off her boots and neatly stood them by her hat. She settled herself as comfortably as she could on the thin bedding, tugging the blanket over her and turning her back to the fire. Despite all the trouble she was in, she knew sleep would come quickly. It was just weighting her body when she felt Revan slip under the blanket and lay down beside her. Wide-eyed with shock, suddenly alert, she turned to stare at his broad back.

''What are ye doing?'' she squeaked.

''Going to sleep.''

''Ye canna sleep here.''

'''Tis the only place to sleep there is. Wheesht, I am too weary to bother with some fool lass's outrage. I am also too weary to be any threat to any female. So ye can just calm yourself down and go to sleep.''

For a brief moment she gave serious thought to continuing the argument, then turned her back to him. He was fully dressed, and she knew he was telling the truth about being tired. She also suspected he meant to keep a close eye on her until he was more sure of her motives. As she closed her eyes, she decided she was also simply too tired to bother with propriety at the moment.

Revan heard her breathing soften and knew she was asleep. He knew he would soon join her, his body aching with exhaustion. For now he felt they were safe, safe enough to rest up and gain some much needed strength for the dangerous days that stretched out ahead of them.

Chapter

◈ 3 ◈

"WELL, NOW THAT YE HAVE RESTED, WASHED, and broken your fast, we can talk." Revan crouched by the fire and poured himself some wine, trying to ignore the way the girl glared at him.

That proved impossible. Since she had awoken, her sullenness had been unrelenting. He had thought a good night's rest would soften her mood, make her see that they were uneasy allies, not enemies. Instead, she continued to regard him as though he were something nasty she had stepped in and could not scrape off of her boots. It was really beginning to annoy him.

"Tess, I think 'twould be greatly to your benefit to aid me."

"Oh, aye? As it was to my benefit to spring ye from my uncle's dungeon?"

She saw his eyes narrow and knew that in this vulnerable situation she ought to tread more warily, just as she knew she wouldn't. When she had awoken, she had slowly studied her surroundings, thought about the situation she was in, and gotten mad. She planned to stay mad, no amount of self-scolding cooling her temper. Although she knew he was not fully to blame for her predicament, he had had a hand in it. He was also there, big as life, a ready target for her frustration-bred fury.

"I am sorry about that, but I didna have much choice. And it looks to me as if ye escaped that keep just in time. Perhaps ye should be thanking me. Dinna forget how your uncle's men were aiming for you as much as me."

"I willna forget that for a minute. Neither will I forget that ye have given him the perfect way to murder me without suffering any consequences!"

He winced at the truth of that, then scowled because it was not the whole truth. "If he is so willing to grab at this chance, then ye canna truly claim ye were safe there. He was obviously thinking about it, might even have tried to kill you a few times ere now. Ye simply failed to see it."

Tess opened her mouth to snarl an answer, then snapped it shut. She felt her anger slowly slip away. The logic of Revan's words could not be fought, especially since their validity had already been proved. Sighing, she refilled her battered tin cup with watered-down wine.

"I saw it. Well, I saw it clearly only yesterday."

"So, he has tried to kill you?" He found her abrupt change in mood a little unsettling but was glad to see those huge brown eyes grow soft again.

"Aye, he has. I thought they were accidents, although something about them made me uneasy at the time. I pushed such thoughts aside. After all, he is my uncle. Blood family. I can think of three times he may have been—well, probably was—behind what happened. He saw a chance and grasped it."

"'Tis quite possible. Do ye have other family?"

"More than most would want. Why?"

"How can your uncle think he will get what wealth ye have? Have ye willed it to him?"

"Nay, never. 'Twas my mother's, put aside by her father and added to by mine. Her father wanted her to have some of her own money. Grandfather Thurkettle never ceased to think of it as 'when' not 'if' she left my father. The money and land was to come to me next. She died and Grandfather Thurkettle controlled it, then he died—''

''And Thurkettle took control.''

''Aye, I fear so. He ruled it until my eighteenth birthday.''

''What happens then?''

'''Tis all mine. Only two short days ago my uncle no longer held the reins.''

''Two days—'' He stared at her in shock ''*Ye* are eighteen?''

The total disbelief in his voice struck her as somewhat insulting. ''Aye, I am eighteen. How old did ye think I was?'' Even as she asked the question, she was not sure she wanted to know the answer.

''Your clothes . . .'' He waved his hand to indicate her baggy male attire. ''I thought ye but a girlchild playing about or the like. Why, in God's good name, is a lass of your years wearing a man's clothes?''

The rather disgusted look in his blue-gray eyes stung. ''I was mucking about in the stables, Sir Halyard, doing various other chores that are apt to make one just a wee bit dirty. I have but two gowns. One plain and one a wee bit less plain. I canna afford to ruin them.''

Suddenly she was painfully conscious of her shabby attire. He was such a beautiful man, and she looked like some ragamuffin. Then she stiffened with pride. After all, he had given her no warning that she was about to take a trip with a gentleman. She could hardly be expected to appear at her best on the off chance that some beautiful man would get chained up in her uncle's dungeon, then drag her off into the night.

Revan knew that he had insulted her, and he almost apologized. Then he recalled what she had just said, and his thoughts were quickly diverted.

''Why only two gowns? What about that money?''

''I told you—my uncle held the purse strings.''

''Aye, but from the little I ken of such matters, he would

be allowed to draw expenses from the fund, coin he would need to house, clothe, and educate you, or the like. Did he have complete control?''

''Nay. There are two lawyers as well who try to keep an eye on it. He would have to tell them if he needed to have some coin and why. Grandfather Thurkettle didna fully trust his son, and there are some restraints upon my uncle. I suppose Uncle felt it was too much to bother with.'' Even as she said it, she doubted the truth of that.

Before she averted her gaze, Revan read her sudden doubt in the expression on her face. He bit back the words he had been about to say. There was no doubt in his mind that Thurkettle would have bled her inheritance of every penny he could. If he was allowed expenses, he would have claimed them. That she would gain no benefit from those claims was hardly surprising. Revan knew her thoughts were just now taking the same route as his. He would not rub salt in her wounds.

He was beginning to think of her more as an innocent victim than as one of Thurkettle's conspirators. Telling himself to cling to his cynicism and mistrust did nothing to change that. It did make him wonder what she could know about her uncle's activities. There was a good chance she would know little or nothing.

Edging a little closer to her, he asked, ''Do ye remember what I said your uncle was involved in?''

Trying not to dwell on what a blind fool she had been—as well as a slight bout of self-pity over how poorly she had been treated—Tess decided to concentrate on what Revan wanted to know. ''Aye, treason against James the Second. 'Tis hard to forget such a crime. Yet, what makes ye so certain my uncle is involved?''

''He has become too well entangled in the Black Douglases' webs not to be. Unfortunately, while all I see and hear points to his guilt, naught touches him.''

''Ah, and ye thought touching Brenda would help.''

''Do ye think we can forget Brenda?'' he said sharply.

"All right, all right. Ye dinna need to get into a black humor."

"I am *not* in a black humor," he snapped.

"Nay, of course not. Exactly what is your interest in all of this?" Quickly thinking over all that had happened, she was not sure she ought to trust him any farther than she could throw him. "How do I ken your interest isna born of a need to stop one of your own from gaining too favored a place amongst the Black Douglases?"

Her suggestion infuriated him, but he forced himself to gain some control over his flare of temper. She had good reason to be suspicious. Considering all that she had gone through and discovered in the past day, it was only natural that she would be wary of everyone—at least for a while.

Then he wondered how much it would be prudent to tell her. A moment later he realized his only choice was the whole truth. Anything less would undoubtedly add to her suspicions and then to his own troubles by making her more foe than friend.

"I have been keeping a close watch upon the Black Douglases and your uncle for months. I am a knight in the service of James the Second, here at his request."

"Oh, aye, and I am queen of England." The man must think she had all the wit of a slug! she thought, faintly insulted. "Ye have proof of all that?"

"Of course not. If I were to carry about proof that I work under the king's own command, 'twould be the same as cutting my own throat. That skinny man working in your uncle's stables was also in the king's service. It can be a good place to hear and see a lot. We had an agreement to share our information. Unfortunately, your uncle discovered the man ere he had told me much."

"And then murdered him."

"I have little doubt of it."

She abruptly stood up and walked to the cave entrance. When he had slipped out earlier for water, he had left a small opening to allow in some fresh air and light. Leaning against the rock, she peered blindly out that small opening and tried to organize her thoughts and feelings. Her world had been turned upside down. Her life was threatened. What she needed to concentrate on was—could she trust Sir Revan Halyard or, in fact, anyone? She also needed to fight a strong urge to cry, an urge that already had her eyes wet and stinging.

And yet, she thought as she angrily wiped the tears from her cheeks with her hands only to have them quickly replaced, if anyone had a good reason to cry, she did. There was only so much bad news a person could be expected to tolerate at one time. She dreaded talking to Revan any more. The man kept pointing out more wrongs every time he opened his mouth.

And what was she to do about him? she thought as she pulled a handkerchief from a hidden pocket in her doublet and blew her nose. She supposed she would have to trust him—but only so far. They did have a bond of sorts. Her uncle was trying to kill both of them. That threat tied them together whether they wanted to be or not.

It was his intention of branding her uncle with the heinous crime of treason that troubled her. If Revan was really one of James II's knights, that was easily explained. However, his interest might be born of darker origins. He could even be as deep into treasonous intrigues as he claimed her uncle was. If that was true, she could well find him as eager to be rid of her as her uncle was. She was going to have to depend on her instincts, and she was not feeling too confident about them at the moment. If nothing else, she could all too easily be led astray by the irrelevant fact that he was far too handsome, in form and face, for any woman's peace of mind.

Revan sighed and stood up, cautiously approaching her. He could tell she was crying, but he was not sure there was anything he could say to soothe her feelings. Her uncle was a traitor, a murderer, and a man greedy for power. There was no denying that. Neither could he tell her they would escape the danger they now found themselves in. He simply did not know. Feeling uncomfortable and a little helpless, he stood behind her and ran a hand through his thick hair.

"I havena lied. I really am one of the king's own knights."

Trying to wipe her eyes dry again, she grumbled, "Ye will pardon me, I am sure, if I am slow to believe you. I dinna ken too many king's knights who kidnap innocent people or threaten to cut their throats."

"I wasna truly going to murder you."

"Nay? What would ye have done if they had called your bluff?"

"Died."

That flat answer caused her to turn. She saw no sign of lying in his face. He looked almost as miserable as she felt. She made her decision. There really was no other choice for her. She would trust him, but while telling him what she knew, she would keep a close eye on him.

"I have seen that my uncle has grown friendly with the Black Douglases. Messengers come and go between them," she said, turning to stare out the opening again. "My uncle has but recently added many new men-at-arms. His armorer works without ceasing. Fletchers have gathered nearby as well. I had begun to fear we were about to be attacked or raided."

"Or were preparing to attack someone else. Have ye seen or heard anything like that?"

"Nay, I dinna think so. I havena seen any army, if that is what ye are asking. If 'tis treason afoot, the ones involved will be careful about what they say or do." She took a deep shaky breath, further subduing her weepiness.

"Aye. However, the Black Douglases have been bold. Sadly not so bold ye ken their every step."

"What can my uncle think to gain from this?" She looked at him. "He isna close to the throne."

"Nay, but the Black Douglases are. After James the First

was murdered, they were but one small lad away from the throne.''

''Aye, and look what befell those who murdered that king. Ye would think their tortured deaths wouldna be forgotten so easily. My uncle has spent a great amount of coin on men and arms. He must be certain of some reward, something greater than he has spent.'' She shook her head.

'' 'Tis all of that coin flowing so freely that led me to him. Ye are certain ye heard no firm plans? Ye said messengers have been sent between them. Did ye never hear what came from the Black Douglases? Or hear your uncle tell his messenger anything ere he sent him off?''

She frowned as she thought over his questions. Leaning against the rock, she tried to grasp at some elusive memory. Then it came. She groaned slightly, lightly slapping her palm against her forehead. It had been right before her eyes all the time.

''The tunnel!'' she cried. ''Where have my wits gone?''

''The tunnel?''

Revan could tell by the look on her face that she had recalled something that could be very important. He felt excitement rise within him. It was impossible to quell it, but he tried. What put that light of revelation on her sweet face might seem important to her but prove nearly useless to him.

''That dark passageway ye dragged me along while tickling my throat with your dirk?''

''Ye arena intending to forget that, are ye?''

'' 'Tis rather hard to forget something like cold deadly steel pressed to the life-giving vein in your throat by some courtier ye had done a kindness for.'' It was odd, she mused, but his annoyance over her references to the incident made her feel she just might be able to trust him. ''Such base ingratitude is apt to linger in one's mind.''

''What about the tunnel?'' he snapped.

''Ah, aye, that. There is a room or two off to the side of it. I have explored them a few times. They are places to store the harvests and tithes paid, things that ought to be kept cooler—like apples or wine. All keeps have them, do they not? Never mind. I was creeping through the tunnel one day, about a fortnight past, and heard my uncle talking.''

''To whom? One of the Black Douglases' men?''

''Aye. In truth, I think he must be someone important within that clan. 'Twasna the usual messenger, and he spoke to my uncle as an equal; nay, as one above him. He also spoke of—well, reminded Uncle of something from the past, a secret my uncle doesna want told. Then he asked if the goods my uncle was sending to the Black Douglases would remain unspoiled, for they wouldna be stored as well as they had been. He wished assurance that they would last until the start of May.''

''Are ye certain of this? Would ye swear to it?''

''Certain. There was a secretive air to their manner. I feared I was hearing words they wouldna wish me to hear. I didna linger but slipped away as swiftly and as silently as I was able.''

''That was wise. They would have killed you if they had thought ye had discovered anything.'' He slammed his fist into his palm. ''Two months. It concurs with the bit I learned.''

''Which is?''

''That an army of thousands is being readied to march against the king.''

''\'Tis so difficult to believe. Why? Why would my uncle risk his life and blacken the name of the family?''

''If ye think on it, I believe ye will soon understand.''

''I dinna have to think on it too long. The man thinks to gain some grand title and rich lands. Yet, what hold do the Douglases have on him? This all seems too great a gamble. My uncle prefers less danger.'' She paled as she heard her uncle and the Douglas man speaking again in her mind, suddenly recalled words she had ignored before. ''This isna the first time my uncle has dealt in treason.''

''Nay?''

''Nay. The hold the Black Douglases have on him is

proof that he has the blood of James the First on his hands.''

Revan felt vaguely stunned. Here was all he had been looking for. He had spent a great deal of time in spying, courting Brenda, and engaging in general subterfuge, yet, in a few minutes Tess had told him as much as he had discovered in months. What was somewhat irritating was that she had not even been trying to find out anything while he had worked so hard to discover so little.

Suddenly he stopped pacing to stare at her. Thurkettle had to know that she could have seen something, would innocently have espied some of his treasonous activities. The man had wit enough to realize she could be a wellspring of incriminating information, that all she needed was to be carefully questioned. It gave Thurkettle all the more reason to want her dead.

She was in as much danger as he was. He had thought so before, but now knew for certain. It meant he was hindered with her until Thurkettle was no longer a threat. Just as there were few he could trust not to betray him, there were few he could trust to keep her safe. Since he had dragged her into the middle of it all, it was his responsibility to keep her from suffering the consequences. At the moment it looked a herculean task. He was not even sure he was going to be able to save himself.

''Ye dinna think that will help you?'' she finally asked, disturbed by the way he scowled at her.

''Oh, aye, 'twill help me—if I can get the information to the king or his men. The information ye have, however, isna going to help *you* at all.''

''Nay. I ken that. 'Tis but another reason for him to try and kill me. Aye, and the Black Douglases will wish me silenced as well.''

''I wondered if ye would understand that.''

''It wasna hard. The very moment I realized I had discovered something that could hurt my uncle, I realized that he would ken it, too. Or he willna wish to chance that I saw something. What difference does it make? Dead is dead no matter what the reason. He may have two motives to kill me now, but he can only kill me once.''

Tess wished she was as calm as she sounded. She walked back to the fire and sat down, staring into the flames. There had been a lot of danger in her short life from sickness to clan feuds and battles. They were dangers everyone faced, however, mostly impersonal dangers. This threat was aimed at her personally. It would not come and go in a winking but linger, pursuing her until her uncle was stopped. It terrified her, but she fought to subdue that. What she faced would require strength.

Returning home became her goal. She wanted the comfort and safety of her father's ever-increasing family. The Delgados and the Comyns would form a tight protective circle around her that her uncle would never dare to confront.

Glancing up, she saw Revan moving toward her again. He crouched by the fire and met her gaze briefly before she returned to watching the flames. She was going to have to accustom herself to the fact that she was dependent upon him, upon his goodwill, protection, and skill. Since she did not really know the man, she could not be sure he was capable of any of that.

''Now, Tess,'' Revan began, then paused to sit down by her side. ''There are two ways this could turn. Your uncle could end our threat to him, or we could end his to us and the king.''

''Are ye afraid I am going to get into the midst of all that, try to stop it? Even try to help my uncle in some way?''

''A wee bit—aye.''

''Well, dinna fret. I regret that part of my family will be harmed—nay, will die—and that the name of Thurkettle will be tainted with the stain of treason. But ye dinna have to worry that I am going to let myself get killed just to save his hide, especially when it would be him doing the killing. Neither will I believe him if he tries to tell me I would be safe if I did what he wanted. Even before this tragedy came about, I kenned my uncle for a liar, not to trust his word for a minute.'' She frowned as she remembered there was more than her uncle involved. ''What about the queenly Brenda, the love of your life?''

He opened his mouth to deny that last remark, then decided it would be better to ignore it. ''If Brenda is involved—''

''Oh, aye, she is. Sweet Brenda is involved right up to her big blue eyes. She could never resist being in the middle of a plot.''

''Then she will meet her downfall alongside her father and the Black Douglases.''

''Brenda willna suffer any downfall, and well ye ken it. She will use the same wiles on her judges as she used on you. Aye, and they will act just as lackwitted.'' She shook her head, not really wanting Brenda to suffer badly but not wanting her to escape punishment for such a heinous crime. ''That is, if ye catch her. She is no doubt busily arranging an escape with as much money as she can grab. I sometimes think she is far more clever than her father.''

''May we forget her? That matter can be tended to later. She isna riding about trying to pierce us full of arrows.''

''Well, what do ye plan to do about the ones who are? Are we to but sit here?''

''For a while.''

''Why? This may be a good defensive position, but it can also turn into a trap.''

''I ken it. I have to stay in this area until Thursday.''

''That is six days away! Ye think we can hide here for that long without being discovered?''

'' 'Tis what I am hoping. I have to meet someone a few miles from here. 'Tis all arranged.''

''Wasna anything arranged in case there was trouble, trouble like we are having now?''

''Aye, he will go searching for me. But I canna allow that to happen. Your uncle would murder him. I mean to stay here for as long as I can. Also, he can take the information

I have gathered back to the king. That can only help us. None of those who hunt us ken this man. He may succeed. Aye, and he could send us some help, too.''

"I can get us help.'' She doubted he would really believe her, as it was too soon for them to trust each other much, but it was the first chance she had had to mention her relatives, to propose going to them for aid.

He studied her closely. There was a look of hope in her expression. There was also a touch of what, on many another, he would have termed cunning. On this open-faced, easily read woman he was not sure what to call it. She was going to try to convince him of something, and he girded himself to ignore the plea in those big, dark eyes.

"How can ye do that? Ye ken someone who might be useful to us?"

"My father's family—the Delgados and the Comyns.'' She could tell that he was going to refuse that source, and she frantically tried to think of what she could say to convince him otherwise.

"Your uncle will undoubtedly suspect that ye would go to them, Tess.''

"I am sure he will, but he will be very careful about drawing too near to any of them, especially if he thinks I have reached them and told them what he is plotting.''

"I am certain they are able to fight and protect you, but this is a matter for the king's men.''

"Even more reason to go to them. Half of them deal in the law. Many of the others are soldiers, skilled men-at-arms. I thought I made mention of that once before. Well, it doesna matter. They truly could aid us. There is certainly enough of them to provide plenty of protection.''

"My allies can protect us.''

"And where are they?''

"With or near the king—Stirling.''

"Mine are nearer—Edinburgh. This side of the city. They have a fine strong keep there.''

"Aye, that is nearer to us, but we have to elude your

uncle's men all the way. And soon, mayhaps, the Black Douglases as well. As I said, he is certain to ken ye will try to reach them and do his best to stop you.''

''Since we have to travel through the enemies' lands to reach the king, we will have to elude them anyhow.'' When he just frowned, she sighed. ''Ye dinna trust me, do ye.''

''Do ye trust me?'' he asked instead of answering. Strangely he did trust her, but he did not want her to know how close he was to accepting everything she said as gospel.

''Nay, not all that much.''

''I will consider what ye suggested. Will that satisfy?''

''Aye.''

He stood up and headed toward the cave opening. ''I am going to find some wood. Ye stay here.''

''The fool speaks as if I have some choice,'' she muttered after he left.

At least he had said he would think about it. It was better than the flat no she had anticipated. She had six days to convince the man, six days to change ''considering'' to conviction.

Chapter

◈ 4 ◈

"I NEED A BATH."

Revan swore softly and turned from cleaning his sword to glare at her. She had woken up with that demand upon her lips and had kept at him ever since. He was in no mood to put up with her stubborn persistence, not after four nights of increasingly disturbed sleep. Somewhere under those ill-fitting clothes she wore was a softness, a softness that kept ending up pressed close to him in the night, a softness that was feeding a growing frustration within him. He was having enough trouble coping with the allure of her thick raven hair and big brown eyes. Feeling those soft curves pressed against his back in the night was almost more than he could deal with.

"It can wait until we are someplace safer," he snapped.

She glared right back at him, her hands on her hips. "It canna wait. I was intending to indulge in a hot bath when you strode into my life and ruined it. I have had quite enough of being filthy, of spending day after day in these dirty clothes. Now, I ken there is a source of water about somewhere near, as ye keep bringing buckets in. Where is it?"

"Curse your eyes." He slammed his sword down and rose to his feet in one angry movement. "Ye can have your

40

cursed bath, although 'tis a very poor time to be so particular.''

''I'm not being particular. I stink.''

''Nay, ye dinna. I havena noticed any smell.'' He rather wished he had, for it might help to stem his errant desires.

''Mayhaps that is because ye have your own aroma to savor.''

She knew that was a lie, and that only added to her annoyance. While she struggled along with inadequate dabbings, he had clearly been bathing. It was unfair.

''Fetch the things ye will need, and I will show you where the water is. Ye can have a quick bath. I repeat—*quick*.'' When all she did was grab the soap she had discovered in his supplies, he frowned. ''Ye will need something to dry yourself with.''

''I will use my clothes before I wash them.''

''Ye plan to wash your clothes as well?''

''Aye, I do, and there is no need to shout. I only have these, and I am not putting them back on dirty.''

''Well, ye arena going to sit about outside—in the open—until they dry, either,'' he grumbled as he moved to his supplies, where he found a clean shirt and thrust it toward her. ''Ye can put this on, then get back here and dry your clothes over the fire.''

She eyed the shirt warily. It would be big on her but not big enough. There would be a lot of her left showing. When she looked at him, intending to protest, she saw him already stepping out of the cave. Deciding she could tolerate a little immodesty for the sake of cleanliness, she hurried after him.

When they reached the small, clear pool, fed by a tumbling rivelet originating from high up in the rocks, she almost hit him. The place was close to their cave and well sheltered from view. As far as she could see, there was no reason for him to deny her access unless he still feared she might run off. She watched him check for snakes for a minute.

"I hope you enjoyed hoarding this all to yourself," she said as she sat down to yank off her boots.

"Now, Tess—"

"Ye had best return to guarding our wee hole in the rocks. I am too eager to get clean to listen to any convoluted excuses for your greediness."

"Well, just dinna dawdle. This place may look sheltered, but it can be reached—very easily," he warned as he walked away.

Fighting the urge to tug her forelock, she looked around again. It was sheltered, but he was also right, much to her annoyance. Since it was at the foot of the rocks, it could be easily reached by horse. Shrugging, she started to undress. Her uncle's men had not been around for quite a while. Although it was possible they could return to the area, she had enough time to bathe. She would not let Revan's ill humor make her fear every shadow.

After scrubbing her clothes out and laying them out in the sun to dry, she jumped into the pool. The cold water stole her breath away for a moment. Once that shock had worn off, she luxuriated in the pleasure.

Idly soaping herself, she began to think about Revan. He was in her thoughts much too often, but what could she expect? They were together night and day. She was far too aware of him as a man, one who made her feel all too much the woman. She was thinking of kisses—and of a lot more than kisses. A curiosity about all that could be shared between a man and a woman, about passion, had risen to a keen edge within her.

Her curiosity was fed by Revan, for he was far too attractive for any woman's peace of mind. Living so close to him for days, she had tried to find fault, some unattractive twist to his character, some flaw that would stem her growing fascination with him. He had flaws, but they were not doing a thing to halt her wanting. Even when she grew annoyed with him, it was only a temporary check. It did not take long for the interest to return in full force.

"He definitely has faults," she muttered as she began to scrub her hair. "I simply must try to concentrate on them more."

He was arrogant, she told herself. Then she reluctantly admitted she had known those more arrogant than he, and he had some right to what he did have.

He had a temper. But then, she mused, so did she.

He was also untrusting, but then, she was finding trust a little hard to grasp herself at the moment.

There was a definite authoritarian streak in the man, but then, didn't the situation call for decisiveness?

She cursed. His faults simply were not deep enough. They were present but too easily tolerated—or too close to her own to criticize without hypocrisy.

There were also too many good things about him. That was the real problem. Faults were the last things on her mind when he looked at her, with his fine blue-gray eyes softened with interest or understanding. Or, she thought with a scowl, when she woke to find that big strong body of his curled close to hers, warming her sometimes a little too much. It was almost embarrassing to recall how she reacted to his smiles. She was soft clay in his hands. Fortunately he did not know that yet.

Even as she ducked beneath the water to rinse out her hair, she amended that last statement to—he could not know for certain. She was not secretive. What she felt or thought was all too often clear to read on her face. It was not beyond the realm of possibility that Revan had gleaned a hint of what she felt. It was up to her to keep it only a hint. That was not going to be easy, not when her emotions were so strong and so tangled. As she lazily paddled about the pool, she hoped he was having as much difficulty as she was.

REVAN sat in front of their hideout blindly staring off into the distance. He tried not to think about what Tess was doing, but it was proving impossible. The softness he had felt curled against him was being revealed, and he ached to take a peek. If nothing else, she might prove far less attractive than his imaginings, which could serve to stem the wanting eating away at him. He badly needed that.

Frustration was slowly chipping away at his common sense. He still found that curious. She was a pretty little thing but had a sharp tongue and, dressed as she was, was not seductive-looking in the least. She was the last woman he would expect to be tied up in lustful knots over. Yet, he was and it was growing worse.

Well, he could just forget it, he thought to himself. Undoubtedly she was a virgin, and feeling lustful over a woman like her would have him standing before a priest before he could spit.

He shook his head. Even that old warning, one that had always cooled his ardor before, did not work. What he needed was to put some distance between them, but that was impossible for at least the next two days. Most likely even longer because she was in as much danger as he was. And he could not just leave her somewhere.

"So rein it in, Revan," he admonished himself. "Then ye will be able to ride away without guilt or regret when this is done."

He scowled at the vista spread out before him. The girl had an unsettling effect upon him. For one thing, he never used to talk to himself.

"Which wouldna be so bad if it helped." He glared in the direction of the pool, then tried to concentrate on watching for any hint of trouble.

She was touching emotions inside of him he really did not want disturbed. He had his life all planned out. He was a knight in service to the king. It was a dangerous position, one meant for a solitary man with no ties. Lust was acceptable, a shallow if sometimes fierce feeling that could be enjoyed, then discarded. He did lust after Tess, but there was more, too much more. No matter how hard he tried to deny it, fight it, ignore it, he knew she was stirring far more than his lust. That was dangerous. That made her someone to avoid. Unfortunately, he could think of no way to do that—not for some time, anyways. So he was stuck, stuck within reach of those huge brown eyes which seemed to look right inside of him and demand he feel more than passion, more than an ache in his groin.

Like protectiveness, he mused, and cursed. She also held his interest. He knew there was a sharp mind behind those beautiful eyes. He found himself wanting to know its twists and turns. At times she could stir what could only be termed tenderness inside of him. That could prove a real threat.

"Almost," he grumbled, "as big a threat as those five horsemen riding toward her bathing pool."

It took a moment for what he was seeing, for the import of his own words, to sink into his mind. Then he gaped, coming to full attention. Ambling straight toward Tess were five horsemen. Despite the distance, he recognized the slovenly riding style of Thurkettle's men. As he raced down the steep path to the small pool, he prayed for time. He would need it in order to get Tess safely out of sight.

The instant he reached the edge of the pool, he started to pick up her clothes. "Come along, Tess. Ye have to hie back to the cave—now."

Crossing her arms over her breasts, Tess crouched in the water up to her neck. "What are ye doing?"

"Thurkettle's men are headed straight toward you."

He was gratified to see an appropriate look of alarm on her face. What annoyed him was that, even now, with danger but yards away, he was thinking about things that had nothing to do with that danger. Things like wanting to shed his clothes and climb into the water with her, like how much more they could do besides swim.

"Well, let me have my clothes," she snapped. "And turn your back."

"There is no time to get dressed! As it is, we will be fortunate to reach the cave without being seen. There is no time for some cursed maidenly modesty."

"I canna simply run out there. I am naked."

"God's beard, lass, five men will be riding through the scrub any moment now. If ye hesitate much longer, your modesty willna be the only thing slighted. Ye have got a choice. Either show me some bare skin as ye hie to safety or stay here and be murdered. Which is it? Bare arse or dead arse?"

"Bare."

She bolted from the water, grabbing her shirt as she ran by him. It took Raven a moment to follow. The sight of her slim naked form had knocked all good sense from his head. By the time he started after her, she had his shirt on, lacing it up even as she ran.

When they reached the cave, he was right behind her. He gave her a nudge inside, then turned to see where Thurkettle's men were. He pressed himself against the highest point of the rocks and watched as the five riders found the small hidden pool. He inwardly cursed when one proved alert enough to find the footprints he and Tess had just left. That ensured that the men would linger in the area, stay far too close for comfort. While it was true they had been close before, they had never been given such a clear reason to stay around. Those tracks gave them one.

Dashing back into the cave, he came face to face with a wide-eyed Tess. She looked far too distractingly enticing clad only in his shirt. He wanted to order her to get dressed but swallowed that urge for two reasons. Her clothes were still wet, and he was sure he would deeply embarrass her. It was not really her fault he could not control his baser emotions. Although, he mused with a touch of irritation, it would help if she did not have such long, slender, beautifully shaped legs.

"Did they leave?" she asked.

"Nay. They willna. We left our marks all around that pool, and one of the fools has spotted them."

"I am sorry."

"'Tis not your fault. I wasna keeping as close a watch as I should have. I was too slow to see them. That error meant

I didna gain myself time enough to take all the precautions I could have—like brushing out our tracks.''

"So ye feel they will linger here, search for us."

"By now Thurkettle must be getting very annoyed."

She grimaced. "They will stay."

"Aye, so I thought."

"And they will look very hard. So now what do we do?"

"For now we stay here." He moved to the fire and started to put it out. "This isna an easy place to find. If we hold quiet and remain out of sight, they could yet miss us." Once the fire was out, he led his horse to the far back of the cave, then saddled it.

"Do you expect to have to make a run for it?" she asked as she watched him.

"'Tis always best to be prepared."

"Mayhaps we should just leave now."

"The moment they found the pool, we lost all chance to do so without being seen. They havena found us, just ken that we were about. We may get lucky. They could easily quit the game, decide we moved on."

"We havena had a great deal of good fortune."

"True," he said as he returned to the mouth of the cave, "so I have another plan or two in mind."

"And what are they?"

"Dinna fret about it. Just stay right here and be quiet."

"Ordering me about again," she muttered as she watched him crouch down at the cave's opening.

Sighing, she wrapped her arms about herself. Now came the waiting—waiting for discovery or waiting for their tenuous safety to return. She feared it would be the former. Her uncle could be impressive when he was furious or in fear of his own safety, as she was certain he was by now. Four days of fruitless searching would surely have strained her uncle's none-too-well-controlled temper. And her uncle's men would not want to return unsuccessful. They would look hard. Fools though they were, they were also stubborn. There was a sign for them to follow now, a hint that the victims they sought were close at hand.

She began to pace, careful not to make a sound as she walked out her tension.

"CURSE them. Curse them all to hell," Revan hissed as he stood up, rubbing the stiffness out of his body.

"They are still there?" Tess spoke as softly as he did even though she sat by his horse.

"Aye and it looks as if they plan to camp here tonight."

"I see. They mean to sit right here until they find something—anything."

"Aye—us or our trail. Ye would have thought, after all these hours, they would have given up. I fear one of them has enough knowledge about tracks to ken those by the pool were very fresh—too fresh for us to have gotten far away."

"Well, Uncle occasionally found a lout with a hint of wit in his fat head."

"That hint could mean our death," he said darkly. He frowned for a moment, continuing to work the stiffness out of his body.

"Mayhaps I should just go to them," she said at last.

Stopping abruptly, he scowled at her though he knew she couldn't see him in the shadows. "Ye have the wish to be a martyr, do ye?"

"Oh, aye, 'tis ever been my plan to die young by some dramatic self-sacrificing gesture," she drawled. A minute later she sighed, knowing their precarious position was straining her temper. "I but thought I would have a better chance of staying alive—at least for a while. They would cut ye down without a moment of hesitation."

"And how do ye think ye could save yourself in what little time ye might be granted?"

"I havena even a hint but I suspect I could think of something. And then, there *is* my family."

"Who are days away *if* ye could even get word to them. I couldna get help for you for days, either, and I truly doubt ye would be given even a few days by Thurkettle. I am still certain that his plan is to use this incident to be rid of you. 'Tis too good a chance to gain all he wants yet come away looking as if he is a victim.''

''Aye, and that is something Uncle would dearly love. Well, what do *ye* think we ought to do?''

''Not we—*I* will do something. *Ye* will sit right here— safe and hidden away.''

''So now who wishes to be a martyr? Are ye sure ye are a mere knight and not some lordling? Ye spit out orders like some earl.''

''There are times when ye have to be a bit of both,'' he murmured, staring at their belongings as he rubbed a hand over his chin. ''I must lead them away from here. The trick is convincing them ye are with me.''

She stood up and moved a little closer to him. ''What happens after ye lead them away?''

''I will lose them, then make my way back here.'' He crouched to roll up their bedding.

''So simple. Did ye happen to forget that they will be aiming arrows at you, trying their utmost to bring ye down, hurl ye right out of your saddle?''

''Nay, I dinna forget, but we have seen that they are very poor archers.'' Once his bedding was secure, he began to afix her wet clothes to the pile.

Trying to see what he was doing, she edged a little closer to him. ''If Uncle found one man who can read tracks well, perhaps he found one who might be able to hit what he aims for—even if the target moves swiftly.''

''I will have to risk that.''

''Why canna we simply stay here? Isna it a good defensive position?''

He glanced toward her. ''We could make a stand, but there are five of them and only two of us. That is assuming ye can fight with sword, arrow, or dirk.''

''I have a wee bit of skill,'' she said defensively. ''More skill than some of Uncle's men.'' She stared down at her small hands. "My greatest problem is that bows, and other weapons, arena made for people of my stature."

"Well, any skill would help if all else fails, but I would rather not be pressed into such a corner. Even Thurkettle's simpleminded fools could think of smoking us out, setting up a siege until we ran out of supplies, fetching more men if we stayed here long enough."

"Enough." She held up one hand. "I can see it all too clearly. Do ye plan to do this now?"

He nodded as he continued to work. "Where they are now will allow me to slip out, then choose when I let them see me." Standing up, he picked up his clothed bedroll. "There, how does that look?"

She frowned. The cave was too dark to see his invention clearly. It appeared vaguely human in form. "Is it meant to be me?"

He nodded.

"Well," she said slowly. "I am a wee bit limp about the arms and legs . . . and where is my head?"

"I will place your hat on top of it. Since I will have it in front of me I hoped they wouldna notice it's, er, a wee bit limp. They will be behind me, their view of this severely hindered."

"And 'tis growing darker out," she murmured. "'Twill probably work," she reluctantly admitted, not wanting him to do as he planned.

After setting his odd creation back down, he picked up a stick and began to write in the dirt. "Now, if I dinna return . . ." he began as she drew closer to watch him.

"That isna the wisest thing to say if ye intend for me to maintain some air of calm," she muttered as she sat by his side.

"Ye dinna seem the sort to suffer from swoons or the like."

"I am not. However, I am also not some hardened knight with a strong sword arm. Nor do I wish to be one who waves the men off to battle with smiles and pride. There may be no choice left us, but, necessary as it might be, I dinna like this. I ken very well it can go all wrong. Ye could at least act as if there is little chance of failure. I willna believe it, but it would give me something to use to lie to myself.'' She sighed when she saw the brief flash of his smile. ''What are ye writing?''

''Here is the way to reach my ally—Simon. Also, this tells you what to say so that he kens ye are one with us, an ally as well. He could take you to your family and safety.'' He waited until she studied it, then nodded. ''Ye have a dirk, aye?''

''Aye. Do ye?'' She struggled to hide her fear.

''Aye. I have my sword, my bow, and my dagger. I doubt I shall use any of them. S'truth, I dinna plan to let them draw that close to me.'' He smoothed his hand over her damp hair. ''I will be back, Tess.''

She did not believe a word of it. Looking up at him, she studied his shadowed face. She was terrified. It could all too easily be the last time she ever saw him. Impulsively, she cupped his handsome face in her hands and kissed him. It startled her a little when he swiftly wrapped his arm around her shoulders and returned her tentative kiss with a deep, fierce one.

''Good luck,'' she managed to whisper when the kiss ended.

Revan stared at her. A moment ago his mind had been filled with his plans for pulling them free of the danger they were in. Now it was filled with Tess and the heady warmth of her kiss. He did not want to ride out and play hide-and-seek with Thurkettle's men. He wanted to stay with Tess. He wanted to see what little his shirt covered of her lithe body. He wanted to kiss and touch every silken inch of her. That kiss had been sweet—dangerously sweet. Inwardly cursing, he grabbed up his lifeless riding companion and strode toward his horse, forcing his thoughts back to survival.

Tess said nothing as he prepared himself. She just sat where he had left her.

"Revan," she finally said as he stood at the mouth of the cave. "Mayhaps it willna mean much, but if this does fail, if ye dinna return, I will make very sure they all pay dearly."

He stared at her for a moment. "It means a lot," he murmured, then left.

Picking up her dirk from the cave floor, Tess set it in her lap. For a while there was silence, then came shouts and the sound of galloping horses. She closed her eyes and prayed. It was going to be a very long night.

Chapter

❖ 5 ❖

"TESS?"

"Revan, ye fool," she hissed, carefully easing her grip on her dagger, "I almost threw this at you."

Edging into the cave and tugging his tired mount in behind him, Revan murmured, "Well, at least ye were alert."

She watched his shadowy form as he moved to light the fire. A hundred different emotions assaulted her as the firelight revealed his weary face. She could not make herself move from where she still crouched at the back of the cave, but simply stared at him as he unsaddled his horse.

"I finally lost the fools through pure good fortune and the help of darkness."

"Good," she managed to croak out. She wondered how one person could look so good to her.

"Alert," he had called her. She had spent so long tensed and afraid, she ached. Sometime during the long night hours she had moved to the rear of the cave, although she could not explain why. Now, though, she was not sure she could move. She feared she would do something mad—or humiliating—when and if she did.

What she ached to do was touch him, listen to his strong heartbeat, feel his warmth. That would still the fear that he

53

hadn't really returned, that this was only a dream born of a terror-fevered mind. She was afraid, however, that she might take it too far. So, cowardly, she sat still.

"Now that I see this in the light," Revan said, laughing as he sat before the fire and began to dismantle the large doll, "I dinna ken how it fooled them. Your clothes are dry now."

"That is nice."

"Do we have enough water for me to wash myself?"

"Aye."

Revan briefly frowned at her as he filled a large wooden bowl with water. She was behaving strangely, sitting in the dark and hardly speaking. Inwardly he shrugged as he yanked off his boots, then stripped to his hose. It must have been hard for her to wait, alone and in the dark, he decided as he began to wash the dust off himself. She probably just needed time to compose herself.

"They willna come looking for us here again," he said in reassurance. "They will think we are miles away. I left many a false trail for them to puzzle over."

"Good."

Finished with his washing, he turned to stare at her. "Tess? Is something wrong?"

"Nay, nothing is wrong."

"Ye are lying. Now"—he held out his hand—"come here into the light, where I can see you."

She stared at him standing there, his broad smooth chest bared and his hand held out to her. It was a sight that broke what little control she had gained over herself. With a soft, inarticulate sound she raced toward him, flinging herself against him, her arms around his neck.

Startled and unbalanced by the sudden charge, Revan stumbled. He sat down, hard, on their bedding. Although he put his arms around her to keep her from tumbling, she showed no signs of awkwardness. Instead, she continued to cling to him, settling herself comfortably on his lap. He began to become far too aware of how good she felt in his arms, of how little she was wearing, and, even more dangerous, to recall how sweet it was to kiss her.

"Sweet Mary, I thought ye werena coming back," she whispered in a rushed voice. "I thought they had murdered you. I began to see the wolves gnawing on your bones."

"Wolves gnawing on my bones?" He laughed shakily.

"I dinna think I have ever been so scared in my whole life."

"I had to leave you here alone." Despite sternly telling himself not to do it, he slid his hands over her slim legs, finding her skin as silky and warm as he had imagined it would be.

"I wasna scared about that. Well, not much. 'Twas for you. I was scared for you. Ye were the one being hunted down."

It occurred to her that she ought to slap his hands away. She might not know much, but she did know it was not proper to let him touch her legs as he was doing. Then she decided "proper" could go to perdition. The gentle stroking felt too good to put a stop to it.

"Well, as ye can clearly see, I have returned hale and hearty."

Revan found clear speech a little difficult. It felt so good to touch her, he wanted to touch more of her. He could feel the shape of her small firm breasts against his chest. The way her shapely little backside pressed against his groin made him ache. If he did not get some distance between them soon, he would forget all the reasons why he should *not* touch her as he craved to.

"There are no cuts, no flesh wounds, no bruises . . . ?"

"Nay, not a scratch."

He could feel her soft full mouth move against the side of his neck as she spoke. It increased his aching need to kiss her tenfold. When she shifted ever so slightly in his lap, rubbing her tempting derriere against him, he barely stifled a groan. Matters were getting completely out of hand. If he did not put a halt to this closeness, and soon, things would be past redemption.

"Well"—he inwardly cursed the husky unsteadiness of his voice, a condition worsened by the way she had begun to move her small hands over his back—"why dinna ye sit by the fire, and I will prepare us a meal."

"I am sitting by the fire."

The movement of her lips against the side of his neck was one time too many. Had he really felt her tongue briefly, tentatively, stroke his skin? Every desire he had tried to control during their sojourn in the cave was running wild.

"Dinna do it, Revan," he muttered to himself even as he smoothed his hand over her thick unbound hair.

Leaning back just a little, Tess stared up at him. "Dinna do what?"

His eyes were a stormy gray, and the look they held stirred her blood as much as his hands. She placed her hands on his chest, lightly caressing its smooth, taut breadth. Beneath her hand she could feel the quickening of his heartbeat. He wanted her. It was a heady realization.

"Kiss you," he whispered, his gaze falling to her full mouth. "Dinna kiss you."

Despite her innocence, she knew he was hungering for far more than a kiss. If they did kiss, it would not stop there. She told herself what she was thinking was sinful. It was not right. It was not wise. It was simply asking for trouble and heartbreak. None of that mattered. She slowly ran her tongue over her lips and heard him inhale sharply. Seeing how she could affect him helped make her decision. It might be only passion, at least on his part, but instinct told her she would find none to equal it. She would take whatever was offered, take it now and worry about the future later. As her father had always told her to, she would follow her heart.

Slipping her arms about his neck, she brought his mouth close to hers. "Then mayhaps I will kiss you."

"'Tis not a very wise plan."

Since he was brushing light, nibbling kisses over her

mouth, she did not take his protest seriously. "A tempting one."

"Too tempting, curse it. Tess." Her name escaped him as a soft groan when, as he ran his tongue over her lips, she lightly touched her tongue to his. "A kiss could be dangerous just now. 'Tis not the only thing I am thinking of. I want more."

Sitting on his lap as she was, she was quite aware of that. She rubbed her bottom against him. He shuddered and she faintly echoed the reaction.

"Ye are playing with fire, lass."

"I ken it—I feel the heat of it."

"I am not a man for marrying, Tess."

"I dinna believe I asked you."

His brief startled laugh was unsteady. "Do ye ken what ye are headed for? I wasna jesting when I said I want more than a kiss."

"How much more?" She continued to move against him, liking how it felt and how it so clearly made him feel.

"A great deal more. I want it all."

He grasped her by her slim hips to halt her tormenting movements. There was a slight flush to her cheeks. Her beautiful eyes were heavy-lidded, the rich brown darkened nearly to black. Her breathing was as erratic as his, the pulse in her throat quickened. They were signs he knew how to read. Her passion was running as hot and mindless as his. It was his place, as the one with experience in such matters, to exercise a little restraint. Unfortunately, he did not possess an ounce of it.

"Tess," he murmured, "I want to touch you. I want to taste every soft, sweet inch of you," he whispered in a hoarse voice. "I want to bury myself deep inside you. I want it badly, so very badly. Have ye ever been with a man before?"

"Nay," she managed to say, enflamed by his words.

"Well, lass, if ye dinna get far, far away from me—and fast—ye willna be able to say that come the dawn."

She stared at him, briefly reviewing her decision. He had said he was not a marrying man. Becoming his lover was not apt to change that. All she could be sure of was his passion while with her body went her heart. It was not the best of situations, but she knew it would not change soon. To hesitate was to be lost, she told herself and brushed her lips across his.

"For a man who claims to want so much so very badly, ye are taking a fair long time in reaching for it."

"Oh—curse it."

Cupping the back of her head in his hands and burying his fingers deep in her soft hair, he held her mouth against his. Tess moaned softly as he kissed her. She opened her mouth quickly, eagerly, to his tongue. His kiss was one of barely restrained hunger, and she welcomed it, heartily returned it. When he moved, pressing her down onto the bedding so that she was sprawled on her back beneath him, she offered no resistance.

He shed the last of his clothes as she watched, wide-eyed. She had never seen a naked man before but decided he had to look as fine as any man could without clothes. Despite his blondness, his skin was all-over dark, even in the white-washing effects of the firelight. A thin line of light hair began at his navel, went straight down to his groin, where it thickened as a cushion for his manhood, then thinned to a light coating over his strong, long legs.

When he laid down, she wrapped her arms about his neck. As he kissed her, he undid the shirt she wore. He propped himself up on one elbow to slowly remove her shirt, and she tensed. She was no Brenda, had no lush curves he could delight in. The longer he stared at her, the more nervous she grew, the more sure she was that the sight of her naked form had cooled his desire. Then he met her gaze. The passion she had read there before was still there but so much stronger. Such was the heat in his gaze she lost all doubt. He liked what he saw. It bred within her a feeling of pride and heady excitement. What embarrassment she had suffered quickly faded.

"Ye are finer than any of my imaginings."

"Ye imagined me naked?" she whispered, shivering with delight when their flesh met as he settled himself in her arms.

Brushing light kisses over her face, he murmured, "Ever since I woke up to find this soft wee body curled up against me."

What she planned to say was lost as he kissed her. When he cupped her breasts in his big hands, brushing his thumbs over the tips until they ached, she moaned softly and closed her eyes. The swirling caress of his tongue that followed made her squirm.

"Tessa," he murmured against her breast. "Sweet Tessa, I never tasted any sweeter."

She cried out, arching against him, when he slowly drew the swollen tip of her breast into his mouth. Burying her fingers into his thick hair, she held him close as he suckled. She trembled from the strength of the desire that rushed through her. Blindly she opened herself to his caresses, his kisses. So caught up in her passion was she, she barely flinched when his stroking hand slid down over the tight silken curls at the base of her abdomen and he began to stroke her intimately. She began to whisper his name, urgency filling each syllable, prompting her every touch.

Then, suddenly, he was crouched over her, urging her legs about his waist. She inhaled slowly as he began to join their bodies. The slow rocking motion he used was intoxicating. The breath escaped her in a startled rush as she felt a quick, sharp pain. He went very still. She could feel him staring down at her. Cautiously she chanced a peek at him from beneath her lashes.

"Tessa," he whispered, "have I hurt you?"

"Nay, not truly." She spoke as softly as he did, wondering if he shared her fear that speaking too loudly could ruin everything, could drag them back to reality and sensibility with a painful abruptness. "'Twas but a twinge."

He touched his mouth to hers, easing his tongue between her lips. As he began to move his body, he mimicked the intimate strokes with his tongue. She clung to him as she caught his gentle rhythm, arching greedily as her passion mounted. With his arm beneath her hips he enhanced the close press of their bodies. As his movements grew fiercer, so did his kiss. Tess welcomed the change, craving the heightened intensity. When she was not sure she could bear any more, her whole body taut and painfully alive, she felt herself yanked into a blinding maelstrom of sensation. She heard herself cry out his name, heard his husky words of delight and encouragement, as she tried to take him with her. A moment later she heard him call out her name, felt him hold her tightly against him as he tensed and shuddered. Feeling exquisitely weak, she kept a limp grip on him as he collapsed in her arms.

The first clear thought Tess had was a sudden understanding of all the looks and smiles her parents had so often exchanged. This was what they had been thinking of, either remembering or anticipating it. Smoothing her hands over his broad warm back, she then pondered the loss of her maidenhead. It troubled her little. Even if all she was to know was this one sweet time with Revan, it was a small price to pay. She briefly, cynically, reminded herself that, with her fortune, she could always find a husband when and if she decided she wanted one.

She murmured a protest when he eased free of her hold, lazily watching him from beneath her lashes. He moved to wash himself off, rinsed the rag out, then returned to her side. When he proceeded to clean her off, she blushed over the intimate service and closed her eyes. The moment he laid down at her side again, she returned to his arms but sensed a tension in him that made her frown.

Revan pressed a kiss to the top of her head. "Tessa, I should never—"

Quickly she pressed two fingers against his lips. "Dinna say it."

Taking her hand in his, he kissed her palm. "I dinna think ye understand. Ye were untouched. I am no lecher, but I am no innocent, either. 'Twas my place, my duty, to halt this, yet I didna."

"Please, Revan," she whispered. "Dinna say ye regret it. I dinna wish to hear that even if it is true."

He briefly kissed her, then held her close. "I dinna regret it."

"Good." She began to shyly dot his chest with kisses.

"—but I should."

Muttering a mild curse, she sat up, grabbing their thin overblanket and modestly tucking it up over her breasts. She did not want him to talk about it, at least not in that way. He could too easily say things that would hurt her.

It was also annoying. He was saying, more or less, that she did not have the wit to make her own choices or decisions. In truth, she mused as she frowned down at him, it was insulting. She did not need him to help her make decisions about herself.

Revan eyed her warily. He had never bedded a virgin before, but he had heard a few things concerning them. It was said that they could be warm and willing one moment, then turn against a man, blaming him. He wondered if Tess was doing that.

"This is why," he said, "I should have held firm to my intention to leave you be." He smiled faintly, hoping to smooth over what appeared to be troubled waters. "'Tis just that I lost all control when ye kissed me so warmly."

"'Tis a shame ye didna lose a bit of that arrogance as well."

"Pardon?" Revan felt lost and confused, no longer sure of the cause of her annoyance.

"Ye ken what I said—*arrogance*. That which makes ye believe I need *you* to guide my every step or that I need your great worldliness to aid me in deciding what I do or dinna want.'' She looked away from him, his stunned expression making her sorry that her temper was spoiling what had been so beautiful, yet she felt unable to hold her tongue.

''That is why ye scowl at me so?'' he asked as he slowly sat up. ''Ye think me arrogant?''

''Well, I dinna ken what else ye would call it. I may not have rolled about in the heather before, but I do possess the wit to ken when such as that is being offered and to decide if I wish to say aye or nay.''

Moving slightly so he sat behind her, he wrapped his arms around her and ignored how stiffly she sat in his hold. He smiled as he nuzzled her thick hair. Amusing though it was, he knew she was also right. She did have the wit to know what was being offered and what was lost. He could not, however, fully quell his guilt.

''Aye, ye have the wit to ken that. Truth is, ye have more wit than is comfortable in a lass.'' He kissed her shoulder and ran his hands over her bared arms. ''I but felt the pinch of guilt, for I can promise you nothing in return for this precious gift.''

''I didna ask ye to promise me anything. And ere ye ask, I did hear you when ye said you were not a man for marrying.'' She relaxed in his hold, seduced by his touch and gentle nibbling kisses on her shoulders. ''Ye dinna expect me to promise anything, do ye? And I havena, have I?'' Leaning her head against his shoulder she looked up at him wondering why he was frowning at her.

''This will cause you trouble with the man ye may choose to wed some day.'' He felt a strong twinge of protest at the thought of her belonging to any other man but hastily pushed it aside.

''Revan, this will undoubtedly sound cold, mayhaps even unfeeling, but if and when I decide to wed, I ken that my fortune will soothe any offense.''

For a moment he just stared at her, a little stunned by the hard, cold truth. She looked so sweet, so innocent, yet was clearly not naive. When or if she decided she had need of a husband, she could, quite simply, purchase one. It was done all the time, although no one usually spoke of it with Tess's bluntness. What troubled him was that he felt she deserved so much more.

In an attempt to clear his mind of such puzzles and questions, he turned his attention to the soft slim body he held. Slowly he moved his hands down from her shoulders to cup her breasts. He circled and stroked the tips with his thumbs, watching as they hardened with invitation.

"If ye ask for no promises nor give any and dinna look for love nor marriage, then why? Why give yourself to me?" He briefly glanced at her face to see that she had closed her eyes and her cheeks were lightly flushed with renewing desire.

Tess hastily swallowed the words of love that rushed into her mouth. He wanted to hear sighs of passion, the heated murmurs of desire, not vows of devotion. If she was lucky, there could come a time when he welcomed knowing all that rested in her heart. Now such declarations could all too easily push him away. That would gain her nothing.

"I wanted you." Her voice was soft and husky.

"'Tis all?" That answer left him feeling keenly disappointed. While he had to eschew love and marriage, he wanted more than some simple common lusting on her part. What he felt was far from simple and common. He wanted her to share the depth of the hunger he suffered, to know some of the aching need that had been twisting his innards for days. He had never desired a woman as fiercely as he desired her, never tasted such a full, rich pleasure. It stung to think her passion might not be as strong.

"Nay, but 'tisna easy to explain." She trembled faintly as he moved his hands down her body to her stomach. "'Tis such a great want, a fierce goading hunger." He moved one hand lower, and his gentle, intimate caress made it very hard for her to carefully measure her words. "I have had a fancy or two, an interest, but this was the first time I ever thought on giving myself to a man, the first time I ever kenned that I might never find it so fine again."

"Oh, aye, very fine," he murmured as he nibbled her ear. "The sweetest, the richest, the best."

"Aye—just so. I didna think it could be measured so for a man. I thought 'twas all the same to him."

Turning her in his arms, he brushed his lips over hers. "So did I—until now. I have never felt the hunger so badly before."

He kissed her as he gently eased her down onto their rough bed. Tess clung to him and decided *hunger* was a very good word for what she suffered. He made her feel as if she would starve, would wither away and slowly die without the delight he offered.

When he ended the kiss and looked at her, idly brushing stray wisps of hair from her face, she could see the hunger he spoke of reflected in the warm, smoky-blue depths of his eyes. It puzzled her that he could feel only hunger. How could such a strong feeling stand alone, without feeding or being fed by other emotions? For her it was all so entwined that one would be lost without the others. Revan's passion could be a thing apart, untouched by more complicated emotions.

"Aye—hunger." She traced his finely arced tawny brow with one finger, then lightly trailed it down his long straight nose. "'Twas so strong I had to fight it each and every minute. Then ye went out to make yourself a target for those men. Ye were gone so long, I was sure they had won, that ye were dead and I would never feed that hunger. When ye returned, unharmed, 'twas as if I had been given a second chance."

"And ye took it." He caught her hand in his and kissed her palm.

"Grabbed it with both hands and all the greed a strong hunger can inspire. The touch of sin suddenly didna mean so very much, didna seem such a great price to pay. In truth, I had already sinned by thinking on it."

"Ye have been thinking on it, have ye?"

"Oh, aye."

"'Tis good to learn I wasna alone."

"Ye thought about it, too?"

"From the first time ye curled up against me in the night." He brushed soft kisses over her face. "Then I never ceased to think about it. I found it difficult to think about anything else—even the danger we were in." He began to slowly cover her slim, long neck with kisses. "It made the days and nights we have spent here seem like years. Long, hellish years."

Slipping her fingers into his thick hair, she murmured her pleasure as his lips touched her breasts. "Did I torment you, then?"

"Night and day."

"Good." She grinned when he gave her a look of feigned reproach. "Well, ye were tormenting me some." She trailed her fingers down his spine. "I am glad to hear I wasna alone in thinking some of those days and nights were longer than they ought to be."

"I think that the rest of our stay here will seem all too short," he whispered as he touched his mouth to hers.

As Tess accepted and returned his passionate kiss, she prayed the time would be long enough for her to get at least a tentative grasp upon his heart.

Chapter

❖ 6 ❖

"ARE YE CERTAIN YE HAVE THE RIGHT MEETING place?" Tess sat and idly plucked at the mossy ground that made a slight clearing in the trees.

Sitting at her side, Revan put his arm about her shoulders and kissed her cheek. "Aye, in this forest at the place where ye can look through the fork of two trees and see the hill."

"Ah, of course, there being so few forked trees and hills in Scotland, 'tis foolish to think ye might be wrong."

Revan laughed, tugged her into his arms so that she was sprawled across his lap, and heartily kissed her. "Such a tart tongue yet such sweet kisses," he murmured as he diverted his kisses to her throat.

Realizing what Revan was contemplating as a possible way to pass the time, Tess wriggled in his hold until he looked at her. "Wasna your friend supposed to be here by now?"

"Aye." He gently pulled at the front of her doublet. "Why not loosen this? Ye must be feeling warm." He winked at her.

"Rogue. Not so warm I wish your somewhat tardy friend to catch us tussling about amongst the trees."

"Old Simon willna mind."

66

"Och, well," drawled a deep voice, "I think 'old' Simon would mind just a wee bit."

Tess gave a startled cry. Revan abruptly turned toward the voice, reaching for his sword with one hand, and unceremoniously dumping her off his lap. She realized she had been forgotten as Revan gave a glad cry, then rose to embrace Simon, both men clapping each other on the back with a rather boisterous camaraderie. As she stood up and brushed herself off, she told herself it was foolish to feel hurt. Revan was simply acting like a man. She did, however, retain the right to be annoyed.

As she waited to be remembered, she studied the man called Simon. He was built much like Revan but a few inches shorter. From his rich attire, she guessed that Simon had a taste for finery. She judged him to be of an age with Revan. Whereas Revan was fair, however, Simon was as dark as night. She could almost think him some unknown kin of her father's.

"Come, Revan, introduce me to your fair companion," Simon said at last.

When Revan drew Simon closer to her, Tess saw that the man's eyes were fine and green. His warm smile lightened his swarthy, somewhat sharply cut features.

"I assume ye are Mistress Contessa Delgado," Simon murmured, bowing slightly then taking her hand in his to lightly kiss the back of it. "May I say that my friend has never stolen a fairer maid."

"Aye, ye may," she replied with a grin as Revan moved to her side and pulled her hand free of Simon's grasp.

Keeping hold of Tess's hand, Revan asked, "So the tale of her 'kidnapping' has already been spread about, has it?"

Simon quickly grew solemn. "I fear it has. Come, 'tis late. Let us make camp, eat, and then we can make plans."

Leaving the men to that, for they were far more adept at it, Tess sat down and watched them. Simon's grave demeanor began to make Revan tense. She noticed Revan's wary expression and his careful movements. She also began to share his uneasiness. Try as she would, Tess could not convince herself that Simon's gravity was caused solely by the dire threat of treason.

They ate a light meal mostly in silence. Tess found that even more ominous. It was as if Simon did not want to speak and Revan did not dare ask any questions. The tension became so taut that even terrible information would be better than not knowing.

"Ye kenned who Tessa was," Revan said at last. "Her uncle has spread word that she was kidnapped."

"Aye." Simon sighed as he took a bracing sip of wine from the wineskin. "He not only says ye have kidnapped the lass, but that your intent is to rape and murder her."

"Does he give me some reason to commit such a vile crime?" Revan asked through gritted teeth.

"Oh, aye—vengeance. Ye did this when Brenda spurned your attentions."

Revan cursed creatively. "And this is believed?" he demanded. "Why would anyone believe it?"

"Mayhaps some have seen Mistress Brenda. She is said to be most beautiful."

"I have seen bonnier," Revan grumbled. He took a long drink.

Deciding now was not a good time to ask *who* was bonnier, Tess simply murmured, "Mayhaps those who have seen Brenda havena been as blessed as you."

Revan glared at her.

"I dinna see what is troubling you so," Tess continued. "I can easily refute the kidnapping charge. Although," she drawled, "there is a *wee* bit of truth to it. A knife at one's throat canna honestly be called a courteous invitation."

"Ye mean to belabor me with that till I am dead and buried, dinna ye?"

"Oh, nay, never that long. But it deserves recalling now and again."

"Ye held a knife to her throat?" Simon asked, his expression a mixture of concern and amusement.

"*I* will tell the tale," Revan said when Tess opened her mouth. "If I had*na* done it," he concluded after a terse relating of his escape from Thurkettle, "I would be a dead man."

"Ye forgot the part where ye threatened to give me a new smile," Tess murmured helpfully. Simon grinned.

"I had to appear really threatening or they wouldna have believed me. What was I to say? Pardon, sirs, I dinna truly intend to hurt the lass? I would have been dead ere we stepped out of that cell!"

"Reminders of the kidnapping do irritate you, eh? Not to worry," she hurried to say, "'tis a charge easily cast aside."

"Ye must get the king first."

"'Tis where we head now, is it not? Do we not travel with Simon now?"

"Nay. 'Tis best and safer if we travel separately, especially since we have people hunting us."

"Then I shall write to the king, and Simon can take him the message."

"Ye can write?"

Tess found his surprise mildly insulting. "Aye, I can write."

"That would help," said Simon, "except that I dinna have quill nor ink nor anything to write upon. Do ye?"

"Nay." Revan ran a hand through his hair. "Your word on this may do as well—for now."

Simon nodded. "'Tis a pity that isna all of it. Ere I tell you the worst of it, I assure you that many do not believe these lies. Many speak out on your behalf. Your family decries each charge and black rumor."

"What other crimes have been lain at my feet?"

"The murder of Leith MacNeill."

Revan looked shocked. "Why should I kill one of the king's men? One who aided me, worked with me?"

"Because he found out ye were no king's man but one of Douglas's."

"They try to brand me a traitor!"

"Only softly, at least when I left, but that was a fortnight ago. Those scurrilous whispers could have grown louder. Of course, the ones who decry those whispers as lies and slander were loud themselves."

"'Tis good to ken it takes *some* work to blacken my name so vilely. But with traitors at every turn and the Douglases in open revolt, it could work. The king has been taught the bitter lesson of trusting too freely."

"And has a very black temper," mumbled Tess.

Both Revan and Simon frowned at her.

"'Tisna treasonous to say so but the simple truth, and a truth it wouldna be wise to ignore. 'Twas the king's rages that helped stir up this trouble. Did he or didna he stab the earl of Douglas in a fury because the man wouldna end his alliance with the lord of the Isles? And the earl was under a safe conduct. A man who lets his rage run so hot and free might not have the patience needed to ken the truth or to wait out whatever doubts he may have. Ye may not wish to speak such truth aloud, but ye should still weigh its worth. 'Tis yet another thing that could work against you, Revan."

"The lass has the right of it," agreed Simon, "though it shouldna be spoken of so freely. If the king has some doubts, then in a moment of black rage he could cause some grievous trouble for you, Revan."

"Ye mean I could well find the king's own men and allies eager to part my head from my shoulders."

"Exactly—and ye already have quite enough people eager to do that."

"Aye, Thurkettle and no doubt the Douglases, too," Revan muttered. He was beginning to feel as if he were neck deep in a bog and sinking fast. "At least"—he took Tess's hand in his—"the taint of treason hasna touched you." He looked at Simon. "Has it?"

"Nay, she is seen as but a victim," he said cheerfully. "But," he continued, "I should be wary around any of the king's men or allies. Some may not ken that 'tis all but rumor, still hotly argued. Some may feel rumor is enough when war darkens the horizon."

Revan nodded, staring at his and Tess's clasped hands. They were in danger—both of them. He cursed inwardly. Every bow and sword threatening him threatened her as well.

"I should have left you behind," he grumbled. "I have plunged you into the thick of it, Tessa."

Tess opened her mouth to protest. But she remained silent. It would be a lie, empty words mouthed to soothe him.

He would not believe it any more than she did. He had dragged her into a great deal of trouble, but he had not caused that trouble. She felt sure she would have been caught up in it all eventually anyway. Revan should not blame himself.

"Aye, ye have. But I couldna have escaped most of this. I would have stumbled onto what Uncle was plotting sooner or later. Then I would have had to stand against him. Also, we ken now that he has always wished me dead."

"Why does your uncle wish you dead?" asked Simon.

"I have a small fortune and some land."

"And," added Revan, "she kens a few things about Thurkettle and about the Douglases that he doesna wish told."

"That explains it," muttered Simon, then paused for another drink of wine.

"Explains what?" Revan demanded, wishing it wasn't going to be another answer he was not going to like.

"There is coin offered for your deaths by Thurkettle and by the Douglases."

"For *both* of us?" Even as he asked, Revan put his arm about Tess's shoulders, holding her closer to his side.

"Aye—for both of you. That they would offer a bounty for *her* head puzzled me. But our compatriot within the Douglas camp assured me it was true. They badly wish to catch both of you ere ye can reach the king. From what our friend said, word of it is spreading swiftly. Ye willna be able to trust anyone.''

"Surely, if the king heard of that, he would realize that my uncle was spreading lies," Tess said. "If Uncle claims Revan wishes to murder me and plays the wronged party, then later offers money for my death, that alone exposes him as a liar.''

"It should," agreed Simon, "but the accusations against Revan are all that reach the king's ear. And 'tis just as much a rumor as all the rest. More so. There is, after all, the fact that ye are gone to give the hint of truth to the tales Thurkettle spreads.''

Tess remained unconvinced. "Ye can weaken that hint of truth when ye return to the king. Ye can say that I am well, that Revan isna the one who seeks to kill me. Ye can say that I vouched for all Revan said.''

"I will and it may help. I would still be wary of the king's men. There is much confusion and mistrust just now." He looked at Revan. "Now, mayhaps ye can tell me all ye have learned.''

"Are ye certain it will be heeded? If my loyalty is now in doubt, then my information will be as well.''

Simon grimaced and rubbed his chin. "'Tis possible. But I feel certain ye have supporters enough to make all ye can tell me useful. And, too, if it's proved true in the end, it proves your loyalty.''

Tess tugged free of Revan's hold and stood up. "Well, I will leave you men to discuss the details and seek my bed. 'Tis certain the days ahead will be ones demanding all the strength and wit I can muster." After murmuring good sleep to both men, she went to where Revan had laid out their meager bedding.

"A pretty lass," Simon murmured, watching Revan closely.

"Aye, and if I am fated to be hindered with a lass during this trouble, she is the best of the lot.''

"I could see how ye *appreciated* her." He ignored Revan's scowl. "The question is—can ye trust her?"

Revan hesitated only a moment before he nodded. "Aye. I didna at first, but she freely shared all she kenned about Thurkettle's intrigues. And she kens that her uncle wishes her dead, that he has done so for quite a while. As she says—'tis a fool who gives loyalty to a man who seeks to murder her."

"And is her loyalty now to you?"

"She kens I will do all I am able to keep her safe. What I *am* sure of is that her loyalty lies with the king."

"'Twill do. What have ye discovered, then?"

"A lot and yet, mayhaps, not enough."

Careful to include every fact as well as all possibilities, Revan told Simon all he had learned from his spying and from Tess. Simon had gathered some information as well, much of it confirming what Revan had discovered. A war was in the offing, and it looked as if it would be soon.

"Is the king prepared? Does he have the men to face Douglas's army?" asked Revan after they spent several moments silently mulling over the information.

"He works hard to gather enough." Simon idly poked at the dying fire with a slender twig.

"Douglas thinks to snare the throne for himself."

"Aye. He was so close just after James the First was murdered that he has gained a fever for it. And, though I should only admit so to you, the ninth earl of Douglas has a righteous grievance. The king's minions butchered the sixth earl and his brother, mere lads, at the 'Black Dinner,' then the king himself killed the eighth earl. Both times the promise of safe conduct was treacherously ignored by the crown. If the crown itself was not on the bargaining table, this would be naught but a simple blood feud."

Revan nodded slowly. "And Douglas lands have been taken. Aye, true enough, there has been wrong on both sides. I, too, have seen it. But I believe the earls of Douglas dealt in treachery ere the murders began."

"They did, indeed. They were allowed to grow far too powerful, far too rich."

"If we are the victors, 'twill be an end to these cursed Douglases."

"Ah, my friend, the Black Douglases will fall, but the Red Douglases of Drumlanrig, of Dalkeith, and of Angus are poised to rise up upon the ashes of their kinsmen. They will surely profit from the fall of the Blacks."

"Surely the king has the wit to keep them from growing as powerful."

"Let us pray that is so." Simon studied Revan a moment before adding, "Ye could gain if we win this approaching war."

"If I am not cut down as a traitor?" Revan grimaced. "What gains there might be obtained from my kinsmen's staunch support willna come to me. My father and my two elder brothers will reap the rewards—as is right. I have gained a knighthood and some coin. That is enough. I shall never be a rich man."

"Then ye must wed to gain it. Ye should be more than a man-at-arms to fickle kings all of your days."

"I have no quarrel with my life as it is."

Simon shrugged. "To marry wealth and land which one is denied by some accident of birth or by circumstance is seen as a wise step to take, a fortunate one, and carries no shame. Ye are not ill-favored. Most maids with coin and land must wed men with far less to offer than you. Ye should barter what ye have ere ye age or the trials of battle steal it from you. Ye could well find ye regret your fine sentiments when all chance has passed."

"What? That I may be aged or crippled some day and pine for some pinched-faced, shrewish wife?"

"Not all maids blessed with a fortune or land are sour of face and nature."

Thoughts of Tess suddenly filled Revan's head, but he forced them away. She held a beauty and a nature he could easily be comfortable with as well as all the passion he needed. There was all he could wish for in a woman, in a mate, plus coin and land. There was temptation and one he felt he had to resist.

"I canna help how I feel, Simon. To me such a mating is distasteful. I would gain all but give nothing. 'Twould be if I were no more than some whore."

"I can see that your heart and mind are set firm. Nevertheless, I shall ask you to think upon it, ponder it some. I dinna see it as an uneven trade. Aye, and think on this—any maid with coin and land *will* be made to marry, and ye would do a lot better by them than many another man. I press you on this, for 'tis my belief that such marriages are the only way younger sons, such as we are, will ever gain more than honor. And honor doesna give a man much fleshly comfort."

"Why do I begin to feel that ye press me on this—now— for other reasons?"

Simon grimaced faintly, then sighed. "Aye, mayhaps I do. Ye could but reach out and gain all ye need—now."

"Ye mean Tessa."

"Aye—I mean Mistress Delgado. Ye are lovers already—"

"I ne'er said so," Revan said quickly.

"There was no need. 'Tis clear to see. No need to look so fierce, my friend. I would never blacken her name. 'Tisna my way and ye ken it. I but saw the—shall we say camaraderie?—between you, the way ye look at each other, and even the way ye bicker. Mayhaps only a friend such as I am can or would see it. And, as a friend, I seek to advise you to grasp what is at hand."

"Tessa deserves much more than some mercenary mating."

"And though I have watched you together only these few hours, I say ye would give her more. Mayhaps much more than ye wish to admit even to yourself." Revan remained quiet, so Simon shrugged and abruptly changed the subject. "Where do ye ride to next?"

Revan eagerly pursued this new conversation. "'Tis a difficult choice. There are many paths to take, but I think all of them will be watched."

"There is little doubt of that, but I think the straightest route to the king will be the one most closely guarded."

"I agree. I mean to take a very twisted route. First I thought I would hie to my brother Nairn's keep."

"That place must be watched as well."

"Aye, but unless a full army encircles him and holds him under siege, I can slip within his walls. I need another horse and more supplies. My hope is that my enemies will decide it is too out of the way, even too simple and clear a choice, thus only place a light force to watch there."

"And then what? Do ye mean to leave the lass there?"

"Nay." Revan sighed and ran a hand through his hair. "Nairn has sent the best strength of his fighting men to the king's side, and I'm sure he means to join them himself soon. Even if he offered to hold Tess, she wouldna be safe there if Thurkettle set after her in force."

"Which ye believe he will."

"Like a starving wolf after a fawn. And not simply for all he would gain upon her death. With each day that passes, he must begin to realize how great a danger she is to him. He will start to recall all she may have seen or heard."

"Well, if ye reach the Comyns or Delgados, there will be help aplenty there for you."

"I hadna yet decided to go to them. Tessa says that they can be trusted, but she hasna lived with them for five years, mayhaps longer."

"They can be trusted. Have no fear of that. They are neither very wealthy nor very powerful, but their loyalty is something I would be willing to swear by." Simon smiled briefly. "'Tis often jested that they strive to atone for their ancestor's taking up of arms against Robert the First. Many of their men are close to the king, many are in the church, and many are in some work that touches upon the law. Aye, ye can trust them with your life. Go to them. They will surely aid you in getting to the king *and* in ending these black accusations against you.''

"Ye are well acquainted with them?"

"Well enough."

"How is it I can bring none to mind, then? I faintly recall the court painter Delgado, Tessa's father, but no others.''

"Well, they dinna often remain Delgados. They are quick to take on a good Scots name if they wed or gain some land." Simon began to bank the fire. "Aye—go to them. They are en route to the king. Once on Silvio Comyn's lands ye are almost in reach. Silvio will see that ye complete the journey alive.''

"Unless he, too, has heard the black accusations against me.''

"Rumor and accusation willna sway these men. They may be wary, but ye have all they will need to believe in your innocence—Contessa and her word upon it. Now, to bed, my friend. Ye sorely need to rest.''

"I should take a turn at watch," Revan murmured as he stood up and brushed himself off. "But selfishness prompts me to accept your offer.''

"Good sense does. Ye ken the truth of what I say."

Revan grinned briefly. "Aye."

"One other word of caution—the Delgados and the Comyns feel very strongly about the chastity of their women.''

"Do ye try to warn me that I could find myself forcibly set before some priest?''

"Ye may wish to consider the possibility."

"Well, I need not worry about that. I will say naught, nor will Tessa speak. So how could they ken what has passed between us?''

"Mayhaps the same way I did."

That possibility was not one Revan felt inclined to

consider, so he quickly turned the subject. "When we meet again, my friend, 'twill be to fight at the king's side." He briefly clasped Simon's outstretched hand.

"If we must. I pray it will never come to a bloodletting."

"I fear God willna heed your prayers this time, Simon."

Chapter

❖ 7 ❖

"DO YOU THINK SIMON CAN REACH THE KING—
safely and in time?" Tess hoped that talking would take her
mind off of how meager a protection her clothes were
against the cold, damp afternoon. The weather had worsened steadily since they had left Simon at dawn.

Carefully urging his weary mount down the rocky slope,
Revan nodded. "Aye. Simon is clever at hiding, slipping
away unseen, losing his pursuers, and all of that. If any man
can make it to the king, 'tis Simon." Then he paused.
"Unless James takes flight."

"He fled once before, did he?" She decided the power of
the Douglases was worthy of inspiring fear in the king.

"Aye—in fifty-two when the Tiger earl of Crawford
raised his army against him. The king thought to flee to
France, but the good Bishop Kennedy persuaded him to stay
and stand firm. Crawford was then beaten at Brechin. Then
the king foolishly forgave the Douglas. Ye can now see
where that has led us."

Tess sighed and nodded, her cheek rubbing against his
damp back. "Peace never seems to visit Scotland for long."

It was true; Revan had no encouraging words to offer, so
he concentrated on getting them through the thick scrub
forest at the base of the hill. He had known little peace in his

lifetime. Although he was not adverse to fighting, he did, at times, grow heartily sick of it.

Glancing up at the sky, he frowned. The sky grew blacker, the storm clouds churning ominously. Soon there would be far more to contend with than the cold misty rain.

"There is a small crofter's hut ahead. I passed a night in it as I traveled to your uncle's. We will pause there."

Although she frowned up at the threatening sky as well, she murmured, "'Tisna night yet."

"Nay, and I would dearly like to travel farther, but I dinna believe the weather will abide by my wishes."

"Aye, I fear ye may be right."

Grinning faintly, Revan patted her slim leg where it rested against his. "I ken well how that must pain you."

She bit back a laugh. "Keep your eyes upon this trail—if ye could grace this precarious path with such a grand name."

The path was pathetic, Tess mused. There were few roads in the border counties, most cut through the rough terrain by drovers taking their cattle or sheep to market, but they could not even use those. They had too many enemies to elude. That forced them to pick their way through little-used paths, sometimes lacking even those. She wondered how she could ever have been so foolish as to think she would like to travel. Seeing new places may well be fun, but getting there was more trouble than it was worth, especially under their present circumstances.

When she saw the crofter's hut, she inwardly sighed, then told herself not to be so particular. It was a tiny earthen-walled hut with a rough thatched roof, but it was shelter. They needed protection from the impending storm far more than they needed finery or luxury. If she could somehow have a wash in heated water, she would be content.

After dismounting before the poor house, Revan helped Tess down. "'Tis a mean place, but it can be made warm and dry. Just allow me a moment to be sure no animals have nested within since I was last here."

Tess waited patiently by his tired horse as Revan stepped inside. The door was little more than a stiffened oiled hide but it could be secured to keep out the wind and rain. She was not surprised when Revan returned and led his mount inside. The horse was vital to their success. It was necessary to pamper the animal.

Stepping inside, she looked around the small, dark interior as Revan tended to his horse. Either the house had not been deserted for long or each wayfarer who made use of it kept it clean. There was a central hearth and a rope-sprung bed up against the wall with what looked to be a thin, straw-stuffed mattress. Ah, well, it would be better than the ground, she told herself as she moved to start a fire.

"I will get some wood," Revan said. "There is a small byre here with a few supplies."

Glancing around, Tess saw enough pots to heat water. "Can ye see if there is a large tub or even a barrel?"

"What for?"

"A bath—a *hot* bath."

"Ah, now, that would be fine. Aye, I will see what I can find. First, though, we need wood or peat for the fire and feed for the horse," he murmured as he stepped outside.

Tess decided to heat some water right away. Even if he found nothing to use as a tub, she wanted hot water to wash up with. She was brushing the snarls from her hair when Revan dragged a large wooden vat into the house. She was barely able to contain her delight.

Setting it near the center hearth, Revan grinned at her. "I cleaned it out, and it seemed watertight."

"Oh, this shall be near to heaven." She grabbed a bucket to get some more water. "It feels as if it has been years since I have had a hot bath."

It was not until the vat was filled that she became aware of the complete lack of privacy she would have. She looked at Revan, who squatted by the fire preparing them some porridge. Although the full fury of the coming storm had not yet struck, she could hear the rain was pounding on the ground. She could not ask him to go outside. Telling herself that there was no need for modesty since they were lovers did very little to ease her mind. She felt awkward.

"Can ye move so that your back is toward me and I can enjoy some privacy?" she finally asked him, cursing silently when she felt the tingle of a blush upon her cheeks.

Looking at her, Revan slowly grinned. "I believe I have seen all your fair charms, dearling."

"Aye, but those times ye were privy to them, I wasna of a mind to care."

He laughed softly but moved so that his back was toward her. Tess eagerly stripped out of her clothes. She sighed with pleasure as she lowered herself into the heated water. Closing her eyes, she lay there enjoying its soothing, cleansing warmth. Soon growing pleasantly drowsy, she was startled by a soft splash and the sudden movement of the water. Opening her eyes, she nearly gaped as she watched Revan lower his long body into the water.

"What are ye about?" she whispered, moving so that he could squeeze his body in.

"Joining you. The way ye were lolling about, I feared the water would cool ere I could enjoy it."

"I would have heated more," she said nervously, struggling to remember she was intending to have a bath and not be distracted by his lean, masculine beauty.

"I have saved you all that extra labor."

"Somehow I dinna think that was your sole purpose."

"Ye may well be right. Turn round and I will help you bathe, then ye can assist me."

Carefully she turned. Looking away did not help much, for soon his hands were moving over her. The way he washed her back was pleasant, gently seductive, then he tucked her up against him so that he could reach around to the front of her.

Tess soon found her passions growing hotter as he slowly rubbed his soapy hands over her body. then trickled water over her to rinse away the soap. All the while he kissed her neck, her shoulders, and nibbled at her ears. She trembled, slowly closing her eyes as he used both hands to spread lather over her breasts, then ever so slowly rinsed it away. Her breathing grew heavy and unsteady. A soft groan of hunger escaped her and she readily opened to his touch as he took his tormenting strokes even lower.

When he grasped her by the shoulders, she responded to his silent urging and turned to face him. She met his gaze and felt her desire grow as she read the want reflected there. He gave her a gentle yet inviting kiss even as he pressed the soap into her hands. Smiling faintly, she began to wash him.

Rising up on her knees, she reached behind him to wash his back. He took quick advantage of her position, lathing and suckling her breasts as she freely caressed her. With unsteady hands she made swift work of that chore and quickly returned to crouching in front of him.

Deciding he needed a taste of the torment he so gleefully meted out, she started by washing his arms. She used the same tantalizing methods he had as she bathed his broad chest, then his strong legs. All the while she meticulously avoided his groin. Finally she smiled at him, watching him closely as she soaped her hands. She lightly brushed her lips over his as she curled her fingers around his erection. The way he groaned, trembled, and closed his eyes told her clearly how he enjoyed her slow stroking touch. She found his delight exciting, increasing her own desire.

She leaned forward to press soft, lingering kisses against his throat and chest. He made a low rumbling sound as he threaded his fingers through her hair. His agitated movements told her that he was struggling to hold back, to control his desire. Tess hoped he would lose that control soon, for she had none left.

Just as she began to wonder if she imagined his hunger for her, he grabbed her by the waist. She gasped as, in a few short moves, he joined their bodies together. Tess sat still, surprised at this new way of uniting their bodies, and savored how good it felt. After he cupped her face in his

hands and gave her a slow, searing kiss, she met his gaze.
Dazedly she noticed how passion caused the gray to
overwhelm the blue in his fine eyes, turning them a dark,
turbulent color.

"Ah, sweet lass," he murmured, sliding his hands down
her sides until he clasped her by her slender hips. "Ye fit so
well. Like a finely made glove—soft, warm, tight yet
supple."

"A glove, eh? There is something I can do that no glove
can, Sir Halyard."

"Aye? And what is that?"

Touching her mouth to his, she whispered, "Move."

Tess relished the soft groan that escaped him when she
began to move. Their kiss was an imitation of their intimate
movement, echoing the growing ferocity of their lovemaking. As the gratification of her hunger swept over her, he
tightened his grip upon her hips. She greedily pressed down
as he bucked upward in response to his own release. As she
struggled to recover, she clung to him, her cheek against his
shoulder.

Revan idly caressed her back. "I believe I can rightly say
that ye have never had a bath like this before."

"Nay, that is true enough. I usually wash my hair." She
smiled against his skin when he laughed.

"Wretch. I dangle for flattery and ye give me impertinence," he murmured and subtly eased the rich intimacy of
their embrace. When she sat looking at him with a quizzical
expression, he warily asked, "What is it?"

"I was but puzzling over how pleased ye are to be the
first man to do this for me."

"Well, 'tis pleasing. 'Twould please any man."

"Why?"

"What?"

"Why would it? I doubt many women are the first. In
truth, by the time some men wed, I doubt there is much left
they havna done—in this matter at least. Yet, a man finds
great pleasure in learning that he is the first for his woman.

Aye, most times he demands to be and faults her if he isna. Indeed, men try to cast aside all chastity as soon as they are able, dinna like any woman to ken that she is the first. So why do men find it such a source of pleasure to be the first for a woman?''

'''Tis a fair question,'' he managed to say after a long moment of silence.

Silence resumed and, after a minute or two she drawled, ''Aye—fair, yet one ye seem most reluctant to answer.''

''Mayhaps that is because I have no answer. Turn round and I will wash your hair.''

She turned so that her back was toward him, quickly deciding that she liked the arrangement as he began to massage the soap into her hair. ''So, are ye saying that 'tis one of those facts, indisputable and unalterable, that actually has no reason to be?''

He gave her hair a brief tug and grinned at her soft curse. ''Though I am loath to admit it—aye, 'tis probably so. But we Scotsmen are far less particular than many another such as the English or the Italians. Mayhaps 'tis best compared to a man's feelings in battle. Most men take great pride in being the first to breach an enemy's defense, yet, more often than not, the price he pays for that privilege is a swift and bloody death.'' He began to slowly rinse the lather from her hair.

''Ah, now there is a thought to warm a lass's heart. 'Tis wondrous fine to be compared to a suicidal charge.''

Revan laughed, then grew serious again. ''Ye ask me to answer a puzzle I have never given a thought to—simply accepted as truth. Mayhaps later, after I have thought it over for a while, I can give you a better reply. Now 'tis your turn to wash my hair, and then we may have our supper.''

Since the bathwater was growing cool, Tess readily did as he asked. They used their clothes to dry themselves off, then wrapped themselves in blankets. Tess quickly scrubbed out their clothes before helping Revan empty the water, using buckets at first but then dragging the vat to the doorway to tip the remainder out. Revan set the vat near the fire, and

Tess draped their clothing over the rim so that the heat of the flames could dry them.

Their supper consisted of porridge supplemented by a little of the cheese Simon had given them. It was a poor meal and one Tess was finding tiresome, but she knew it would do no good to complain. At the first opportunity she vowed to have a meal fit for a king.

Outside the storm grew fiercer. Soon the howling wind and driving rain chilled the small cottage until the only real warmth was close to the fire. As she washed out their bowls, Revan dragged the straw mattress from the cot and set it before the fire. She eyed it warily as he spread a blanket over it.

"Are ye certain that it is free of vermin?" she asked even as she cautiously sat down on it.

"Aye." He sat beside her and put his arm around her shoulders. "As certain as one can be. When I slept on it before, I gained no new companions. I believe it is still free of such wildlife. In truth, I dinna think anyone has been here since I was as everything is just as I left it." He picked up his wineskin, took a drink, and passed it over to her.

After helping herself to a drink of the warm, sweet wine, Tess gave it back to him. "Do ye think the storm will end by the morning?"

"The fiercest storms are ofttimes the shortest. I hope 'tis true this time." He frowned, hoping they wouldn't lose time.

"It could bring our enemies closer to us?"

"Nay, if the storm is so fierce that it binds us to this place, 'twill also force them to seek shelter and stay there. This storm could even be to our benefit, as it will surely wash away any trail we may have left for them to follow."

"Then why did ye frown so when ye mentioned the possibility of being stuck here?"

He rubbed his chin with the palm of his hand as he stared into the fire. "'Twould be precious time lost."

"Ah—time. If the information ye gathered is correct,

then we still have six weeks, mayhaps longer.'' She could tell by his face that he did not find that comforting.

''Aye. *If* we have six weeks. *If* our information is correct. Even if it is, 'tis still important to get our news to the king as soon as we can. One needs to prepare for battle. True, the king works to gather an army, and all ken that this confrontation is past due, but they canna say just when. A man willna put aside his planting on a guess. No man will risk his family starving come winter because the king 'thinks' there will be a battle.''

''Nay, of course not.'' She took his hand between her own. ''Well, ye have Simon. Ye did feel he would get word to the king.''

His expression lightened slightly. ''Aye, he can. 'Tis but difficult to ignore one simple fact. He is in the heart of the Douglas lands and will be riding toward the king. Anyone doing that will be suspect. The Douglases willna let anyone do that if they can stop it.''

''He is but one man. In this wild country that can be a great advantage. There are many places for him to hide.''

''Ye seek to ease my worries.'' He smiled down at her.

Tess kissed his cheek. ''Aye, I do, and ye shouldna cast aside my efforts so quickly. 'Tis a dark time we are caught in. Worrying will do no good. Ye said Simon was clever. Remember that and set aside the matter. I believe we ourselves have more than enough to prey upon our minds. Why add to it by fretting over something ye can do naught about?''

''How very sensible.''

''I thought so.''

Revan chuckled. ''By needing to huddle here for a while, I have been given time to think too much.''

''Then mayhaps the answer is to distract you.'' She nibbled gently at his earlobe.

''Tis a possibility.''

''If ye prefer sitting and fretting, ye need just say so.'' She began to cover his strong throat with soft heated kisses, and the arm he had draped about her shoulders tightened slightly.

"Nay, I believe I should prefer being distracted."

His hand on the back of her head, he turned her mouth toward his. The hunger behind the kiss they shared startled him a little. After two days and nights in the cave where they did little more than make love, he had expected that hunger to wane some by now. Instead, it was richer, deeper. Knowing the pleasure he could find in her arms only made him want more. It worried him, for he could foresee no future for them, yet the need she infected him with seemed to demand one. Good sense told him to distance himself from her before it got worse, but he could not, would not heed it. Instead, he began to consider glutting himself, of taking all he could before it had to end.

Tess moved her soft, small hands down his body, easing off the loosely secured blanket he wore. He trembled beneath her touch and wished she would be bolder, yet enjoyed her lingering innocence. Revan continued to kiss her, to sit still as she tested her skills, until his desire demanded more. He eased her down onto her back and crouched over her as he opened her blanket wrap. Lowering himself down into her welcoming arms, he began to kiss her throat as he ran his hands over her slim body.

"Was I not supposed to distract you?" Tess found speech a little difficult as he leisurely toyed with her breasts using his hands, his lips, and his tongue to send her passions soaring.

"Oh, ye are, lass. There has never been a woman so sweetly distracting."

"Well, that was easily done. It appears I but needed to say 'aye.'"

Revan smiled briefly against the warm silken skin of her midriff. "Actually, ye but need to say 'mayhaps.'"

That flattery, spoken in his passion-roughened voice, combined with his caresses to finally rob her of the power of coherent speech. She curled her fingers in his thick fair hair and gave herself over completely to his lovemaking. The only sounds she made were soft, mostly mumbled assertions of how much delight he gave her. Even that died, choked off by shock, when the hot touch of his lips and tongue slid upward from her inner thighs.

She bucked in rejection of the deeply personal caress only once. He grasped her by the hips to hold her still, and an instant later she had no wish to retreat from the intimacy. Tess melted to his will, opening to his intimate kiss and arching greedily as her passion grew. When he felt her release draw near, she called to him, crying out with pleasure as he swiftly united their bodies. She clung tightly to him as he drove them both to the full gratification of their needs.

It was not long after Revan had briefly left the bed to wash himself, then return to gently bathe her that Tess began to feel embarrassed. He took her into his arms, and she kept her cheek pressed against his broad chest, unable to look at him. It was difficult to meet the gaze of a man who had just seen her behave with such a lack of restraint and, she feared, perhaps even in a manner better fitted to a common whore.

As he combed his fingers through her thick, lightly tangled hair, Revan frowned. Tess was holding herself a little tensely. He hoped he had not shocked her too badly. The last thing he wished to do was chill the heat of her passion by expecting too much of her too quickly. Her desires matched his in strength, and he had trouble recalling that he still needed to go slowly with her.

"Is that a whore's trick?" Tess whispered, finally pushed to voice her greatest fear.

"Nay. In truth, any man with sense would hesitate to give one of those wenches such loving." He grasped her by the chin and turned her face up to his, smiling faintly at her blush. "Ah, but ye, wee Tessa, are very sweet." He grinned when she blushed even more, then brushed a kiss over her mouth. "Ye tempt a man to be very creative."

She shook her head before resting it against his chest
again as she tried to smother a yawn. "Creative, is it? I had
meant to distract you."

"Ye did that very well, lass." He saw her try to hide
another yawn and pressed a kiss to the top of her head. "Get
some rest, loving. Dawn isna so very far away."

Tess groaned and ignored his soft chuckle. "That is the
second thing I promise to myself," she muttered. "As soon
as we are safe, I shall sleep late for a week. In fact, I believe
I will simply stay abed."

"Aye, that does sound a fine idea." He gently smoothed
his hands up and down her slim back. "But ye said that was
the second thing ye promise to yourself. What is the first?"

"Ah, the first." She curled herself more comfortably
around him, yawned, and closed her eyes. "The first is a
sumptuous feast, and I shall eat so much that they shall need
to carry me to my bed. I shall have fruit and cream and
cheese and meat. Aye—a great deal of meat."

"Well, porridge does grow a bit tedious."

"I meant no criticism."

"I ken it. But I may be able to satisfy at least one of your
wishes. If we wake early enough and the storm has cleared,
I shall go hunting."

"Would that be wise? Or safe?"

"As wise or safe as it will ever be until we reach the king.
Our enemies hadna found us ere this storm descended, and
it has washed away our scent. I will get us some small fowl
or meat, and we can prepare it for cooking ere we ride
away."

"I can wait until we are with the king."

"Aye, but I can see no true harm in pausing a moment to
supplement our meager fare. 'Twill do us good, give us
some needed strength, and—" he grinned—"I ken that ye
will be most grateful to me."

She briefly looked at him with mock disgust before
closing her eyes again. "Aye, I would be grateful, but *how*
grateful shall depend upon the fare."

"How grateful would ye be for a nice plump grouse?"

The mere thought of it made her mouth water. "Very grateful, indeed. So much so that I need to think long and hard on a suitable reward."

"Ye mean to go to sleep."

"Aye, but if ye bring me back something heartier than porridge, ye will soon see that I can think whilst asleep. I need not stay awake all night to decide upon a reward."

"Intriguing. Sleep well, then. I may bring back a full brace of birds."

"One will do. And pray that ye dinna bring back any two-legged carrion trailing at your heels."

"Dinna worry. For a wee while I mean to be the hunter, not the hunted."

Chapter

❖ 8 ❖

AFTER SETTING THE SADDLE PACKS BY THE
doorway, Tess frowned and hooked up the stiffened hide
that served as a door. She stood on the worn threshold stone
and stared out toward the wood encircling the small cottage.
What fields may have once been cleared had become badly
overgrown. But she was only partly aware of the rain-
washed beauty around her. It had been hours since Revan
had left.

Revan had set off when the sky was only faintly lightened
by the coming dawn. The moment he had left her sight, she
had wanted him back. She was unable to think of anything
but the dangers he might face. Although they had seen no
sign of their pursuers, even Revan had been unable to say
that they were safe. Suddenly she wanted to be gone from
the cottage, wanted to be fleeing toward the king again.

Sighing, she went and sat by the fire. She had dressed,
packed up their meager supplies, and now could only wait.
After yanking off her cap, she finger-combed her hair and
began to braid it. It would probably not fit her cap and have
to be undone, but she badly needed something to keep
herself busy.

When she was only halfway done with her braid, she
tensed. A soft sound like a boot scraping across stone

distracted her. Even as she looked up, she knew it was not Revan. He would have announced himself in some way. She was not surprised to see her uncle's man, Thomas, but alarm quickly seized her.

Tess cursed and leapt to her feet, but she was a moment too slow. Thomas, followed by Donald, swiftly crossed the room. She eluded them, but when she turned to bolt for the door, she found her way blocked by two more of her uncle's men-at-arms. There was no chance of escape. Her only clear thought was to delay until Revan returned. Although she was not sure what Revan could do against such odds, it was her only plan.

Thomas lunged for her again. She ducked out of his reach. There was not much in the tiny poor cottage, but she grabbed what little she could and hurled it at them, including the peat and wood Revan had brought in for the fire. It kept Thomas and Donald at a distance as she pelted them with all she could put her hands on, but it afforded her no opportunity to flee. The two men swore and called for their companions in the doorway to aid them. That pair answered with hoots of derision and laughter.

The moment she ran out of things to throw at them, both Donald and Thomas charged her. Tess danced out of Thomas's reach, but Donald was able to trip her. She hit the packed earthen floor hard, and before she could catch her breath and scramble to her feet, the bulky Donald sat on her. It took her a moment to catch hold of enough breath to speak.

"Get off of me, ye great hulking oaf," she snapped.

"Ye stay right there, Donald," ordered Thomas as he crouched before Tess and grabbed hold of her wrists, yanking her arms in front of her.

"Ye canna take me back to Uncle Fergus," she protested as Thomas tightly bound her wrists together with a length of coarse rope.

"I can and I will. She is secured, Donald. Ye can get up now."

Donald hopped to his feet, and Thomas dragged her to hers by the rope about her wrists. Tess tried to kick him, but he held her at a safe distance from him. She knew she would get no sympathy or mercy from the man. However, she decided to test his love for his own skin by reminding him of how he was aiding her uncle in his crimes.

"Ye will be a party to murder, Thomas." She felt her brief hope die when he just smiled.

"'Twill be your fine knight who is blamed for whatever fate befalls you."

"My *uncle* is the one who wants me dead."

"Canna say I much blame him for that," muttered Donald.

"Ye willna find it such a great jest when ye are dangling from the gibbet for this crime. Aye, hanging like carrion and without having enjoyed any gain for all you did."

"'Tis your pretty Sir Halyard who will hang," snapped Thomas as he dragged her toward the doorway.

"Aye, Sir Thurkettle has it all planned," agreed Donald as he fell into step behind them.

The two men in the doorway stepped back outside. Tess cursed viciously as she was tugged out of the cottage, stumbling over the threshold. The fools thought her uncle so clever he could consistently thwart justice. She tried very hard not to think about how often her uncle did just that.

"My uncle will be caught some day, and ye will both fall with him." She tried to drag her feet, to slow Thomas's dogged march toward the tethered horses. "He would throw both of you to the dogs without hesitation if he thought he could save his own hide."

"Shut your mouth, wench." Thomas picked her up and roughly set her on a horse as Donald and the other two men mounted theirs. "Ye willna talk us out of this, and if ye keep trying, I will shut your mouth for you." He briefly shook his fist at her before mounting behind her.

Tess decided to be quiet. She did not know what sort of hold her uncle had on his men. It could be a simple matter of their believing that they were already so deeply involved in her uncle's plots that they could not untangle themselves now. They could also believe that Sir Fergus could do exactly as he pleased, especially since Fergus had already broken many a law over the years without suffering in the slightest. Unless she knew why they would not heed her, she could make no substantive arguments. Even if she did know, it might not do her any good anyway. Her uncle could have as deadly a hold on these men as the Douglases had on him.

"He means to drag you into treason against the king," she said. She wanted to make one last attempt to sway them from blindly obeying her uncle.

"I told you to shut your mouth."

She gasped and quickly grasped the pommel of the saddle when Thomas suddenly kicked his horse into a gallop. As her four captors made their somewhat reckless way through the wood, she chanced a brief glance over her shoulder. The cottage was almost out of sight. Thomas cuffed her offside the head, and she faced front again, her head throbbing slightly from the blow.

It puzzled her a little that the men were not setting a trap for Revan. She knew her uncle wanted Revan as much—if not more—than he wanted her. Tess prayed the four men she was with were all there was, that no more waited out of sight at the cottage for an unwary Revan. It was important that Revan remain free, important for Scotland. She was but one tiny cog in the wheel. Her life was nothing compared to the need to stop the Douglases from grasping all of Scotland. That would be the way Revan would—indeed, *had* to—see it.

A sense of utter defeat washed over her. She fought to push it aside. It was true that Revan could not risk himself to save her, that he had to think of Scotland and King James before her, but that did not mean she was ultimately doomed. She was still alive. Where there was life, there was hope. That was the thought she had to cling to. She must not let despair weaken her.

Tess forced her attention to studying the trail they took. She knew she had an abominable sense of direction, yet knew she would have to find some scrap of one to depend upon. If she was able to extract herself from her predicament, she would have to make her way back to Revan or to her father's kin. She tried her utmost to keep her full attention upon the route they took and not on the fact that she might never see Revan again.

REVAN pulled his mount to a halt and stared harder at the ground. For several moments he had been watching the mossy damp ground beneath his horse's hooves. Now, with a thrill of alarm, he realized what it was that had caught and held his attention—hoofprints. Since he was certain they did not belong to his mount, it could only mean that someone was or recently had been in the area.

The joy he had felt over catching two birds faded immediately. Whoever had drawn near *could* be an innocent traveler, but Revan dared not trust in that. There were far too many people hunting him and Tessa. While still out of sight of the cottage, he dismounted and secured his horse to a stunted hawthorne tree.

When a closer inspection of the tracks revealed that four horsemen had approached the cottage, Revan's alarm grew. As he crept up to the tiny house, being careful to remain hidden, he searched for some sign of the intruders themselves.

By the time he was able to see the cottage, Revan was certain that whoever had ridden up to the house was no longer nearby. He remained watchful as he hurried across the clear front yard. The moment he stepped inside the tiny cottage he knew Tess was gone. He discarded caution as he searched the place and its surrounding lands to gain some idea of how she had been taken and in what direction.

It was easy to see from the devastated house that Tess had

gone unwillingly. Tracks outside of the cottage revealed that she had briefly dragged her feet from the threshold to the men's waiting horses. The men had then ridden southward, back over the trail he and Tess had ridden, back toward Thurkettle. There was only one thing Revan was able to find some comfort in—there was no blood, no sign at all that Tess had been hurt. As he scooped up their belongings and hurried back to his mount, he used that knowledge to calm his fears. He may yet have a chance to save her.

Once mounted, he followed the men's trail. They had made no attempt to hide their tracks; the damp muddy earth was clearly marked by their passing. When he was certain there were just four men, Revan began to plot.

Although he felt a twinge of discomfort over turning his back on the king for even a short time, Revan decided he had no choice. Without his help Tess would die.

"WE will camp here," announced Thomas as he reined in his mount and looked around.

Tess almost thanked the man but told herself not to be such an idiot. They had ridden all day over rough and dangerous terrain. She was relieved to be through with that for a while—but not grateful. After all, if these curs had not kidnapped her, she would not have had to suffer through the uncomfortable ride, she thought crossly. She glared at Thomas, who, after he dismounted, roughly yanked her out of the saddle.

"Be careful, ye great boar," she snapped as she fought to stand despite a trembling weakness in her legs.

"I would watch how ye talk to me, woman."

"Would ye, now? And just what can ye do to me? Ye are taking me to my execution. There canna be much worse than that." Tess struggled to maintain her haughty calm when Thomas narrowed his beady eyes.

"I can make your last miles pure hell, lassie."

"Since I have to make my journey within sniffing

distance of you, I would say that ye have already done that.''

Thomas flushed as his companions snickered. ''Shut your mouth and go sit by that tree.''

''What tree? We are in a forest, fool. There are dozens of them.''

He shoved her toward a stunted pine that was more dead than alive. ''Sit there.''

She decided to do as she was told. It gave her some mild satisfaction to insult and harass the man, but it was dangerous. Carefully, her bound wrists making it a little awkward, she sat down by the gnarled tree. For a little while she rested, paying no heed to the four men setting up camp. Then her attention was firmly caught by what they were saying.

''He *will* come after her,'' Thomas insisted as he squatted by the newly made fire and took a long drink from his wineskin. ''A man like Sir Halyard will believe it his duty.''

Donald shook his head, his stringy dark hair swaying with the movement. ''He has to get to the king. That is what his duty is. He willna set that aside for some wee brown lass.''

''Nay, but he is arrogant and will think he can rescue her without losing much time.''

''Well, 'twillna hurt to be ready,'' grumbled one of the two men Tess did not recognize. ''None of us can say for certain what the man will do.''

Thomas nodded vigorously at this sign of support. ''Heed our friend John, Donald. I may be wrong to think we can entrap that knight by holding the lass, but we canna take any chances now. Time is running out. Thurkettle is getting very nervous.''

''So, how do we set this trap?'' asked Donald. ''The man willna just walk into our grasp. If he is after the lass, he will be wary. Halyard has enough wit to ken that we will try to use her to reach him.''

''Aye, but there are four of us and only one of him. Two of us will keep watch just beyond the campsite. And two of us will remain close to the lass. We can change watches every few hours.''

"And when do we sleep?'' demanded John.

"There willna be much of that, I fear,'' admitted Thomas. "But if we gain hold of both Halyard and the lass, Thurkettle will be certain to reward us well, indeed. A night without sleep willna kill us.''

Tess battled to hide her fear. Incompetent though they were, they did have the advantage of numbers. No matter how good a soldier Revan was, he would be but one man against four. She prayed she had been right when she had decided he would not come after her, that aiding the king and Scotland would be the path he chose to take. Tess shuddered at the thought that she might be the cause of Revan's capture and, far worse, of his death.

REVAN cursed as he overheard Thomas's plan. He had hoped that the men would not have expected anyone to chase after Tess. That they had not only expected it but wanted him to do so would make Tess's rescue much more difficult—if not impossible.

Lying on his stomach in the midst of a thicket and hidden from sight, he had a good view of the campsite. He tried to bolster himself with the fact that he had managed to draw so close to the camp he could hear the plots against him yet had not been espied by his enemies. There was too much to worry about, however. Was his mount far enough away to remain undetected? Would Tess be hurt or killed in the course of any rescue attempt? Each plan of action he devised held more chance of failure than he would have liked.

The plan he finally chose also held a great opportunity for utter failure, but he had no choice. He would decrease the numbers arrayed against him by silencing the two men sent outside of the campsite. Revan was confident he could do that much without difficulty. The problem would come when he went to fetch his horse. He would have to hope that, in the interval between silencing the guards and riding in to grab Tess, no one thought to check on the two sent out to be sentries. He also had to hope that Tess had the wit to react immediately and properly when he did ride into camp. Bursting into the camp would give him the element of surprise, but that would be lost if Tess did not react as he needed her to. All he could do was pray that all went well, and that Tess's wit was as strong as ever.

He silently cursed again. His chosen hiding place was almost painfully uncomfortable. Sharp sticks and thorns jabbed at him from all angles. It was going to be a long night, he decided as he prepared to await his chance.

WHEN Thomas set a tin plate of lumpy porridge in her lap, Tess stared at it a moment before looking up at him. "I canna eat this."

"'Tis all ye will get, wench. So eat it and shut your mouth."

"I intend to eat it, ill-made though it is. But I canna do so with my wrists bound, can I?"

"Ye must think I am as dumb as mud."

Tess forced herself not to respond. Insulting Thomas was all too easy, but it would gain her nothing. She needed her wrists untied and not simply to eat the poor fare he had set before her. Her hands would soon be useless, and, when and if she had a chance to escape, she might not be able to grasp it if she did not get some respite from her bonds.

"If ye willna untie me, then someone must feed me. I canna feed myself with my wrists bound like this."

"All right, curse you, but just until ye have finished eating." He untied her, then ordered, "Donald, ye come and sit by this wench and watch her closely." The moment Donald was squatted by Tess, Thomas went back to the campfire to talk to the two men still seated there.

It was several moments before Tess could even begin to eat. She needed to rub the feeling back into her hands. Grimacing as she picked up the spoon, she ate the porridge, idly wishing that her ability to taste had become as numb as her hands had been. The porridge was gray, stodgy, and lumpy, as well as cold, but she was hungry. It was undoubtedly the worst porridge she had ever eaten. She concentrated on what Thomas and the other men talked of in the vain hope that she could forget what she was putting into her mouth.

"John, I want you and Wallace to take the first watch outside the camp," ordered Thomas.

"Why must we be the first?" complained John.

"First or last—what matter?"

"If it doesna matter, then ye and Donald can take the first one."

Thomas spat out a foul oath, then called to Donald, "Come with me. We are to take the first watch." When Donald stood up and started toward him, he snapped, "Tie the bitch back up first, ye great fool."

Tess winced as Donald roughly yanked her hands in front of her and tightly rebound them. She had not been granted as long a respite as she had hoped for. As Donald and Thomas disappeared into the night-shrouded forest, she looked toward John and Wallace. The way the two men were staring at her and exchanging hurried whispers made her nervous. She was suddenly convinced that the condition of her hands and wrists would soon be the very least of her troubles. Tess recognized the narrowed glances they were slanting her way. Lust, in its ugliest form.

Attempting to distract them, she struggled to her feet. Both men immediately stood up and took a few steps toward her. For a brief moment she thought about calling out to Thomas and Donald but quickly discarded the idea. She could not be certain those two would stop these men from raping her. They could just as easily join in.

"And just where do ye think ye are going?" demanded John as he cautiously edged toward her.

"To Canterbury to have a wee chat with the archbishop." That he was so clearly prepared for her to try and bolt did not bode well for her chances of eluding him and his hulking companion. "'Tis about time I took myself a pilgrimage."

"Ye are a saucy wench. Too quick of tongue by far."

"I need to walk about some. Riding all day as we did has left me sore and cramped." She began to slowly pace in a circle; John and Wallace moved to flank her.

"A wench like yourself ought to be well accustomed to that. I wager ye have been riding Sir Halyard day and night."

"Such wit. Ye must have the guardroom at my uncle's keep rocked with hilarity day and night."

Wallace chuckled and John flushed, glaring even harder at Tess. "Ye are a sour-tongued wench. I mean to mend that, I do. I have got something here that will sweeten you up." He leered at her.

It was difficult to stifle her panic, but Tess maintained a calm facade as she continued to idly pace. "So, ye mean to rape me. My, how surprising." She paused briefly to send him a hard, cold stare. "Ye touch me, lay even one filthy finger upon me, and I shall see ye roasting in Hell's fires."

For a moment both men simply stared at her, their mouths slightly agape, with a look of shock and a hint of fear. Tess began to walk again. She knew that soon their torpid minds would conclude that her threat was heartfelt but empty. Since the moment she reached her uncle's she would be murdered, there would be no chance for her to avenge whatever indignities they now forced upon her. As far as she could see, only a miracle could save her now. Such things had been very scarce in her short life. She prayed that, if she was unable to escape rape, it would not scar the memories of all she had shared with Revan.

REVAN carefully lowered Thomas's limp body to the ground. He knew it would have been wiser to kill both Thomas and Donald instead of just rendering them unconscious. However, he had never had the stomach for slipping a knife into an unsuspecting man. Wrapping his arm about their throats and banging them offside the head with a rock was about as underhanded as he could tolerate. As he took one last look at Tess before he retrieved his horse, Revan decided it was time he overcame such niceties of feeling.

When he saw what was happening in camp, Revan nearly charged straight in. Neither man was touching Tess, yet their intentions were blatantly clear. He ached to end their slow advance on Tess, wanted to stop them before they could even lay a hand on her, but he knew that would be a mistake. The two men had the look of mercenaries and were both older and heavier than he. For them to have survived so long in such a brutal craft, they had to have skill. He dared not chance a direct battle with war-hardened men. It might be more heroic, but right now it was far more important to free Tess.

He took one brief but close look at her. She appeared unaware of the danger, calmly walking in a circle, but then he saw her hands. Tess had them clasped together so tightly her knuckles were bone white. She knew exactly what was about to happen and was fighting to be brave. He was filled with admiration for her but knew now was not the time to indulge in it. She was more in need of rescue than respect.

With extreme care Revan crept away from the campsite. As soon as he felt confident that no one there could hear him, he began to move faster. He soon raced for his horse. Time was not something he had much of, not if he was going to stop those men from touching Tess. He admitted to himself that, while fear for Tess was certainly part of what drove him, so was possession. The thought of another man touching Tess, especially if she was unwilling, brought forth a strong emotion within him, and it was sheer blinding rage.

Revan threw himself on the back of his mount. For a little while he held the horse to a slow and cautious pace through the wood. As he drew closer to the small clearing where the camp was, the trees began to thin out. He urged his horse to a faster pace until soon he was racing toward the camp at a full gallop, his mount's pounding hoofbeats echoing through the night-shadowed forest.

Tess stiffened as John reached out for her. However, his hand never touched her, for he paused, frowning as he looked toward the woods that encircled them. It took her a moment to still the pounding in her ears caused by her growing fear, but then she heard what he had—hoofbeats. The sound echoed through the wood in such a way it was difficult to tell from which direction they came or even how many horsemen there were. An instant later a lone rider burst into the clearing, and Tess knew the sweet, heady taste of renewed hope.

"Revan," she whispered as he rode straight toward her and her two erstwhile assailants.

Wallace flung himself out of harm's way, but John stood where he was, gaping. Revan kicked him full in the face as he rode by. He sped past Tess, then turned his mount and headed back in her direction. She held out her bound hands. Easing the pace of his horse, Revan grabbed her by the ropes about her wrists and yanked her up across the saddle in front of him. He had to grasp her by the hem of her doublet and give her an added boost to steady her before he could urge his mount to a greater speed.

Wallace and John were on their feet and drawing their swords by the time Revan had his horse up to a pace that enabled him to elude them. Keeping his mount at a speed that allowed for some small measure of caution, Revan plunged back into the wood, leaving Wallace and John bellowing for Thomas and Donald. He knew all four men would be on his trail as soon as they were able.

Tess struggled not to complain and thus distract Revan as they made their swift but precarious way through the trees. For as long as she could she endured being flung over the saddle like a sack of grain. Her stomach was roiling from being bounced against the hard saddle, and her head pulsed with pain. Finally she had to speak out. Even if it cost them a few precious moments of delay, she had to get upright.

"Revan." Her voice wavered in time with the horse's pace and was weakened by her breathlessness. "I canna bear it any longer. Let me up."

"Sorry, lass," he said as he quickly reined to a halt, then helped her sit up. "We canna pause to rest," he added as he neatly untied her wrists. "Those fools will soon be after us."

"Ah, so after riding all day, they now force us to ride all night."

"I fear so, loving. We will rest when I feel certain we have placed a safe distance between us and them and find a secure place to camp."

She sighed with resignation as he spurred the horse onward again. All she could do was hold on and pray that they did not have some terrible accident while riding in the treacherous shadowy landscape of night.

Chapter

◈ 9 ◈

THE LIGHT HURT TESS'S EYES. CURSING SOFTLY, she closed them again. It could not have been more than a few minutes since they had stopped fleeing her uncle's hirelings. Revan could not be so cruel as to make her rise so soon after she had lain down, yet that had to be his booted foot nudging her in the back. As she turned onto her back, she mused groggily that the moss-covered ground did not feel as soft and welcoming as it had when she had first spread a blanket over it and collapsed onto the rough bed. She glared at Revan.

"Ye said we would rest," she grumbled. "I have barely gotten myself settled."

"I fear ye are in error, dearling. Ye have been deeply asleep for nearly six hours. Can ye not recall that 'twas just dawn when we halted, yet 'tis now high nooning." He pointed up at the sun.

"It doesna feel like hours since I closed my eyes, but mere moments."

He gave her a smile full of sympathy as he helped her to her feet. She stretched and rubbed the small of her back as she looked around. They were in a gully between two hillsides, probably the result of past, heavy winter runoffs. It was a good hiding place, but, seeing Revan already packing up their meager belongings, she knew they had lingered as long as he could allow them to.

She quickly moved to the shelter of some scrub bushes to relieve herself. Returning to their small campsite, she took the waterskin from Revan's mount and sparingly washed up. She was still too sleepy to talk so ate in silence as they shared a small breakfast of the ever-present porridge. It was not until they were mounted and on their way that she saw the bald carcasses of two birds dangling from a rope tied to his saddle.

"So ye did catch some game," she murmured, idly deciding that, although it was pleasant to ride along wrapped in his arms, she preferred riding behind him. It was far less confining and she could hang on to his strong body if the need arose.

"Aye. When we camp for the night, we can have ourselves a fine feast."

"There is something to look forward to."

"'Twas tempting to cook them this morning, but I dared not build too large a fire. So I but readied them for roasting as ye snored."

"I dinna snore."

"Nay, of course not."

She ignored his soft laughter. "I thank ye for coming to my rescue. In truth, I didna expect ye to. After all, ye must get to the king. Then, too, ye had to ken that they would set a trap for you."

"Oh, aye. I could see how they could use you to bait it, although I was a wee bit surprised to find that they had the wit for such a plan. If I had had any doubts about your fate, I wouldna have come after you." He was not so sure he spoke the truth but forced the weight of confidence into his voice. "If pressed, I can claim ye were needed to further the cause of King James. After all, ye were privy to much of what was said and done at your uncle's."

"'Tis ever wise to plan one's excuses beforehand." She

smiled faintly when he chuckled. "I dinna think I was ever so pleased to see anyone in all my born days."

"'Twas clear to see that ye were in some trouble."

"Aye, but I was planning my escape."

"Ah, of course."

The sarcastic tone of his voice prompted her to insist, "I was."

They began to amiably argue the chances of her escaping without his aid. Tess knew she had had no chance at all but felt obligated to diminish his arrogance. It struck her as decidedly odd that their pleasant bickering should make her feel good. His somewhat bland explanation for why he had come after her had stung a little. This evidence of an easy camaraderie between them soothed that. He might not feel the depth of emotion she wished him to, but he was not indifferent, either.

It was not long before she became drowsy. Resting against Revan's broad back, she gave in to it, slipping into a pleasant state of half-sleep. She knew he would warn her when and if she needed to be alert.

"Tess," whispered Revan. "Tessa, ye must wake up. We need to hide ourselves for a while."

Surprised that she had fallen completely asleep yet not fallen off the horse, Tess struggled to fully wake up. Revan was urging his mount through a thick copse of trees on the brow of a small hill. A quick glance up at the sky told her it was midafternoon. She wondered briefly how far they had managed to travel while she had been slumped unawares against Revan. What she did not immediately see was why Revan believed they had to hide themselves away for a time.

Revan halted his horse, dismounted, and quickly helped her down from the saddle. "There are some men in the hollow."

"Douglas men? Or my uncle's?" she asked as he looped his mount's reins over a branch of an alder tree.

"I didna wait to see." He took her by the hand and led

her toward the edge of the hill overlooking the hollow. ''I thought it best to try and judge that whilst still unseen.''

He laid down on his stomach, and she did the same. Tess inched forward over the rocky ground right along with him. She wondered why he did not wince and decided his front was a lot harder than hers. Once at the very edge of the hill she looked down into the hollow but saw nothing. She frowned at Revan.

''I see no one. Are ye certain there are men near at hand?''

''Very certain. I was about to take the same path they are. They startled some birds, and so I saw them in time to elude them. I turned round and set this hill between us. There— look.''

Tess strained forward to get a better look as riders entered the hollow between the hill she and Revan crouched on and the one opposite them. There were at least twenty men. She frowned at the pair who led the small force. Something was very familiar about the man who rode the heavy-set black stallion with the white stockings. She was not sure if it was the horse she recognized or the man who rode it, but the shock of familiarity could not be denied. Tess wished she could remember where or when she had seen the man. It would explain why the sight of him with this small force alarmed her so.

''Douglas men,'' Revan hissed. ''They ride to join the earl's traitorous army.''

''Are ye certain, Revan?'' Tess thought she recognized the colors the men wore as those of the Douglases, but she was not sure. She had never done a serious study of heraldry.

''Aye. Though they dinna fly his banner, most wear the earl's colors. Except for the man on the black stallion and the two men riding directly behind him. They wear no man's colors,'' he muttered.

''And that is a bad thing?'' She began to wish she had paid more heed to the ways of knights and soldiers so that she did not have to ask Revan so many questions now.

"'Tis suspicious. A man wears his colors to be marked as friend as well as foe. Such markings can save him from being struck down by his own allies. Nay, a man usually has a good reason for not wearing his colors when he goes abroad. He clearly feels he risks more by being identified."

"Simon wore no colors," she murmured, staring at the man they discussed.

"Simon was spying." He frowned. "A spy marks himself as no man's or any man's. He must not be seen as an enemy to those he would spy upon, and he doesna want his friends to see him with the enemy and thus mark him as a traitor. The question must be—which does this man fear? That he is exposed to his friends or to his foes?"

"Such intrigues. Why must they go on?"

"Power, loving. Those who have none crave some, and many who have some crave more."

She glanced at him to catch him frowning at her. "Is there something wrong?"

"I but puzzled over the way ye stare at that man so hard."

Tess sighed. "I canna shake the feeling that I have seen him before. The pity is, I canna recall the when nor the where. Yet something within me tells me 'tis very important that I do. I feel both recognition and alarm when I look upon him. 'Tis so important, I ken it, yet, curse my addled brain, the memory willna come."

"Mayhaps if we draw closer." Taking her by the hand, he urged her to follow as he crept through the undergrowth covering the rocky hillside. "Ye may just be too distant to see what would bring forth the memory."

"Is that not a bit risky?" She struggled to creep along, keeping hidden in the trees and undergrowth but not stumbling, thus giving them away. "I thought we were supposed to be hiding."

"'Tis best if we are unseen, but this could be very important."

"This could also be but foolishness, simply my mind playing tricks upon me."

"I canna believe ye are subject to such fancies."

"I thank ye for that confidence in me. I pray it isna unearned."

Tess studied the man when they paused halfway down the hillside. He was tall and bone thin. His face was of a hawkish cast. The closer look did bring a stronger sense of recognition. It also increased her sense of alarm.

She edged even closer. To her horror her foot loosened a few stones, and they tumbled noisily down the hillside. She and Revan held themselves tensely still, but it did no good. A man heard, then saw the stones, and his gaze followed their path back up the hill. Despite their cover, he saw Revan and Tess and cried out an alarm.

Revan cursed, grabbed Tess by the hand, and raced back up the hill. The few times she stumbled, he did not hesitate but dragged her along until she regained her footing. Once he reached his horse, he threw her into the saddle, unhitched the animal, and flung himself up behind her.

"Hang on, lass," he ordered as he urged his steed down the hillside away from those men now racing to catch them. "We shall have a hard ride to shake these curs."

Since he had put her in front of him, she had only the saddle pommel or the horse's mane to cling to. She chose the mane, for it gave her a better hold. It also forced her to lean forward out of Revan's way.

As they came down off of the hill, men closed in on them from the right and the left. More came from behind, having charged up the hill only to chase Revan back down another slope. Revan spurred his mount forward through the only opening left—straight ahead. Tess felt the wind stirred by the swing of swords, but she and Revan slipped through the closing net unscathed. Douglas's men bellowed their frustration and, despite a moment's confusion as they all fought to change direction, were soon after her and Revan.

She began to fear for Revan's poor horse as they

thundered over the rough ground. It could not possibly carry the two of them for very long at full speed. They kept a safe distance between them and their pursuers, the occasional arrow shot falling uselessly short, but they could not lengthen that span. It seemed to her that it was simply a matter of whose mount began to tire sooner. Tess prayed it was not Revan's horse that faltered first.

"'Twill be hazardous ahead, loving!" Revan shouted. "Hold tight, for I mean to try twisting and turning until I lose them."

Ahead of them lay a thick wood. It would take skill to wend their way through, and Revan intended to make it even more difficult for them by veering erratically. Tess closed her eyes and began to pray as they plunged into the forest.

Finally the horse's pace eased, and she no longer needed to concentrate on staying in the saddle. Little by little she eased the stiffness within her body, a stiffness born as much from fear as from holding the same awkward pose for too long. By the time she was sitting upright, Revan had reined his horse in to a slow walk. The poor animal was weary, but Tess felt confident that it would recover. She turned her thoughts to their pursuers but could neither see nor hear them.

"Have we lost them, then?" she asked and slumped against Revan.

"Aye, dearling, I believe we have."

"So your weaving and veering worked."

"Well, aye, though a bit of luck didna hurt, either. The poor fools got themselves all atangle. The last I heard, their leader was bellowing for them to rally round him, that they didna have the time to waste on such a mad chase."

"Which would mean that they are expected to be at a muster somewhere and soon."

"'Twould seem so. They could have run us down, but they didna wish to spend any longer at the game."

"Do ye think they recognized us?"

"Nay. They would never have given up the chase had they kenned who we were. They probably thought us just curious lads and decided we couldna have heard anything of much importance."

"Yet they chased us." She did not dare to think the danger had passed quite so easily.

"Well, we bolted. 'Twas natural for them to give chase. It may have just taken them a while to decide that we couldna have learned anything worth tiring their horses over."

"I pray ye are right. 'Tis difficult to set aside one's fears, though. So what do we do now? Stay within the forest?"

"Not in this part. 'Tis so close to where we finally shook our hunters that I wouldna dare to light a fire. And we have some fowl to roast, aye?"

"Aye." She smiled when she felt him kiss her ear. "I do look forward to that."

"And ye shall have it as soon as I can find us a clearing. This poor lad needs a rest and some water as well." He reached around her to pat his mount's neck. "I hate to lose the last hour or so of daylight, but I canna push him any harder."

"Nay, he must rest. What is his name? I have never heard ye call him by any name."

Revan cleared his throat, then grimaced when she looked at him over her shoulder. "He doesna have a name."

"Ye havena named the poor fellow? Everyone names his mount. Is he a new one, then?"

"Nay, I have had him for nigh on three years. I just havena given it much thought. So I just call him Horse."

"That is no proper name! Nay, especially not after all he has done for us. I shall have to give the matter some thought. He needs a name to suit his skill and speed. Horse—humph! I am amazed he hasna tossed ye right out of the saddle ere now. Ye have no doubt sorely bruised his pride and vanity." She patted the animal's neck. "I shall think of a name that will make this poor gelding feel the stallion again.''

"Fine. Setting a name to things has never been my strength. There is something else ye can think on. Who was that man ye thought ye had seen before?"

She nodded. "I mean to remember. Sometimes the memory one finds elusive returns more easily if one doesna try so hard to grasp it. 'Tis the way I have found it to be.''

Revan held back a groan. "I willna press you on it anymore. Dinna get too comfortable, loving,'' he murmured when she nestled against him. "I believe there is a place to camp not far from here. It has been a long time, but I did travel this way once or twice in the past.''

It was only a half hour later, or less, when they reached a clearing that was perfect for their campsite. A circle of stones about a shallow hollow in the ground was ample proof that other travelers had decided the same. The moment her feet touched the ground, Tess realized how weary she was. Revan handed her a blanket, flint, and tinder. After picking up a few sticks, she went to sit by the circle of stones to begin a fire.

As soon as he had tended to his horse, Revan joined her, bringing wood to feed the fire and make a spit to cook the fowl on. Tess slipped away into the surrounding thickets to see to her personal needs. She then used the water from his waterskin sparingly to lightly wash herself. By the time she was done and returned to sit by his side, the smell of the roasting birds was enough to make her stomach rumble noisily. She ignored Revan's grin and had a small drink from his wineskin.

Tess soon decided that waiting for those birds to cook was the hardest thing she had ever done. When Revan finally pronounced them ready to eat, she feared disgracing herself, sure that she was so hungry she would forsake all good manners. One glance at the way Revan was devouring his share relieved her of that concern. They ate in silence, only occasionally exchanging a grin, as they made complete pigs of themselves. Tess did not think she had ever enjoyed a meal more.

"That was delicious," she murmured as she tossed the last bone into the fire and used a little water to wash off her hands and face. "'Twas also very swinish of us."

"Aye. After days of naught but porridge, I believe one is allowed such graceless gluttony." Revan took the waterskin from her and also washed up.

"One certainly should be. In fact, I think it should be a law."

"I shall mention it to the king when next I speak with him. Wine?" He offered her the wineskin.

"Thank ye." She took a small sip, knowing their supply was dwindling, then handed it back to him. "I ken that days of deprivation may make my judgment questionable, but I dinna think I have ever tasted anything so fine, at least not since my cousin Tomas's wedding."

"Tomas?"

"Aye—Tomas Delgado Mackintyre." When he grinned, she gave him a mock look of severe reprimand.

"Mackintyre, eh? Ye are kin to them, too?"

"Through Tomas's marriage to a Mackintyre heiress, but that is all. He took the name Mackintyre, for there was property involved. 'Twas a grand feasting and such a gay time. Many people from the king's court were there, for Tomas was well liked amongst the courtiers. 'Twas the last time I was amongst my father's kinsmen. My parents died soon afterward. A storm and heavy flooding had weakened the bridge they rode over one night," she murmured.

Lost in her memories, she was only faintly aware of Revan's soft words of condolence and nodded absently in response to them. She could easily recall the handsome Tomas's wedding. While she had romped with her younger cousins, her parents had visited with all their friends, laughing and dancing as if it was their own wedding day. The images in her mind were painfully distinct. Tess could see her mother and father toasting the bride and groom, could hear them laugh at her uncle Comyn's wry jokes, could see them standing with a tall, dark courtier who clapped her father on the back and flirted with her mother . . .

Tess froze as her mind clung to that image of the courtier. She saw him with increasing clarity. He was thin, almost too thin, and had hawklike features. It was, without question, the same man she had seen from the hillside. But at the wedding he had worn his colors, proclaiming his allegiances proudly with his dress.

"Oh, sweet Mary," she whispered.

"Is something wrong, Tess?" Revan asked as he gently grasped her by the arm. "Ye have grown quite pale."

"I ken why that man we saw today was so familiar."

Revan gripped her by the shoulders and forced her to face him. "Ye ken his name?"

"Nay, not his name. He was at my cousin Tomas's wedding. He was one of the courtiers."

"Well, that need not be very dangerous. There are hundreds who linger about the king's court. Some never even speak to James. Was he wearing any colors ye can recall or recognize? That would help."

"Oh, aye, he wore his colors. He saw no need to hide who or what he was on that day. I fear this courtier could be most dangerous, Revan. He was dressed as one of the king's own household guards."

"Lord save us." Revan took a full minute to overcome his shock. "Are ye certain, Tessa? Very certain?"

"Very certain. My uncle Comyn told me so himself. There is a Comyn or two so honored. Mayhaps he but does as ye and Simon—spies for the king."

"I would pray that was so, but 'tis too unlikely. Simon and I were chosen not only for our skills." He released her and ran a hand through his hair. "'Twas felt that, as mere knights in the king's army, we wouldna have been as closely marked by his enemies as others within the court might have been."

"Others such as the king's own household guards." She knew now why seeing that man with the traitors had alarmed her so.

"Aye—just so. This is dire news, indeed."

"Mayhaps I am wrong."

"I can hear in your voice that ye dinna believe that."

"Nay, I dinna. I dinna wish it to be so, but the memory is too clear, too strong, to be denied. I can see him standing there, tall and reed thin, slapping Papa on the back and laughing at some jest. God's tears, do ye think he was a traitor even then?"

"Nay, or the Douglases would have made use of him before now."

"Can ye not guess at who he is? Ye are a king's knight. Ye must ken many of those at his court."

"Those at court are ever changing. It also takes a long while to gain any recognition or be drawn into the inner circle about King James. I wasna unseen, let us say, but I wasna embraced by all, either. Since my place was to wield my sword in James's name, I was often from court as well. This position was going to draw me closer to the throne. Aye, I ken many at court, but those men who guard the king even in his privy chamber were still beyond my touch. I ken a few but"—he shrugged—"sadly I dinna ken that man. The few times I was drawn close to the king, the man must have been elsewhere."

"Is all of that why ye could be so easily accused?"

"Mayhaps. But my name and that of my kinsmen was familiar in the court. And this last year even the king came to ken my face as well as my name."

"What game could this man be playing, then?"

"There are many to choose from." Revan absently poked at the fire with a stick. "There is one in particular that worries me the most."

"And what is that?" she pressed.

He stared into the fire, lost in his thoughts. "That he is meant to kill the king. Even if the Douglases win the coming battle, they canna truly claim victory as long as James is alive. Ye dinna leave the rightful king alive when ye mean to grab and hold his throne.''

"Nor his heirs," she whispered, terrified by the plot they may well have uncovered.

"Nay, nor his heirs. If this battle does come to pass and the Douglases appear to be losing it, what better way to turn it in their favor than by murdering the very man the opposing army fights for. It could turn a Douglas defeat into a victory. And if the Douglases win the battle, murder may still need to be done to secure the throne. Aye, murder seems the best reason for the Douglases to enlist the loyalty of a man so close to the king.''

"He would also make a very good spy."

"The best. He would be privy to a great deal of what is said, done, or planned by the king and his allies."

"What are we to do?"

Revan grimaced and put his arm about her shoulders. "Just what we are doing now—trying to get to the king as swiftly as we are able. We can no longer excuse delay by claiming Simon kens all that we do."

"'Tis certain they didna recognize us, then. If they had, they would have hunted us to the depths of Hell and beyond."

"Aye, for they would ken that we might have recognized that man and would hie to the king with the news." He kissed her cheek, then pulled away slightly. "Time for us to seek our bed. We need rest. These last two days have been exhausting ones, and those ahead will probably be equally as harried. 'Tis best if we catch all the sleep we can when we have the chance."

She yanked off her boots, then laid down on the blanket. Revan did the same and spread a second blanket over them before tucking her up against him spoon fashion. It felt good, but her desire was sadly dimmed by her weariness. Revan made no overtures toward her, and she realized he was suffering in much the same way. Exhaustion was proving to be an excellent cure for passion.

"Dinna ye think we ought to keep a watch?" she asked even as she closed her eyes and prepared to go to sleep.

"Nay. Those men arena searching for us. Also, my horse is as good as any watchhound. It has been trained to warn me of any approach, and I have trained myself to wake at his slightest sound. 'Tis why I tether it so nearby despite how it befouls our campsite. The beast can scent or hear a man ere I could ever see him."

"Yet ye dinna even grace the poor beast with a proud name."

"Ye are right. 'Tis shameful. But, there is little time for that game now. We have a much darker one to play, one whose outcome could change the fate of all Scotland."

Tess huddled closer to Revan. She did not like to think of the treacherous game they were caught in. She especially did not like to think of what they could face if they lost. It was only when Revan was so close that she could find the strength to believe that they could win.

Chapter

✧ 10 ✧

IT WAS NOT EASY, BUT TESS RESISTED THE urge to kick the calmly grazing horse as she paced around him. After only two and a half days of trouble-free travel, the horse had thrown a shoe. It was not the animal's fault, but there was no one else to take her ill-temper out on. Fate held a snare for her and Revan at every turn.

Not only did this delay threaten their mission, but she was on her own with the placidly munching horse. Revan had left her concealed in the wood while he had gone on ahead to the village she could just glimpse through the trees. He wanted to be sure that none of his enemies were in the village and that there was a blacksmith who could tend to his horse with speed and skill. His only instructions to her had been for her to wait until nightfall and, if he did not return, to try and find her way to her father's kinsmen. She did not find his parting words very comforting.

She tensed, stepping a little closer to the edge of the wood, as she espied someone emerging from the village. It was a moment or two before she was certain it was Revan trotting toward her. Tess sagged a little with relief, then fought the urge to go out and meet him or to call to him. He seemed unconcerned, but she wasn't certain.

The moment he stood before her, she asked, "Is it safe?"

"Aye, safe enough. There doesna appear to be anyone in the village whom I recognize or who recognized me."

He took up his horse's reins, then held out his other hand to her. She hesitated a moment before putting her hand in his and letting him tug her along as he headed back toward the village. In the village she could get a hot bath and a hearty meal, perhaps even a decent bed for the night. Unfortunately, she and Revan would also be seen by far too many people. She did not like it. Neither did she like marching into the place still dressed as scandalously as she was in her lad's clothing. Sensing Revan staring at her, she warily met his gaze.

"I am not very pleased about this either, but Horse needs the services of a blacksmith, and the blacksmith is in the village," he said.

Tess sighed and nodded. "I ken it. Are we to stay the night?"

"Aye, I have found us a room at the inn."

"A room all to ourselves?"

"All to ourselves. I thought it a wee bit grand myself for such a wee town, but the innkeeper claims many a fine gentleman wends his way through the village." He winked at her. "In fact, he said the Douglas himself even stops there now and again."

"So, 'tis a Douglas village. That doesna make me very happy."

"I, too, wish we could have gotten out of the Douglas's lands ere we entered any village, but need forces us to risk it. Whilst I have my horse tended to, ye can fetch us some supplies." Releasing her hand, he unhitched his purse from his belt and handed it to her. "We dinna need too much, for we should reach my brother Nairn in two or three days. We can resupply there ere we travel on to your uncle Comyn."

She faltered slightly, surprised into a brief clumsiness, and gaped at him. "When did ye decide we would go there?"

"Truth tell, when we met with Simon. He assured me that they could be trusted."

"My assurance wasna enough?" Tess felt both insulted and a little hurt.

"Well—nay. They are your kinsmen. Ye could be blind to a lot concerning them and their loyalties." He could tell by the look on her face that his words had stung, and he tried to soothe that. "Ye didna think your uncle Thurkettle was a traitor, did ye?"

"Nay." He had made a telling point, and she calmed down a little. "But I wasna too surprised, either. The knowledge was there, I just hadna brought myself to accept it yet. With my father's kinsmen I dinna think I would ever believe it of them, not until I saw one of them actually plunge a dagger into the king's heart."

"I had guessed as much, which was one reason I felt I needed another to vouch for them."

"Aye, I suppose the tangle we are caught up in requires such caution."

He took her by the hand and pressed a kiss to her palm. "It does—if only for our own safety. Now, after ye buy the supplies we need, ye are to try and find yourself another outfit of lad's clothing. Forced to twist and turn over the countryside as we are, we still have a long journey ahead of us. 'Twould be best if ye can play the lad as well as is possible. We dinna draw quite so much attention to ourselves that way." He waited as she paused to tuck her braid up into her cap.

"'Tis scandalous," she murmured as he took her by the hand again, and they started across a heather-covered field that bordered the tiny village. "And I think it may be against church law."

"I believe ye will have no trouble gaining absolution. After all, ye sin in service to the king."

"And that makes it all right, does it?"

"Well, 'twill ease the penance asked of you."

She wanted to ask if the penance she would pay for

bedding down with him could be eased as well, but bit back the words. It would begin a discussion she was not prepared for, or, worse, bring a response from him that would cut her deeply. Instead, Tess concentrated on the sight of the heather in bloom all around them. There was pleasure to be found in that sign of warmer weather.

They were barely inside the confines of the village when Revan released her hand, gave her the wineskin to be filled, and told her, "The inn is on the market square just ahead. Tell the innkeeper ye are with Wallace Frazer."

"Wallace Frazer?" She grimaced. "Could ye not think of another name?" She looked at him. "It doesna really suit you, either."

"'Tis a good common name that no one will question."

"I suppose one canna expect much from a man who canna even name his own horse."

Revan gave her a mock scowl, then nudged her toward the market center prominently marked by the large common well. "Enough of your impertinence. I shall join ye at the inn as soon as I am able." He turned to the left to urge his mount toward the blacksmith shop set at the very edge of the village.

Tess took a deep breath to try and banish her nervousness and walked on alone. A woman paused in scrubbing her threshold stone to stare at her—hard—and Tess inwardly grimaced. When the woman suddenly gaped, Tess knew her thin disguise had been penetrated already. She could only pray that most of the other villagers were either too blind or too busy to notice. If not, there would be a stir which none of Revan's sweet talk or "good common names" could settle.

She hurried from shop to shop collecting supplies. The way the merchants stared at her made her even more inclined to hurry. As she stepped into the mercer's, however, she knew she would linger a while. He had a surprisingly good selection of clothing bought from those either too wasteful to reuse it or from ones who needed what little coin he would offer. She found a full set of lad's clothes, although the doublet was painfully dull, being of a brownish hue and having had all the fine trim removed.

Her greatest find was a lady's gown of a rich blue that was only slightly faded. It was a little dated, with short sleeves and a tight laced bodice, but the linen underdress was still with it. As she gathered it up, she could almost hear Brenda shriek in dismay over the fact that her cousin would dare to wear some merchant's wife's gown, but Tess ignored the image. She also ignored the instinct that told her Revan had not intended her to spend his coin on such things. He had not ordered her one way or the other in the matter.

After bickering with the mercer until she got a reasonable price, Tess hurried away with her new purchases. She made her way to the small inn with a nervous eagerness. The overweight innkeeper showed her to the room with no hesitation until she asked for a hot bath to be prepared for her. He shook his head as he left, clearly of the opinion that taking a hot bath was far stranger than a lass wandering about dressed as a lad, something Tess knew he had guessed at once. Tess shrugged and set out her new clothes. She could not wait to show Revan how she could look when dressed as a lady ought to be dressed.

REVAN grinned as he watched the innkeeper waddle away. The man had shrugged off the strange puzzle of a knight wandering the countryside with a girl dressed like a boy. However, the hot bath Tess had asked for had the poor fellow questioning Tess's sanity.

Revan sprawled more comfortably on his bench, resting his back against the cool stone wall. The innkeeper had been as shocked as the blacksmith had been when Revan had used one of his huge vats to wash in. Tess had done exactly as he had thought she would, so he had decided to bathe elsewhere before joining her. It was evident, however, that the villagers held the common belief that immersing one's body in water was a sure way to catch the ague and die. He had worried that Tess's scandalous attire, a thin disguise seen through by many, could make them too well remembered, but it was clear that their penchant for cleanliness had overridden that. Revan chuckled again and sipped his ale.

"Ah, Revan, my gallant stallion. It has been a very long time."

The sultry voice speaking his true name startled Revan so he choked slightly on his ale and abruptly sat up straight. He stared at the buxom brunette leaning against the small rough table in front of him and struggled not to reveal his horror. The very last thing he could afford at this time was to be recognized. As he forced a smile for her, he tried to think of a way to make her hold her silence.

"Mary, what are ye doing here? The last time I set eyes upon you, ye were living in Edinburgh."

"Aye, but there was a wee bit of trouble, and my protector took to wife a very jealous lass." She reached out to thread her fingers through his still damp hair. "This poor spot is where I was born. I came home for a time." Mary trailed a finger over his cheek as she leaned forward, allowing her low neckline to gape open. "Ye canna ken how very pleased I am to see you again. I have been stranded here for months with naught to entertain me save farmers and drovers."

Revan grunted in surprise when she settled herself upon his lap and wrapped her arms about his neck. Her kiss was one of skilled passion. It did nothing for him. The narrow-eyed look she gave him when she pulled away told him she not only had sensed his complete disinterest but was infuriated by it. He struggled to think of a way to soothe that anger. Revan recalled that Mary could be as wild in her fury as she was in a bedchamber. She felt insulted, and that could make her very dangerous.

"'Tis good to see that ye are well, Mary," he said as he gently set her away from him.

"Is it? Ye dinna seem too pleased to me. I remember when—"

"I remember it as well," he said hastily, "but 'twas six

months ago or more. My life has taken a new turn since then. I have a new lover.''

"Do ye mean that wee brown lass dressed as a boy?'' She stood before him, her fists planted firmly upon her full hips. ''Ye would choose that skinny, flesh-bare child over me?''

It was hard for Revan to soften his words. Her disparaging remarks about Tess infuriated him. He looked at the full-curved Mary and felt no desire. Her scent was one of heavy perfume poorly disguising the aroma of rarely washed clothes and skin. She had more for a man to hold on to, but Revan could not remember a single time when she had fit in his hold as perfectly as Tess did. Mary had skill and a hunger to satisfy many men, but Revan no longer counted himself one of those. The way she glared at him made him realize his less than charitable thoughts were being reflected in his face.

"'Tis the way of it, Mary. I owe you no explanation.'' He immediately saw that he had taken the wrong tack with the woman.

"We were lovers. I gave myself to you.''

Since he was caught up in the argument already, he decided to see it through. ''Ye were well paid for that 'giving.''' He swiftly finished off his ale, slammed the dented tankard down onto the table, and stood up. ''I have no need for a lover now. Ye demean yourself by pressing the matter. Find yourself a man with the will and the purse to pay for it.''

Mary slipped her arms around his neck and rubbed her body against his. "Faithfulness is very admirable, Sir Halyard, but ye shouldna allow it to steal all pleasure from your life.''

"I wouldna practice faithfulness if it didna pleasure me. I am not so unselfish.'' He tugged free of her hold and grasped her tightly by the arms. ''Now, heed me, my fair Mary,'' he said, making his voice cold. ''While I abide here, I am not Sir Halyard but Wallace Frazer, a common man-at-arms. Ye best recall that upon what few occasions ye may need to address me. Ye will also forget my companion. I had none with me should any ask. Ye will do as I command, or ye will forfeit that beauty ye use to ply such a fine living.'' Despite the way she glared at him, he saw the hint of fear in her eyes and believed his warning would be heeded.

''Ye ask a great deal of me, yet I see no profit in obedience.'' She yanked free of his grip and rubbed her arms.

With a soft curse Revan extracted a few coins from his pocket and thrust them into her hand. ''There, woman. Ye are now better paid to hold your tongue than ye ever have been for your reputed charms.''

Although she closed her fingers tightly over the coins, she hissed, ''This insult will be remembered.''

''It had best be forgotten. This game ye have stumbled into far outweighs your petty jealousies and tantrums. If I ever have reason to believe ye have been the cause of trouble for me, I shall still that clattering tongue of yours forever.''

Revan pushed past her and headed toward his chambers. He ignored the insulting and ribald comments of the group of men he passed who loudly questioned his manhood because he had pushed the fulsome Mary away. As he hurried up the narrow wooden steps to the room where Tess was waiting for him, he tried to think of a way to explain why he stank of Mary's somewhat cloying scent.

The moment he stepped into the room he had bought for the night, he forgot all about Mary, the trouble she could cause, or any explanations. Tess stood by the bed, smiling faintly and nervously, dressed as a woman should be. Her thick midnight hair tumbled over her slim shoulders and was gently held back from her face by two hairpins of bone. As he shut and bolted the door, she gathered up a little of her skirts in each hand and turned in a circle. The gown could not be considered in fashion, it was faded and it did not fit her perfectly, being a bit too long and too wide at the waist, but he thought she looked endearingly lovely.

"Ah, lass, when ye finally gain the gowns your fortune and birth can fetch you, every Scotsman with blood in his veins will be rendered speechless." He tossed his cape and hat on a stool by the door and took a step toward her. "I ken it because of how ye flatter this wee pretty dress."

Tess could feel the tingling heat of a blush cover her cheeks. "Mayhaps 'twas wrong to spend your coin so, but I saw this in the mercer's shop and suddenly ached to be rid of my lad's clothes, if only for a wee while."

"Seeing you like this, how can I begrudge the cost?"

He took her into his arms and combed his fingers through her hair. Tess's pleasure abruptly ended as she caught the scent of another woman upon his clothes, a heavy flowery scent that made her wrinkle her nose. In her mind the voice of caution advised her to ignore it. The woman's scent might cling to his doublet, but the woman herself was not there. It was Tess he held. Then came the crisp voice of jealousy echoing through her mind, demanding to know just where he had been before he had come to her. Just where, when, and how had he gained the perfume upon his clothes?

"The blacksmith of this village must be a very odd fellow," she murmured.

Revan pulled away a little to look down at her. The way she crinkled up her pretty nose and scowled at his doublet explained her strange words. He had briefly forgotten how Mary left her heavy scent on a man. It had been the one thing that had often left him displeased when they had been lovers.

"I fear I was accosted by a wench eager for a bit of coin."

"Ye need offer me no explanations." Tess suddenly began to heed the voice of caution.

"Nay, I dinna, but I will. The reasons I feel I owe ye one are too many to list, the greatest being that we are bound together in this time of danger and treachery."

It pleased Tess to hear him speak of a bond even if it was not the sort she wished to share with him. She was also pleased that he felt there was reason to explain himself to her. He could just as easily have agreed that he owed her nothing. She much preferred this display of honesty. Yet, she inwardly grimaced, she prayed she would continue to be pleased after she had heard what he had to say.

"So ye were accosted, were ye?" She smiled faintly, finding it easy to believe that a woman would work hard to try and catch Revan's eye.

"Aye. I fear she scented the coin in my pocket." He was debating the wisdom of admitting to his past relationship with Mary when there was a rap at the door. "That should be our meal."

"More than porridge, I pray."

"Much more," Revan answered as he opened the door, and two young boys hurried in with heavily laden trays.

Tess clasped her hands in delight and anticipation. The trays were loaded up with meat, bread, cheese, and wine. The boys had barely set them down upon the table near the window when she was there to inspect the feast. She ignored Revan's soft laughter as he pressed a coin into each lad's hand, then ushered them out of the room.

"Dinna wait upon me—begin," he said as he shut and bolted the door.

After she set the tiny wooden bench closer to the table, Tess sat down but did not immediately start to eat. "I am not sure which to savor first."

Revan sat on another small bench opposite her. "Ye had best not hesitate too long, or I shall have eaten it all." He grabbed a still-warm loaf of bread and, after slipping his eating knife free of its sheath at his waist, began to slice it.

She helped herself to one of the thick slices of bread he cut and spooned some honey over it. Revan poured them each a tankard of wine. With only the occasional exchange of smiles over their gluttony, she and Revan proceeded to eat every morsel of food upon the trays.

When Revan offered her the last slice of bread, Tess shook her head and placed her hands over her stomach. "I am full nearly to bursting."

"There is a cure for that." Revan finished the last slice of bread and took a hearty drink of wine.

"Oh? And what might that be, other than to cease indulging in such wanton gluttony?"

He stood up and moved to stand beside her. "Well, first we must remove this tight bodice." He began to unlace it.

As she watched him undo her gown, Tess smiled faintly. She did not need to see the look in his eyes to know that he was no longer thinking of her overindulgence at the table. His hope was to inspire her to another overindulgence—in the bed. That husky note of rising desire was in his voice. She felt her body begin to respond to it.

"Ah, so that I might breathe with more ease?"

"So I may breathe with less ease." He picked her up in his arms and carried her to the high, curtained bed.

"And that will help to cure me of gluttony?" she asked as he laid her down on the bed, then sat down on the edge of it and began to tug off his boots.

"Let us say I hope to change the source of your gluttony from that of one for food to one for something else." He laid down on his side next to her.

"I had suspected as much." She put her arms about his neck and tugged him closer. "We are to halt here for the night?"

"Aye." He began to brush soft, light kisses over her face. "The horse has been reshod, but so few hours were left to the day that there didna seem much point in moving on. Though the night will be a short one, as we must leave at first light, I saw no harm in our spending it in comfort."

"Ye shall hear no complaint from me, but—are ye certain we can be safe here even through a short night?"

Only briefly did Revan consider Mary as a possible danger. The woman was uncommonly fond of her own skin. She may doubt the truth of his threats, but she would not dare to risk her life or beauty in challenging the worth of them.

"Ay, 'tis safe enough. No one shall disturb us."

MARY cursed under her breath as she eluded the grasping hands of the two men she was serving. She slammed the tankards of ale down in front of them. They were handsome enough, but they had little coin to spare. And coin was what she needed. Without it she would be stuck in the tiny village until age robbed her of her beauty. When she'd seen Revan, she had thought he was the answer to her prayers, that he would free her of the bonds of boredom and toil she was caught in all the while she lingered within the village.

She strode back to the bar, slouching against it, and cursed Revan yet again. He had scorned her, even threatened her. It infuriated her, but there was nothing she could do, no way she could make him pay for the insult he had dealt her.

The arrival of four well-armed men drew her out of her angry thoughts. They demanded ale, and she quickly filled tankards for them. Their armor was not that of a full knight but fine enough to hint at some coin in their purses, coin enough to be of use to her. As she neared the table the men sat round, she noticed that they wore the colors of the Douglas, and she saw the chance for even more gain. The Douglases owned nearly half of Scotland. The men who worked for such a powerful family had to be well paid and could even have some power themselves, if only through their liege lord. A little flattery, a little catering to their passions, and the day could yet prove to be a profitable one.

"Here, my fine stalwart soldiers," she said, smiling invitingly as she set their tankards down on the table before them. "'Tis the sweetest ale in all of the borderlands."

The tallest of the four wrapped his arm about her waist and tugged her close to his side. "And a fair maid to serve it to us. I can think of no better way to end *my* searching than to rest a night in your fair arms.''

"Spend the night where ye will, Howard," said a short, burly man at his side. "But 'twill not mark the end of this search.''

"God's tears, we have searched every inch of the borderlands and gained naught for our troubles.''

"Not *every* inch, and we had best not return to the Douglas with empty hands until we can swear to just that. He will hang us from his keep's great walls and leave us there for the corbies to feast upon if he thinks we were slack in our duty.''

"What do ye search for?" Mary asked, allowing Howard to tug her down onto his lap.

"'Tis none of your concern, wench," grumbled the short, burly man.

"Nay, yet I could be of some help.''

"Hah! Have ye heard of the reward offered? Is that it?''

"Nay. A reward, is there? Well, I should like a fair chance at it.''

The man opened his purse and set twenty-five gold riders upon the table. "This is the reward offered for aid in capturing or killing Sir Revan Halyard and his companion. And, so, wench, take your chance.''

Mary could not believe her luck. She reached for the coin only to have the man grab her tightly by the wrist, halting her. "The coin is mine.''

"Not until I am certain ye have earned it, wench. Ye have told me naught yet, if ye even ken anything of any worth.''

"The man ye seek is right over your heads, ye great fools." She chuckled when each of them glanced upward.

"Ye mean Halyard is here—in this very inn?''

"Aye. He has taken a bedchamber above. He and his wench.''

"The lass is with him?''

"Oh, aye. The lass is dressed as a lad. She is the one ye look for, aye?''

"Aye." He released her hand but quickly took up ten of the coins, allowing her to grab only fifteen.

"Here!" she cried and leapt to her feet. "Ye said the reward was all of that."

"I have yet to see the proof of what ye have told us. In truth, why should I believe ye at all? How could some common tavern wench ken a king's knight? Aye, and his secrets, his comings and goings?"

"Common tavern wench, am I?" she snapped. "I have refused far better men than you. Sir Revan Halyard was my lover for nigh onto a sixmonth when I was in Edinburgh. I ken the man very well indeed. He calls himself Wallace Frazer for the moment, but I wasna fooled. He and the skinny wench are in the best chamber. Just go up the stairs, and 'tis the door to your right. I will have the rest of that coin now."

"Ye will have it when I have them. Come on, men," he ordered the other three as he stood up and strode toward the narrow stairway. "This may be the night we can end this thrice-cursed search."

Mary smiled as she watched them hurry up the stairway. She sat down and helped herself to one of their tankards of ale. When she heard them begin to try and break down the door, she wandered outside to stand beneath Revan's window. If he was to die, she at least wished to hear it. It would pay for the insult he had dealt her.

Chapter

◆ 11 ◆

"OPEN THIS DOOR, HALYARD!"

A thundering crash against the door followed that bellowed command. Revan leapt from the bed, cursing himself for a fool. He had heard sounds, noises that had alerted the soldier within him, but his hunger for Tess had held him in her arms. Instead of heeding what had been the sound of four well-armed men hurriedly approaching their room, he had continued to stroke and kiss Tess. That distraction had cost them a valuable minute or two. He yanked on his boots, grimly determined not to let his error cost them too dearly now.

"We are trapped," Tess whispered even as she scrambled off of the bed and swiftly donned her boots.

"Nay, dearling. We may yet escape if we act swiftly." He buckled on his sword. "Grab up all ye can safely carry and slip out through the window."

"Halyard!" one of the men bellowed while they continued to hurl themselves against the door in an attempt to break into the bedchamber. "We ken ye are in there. Your Edinburgh whore told us."

"Mary. That she-devil!" hissed Revan. "'Tis clear I didna pay her enough for her silence."

Tess hesitated only a moment over the indication that the

134

woman who had left her scent on Revan had been more than some unknown tavern wench. Now was a poor time to delve into the matter. The woman had betrayed them, and it was time to flee. With the saddle pack draped about her neck, the wineskin over her shoulder and a blanket tied about her waist, Tess hurried over to the window. One glance out of it left her certain that Revan had taken the room because of the ease with which they could flee it if the need arose. A series of shabby outbuildings cluttered the area below and provided an odd stairway to the ground. After shoving the table out of her way, she gathered her skirts, swung her leg over the sill, and looked toward Revan.

"Where to once we are on the ground?" she asked.

"Head to the blacksmith's," Revan answered even as he piled what little furniture there was in front of the door. "The horse will be tethered in back of his forge, saddle at hand. It seems the blacksmith smells the stink of treason in the air and wants no part of it. Go, Tessa. I will follow in but a moment."

She cautiously climbed out of the window. It was necessary to tread warily for the roofs were of thatch. By the time she lowered herself from the last roof onto the ground, Revan was nimbly following her. She turned to start on her way to the blacksmith's—and saw the woman.

Tess knew, instinctively, that it was Mary. A twinge of jealousy tore through her as she quickly surveyed Revan's old lover. Mary was fulsome, possessing the sort of full, tempting curves Tess doubted she would ever have. Seeing what Revan was accustomed to, Tess began to seriously doubt her chances of holding on to the man. She was yanked from her dark thoughts by the sound of Revan jumping to the ground from the roof. Mary looked terrified.

"Ye betrayed me, Mary." Revan grasped Tess by the arm, knowing he had no time to deal with Mary but needing to strike back in some small way. "Ye came here to listen to my death screams, but now 'twill be yours that will rent the night."

"Nay, they forced me to tell them where ye were." Mary held out her hands in a gesture of pleading as she cowered against the ivy-swamped wall of the inn. "I swear it. I had no choice."

"How quickly and smoothly the lies fall from your lips. I have no time to deal with ye now, but I willna forget this betrayal. And, my greedy whore, by this act ye have placed yourself upon the side of treason against the king." He nodded when she gasped in terror and fear. "Aye—treason. The Douglas plots against James the Second, and ye have just aided him. 'Twill be no simple, merciful hanging for the likes of you."

"Nay! I didna ken their reasons for wanting you," she protested. "I would never betray our king."

"But ye just have. I hope your petty vengeance was worth the cost ye may yet have to pay."

Revan heard the bellows of the men as they finally crashed into the room above and stumbled over all the furniture he had set before the door. Yanking Tess along after him, Revan sprinted toward the blacksmith's. Mary's pleas for forgiveness and pity were soon overridden by the cries of the men hunting him and Tess.

His horse was exactly where the blacksmith had promised it would be. Revan saddled it, securing the cinches even as Tess secured their belongings on the back of the animal. They had just mounted, Tess seated behind him, when four armed men rounded the corner of the smith's forge. Revan spurred his horse right toward them, causing them to scatter out of the way. He heard their cries for mounts as he thundered toward the forest and, he prayed, safety.

TESS was more asleep than awake when she felt Revan rein his mount to a halt. Rubbing her eyes, she looked around. They were still surrounded by trees, but she was not sure which wooded area they were now sheltered in. She was not even sure which direction they had ridden in or for how long. That, she decided as she dismounted, was

Revan's concern and could remain so. She would only get them lost.

As Revan tended to his weary horse, she sat down. She had looked forward to a night in a real bed. It made her feel even more weary to have been thrust out of it into the night. The thought of another night spent on the ground was enough to make her want to scream.

That inclination increased tenfold when she glanced down at her dress. It had not been the finest of gowns, but it had made her feel like a lady for a little while. She had seen the appreciation in Revan's eyes. There would be none there now. Her new gown was ruined. It was splattered with mud and torn in several places. It looked worse than her too-large boy's attire. She looked a poor ragamuffin child again.

The urge to cry became achingly overpowering. Tess struggled against it as she tried to brush off some of the dirt upon her gown, but it was difficult. In her mind was the image of Mary and how very womanly she had appeared. The reminder that Mary was certainly a whore and had betrayed Revan did not help to dispel the image or ease the sadness it inflicted Tess with. She had wanted to be pretty for just a little while, to show Revan that she could do him proud. Instead, she sat there on the leaf-covered ground mud-splattered, ragged, and smelling like a horse. The quivering in her chin and lip told her she was rapidly losing the battle against tears. She cursed, for she badly wished to be strong, yet also ached to have a good wailing cry. Her hope that she could pull her tattered emotions together before Revan joined her proved a vain one. He strode over to sit at her side and stare at her.

"I fear we dare not light a fire." Revan frowned as he studied her, trying to see her expression clearly in the dim light of a three-quarter moon. "Are ye all right, Tessa? Did ye hurt yourself climbing down from that window?"

Tess only shook her head to answer no, sure that her urge to cry would be clear in her voice if she tried to speak.

Revan reached out, gently grasped her by the chin, and turned her face directly toward him. He could only see her expression a little more clearly. Despite that he knew she was upset. To his surprise, and with a touch of dismay, he realized he could sense her mood, could almost feel it himself.

"I am sorry we were driven from our fine room at the inn. I truly thought I had paid Mary enough, aye, and threatened her enough, to silence her."

"She recognized you, didna she?" Tess wondered if she would get the full truth about Mary now, and if she really wanted to hear it anyway.

"Aye, she did." He grimaced and ran a hand through his hair. "One's past can sometimes be a troublesome thing and return to haunt one at the most inconvenient of times. Many months ago she and I spent a brief time together. I traveled to and from Edinburgh a great deal, and she was my lover there."

"Edinburgh? Then why was she serving ale at a poor inn in a wee village?"

"She has kinsmen here, it seems, and she needed to flee Edinburgh. I didna ask why. That was of no interest to me. From what little she did say, it had something to do with her protector, his marriage, or mayhaps his new wife. 'Twas clear that she thought to take up with me again."

"She was fair. And fulsome," she muttered, unable to resist a brief glance down at her own small, slender body.

He put his arm about her shoulders and tugged her close. There was the hint of jealousy in her mood, and Revan discovered that he appreciated it. After the deep fear and rage he had experienced when Thurkettle's men had planned to rape her, it was soothing to see that she, too, could suffer from the twisting bonds of possessiveness. At the moment, however, hers was breeding sadness, a sense of unworthiness, as she looked to herself and found herself lacking. It was nonsense, yet he found that he understood it. Inwardly he shook his head over his own vagaries.

Common sense told him to make some bland remark, some mildly flattering nonsense she would know meant nothing. He knew he would ignore common sense. Her sadness touched him, and he needed to soothe it.

It was yet more proof of what he had begun to suspect back at the inn. The suspicion had been born when he had turned aside Mary's invitation. Mary was fulsome and skilled, a woman he would have bedded without hesitation before meeting Tess. Then he had seen Tess in her gown. There was no denying the sort of emotion that had gripped him then. He cared for the girl. It could be even worse than that, but he shied away from that knowledge.

"Aye, Mary is fulsome, but she is also a whore." He kissed the tip of Tess's nose when she glanced at him. "Ye dinna have the same curves as she, but that doesna dim the beauty of what ye do have. Aye, and I think it is perfection." Although she blushed, she gave him a look of mild disbelief. "Did I not turn from that fullness to come to you? Mary couldna raise a spark of interest. All I thought on when I espied her was how to shut her mouth. I didna do that very well, either."

"And so we had to run for our very lives yet again."

"We shall be doing that until we reach the king."

"Well, at least we have shaken this pack of hounds."

"So it would appear, but I still do not dare to light a fire. The dark hides us, but it can also hide them. I dinna wish to give them a pretty beacon to follow straight toward us."

"Nay, of course not." She sighed and stared at the tattered hem of her gown. "That ride ruined my gown, poor old thing though it was."

"Ye looked beautiful in it. If our fine supper had not been due, I should have shown my appreciation far more swiftly than I did."

Tess was able to smile. He spouted no flowery phrases; his flattery was simple and unencumbered by any grand protestations. It made it much more believable. So did the memory of how he had looked at her when he had first seen her in the gown. His ardent gaze had made her feel beautiful. That was worth more than any pretty words.

"I am sorry I spent your coin without asking first, but when I saw it, I so wished to have it, I couldna resist. Just once I wanted ye to see me dressed as a lady should be, to see me as a woman." She frowned when he slowly grinned, as it was an odd response to her soft admission.

"Tessa, after the first night we spent curled up together beneath the blankets, I have never had trouble seeing you as a woman. In truth, after my first surprise over seeing a lass dressed as a lad, I never gave much thought to what ye were wearing." She shivered slightly, and he stood up. "I will fetch our blankets."

She watched him as he got the blankets and spread one out upon the ground. It was nice to know that he felt no shame over her appearance. Yet, she was not sure it was particularly good that he had apparently paid little heed at all to the matter. Indifference was certainly not what she was longing for.

When the blanket was properly laid out, she moved to sit on it and tug off her boots. She lay down on her back and watched as Revan did the same. He settled himself at her side and spread two blankets over them. She smiled faintly when he next tugged her into his arms.

"Did ye truly take no notice of what I wore?"

"I will confess that I am not a man who pays much heed to fashion anyway. But I doubt that ignorance would make much difference. I truly gave it little thought. Occasionally I did think it more suitable for the trials we have been forced to endure." He idly nibbled her ear. "One thing I did think on when I saw ye in this gown, besides deeming ye very lovely, indeed, was how ye should have chests full of fine gowns."

"Chests full?" She began to unlace his doublet. "What should I ever do with so many?"

"Blind near every man in Scotland, as is your right, a right Thurkettle and his cursed daughter have denied you."

"At the moment that is the very least of their crimes." After he gave her a little help in tugging off his doublet, she began to unlace his shirt.

"There are times I think it the greatest of their crimes," he murmured.

For a little while they said nothing, just quietly worked to undress each other. Tess was moved by his honest concern for how poorly she had been treated by her Thurkettle kin. Even better was that there was not a hint of pity, only outrage on her behalf. She did stir more than his passion. It was not quite the depth of emotion she wanted, but it was enough to give her hope.

The moment she had him undressed to his braies and she wore only her linen shift, she moved to sprawl on top of him. Tess decided it was past time to do more than hope. She was going to work a little more assertively to reach his heart. And, she mused, if she still hadna won his heart at the end of this travail, at least she would have set herself firmly in his memory.

"And this Mary was skilled, was she?" She brushed her lips over his.

"Aye, as any whore must be. But 'tis not necessarily skill that can fire a man's blood, lass. What ye may lack in skills, ye make amends for in the honesty of your passion. In truth, at times your innocence stirs me more than any practiced hand ever has. Now and again I have even found myself wishing I could have come to your arms with an equal innocence," he whispered, cupping her face in his hands and stealing a fuller kiss before she neatly eluded his grasp.

"That would have been nice," she murmured against his neck as she encircled it with soft, teasing kisses and light strokes of her tongue. "However, 'tis probably best that one of us kenned what we were about."

His chuckle caught in his throat as she moved her warm caresses to his chest. She was being unusually daring tonight. He threaded his fingers through her silken hair and wondered just how daring she might become.

Tess felt him tremble as she touched her lips to his stomach. He groaned softly when she drew idle patterns upon his muscular abdomen with her tongue. The way he was shifting slightly beneath her revealed his growing desire as well. That knowledge increased her sense of daring. If passion was all he could give her, she would learn how to take all he had to give. She was also discovering that actively stirring his passion was having a heady effect upon her own.

As she covered his strong thighs with kisses, she neatly removed his braies. He groaned his approval when she curled her fingers around his erection. Recalling how he had loved her back at the deserted crofter's hut, she hesitantly replaced her hand with her mouth. The way his body jerked beneath her kiss made her think she had gone too far, but when she started to pull away, he tightened his grip in her hair, silently urging her to continue.

Revan felt a shudder of intense delight ripple through his entire body the first time her soft warm lips touched his staff. He tried to tell her what he wanted but was not sure he was coherent. Despite that, she did everything he could hope for. When she took him into her mouth, he lost all sense   of time and place, knew only Tessa and the exquisite pleasure she was giving him. He fought for some control over the desire raging within him.

Finally, knowing he could not restrain himself much longer, he grasped her by the arms and pulled her up his body to neatly, swiftly, unite them. He cried out his pleasure at the warmth he found there, the sweet heated proof that her passion was as hot as his own. She needed no help from him but rode him with an instinctive skill that brought them both to the blinding release they craved. He caught her in his arms when she sagged against him, holding her tightly as they both trembled and sought to catch their breath. It was a long time before he eased the rich intimacy of their embrace, tucked her up against his side, and pulled the blankets over their cooling bodies.

"Ye still have your shift on," he muttered after several moments of contented silence.

"Well, I canna think of everything." She rubbed her cheek against his chest, enjoying the way he combed his fingers through her hair.

"'Tis a good thing, too. They no doubt heard the result of that thinking clear into Edinburgh." He shook his head. "We had best save such delights until we are more certain of our safety."

"So, ye found it a delight, did ye?" She inwardly cursed her own doubts yet was driven to voice them.

"For a clever lass ye do ask some very foolish questions." Revan laughed softly and kissed the top of her head.

"Mayhaps. My cousin, Tomas, always says not to let the fear of appearing foolish stop ye from asking questions. He told me that a wee bit of embarrassment was easier to endure than ignorance or doubt."

"And ye have a doubt or two, do ye? Sweet Mary's tears, dearling, if anyone had stumbled upon us just now, I would have had trouble recalling my own name. I was so blind to all about us, I howled my pleasure to the moon. If Douglas's men had been with a mile of this place, they would have found us easily. Aye, and I would have been too weak with delight to even try and save us. Does that answer your doubts, Tessa? I have never kenned such pleasure before," he murmured when she lifted her head to look at him. "Ye make it very difficult for a man to keep his mind upon his duty."

"I think ye have been dilligent. The king should reward ye well. Aye, especially after he has paused to heed those lies about you. I dinna ken how he can even once think that ye would betray him."

"Everyone else has, or so he believes at times. Dinna forget, his father was cruelly murdered. As a child, James the Second was used as a pawn by Livingston after that man violently abducted the young king and his mother. The Douglases have ne'er ceased to be a trial. Nor have the lords of the Isles. Even some of James's allies, such as the Crichtons, have doubted him at times. Nay, he has a right to his suspicions. It stings to have them directed my way, but I can understand it.''

"Mayhaps. Well, soon ye shall prove to him just how firm an ally ye have been.''

"Aye, but in doing so I must mark your kin, the Thurkettles, as traitors.'' He lifted his hand and smoothed away the tangled hair from her face. '' 'Tis a mark that isna easily washed away.''

"Ye dinna put it upon them falsely. They take the chance themselves by dabbling in treachery. If the name is stained, 'tis their own fault. Aye, it sorely troubled me at first, for their blood runs in my veins and my mother was one of them. But, one cannae take on the guilt of all one's kinsmen. 'Tis their crime, not mine nor my mother's, and they must pay for it.''

"True, but not everyone will think like that, dearling. Ye will be made to pay for your Thurkettle blood, in small ways, at least. I shall be the cause of painful words, mayhaps even a slighting or two.''

"Nay, ye willna be the cause. Uncle Fergus will be.'' She brushed a kiss over his mouth, touched by his show of concern and unnecessary guilt. "He commits this foul crime. Ye but bring him to justice, expose his treason, as ye must. Dinna fret over me. I have more kinsmen left than most think is proper or wise, and there is no stain upon the names of Comyn or Delgado. Well, not since the Comyns sided with England in the Bruce's time.''

"Too many others did the same for that to weigh too heavily anymore.'' He gently pressed her head back down against his chest. "Sleep now, lass. We must be away at dawn's first light.''

"As ever.'' She huddled closer to him to stave off the chill of the night air. "I hope all those treacherous dogs trying to hunt us down are getting as little sleep as we are.''

"So do I.'' He idly checked to be sure his sword was

within reach. "When we get to my brother's, we shall rest a while ere we set out for your kinsmen's. We will be safe enough there."

"They must ken that ye might go there. Once they guessed who ye really were, they would easily find all your kinsmen."

"True enough, but they canna put too many men at each place or the Douglas willna have any left for his army. Dinna fret. We have eluded them so far. We will continue to do so."

Tess nodded and closed her eyes. She did not fully trust in their luck to continue, but she also believed it was foolish to worry over something that had not happened and might never happen. There was more than enough to be concerned about without adding a lot of *what ifs*. Rest was important now, and that would be elusive if she let her mind prey on the problems yet to come. She cleared her mind of all thought save of how good it felt to be warm and sated in Revan's strong arms. It was not long before she felt the strong pull of sleep.

Revan stroked her hair and stared up through the treetops at the clear night sky. He could feel her body grow limp and her breathing become soft and even as sleep crept over her. That peaceful haven eluded him.

"Ah, Tessa, what am I going to do with you?" he whispered, knowing she could not hear him.

She was proving to be an intricate problem. At every turn she tugged at his emotions. She had him breaking nearly every rule he had ever made concerning women. There also seemed to be no way for him to stop himself, to draw back and behave as he knew he should, as he knew would be best for both of them.

He found himself wishing that she were poor. It would solve so many problems. He would not have the worry of possibly offending some powerful family's honor by taking her as his lover. Right or wrong, bedding a poor virgin did not stir the outrage bedding a wealthy one did. And if he decided he did want her as his wife, he would not have to worry about compromising his honor. They would come to the marriage with equal dowries—nothing. Unfortunately, his association with Tess held nearly as many dangers as the tangled web of treasonous plots they were caught up in.

Guilt pinched at him as well. He was not being fair to her. Tess loved him or was very close to doing so. He was certain of it. Yet he would not, could not, offer her any future with him. Fairness, even honor, demanded that he set her away from him, but he could not find the strength to do so. She would look at him with those beautiful brown eyes, and he could not hold himself at a distance. As he had done tonight, he would comfort or confide, hold her close and murmur sweet words, and do all that could give her hope that they would stay together. It was almost cruel, he thought with a wince of self-disgust. He prayed that she would not think that of him when he finally had to leave her.

Chapter

❖ 12 ❖

AFTER TWO DAYS OF RIDING, TESS NO LONGER paid much attention to the scenery. But the ruined priory caught her interest immediately. For the first time since they had fled the inn, there was a sign that they were not lost in the depths of some never-ending forest. She also recognized the place. Five years ago she had seen it when she was being taken to the Thurkettles. It had not been in complete ruin then. Some English raiding party had burned it a little. In the intervening years another had clearly finished the destruction. The borderlands were full of such ruins, but it still made her sad.

What puzzled her was that it had taken her and Revan nearly twice as many days to reach it after leaving the cave near Thurkettle's keep than it had taken her to go in the other direction all those years ago. She suddenly realized just how twisted a route they had been forced to take by their pursuers. If they were not being so assiduously hunted, they would probably have reached the king by now.

"Your brother's keep lies in the direction of my kinsmen's."

"Ye have been this way before?" Revan asked.

"Aye. Five years ago when my father's kin took me to the Thurkettles. My father's kinsmen are three days' ride

147

from here, but I canna be sure whether 'tis north or west or a bit of both.''

"The latter I believe." He glanced at her over his shoulder and grinned. "'Tis good that ye arena leading us."

"Rogue, but, aye, I fear ye are right in that. I was but thinking on how much longer it has taken us to get here. I see the need to travel a twisting route, but I hadna realized just how much time such machinations have cost us. Thurkettle could keep us from reaching the king simply by chasing us hither and yon."

"We have been forced south when we should have ridden north, and east when we needed to go west, but only a time or two. The need to hide from time to time also slows us down." He patted his horse's neck. "As does having but one mount between us. We are nearly halfway there. My brother can give us a second horse, and that will gain us some speed."

"I didna mean to sound complaining. 'Twas more surprise than anything else. It feels as if we should be nearer our goal." She grimaced faintly and shifted in the saddle.

Revan chuckled as he felt her movement. "Aye, I ken that feeling well. We will rest for a while at my brother's keep. There is time for that."

Tess prayed it did not occur to him to leave her at his brother's keep and continue on by himself. Thus far, he gave no hint of even considering that possibility. She hoped nothing occurred at his brother's to change his mind about keeping her with him. It was vital that she stay by his side. Although she sensed a softening in him, he still gave her no promises of a future, not even vague ones. She needed more time to try and capture his heart.

"We will reach your brother soon?"

"Aye. His keep lies about five miles west of here. We must keep a close watch now, closer than we have done. There is certain to be someone watching for us. I plan to draw within a mile, mayhaps half a mile, of Nairn's, then wait until dark. We can use the shadows of night to slip inside his keep. There is a bolt-hole we can go through.''

''Where do ye mean to leave the horse?''

''There is an old couple in a cottage near the keep. They will hold the animal until the morning, when one of Nairn's men can fetch it in.''

''If we see any of Douglas's or Uncle Fergus's men, would it not be best to, well, catch them and hold them?''

'''Twould be best to kill the swine, but I have never been one for executions. Nairn is also dangerously close to the Douglas's lands, bordered by them on three sides. Killing or capturing a Douglas man on his land could bring the wrath of the earl upon his head. Since most of Nairn's fighting men are surely with the king, 'tis best if we creep in and creep out and bring as little attention upon my brother as is possible.''

She nodded and felt relieved. Revan would not leave her behind here. That would bring Nairn the very attention Revan spoke of trying to avoid. It would also be dangerous for her to remain so close to the Douglases and, by rescuing her from Uncle Fergus's men as he had, Revan had shown that he would not leave her to her fate. She relaxed, more at ease about the visit they were about to make.

There was still several hours of light remaining when Revan halted. Signaling her to be as quiet as possible, he dismounted and helped her down. He then left her with the horse in a thick copse of pines while he crept toward a small thatched-roof stone cottage. Tess remained tense for several moments after he disappeared inside. The people he sought aid from could easily be startled into giving a warning to whomever might be watching. Tess had seen none of their enemy yet, but shared Revan's certainty that the earl or Uncle Fergus would have set someone to watch Nairn Halyard's keep.

Still holding on to the horse's reins, she sat down on the ground to wait for Revan. It was not very long before he darted back to join her, carrying a small sack she hoped was full of something to eat. It was evident that Nairn and his people had been ready and waiting for Revan's possible appearance.

"Old Colin says three of Douglas's men have been lurking about for nearly a fortnight," Revan said as he sat down beside her. "We should see them very soon after leaving here. They are camped just on the Douglas side of the border." He shook his head. "They just squat there, and no one can drive them away, for they are on Douglas land."

"So what are we to do, then?"

"We will slip by and get as close as we can to the bolt-hole, then wait until dark. I thought we might wait inside Old Colin's cottage, but he says those men come around too often. The old man canna stop them, and my brother's men canna just set here waiting for them. They wouldna come round then, would they?" He gave her a faint smile and held up the small sack. "Some bread, cheese, and apples. At least we willna go hungry while we wait for the sun to set."

"Can the old man care for your horse?"

"Aye. We will leave him here. Old Colin says he has a place to hide it and care for it until morning." He stood up, took her by the hand, and helped her to her feet. "Let us see just how close we can get."

A moment later the keep was in view. It was a tall, square tower house with a high thick wall around it. As she and Revan crept along, trying to stay within the shelter of the thinning trees, Tess could see a few men upon the wall. A moment later she saw the three Douglas men. They made no effort to hide themselves, had even built rough shelters for themselves and their horses. Although they were too distant to be a real threat to the tower house itself, they could see all who came and went from the place. Tess did not envy Nairn Halyard. It could not be easy living cheek to jowl with a man as powerful and treacherous as the Douglas.

It was not until they were actually in it that Tess realized she and Revan had entered a brush-clogged trench. On their hands and knees they crawled along until they reached a somewhat clear spot. The brush around them and growing on the sides and edges of the trench hid them from view. Revan sat down, and with a sigh of relief, Tess sat next to him.

"Does this go all the way round your brother's keep?" she asked as he handed her some bread and cheese.

"Aye. My brother has let it become clogged with brambles and brush so that it might be set alight if the need arose. Ye can see it from where those Douglas men squat, so 'tis no great secret but 'tis still a good defense." He looked up at the sky, now growing clouded with the approaching sunset. "In an hour or two we can make our way to the bolt-hole. 'Tis on the western side, so I fear we have a distance to crawl yet."

Tess grimaced and started to eat her food. "Are ye certain those men canna see us in here?"

"Not with all this brush and debris, and if we sit very still, keep low and all."

She nodded and silently continued to eat. When she was finished with her light meal, she leaned against Revan and closed her eyes. She huddled closer to him when he put his arm about her shoulders. She felt weary to the bone, weak, and chilled. It seemed only minutes had passed before Revan shook her awake and they began to crawl along the trench in the dark.

As she was poked and scratched by sticks and brambles, she struggled not to make any sound. It had rained recently, and the bottom of the trench was increasingly damp and muddy. She was soon wet through to the skin and began to shiver. When Revan crawled out and helped her up after him, she almost wept with relief only to find herself being nudged into a musty-smelling, black hole hidden inside a huge tree stump. She prayed it was not a long tunnel as she inched her way along, fighting to ignore the occasional slimy wriggle of life beneath her hand or the distinct squeak of a rat. A grunt of pain finally escaped her when, just as her muscles began to cramp and she feared she could go no farther, she crawled headfirst into a very hard and solid wall of wood.

"Push, Tessa," hissed Revan. "'Tis the end and that is the door into my brother's bedchambers."

The thought that her ordeal was over gave her the strength to push open the small door. No light entered as the doorway widened. Once sure it was wide enough for her to get through, she edged forward only to stop short as something cold and sharp pricked the end of her nose. She tensed and felt Revan bump her from behind.

"Tessa, ye do have the sweetest tail I have ever seen, but I have no wish to kiss it now. So move." Revan gave her a light nudge only to meet stiff, strong resistance.

"If I move another inch, I shall have three noseholes."

Tess knew her eyes were crossed as she stared at the dimly visible sword point touching her nose. They were starting to sting from the strain. She nearly collapsed with relief when it was pulled back slightly.

"Come on out, woman. Very slowly."

She did not hesitate. The man's voice was like ice. Tess had no doubt at all that that sword point would be buried deep within her flesh if she did not immediately obey. As she crawled out, she prayed the tense confrontation would soon pass, that the man would realize no enemy threatened him. The brief, horrifying thought that somehow the enemy had taken possession of the tower house was one she tried to force away.

The instant she was clear of the tunnel and started to stand up, the man grabbed her. She gave a soft squeak of alarm as he wrapped his strong arm around her and yanked her up against him with her face toward the tunnel. When the cold steel of his short sword was lightly pressed to her throat, she went very still.

"Now you, my good man, will come out of there slowly as well."

Revan did as he was told even as he grumbled, "Dinna ye recognize a kinsman, fool?"

"Ye do sound like one, but 'tis too dark to see. In these troubled times a man canna afford to take any risks. There is a lamp and a flint on a table just to your right," he continued when Revan was out of the cramped space and standing up. "Light it so that I may make sure the face mates with the voice. 'Ware now, I hold a sword to your companion's throat. One false move, and your wee friend shall be wearing a new smile."

The moment the lamp was lit, Revan turned to glare at his brother Nairn. "Well, Brother?"

Releasing Tess, Nairn shrugged as he sheathed his sword. "Troubled times, lad. What's a man to do?"

Lightly rubbing her throat, Tess scowled at the two men. "It appears this love of holding a blade to a lass's throat fair runs rampant in your family, Revan."

"Now, Tessa—" Revan began.

"And your threats carry a tedious similarity."

Nairn gave her a small bow, his dark blue eyes briefly but intently fixed upon her. "My apologies, lass. Danger is all about. One must act accordingly."

She did not have a chance to respond. Nairn immediately turned back to Revan. The brothers embraced and clapped each other on the back. Tess rolled her eyes in a silent expression of disgust as they traded insults as well as assured each other of their mutual good health. Yet again she had been forgotten.

Glancing around, she spotted the large bed and was drawn to it by the sweet tempting thought of sleep. She eyed the bed, noting its clean, lightly scented linens. She was not clean but wet and smeared with mud. It would be ill-mannered to lie down as she so ached to do. A moment later she decided such a breach of good manners was well-earned. Not only had yet another Halyard threatened her life, but she was being thoroughly ignored. No one had yet inquired after her well-being, and, she frowned, she was feeling increasingly poorly.

After flipping one of the light blankets over the clean linen, she collapsed on the bed. It felt to her as if her whole body sighed with relief. She had not had the time to notice how weary she was. That utter exhaustion was why she felt a little unwell, she decided. A long sleep in a warm, dry, comfortable place was all she needed. Closing her eyes, she wondered a little crossly how long it would take Revan to remember her.

"So, the lass dressed as a lad is Thurkettle's niece," Nairn murmured when he and Revan finished their lengthy welcome.

"Aye." Revan turned to look at Tess and gaped when he saw her sprawled on Nairn's bed. "Tessa," he snapped as he hurried over there. "Ye need to clean up first." He grasped her by the arm.

She forced open one eye and tried to glare at him. "Move me from here and it willna be your throat I set a blade against."

"Tessa, I ken that ye are weary, but this is Nairn's bed and ye are a wee bit dirty."

"I am *filthy* and 'tis the least he deserves for threatening my miserable life. Now, leave me be," she muttered, turning on her side so that her back was to him. "I can bathe later," she managed to say before she fell asleep.

"Tessa." Revan started to gently shake her only to have Nairn grasp him by the arm and stop him.

"Leave the poor wee lass be. I suspect ye have dragged her over moor and mountain with little pause to rest. And no doubt Douglas and Thurkettle have been driving ye hard."

"Well—aye—but she shall make a fair mess of your fine bed. She is dusty, muddy, and wet."

"None of which shall ruin my bed. Ye and I can bed down in another chamber."

"Ye can. I shall stay with her."

"Is that wise?"

"It matters little now if it is wise or not. 'Tis beyond mending." He started to undress her, tugging off her boots.

Moving to unlace her doublet, Nairn asked, "Are ye to be wed soon, then?"

"Nay. Ye ken well how I look upon wedding an heiress when I have but a few coins and a fine sword."

"Then ye never should have seduced the lass."

"I didna seduce her," Revan snapped, briefly nettled at the accusation, then he grimaced. "S'truth, we seduced each other."

"Ah, then she wasna a virgin lass."

"She was."

"Virgins rarely seduce a man, leastwise not knowingly."

"'Tis a long story."

"I see. So be it. Ye will be lingering here a while. I am certain we can find the time for you to relate this grand tale." Nairn crossed his arms over his chest and watched as Revan unlaced Tess's chemise.

Revan glared at his brother. "Do ye have a shirt or the like that I can put on her? And something I might use to dry her off?"

The moment Nairn turned away, Revan hurried to tug off Tess's chemise. He tossed it aside and was just reaching to pull part of the blanket over her when he realized Nairn was back standing on the other side of the bed, a shirt in one hand and a drying cloth in the other. Quickly flipping the blanket over Tess to hide her nudity from Nairn's considering gaze, he scowled at his brother.

"I have looked at your women before," murmured Nairn as he handed Revan the cloth to dry Tess off with.

"This time I would appreciate it if ye would cast your eyes elsewhere until I have her dressed."

Nairn looked away, and Revan quickly dried Tess off, rubbing away most of the mud as well. He snatched the shirt Nairn still dangled from his hand and struggled to get it on Tess. By the time he was lacing it up, Tess was rousing a little. To Revan's surprise, she swatted at him.

"Nay, Revan," she muttered. "I am too tired. Mayhaps in the morning."

Nairn laughed softly, and Revan was annoyed to feel the heat of a blush sting his cheeks. "I am just putting some clean clothes on you." She did not respond, and Revan realized she had fallen back into a deep sleep. "There," he muttered as he finished lacing up the shirt. "Ye can look now, Nairn." The expression of amusement on his brother's face irritated Revan.

"Lift the lass up, and I will pull the bedclothes down. Then ye can tuck her in properly."

After they did that, Revan felt Tess's cheeks and forehead. "She feels a wee bit warm yet shivers a little."

"The poor lass was chilled to the bone and exhausted. See how she fares after a good night's sleep ere ye start to worry. Now, come set over here and share some wine with me."

After one last look at Tess, Revan moved to join Nairn at a small table in the far corner of his bedchamber. As he sat down opposite Nairn and accepted a goblet of wine, he hoped his brother would understand if he did not sit and talk for too long. He was feeling somewhat exhausted himself.

"Ye slipped by the Douglas's men unseen?" Nairn asked.

"Aye, I believe so. How long have they been camped there? Old Colin said nearly a fortnight."

"'Tis nearly that. The only way we could have driven them off was to attack them on Douglas land, and I dared not do that."

"Nay, I understand. Ye dinna want the man looking your way, especially not now."

"Is there to be a battle, then? Has it come to that?"

"Aye. I grow too weary to tell it all tonight. The Douglas plans to march against the king in early May. We have seen men riding to muster. Tess's uncle, Thurkettle, was gathering supplies for the men. Do ye ride to join with the king soon?"

"Most of my men are with our liege even now. I, and a small troop of men, will join him in time for the battle. I fear to leave my lands too soon. That might give the Douglas the time and the chance to raze this place or take it and hold it against the king. If I wait until I must hurry or miss the battle, then the Douglas is also too hurried to take the trouble and time to harry my lands."

"'Tis your best hope at least. Your greatest danger is now, as he gathers men yet has no battle to occupy them."

Nodding, Nairn ran a hand through his light brown hair. "That is a worry. I also worry over what might happen here if the king loses or tries to flee as he did once before. Douglas kens that I support the king. He will make me pay dearly for that. He will make my people pay dearly for that. He could do the same if he loses but isna routed. In these last troubled months I have seen, all too clearly, how precarious my position is.

"God help us, Revan. I could suffer even if the king wins for he will surely wish to harry the Douglas's lands. I sit here in the midst of those lands. Soldiers arena always aware of where the boundaries of friend and foe lie. Being an ally could cost me, for they might muster here and demand that I supply them."

Revan reached across the age-smoothed table and briefly clasped his brother's hand. "Ye and your people willna be left to starve. Just remember that. Aye, and dinna forget that ye wouldna stand alone against any enemy."

Nairn smiled faintly. "Aye, I ken it. But I did need reminding. I have set here too long alone. Those three Douglas corbies squatting just beyond my reach havena helped my peace of mind, either."

"And there has been no word from our father or our brothers?"

"A message or two, but the last was three weeks ago."

"Then Simon couldna have reached the court to report on Thurkettle and the Douglas yet. My name hasna been cleared."

"Nay. Rumors about you still abounded but no charges had yet been made. Doubts and questions but no accusations. Thurkettle spat out his slander but has disappeared."

"Aye, he would. The man is hip deep in treachery. He dare not stay too close to the very ones he seeks to betray. Guilt alone would make him fearful. This isna the first time he has played the traitor."

"James the First?" Nairn whispered, his voice softened by shock.

"Aye. Thurkettle had a part in that cowardly murder. 'Tis one hold the Douglases have on him."

"Does the lass ken this?"

"'Twas she who told me."

"Poor lass, to share the blood of such a man. Ah, well, her other kinsmen, the Comyns and the Delgados, are honorable. She can take comfort, and shelter, in their good name."

"How is it ye ken who her family is?"

"I wouldna have kenned it save that Father made mention of it in his last missive. He complained a little over how there is always one of that clan haunting him. He says they take turns, he is certain of it, so that they can dog him day and night."

Revan cursed. "Then they believe I have kidnapped the girl and mayhaps the other black charges Thurkettle made."

"Nay. They but seek some word of her. It seems none of them trusts in Thurkettle's word. Aye, they are angry and concerned, over her safety and her honor, but they have graciously accorded us the benefit of the doubt. Father told them of your mission, and they but wait." Nairn watched Revan closely as he added, "They are as concerned as any kinsmen would be and, mayhaps, more. Her father was a much loved son, and as our father tells it, there are very few lasses born to the family. Father expressed surprise, after seeing their deep concern, that they had ever parted with her."

It was difficult, but Revan hid his consternation. If the

Comyns and the Delgados did hold such affection for Tess, it would not make his meeting with them an easy one. Inwardly he shrugged. There was no turning back.

"Did our father say anything about their trustworthiness?" He ignored his brother's irritated look.

"Aye. 'Tis without question. Why?"

"Because I ride to Donnbraigh and Silvio Comyn when I leave here."

"Is that wise?"

"'Tis necessary. He can aid me in reaching the king, keep Tessa safe, and will have the name of the king's household guard who has turned traitor."

"One of James's own personal guards?"

"Aye. Tess recognized the man. He rode with the Douglas's troops. She canna recall the name, though."

"Sweet heaven, that is a blade a wee bit too close to our liege's throat."

"Or his back." Nairn nodded solemnly in agreement, and Revan fought to smother a yawn. "I have more to tell, but I need to rest. 'Twill have to wait until the morning."

"Of course."

Revan stood up and moved to the bed as Nairn finished his wine. Gently touching Tess's cheeks and forehead again, he still found her warmer than he liked, but her shivering had ceased. He straightened as Nairn moved to his side, watching him with an interest that was unsettling.

"All she needs is some rest," Nairn murmured. "Rest and a few hearty meals. She must be a great deal stronger than she appears to be."

"Much stronger. Some might even say too strong for a lass."

"Then she would make a fine wife for a soldier."

"Aye, she would," Revan grumbled and scowled at Nairn. "Good sleep, Brother. We can talk more in the morning."

"That we can, Revan." Nairn moved to the door, opened it, and paused to look back at Revan. "We can talk about a great many things—battles, traitors, and wee brown lasses. Good sleep to you, Revan.''

The moment the door shut behind his brother, Revan cursed. He did not like the sound of Nairn's parting words at all. Although Nairn was only two years older than he, the man often took his role as elder far too seriously. It sounded as if Nairn intended to lecture him about how he was treating Tess. Shaking his head, Revan began to undress and prayed that Tess would recover soon.

Chapter

✧ 13 ✧

"ARE YE CERTAIN YE ARE WELL ENOUGH?"

Tess rolled her eyes, making no attempt to hide her exasperation. Revan had asked her that same question so many times she had lost count. At first his evident concern had been touching. Now it had her grinding her teeth. He had insisted on showing her something outside of the keep, had had her get all dressed to go out, and yet had hesitated each step of the way. Now they stood at the door leading into the bailey, and he hesitated again. Since he had forced her to dress as warmly as if she were stepping out into the December snows instead of the April sun, she was starting to feel uncomfortably warm. That only increased her mounting irritation.

"I have done naught but sleep and eat for two days. I am completely well."

"I shouldna wish you to take a chill by going out ere ye are ready."

"Take a chill? Ye have me weighted down with a heavy shift, thick petticoats, a winter's gown, a cape, and a cursed wool shawl tied about my head. I could prance about in the January ice and never feel it. But, I am now beginning to feel like a boiled pig. I think my temper will soon be as hot as the rest of me."

"Aye, ye do seem a wee bit sharp," he murmured as he took her by the hand and led her outside.

"Where did ye find all these clothes, anyway? Nairn isna married."

"They were borrowed from one of the women in the village nearby. Nairn went to her whilst we slept that first day. He thought ye might prefer to wear a gown or two while ye are here, that ye would feel more comfortable in women's clothing."

"Aye, but just now I could do with wearing less of them," she grumbled, but he ignored her.

It was not as cool outside as Tess had hoped it would be. As in many tower houses, the door was set up high, entering at the second floor. By the time they descended the narrow stone steps to the bailey, she could feel the sweat trickling down her back. She promised herself she would never again allow Revan to dictate what she wore. The fleeting thought that he had given no indication that he would stay with her long enough for that to become a problem was one she pushed aside. She would not darken her present happiness with worries about the future and possible heartbreak.

Revan led her to the stables at the far side of the bailey. As they walked past the first few horses quartered there, she had to approve of Nairn's selection of mounts. They paused by Horse's stall, and she rubbed his nose, silently apologizing for not having thought of a suitable name yet.

"The rest will do this poor fellow some good as well," she murmured.

"Aye, it has, but that isna why I brought you here." He tugged her over to the next stall, which held a pretty roan mare.

"A fine mount." She stroked the mare's nose and looked at Revan. "Has Nairn just purchased her, then?"

"Nay. She was bred here. Wild Rose is what he calls her. He has chosen her for ye to ride when we leave here."

Tess gasped softly and stared at the horse. "Are ye

certain? 'Tis too fine a horse from which he could breed others.''

''Nairn feels she is the best one for you. She can keep pace with Horse, and if we are forced to take the roughest paths again, she is surefooted and easily ridden. He insists that you ride her.''

''If he is sure . . .'' she began, a little concerned about taking on the responsibility for such a fine horse.

''He is sure,'' interrupted Nairn as he strode up to them and leaned against the front of Horse's stall.

She smiled at him, thinking that the Halyards were unfairly blessed with good looks. It surprised her that the man was not yet wed. A handsome man with property was not usually allowed to run free for very long. Inwardly she frowned, wondering if the Halyard men shared some fierce objection to the state of matrimony.

''I am wary of taking such a fine mount,'' she said.

''Ye are sorely in need of one, mistress.'' He frowned at her. ''Ye are looking a wee bit flushed.''

''I am not surprised. I am fairly roasting. I thank ye for the use of your horse and shall endeavor to return it to you unharmed. Now, if ye would be so kind as to excuse me, I must go and shed some of this crippling burden of clothing.'' She gave him a quick feint of a curtsy and started out of the stable, tugging off the shawl as she went.

''Ye could catch a chill,'' called Revan.

''Twould be preferable to melting,'' she replied and hurried away before he could do more than verbally protest.

''Did ye force the lass to bundle up so?'' asked Nairn, grinning at his brother.

''She has been ill.''

''Not dangerously.''

''Well, I canna afford to let her grow dangerously ill, can I?''

When Nairn just laughed, Revan cursed and strode out of the stables. He was eager to leave and not just because his mission required it. Nairn was gaining an irritating amount of amusement out of watching him and Tess together. So far, in all their talks, he had neatly avoided any discussion of his relationship with Tess. Revan was eager to keep it that way but knew that the longer he stayed with Nairn, the less chance he had of continuing to evade the topic.

TESS nudged her plate away and smiled at Nairn before taking a sip of wine. The man set a good table. After two days of enjoying such fare, she was feeling strong again. The fact that she, Nairn, and Revan were the only ones in the great hall savoring the feast told her several things. Nairn had indeed sent most of his people away, either to safety farther from the Douglas or to fight for the king. It also told her that it was most likely the last night she and Revan would spend with him.

"I shall grow quite fat if we stay here much longer," she said.

Revan grinned, as did his brother, then responded, "'Tis good that we are leaving, then."

"I thought we might be. At dawn?" she asked and gave an exaggerated sigh when both men nodded. "I used to find the dawn such a pretty time when I saw it but rarely." She smiled when both men chuckled. "Do we still ride to my kinsmen?"

"Aye," replied Revan. "They lie between us and the king. 'Twould be foolish to ignore what aid they could give us. Aye, even if it can only be fresh horses and added supplies."

"And, after that, we ride on to the king?" She waited tensely for his reply, although she struggled to look calm.

"I shall ride on. 'Twas my hope that ye could remain safe with your kinsmen."

It stung her to hear him voice what she had suspected—that once with her kinsmen, he would leave her. She knew that when he left her there, he would not be back for her. If he had any plans for a future for them, he would have said so by now. Her kinsmen were barely two or three days away. In two or three days Revan meant to desert her.

"They may all be with the king," she murmured, wondering sadly what good it would do her even if she could gain some more time.

"Some are surely still at Donnbraigh, their keep. They feel as Nairn does, fear leaving their lands completely unprotected. They most surely also wait to see if I will bring you to them ere I reach the king."

"They may believe all my uncle Fergus has said. It could be dangerous for ye to go to them." She knew that contradicted what she had told him once before but hoped he would not notice.

"Nay. They will hear me out first. My father has assured me of that through a message he sent to Nairn."

"Well, aye, they would doubt most anything Fergus had to say," she admitted. "I had thought to see this through to the end."

"The end shall be a fierce battle. 'Tis no place for a lass. Even if ye could persuade me to take such a risk with your life, ye could never persuade your kinsmen." Revan watched her closely as he sipped at his wine.

There was no arguing that truth. Her father's kin would not hesitate to lock her in their dungeons if they thought it would keep her safe. They would never allow her within sight or hearing of a battle.

Tess decided she did not have the spirit to try and talk Revan into keeping her with him longer than he planned. The news that they would part in two or three days had sapped it from her. She began to fear she would reveal the hurt and sadness now gripping her and decided it would be wise to excuse herself. Alone in the chambers she shared with Revan, she would have some chance of recouping her strength. If she and Revan were to part in but a few days, she did not wish to weight what little time she had left with him with sadness and regret.

"I believe I will retire now, if ye would be so kind as to excuse me."

When both men murmured a good night, she left them. She headed for her chambers, determined to conquer her sadness. There would be plenty of time to succumb to it when Revan was gone. Years and years, she thought forlornly as she climbed the stairs.

"Ye are a hard, cruel man, Revan," Nairn said the moment the heavy door of the great hall shut behind Tess.

"What prompts that condemnation?" Revan turned from frowning after Tess to look at his brother in mild surprise.

"The way ye treat that poor lass. Ye have just blithely cut her to the quick and took no notice of it."

"And who says I didna notice?"

Revan had seen the hurt in her eyes, the unspoken sadness. He had wanted to ignore it, to forget it, but Nairn clearly had other plans. This time Revan did not think he would be able to evade a long, difficult discussion about Tess. Briefly he considered simply walking away.

"Dinna cast a longing eye at that door," advised Nairn. "If need be, I will have it barred from the outside."

"What occurs between Tess and myself is none of your concern."

"Nay? Her kinsmen may not make that fine distinction. What ye are doing with that lass has ofttimes led to bloody, unending feuds. From what our father has told me in his last few missives, the Comyns and the Delgados arena ones to dismiss this lightly." When the only response from Revan was a cold, angry silence, Nairn asked, "And what of the lass herself?"

"I didna seduce the lass. I have told you that." Revan took a long drink of wine in the hope of cooling his rising temper.

"Aye, and I am inclined to believe you." Nairn relaxed in his chair, sipped at his wine, and studied Revan. "I have been watching the two of you."

"Like one of those carrion of the Douglas's," Revan muttered.

Nairn ignored his surly interruption. "It was a bit difficult at first to believe that ye—er—seduced each other. Howbeit, I believe it now. Aye, all ye two needed was to be together for a while. I begin to think ye were fated to be lovers."

"Why?" Revan demanded. He had reached that conclusion himself yet had no reason for it and wondered if Nairn could give him one.

"I should think ye would ken the why of it for yourself. 'Tis difficult to explain. There is something between you and that wee lass. A pull? A bond?" Nairn shrugged. "I see you and that wee brown lass together and 'tis right, 'tis proper. Ye ask me to explain what canna be explained. Ye also try to divert me from what I wish to speak on."

"Ye wish to speak about Tessa."

"Aye—Tessa. And—nay." Nairn leaned forward, resting his arms on the table. "'Tis ye who troubles me the most. Let us ignore the chance that these Comyns and Delgados will be . . . shall we say upset? . . . and the fact that, after all these weeks, 'twill be assumed by all that ye have bedded the lass."

"Aye. Let us ignore that." Revan spoke through gritted teeth, infuriated by the way Nairn presented truths he had struggled to forget. "Why dinna ye cease playing about and say what ye mean to—directly?"

"As ye wish. Marry the lass."

"Nay."

"Why? 'Tis plain to any who see you together that ye care for that lass."

"Mayhaps I do." He ignored his brother's short, scornful laugh. "It makes no difference. She is an heiress."

"Even more reason to wed her. Ye have naught, and although being a king's knight carries a lot of honor, it may never give ye much profit. Here is all ye could ever want within your grasp. Any other time ye would never have a chance to wed such a lass. Her kinsmen wouldna allow a landless knight with a light purse to even smile her way. Now they would accept you, welcome you, mayhaps even insist that ye wed her. Take it.''

''I willna wed for money or for land.''

''Then wed her because ye care for her. Curse you for a fool, ye love her.''

''And what if I do? Do ye think that is what people will believe? Nay. They will say I wed her for her land and her purse. That would shame her and me. As she herself has said—if and when she wishes to take a husband, she can buy one. Well, I willna be bought and I willna have folk thinking that she had to pay me to wed her.''

''That pride of yours will choke you some day. Aye, and very soon, too.''

''And what of Tessa's pride?''

''Oh, she has nearly as much as you. I have little doubt of that. But, she isna such a fool as to cut herself on it. If ye refuse to wed her—''

''I willna sell myself or be thought to have done so.'' It confounded Revan that no one else seemed to understand that or agree with his opinion on the matter.

''Then get out of her bed, curse you. Cease using the lass when ye mean to set her aside. Ye are so concerned about looking the whore if ye wed an heiress, ye dinna see that ye are treating her much like one.''

Revan leapt to his feet, his fists partly raised as he fought the urge to strike his brother. ''I have never treated her like a whore nor thought her one.''

''Ye are the only one who will see that fine distinction. She was a virgin and is of a good family. When a man beds such a lass, he should wed her. Ye ken that as well as I do, yet ye merrily go to her bed each night with no intention of marrying her. Ye canna say ye believe that is right?''

''Ere I bedded her I told her I wasna a man to offer her marriage. She understood that.''

''Are ye certain?''

"Aye. She told me that she hadna asked me. She also reminded me that she had offered me no promises, either. That was when she spoke of buying a husband if she ever needed one. Tessa understands that I can offer her no future."

"Mayhaps she does understand," Nairn murmured. "But is that how she wants it to be? Have ye ever asked her that, asked her if she can be happy with naught but a brief affair? I think not. Do ye wish to hear how I see it?"

"I dinna believe I do, but ye will tell me anyways— aye?"

"Aye. I believe she has agreed to your rules because she had no choice. The lass is in love with you. I would wager all I own upon it. She probably loved you when she first accepted you as her lover. Her choice was to have nothing or accept what little ye were offering. Mayhaps she even hoped to change your mind. What she couldna see was that those rules of yours are set in stone, that even if she touched your heart, ye would never change them. Mayhaps, Revan, 'tis past time ye told the girl. 'Tis only fair to let a person ken that they are in a game they can never hope to win."

"I have never let her think those rules would change."

"Nay?" Nairn shook his head. "Ye can be very blind at times, brother of mine. Well, go to her, then. I doubt it matters much now exactly *when* ye set her aside. 'Twill hurt her whether ye do it now or when ye leave her with her kinsmen."

That stung and Revan reacted to it with anger, giving Nairn a mocking bow. "Thank ye. I will rest so much easier kenning that I have your kind permission." He started toward the door.

"There is one last thing I would say, Revan."

Revan yanked open the heavy door, then glared at Nairn. "There is some other crime ye neglected to lay at my feet?"

"Being an utter fool isna a crime, although I ofttimes think it ought to be. Nay, I but mean to remind you that what ye so callously toss aside willna be left to rot. I have had the pleasure of her company for but a short time, yet I can say, with full confidence, that she will not be left to pine for you. 'Twill not be her good blood and purse alone that draws the courtiers to her, either. In fact, once ye cast her aside, I may well think on courting her myself. But then, that shouldna trouble ye overmuch. Ye will still have your pride, will ye not, Revan?''

With a soft curse Revan left. Nairn sighed and picked up his tankard. He took a long drink of wine and, when he had finished, found his sergeant-at-arms, Thorson, at his side.

''Ye have finally had a word with the lad about the lassie, havena ye?'' Thorson helped himself to a tankard of wine.

''Aye. 'Twas like talking to these stone walls. I even tried to pinch at his jealousy by pointing out that she willna be left alone for long. I even said I might take to courting her myself.''

''And would ye?''

''Well, if I thought she had truly shaken the ghost of my brother, I just might. Aye, I just might. Howbeit, I still cling to the hope that my young brother isna quite the idiot he acts like.'' Nairn exchanged a grin with the older man.

TESS slowly sat up in the bed when Revan strode into the room. She had almost buried her hurt. Her determination not to let it spoil what little time she had left with Revan had been the greatest help. The sadness lingered, weighting her heart, but she refused to give in to it. A flicker of hope remained as well, although she cursed herself for a fool for clinging to it. Nevertheless, a part of her refused to accept the end until Revan himself said a final fare-thee-well and walked away. She just prayed that she had the wit to stop hoping then.

She watched him as he washed up. He did not look to be in the best of tempers, and she wondered why. After she had worked so hard to control her own emotions so that she would not ruin what little time they had left together, she did not want him to ruin it with his moodiness. When he sat down on the edge of the bed to tug off his boots, she reached out to lightly stroke his arm. He briefly glanced her way, then continued to undress.

"Has something gone wrong?" she asked.

"Nay. I just had a quarrel with Nairn." He managed a small smile for her as he shrugged off his doublet and began to undo his shirt. "Losing it has put me in an ill mood. I will shake it soon."

Something in the tone of his voice told her that he was not being completely truthful. She did not press him, however. If he wanted her to know, he would tell her. At the moment his secretiveness about what had occurred after she had left the great hall was the least of her concerns.

When he finally slipped into bed and tugged her into his arms, she discovered that her emotions were not as controlled as she had thought. For a moment they overwhelmed her, tearing her apart. She clung to Revan as if she could hold him at her side by force alone. Now that she knew he meant to leave her behind at Donnbraigh, her kinsmen's keep, she saw each moment in terms of his walking away. It would be a slow bloodletting, hour by hour, until he finally left her. She was no longer sure she would be able to pretend that it was not torturing her. It could require far more strength than she could ever muster.

"Tess?" He sensed the desperation in the way she held him. "Ye do ken that 'twill be safer for ye to stay at Donnbraigh than to be dragged into the battle between the Douglases and King James, dinna ye? Ye do understand?"

"Aye. I understand."

The way she said those three words made Revan think she was not really referring to the need to keep her safe. "I have been in more battles than I care to recall, and ye must believe me when I tell ye that ye will be far better off set at a goodly distance from it all."

She wondered why he was trying so hard to make her accept that her safety was the only reason he'd leave her behind. He undoubtedly *did* have an honest concern for her well-being. However, no matter what he convinced her of now, the truth would be painfully clear when he did not return for her after the battle. He had to know that she would not be fooled for long. It irritated her a little that he did not simply tell her the blunt, cold truth, even though she did not really wish to hear it.

"I have heard enough tales about battles to ken that, Revan. I havena argued your decision much, have I?"

"Nay, but I sense your disappointment."

"Aye. I am disappointed." It was a paltry word to describe all she was feeling.

He cupped her chin in his hand and turned her face up toward his. The dim light from a branch of candles next to the bed made it difficult to read her expression. Despite that, he felt her hurt. He tried to dispel his guilt by reminding himself that he had given her no promises, had told her at the start that he was not a man for marriage. It did not help much. He knew she would not blame him, but he blamed himself. The situation had slipped beyond his control. He was no longer sure he had had any control to begin with. If it was fate at work, then fate was exceedingly cruel. It had thrust into his arms the one woman he could not accept no matter how much he might want to.

"But ye will be safe."

"Aye. I ken it." Safe, she thought. Aye, safe; but wretchedly alone.

Tess slid her hand up from his back to behind his head. She pressed his mouth against hers. From the first touch of his lips upon hers, her passion began to stir to life. She let it flow freely through her. It would overwhelm all the rest of her emotions, push them aside, if only for a little while.

For a moment she wondered if it was wise or right to continue to be his lover. He intended to leave her behind. That tainted what they shared. It was no longer love-making, but Revan using her to sate his lusts until he set her aside. Many might consider her the greatest of fools for still letting him share her bed after he had made his plans for her so clear.

Even as he deepened the kiss and her desire rose, she had the sudden urge to violently reject his loving. Her pride was rebelling, and she knew it. It was her pride making her think such things. She held Revan tighter, fully returning his kiss, and refused to let her pride win. For a few days, for whatever meager time was left to her, she would swallow her pride. It could chastise her later, after she was alone. For now she would take whatever Revan had to offer, no matter how fleeting. Once she was returned to her father's family, she would have many a long, cold night to soothe her stung pride.

Revan made love to her tenderly, slowly, yet with a hint of the desperation she felt. He covered her with kisses from her forehead to her toes. Even as she slipped into the mindless realm of her all-consuming passion, Tess marveled at how he could make love to her in such a way yet set her aside. Instinct told her there was far more behind his caresses, his kisses, than passion, but he meant to turn his back on it all. As she succumbed to her desires, she felt an urge to weep.

Chapter

✦ 14 ✦

NAIRN CURSED AND SWATTED AT THE HAND shaking him. It did not stop, simply gripped his naked shoulder harder and shook him more vigorously. He sat up on his bed, one fist raised to clout the intruder, only to pause and frown when he recognized Thorson. The man looked very concerned, and Nairn felt himself wake up even more.

"We have trouble, lad," the graying soldier said and held out Nairn's braies.

"The Douglases?" Nairn quickly stood up and put on his braies.

"'Tisna an attack, but—ye ken those three corbies who have squatted on the border for nearly a fortnight?" He leaned against the bedpost as Nairn tugged on his hose and shirt.

"Aye? What of them?"

"Well, there are more of the devils now. Twenty at my count. They dinna all wear the Douglas colors, either."

"Some of Thurkettle's dogs, no doubt. They have somehow discovered that Revan and Tess are here. But how?"

"One of them must have seen his horse. 'Tis all I can figure. They couldna have seen either the lad or the lass over the walls, and I feel certain we have no spy within the keep. Nay, they had to have espied his horse."

Not waiting to finish dressing except to yank on his boots, Nairn strode out of the bedchamber he had been using while Revan and Tess shared his. Their last night with him was going to come to an abrupt end. Thorson at his heels, Nairn marched into their chambers, over to the bed, and paused to stare at the couple sleeping there.

The pinch of jealousy was sharp but brief as Nairn studied Revan and Tess. She was curled up in Revan's arms, her lovely hair splayed out over his chest. Revan held her close even in his sleep, his cheek against the top of her head.

"Have ye ever noticed, Thorson," Nairn drawled, "how the greatest of fools can often find the sweetest havens?"

Thorson smiled faintly when Nairn glanced at him. "Mayhaps he will prove himself less the fool than he portrays now."

"I pray ye are right, old friend. 'Twould be sad, indeed, to watch one's own brother fatally cut himself upon the point of his own pride." He grasped Revan by the shoulder and shook him. "Wake up, idiot."

Revan blinked, then glared sleepily at his brother. "What do ye want?"

"The number of the carrion roosting on my border has grown—to nearly twenty."

"We have been discovered."

"'Twould appear so. Thorson is certain they espied your horse despite all of our care to hide it. They arena all Douglas men, either. We could make a stand."

"Nay. In the end I must still leave, and there will be more of the dogs sent out or waiting for us at Donnbraigh. Naught would really be gained by fighting this lot, and it would pull you even deeper into our troubles. 'Tis best if Tess and I try to slip away unseen. We have become quite skilled at it."

"Then we will get your horses ready and pack a few supplies for you."

The minute Nairn and Thorson were gone, Revan shook Tess awake. He felt guilty when he saw how tired she was, for he had woken her up several times during the night.

Time and again he had sought to banish the sadness he could sense in her with his lovemaking. Greediness had also prompted him, a greediness born of the knowledge that soon he would no longer be able to reach out in the dark and find her there.

Tess stumbled out of bed and over to the washbowl. Splashing the cold water on her face helped her wake up enough to get dressed. As she tugged on her cleaned and mended lad's clothing, she glanced longingly at the gowns Nairn had borrowed for her use. There had been a sense of normalcy in wearing them. For a little while she had been able to forget the danger and intrigue she was trapped in.

"'Tis still dark," she mumbled as she laced up her doublet.

"I fear we have been discovered, dearling." He yanked on his boots, then began to stuff their belongings into his saddle packs. "There are now twenty men or more squatting on that border and staring at Nairn's keep. We are going to try and slip away while the dark can still hide us. In truth, they probably expect us to try and leave at first light and will be waiting for us then."

"Do ye think they might try and attack Nairn?"

"If they were certain we were here, and Nairn willna give us up—aye, they might do so. But we will be gone, so I believe Nairn will be safe. If we leave without being seen, they canna even accuse him of aiding us. Leastwise, not with any certainty. 'Tis my belief that they willna waste time or men here if they are certain we arena within these walls. Our leaving will be Nairn's best defense. Are ye ready?"

"Give me but a moment or two of privacy, and I will be."

He kissed her cheek and started out of the door, taking their saddle packs with him. "I will meet you in the stables."

Revan made his cautious way through the dark keep. Only a few watchfires burned outside, and he was careful to remain in the shadows as he hurried to the stables. He found the horses already saddled and Thorson and Nairn waiting for him.

"Where is Tess?" asked Nairn as Revan put his saddle packs on his mount.

"She will be along in a moment." He briefly rested his hand on the packs flung over the mare's back. "Supplies?"

"Aye, enough to last ye until ye reach Donnbraigh and beyond, if the need arises. Are ye sure the lass will stay to the shadows? They could catch sight of her if she doesna move cautiously."

"She will be careful. Only once did she give us away, and that was unavoidable. I am more concerned about getting these beasts out of here without being seen. I have never seen Tess ride, so I would prefer not risking a chase just yet."

"The moon has set. That will work to your advantage. We will open the barmkin gates only enough to let ye lead the animals out. I think that 'tis best if ye lead the horses until ye are within the wood to the north of us. If those hounds catch your scent too soon, we will do what we can to slow them down and gain you some lead."

"I would rather you didna get caught up in this at all."

"So would I." Nairn smiled briefly. "But, I was caught in the midst of it all the moment I made my allegiance to James clear. I am but too small for the Douglas to trouble himself with at the moment."

"Let us pray that it remains so. Ah, Tessa," Revan murmured as she slipped into the stables. Once she reached his side, he related the plan for sneaking away from the keep.

"I begin to feel like a thief," she drawled as she took up the mare's reins. "Ye must be well accustomed to this sort of thing, though," she added, looking at Revan.

"Why would ye think that I would be accustomed to such subterfuge?" Revan frowned, mistrusting her faint smile.

"Well, I always saw the courtiers who tiptoed to and

from the regal Brenda's scented bedchambers. And though ye sighed and dribbled about her for so long, I never saw you. So ye must be well trained in it.''

Revan took a moment to glare at Nairn and Thorson, who were badly muffling their laughter, then scowled at Tess. ''I didna sigh and dribble, and I didna tiptoe about, either. Why mention Brenda now? Ye havena spoken of the cursed woman for days.''

''How remiss of me.''

''Tessa, God alone kens why ye should speak of this now. Did ye forget about the twenty or so men looking for us?''

''Not at all. I was but waiting for you to lead us on.''

''Are ye always so irritating in the morning?''

'''Tisna morning yet.''

''I dinna ken how ye can feel so pert when there are a score of men prepared to murder us at first sight.'' Revan began to lead his horse out of the stables.

Tess quickly moved to follow him. ''I begin to think that having a sword constantly at one's throat, having death nipping at one's heels day after day after day, can put one into a very odd humor.''

''Aye,'' murmured Nairn. ''I can understand that.''

''Dinna encourage the lass,'' said Revan, his voice barely above a whisper as he took his first step out of the stables.

They wound their way toward the gates by staying close to the walls. The shadows were the deepest there. Tess kept as close to Revan as she dared, knowing he would speak softly if he spoke at all, and she was afraid she might miss some important command. Fear twisted her insides. She knew that prompted her irreverence. Such nonsense or sarcasm had always been her way of hiding her fears and, at times, easing it. She was also simply tired of it all, weary of constantly running or hiding. Tess hoped that weariness continued to put her into an odd humor. It was preferable to resignation or a dangerous loss of caution.

As they neared the gates, Nairn and Thorson slipped ahead of her and Revan to open them. Tess waited in the shadows behind Revan. She could almost look forward to reaching her father's kinsmen despite the fact that she would then lose Revan. Wrapped within the boisterous protection of the Comyns and Delgados, she would no longer suffer the constant fear she did now, would no longer have to keep running until she sometimes thought she would never rest again.

"Ye can come ahead now." Nairn's voice was a soft interruption in the predawn silence.

Revan moved ahead, pausing only to briefly clasp Nairn's and Thorson's hands and exchange hurried wishes for good luck. He then edged out of the narrowly opened gates. Tess crept after him and stopped in front of Nairn.

"I thank ye for your hospitality and the clothes. Please tell the woman who so kindly allowed me the use of them that I was most grateful." To her utter surprise Nairn kissed her full on the mouth.

"Take care of yourself, Tessa, and of my foolish brother."

Before she could make any reply, she heard Revan sharply whisper her name. She quickly smiled a farewell to Nairn and his sergeant-of-arms before leading her horse through the partly opened gates. Barely three steps outside of them she bumped into Revan on his way back.

"What was the delay?" he asked even as he turned and strode back to his patiently waiting horse.

"I wished to say thank ye and fare-thee-well to your brother."

"Ye must have been fulsome in expressing your gratitude for it to have taken so long." He took up his mount's reins and started on his way.

Tess quickly fell into step behind Revan as he started leading his horse toward the distant trees. "I suspect 'twas not the talking but the kissing that took up all the time." She was not sure, because the deep shadows they huddled in obscured her sight a little, but it looked as if Revan stumbled slightly.

''Nairn kissed you?''

''Aye.''

''I see. Well, a brief peck upon the cheek shouldna have taken so long, either.''

''Very true, but this was no light touch upon my cheek. Nairn kissed me full upon the mouth.''

This time Revan stopped and stood very still for a moment. She waited for more, but he neither spoke nor acted. When he started walking again, she inwardly sighed and followed. She should have waited to tell him about the kiss until she could have seen him clearly, could have read his reaction in his expression. Without words and without seeing him as any more than one shadow amongst many, she could only guess at how he felt. That did her no good at all. In truth, she wondered why she even troubled herself. He intended to leave her behind.

And yet, she mused as she kept pace with him, she did want something, some hint of emotion. She decided that she was searching for some sign that she was more to him than a partner in danger and a warm bed partner. It might prove some comfort after he had left her behind. And that, Contessa Comyn Delgado, she told herself, was the very height of foolishness.

Revan halted, drawing her out of her introspection. They were far enough within the trees to be hidden by them. He walked toward her, halted in front of her, and stared at her. Just as she was about to ask him what was the matter, he pulled her into his arms and heartily kissed her. The moment he ended the kiss, he hoisted her up onto the mare's back. Tess sat, dazed, and watched him return to his own horse, mount it, and nudge it into motion.

''And men have the gall to complain about a woman's odd humors,'' she grumbled as she urged the mare to follow him.

''Did ye say something?''

''Nothing of any importance.'' She noticed with some

relief that the mare needed little direction or urging to follow Revan's horse carefully as well as closely.

"'Tis best if we keep as silent as possible. Those fools hunting us could have had the wit to set spies within these woods. Aye, and at every other route leading away from Nairn's. We shall move slowly until dawn breaks and we have the light to see our path more clearly. Then we shall ride faster and harder. We must put some distance between us and those carrion."

"Ye think they will soon follow us?" She could not resist a quick but fruitless look behind her.

"Aye, I believe so. Once there is no sign of us leaving come the dawn, they will probably approach Nairn to demand that he hand us over to them. As soon as they are sure we arena there, they will be hunting us again."

"Are ye sure they willna harm your brother?"

"Aye, as certain as one can be. Nairn can be clever with words. And he will give them no cause to strike at him. He would dearly like to stand against them, but he has the wit to ken that now is not the time for foolish lance-tilting. That we draw so near to the king also works in Nairn's favor. Those hounds willna wish to waste any time in setting out after us. Aye, they may well promise retribution when they find us gone, but they willna pause to deliver it now."

Tess nodded, even though she knew he could not see her, and hoped that he was right. Thus far they had been hounded, deprived of comfort, and given little chance to rest, but no one had yet lost his life or even been badly injured. She took one last look behind her and prayed that that good fortune would continue to follow them.

NAIRN watched Tess and Revan walk away until they faded into the shadows. With a sigh he started to close the gates. Thorson moved to his side to help him.

"'Tis very difficult to send them off as if they are ill-approved guests one must hide from one's mother."

Thorson nodded as they bolted the gates. "True, but such
stealth must be used. These troubled times demand it."

"Aye. Curse the Douglas and his treasonous plots."
Nairn slumped against the cold damp stone of the wall.
"There is more to do before the dawn. The corbies upon the
border are certain to come banging at our gates when they
catch no sight of their prey. I am sure they expect Revan and
Tess to ride out of here at dawn or soon after."

"Then we are left with little time to clear away all sign of
your brother and his lady."

"Best to set about it, then." Nairn stood up straight.
"The sooner we finish that chore, the more time we shall
have to prepare ourselves."

"Prepare ourselves? For what? Do ye think they will
fight us?"

"Nay. I speak of preparing ourselves to appear properly
astounded when the Douglas's and Thurkettle's lapdogs
come yapping after Revan and Tess." He and Thorson
exchanged a grin.

MORNING was half gone when the small force on
the Douglas border finally rode down to Nairn's tower
house. Nairn sat at his table in his great hall and sipped his
wine, smiling faintly over their bellowed demands to be let
inside. They echoed the arrogance of their liege, the
Douglas. It was past time the great earl was brought down.
Nairn hoped the king did not falter or forgive this time.

It was several minutes before anyone appeared in the
great hall. Nairn was certain that Thorson had delayed and
been as obstructive as possible. When Thorson entered,
followed almost too closely by the Douglas's and Thurkettle's men, Nairn offered the intruders a sweet smile. Inside
he seethed, frustrated by the need to do nothing at all when
he ached to act.

A bulky man of medium height, wearing the Douglas's
colors, pushed by Thorson and strode over to the table.

"Where is your brother?" he demanded as he halted inches from Nairn.

"I believe he is with our father. That is correct, is it not, Thorson? Colin rides with my father?"

"Aye." Thorson moved to stand at Nairn's side, his hand gripping the hilt of his sword.

"Dinna play games with me. I am sergeant-at-arms to the earl of Douglas. I seek Sir *Revan* Halyard. We ken very well that he is—or was—*here!*"

"Thorson, ye never told me that Revan had come by." Nairn affected a look of surprise as he turned to Thorson.

"Mayhaps I never told you because he never passed by."

"Ah, I see." Nairn turned back to the Douglas man. "I fear ye are mistaken, sir."

"Ye willna succeed in keeping him safe from punishment for his crimes."

"Crimes? What crimes?"

"All of Scotland has heard of his black deeds."

"Not all. I have had no word of Revan being cried an outlaw."

"He isna outlawed yet, but he is guilty of kidnapping Sir Fergus Thurkettle's niece, of rape, and mayhaps even murder by now. Aye, and there is talk of treason."

It was very hard not to strike the man, but Nairn took a slow drink of wine to soothe his rage. "Ah, the lass. I have heard of a lass. Mayhaps, sir, they but ran away together. Revan always has had a way with the lasses."

"'Twas *kidnapping!*" The man banged his fist upon the table. "Now, cease this play and give me Sir Revan."

"I fear I dinna have him to give. He isna here."

"He is. His horse was seen. One of your people was hiding it."

"There are many horses that look like my brother's. Seeing a horse tells you little or nothing when no one has seen the man who was riding it. I havena seen Revan for several months. Nor has anyone here. Ask about if ye have a mind to.''

"I mean to do more than ask. I will search this place—now.''

"Well, if ye feel ye must,'' Nairn murmured, affecting a languid, bored attitude.

The moment Douglas's sergeant and his men had left the great hall, Nairn asked Thorson, ''Are our people readied to play the game? Do they understand what must be done?''

"Aye.'' Thorson helped himself to a goblet of wine and sat down at the table. ''There will be people everywhere those fools look. When I finally let those strutting curs into the bailey, it was full of folk and the walls looked to be well staffed with men-at-arms. 'Tis good that they didna look too closely at our soldiers. A sword and doublet canna hide everything. I think I would rather be seen to be under-manned than have it kenned that we had lasses and old men standing guard.'' He grinned when Nairn laughed.

"Rest easy, Thorson. 'Tis clear that they didna see the trick. Let us pray that they continue to be so blind. One of them might have wit enough to realize that he has seen that man or that lass before. Then our deceit will be uncovered.''

"As young Meg assured me, these soldiers will only take a look at the lasses and they willna be allowed to linger at it. She says a change of kerchief, of apron, or of bonnet should be enough. And if one of those men does say that he has seen her before, she can say she has finished that chore and moved onto this one or that the one he saw was her cousin or her sister. Dinna worry on it. Our folk will do very well. In truth, they were eager for the chance to dupe these men. We have suffered this annoyance for too long. Aye, and the threat of their presence all around us.''

Nairn gave a faint nod of agreement and prayed that Thorson was right, that their ploy would work and Douglas's minions would leave thinking that his keep was fully staffed. If he could emerge from these troubled times with his lands unscathed and his people unhurt, it would be some recompense for the need to be so meek and nearly servile toward his arrogant neighbors. Douglas's downfall would not be quite so satisfying if he returned from fighting for the king to find his lands devastated and his people suffering.

As soon as he finished his wine, Nairn strolled out into the bailey, Thorson quietly following him. He watched the number of guards upon his walls begin to increase and knew Douglas's men would soon leave. It was only a few moments later when Douglas's men began to gather in the bailey and the sergeant marched over to him. Nairn could tell by the expression upon the man's face that no sign of Revan or Tess had been discovered. That allowed him the strength to meet the man's insolence with a semblance of calm. He just hoped God would grant him the chance to meet the man on the battlefield later.

"I dinna ken how ye did it, but they arena here," the man grumbled. "We found naught." His gruff voice was weighted with accusation.

"Mayhaps that is because ye were mistaken."

"Nay, I think not. We will find them. Mount up, men," he bellowed. "We set out upon a hunt." He glared at Nairn. "Your brother shall not escape justice and punishment for his crimes, Sir Nairn."

"There is no proof that he has committed any crimes."

"Enough. Mayhaps he didna kill that king's man. Mayhaps that fool niece of Thurkettle's did run off with him willingly. It doesna matter. He has taken the wife of one of the earl's nephews. 'Tis an insult that must be paid for."

"The lass is wed to a Douglas?" Nairn made no attempt to hide his shock.

"Betrothed. 'Tis much the same. Best ye prepare his winding sheets, for Sir Revan Halyard willna see another summer through." He strode over to his horse, mounted, and led his men out of Nairn's bailey.

The minute the gates were shut behind the men, Nairn looked at Thorson, whose weatherbeaten face was wrinkled in a frown. "Revan never said the lass was betrothed or wed."

"Mayhaps she didna tell him."

"Aye, and mayhaps she didna ken it herself."

"I am inclined to believe that possibility. She didna strike me as a lass who would keep such a thing secret."

"Nay. When one considers all she has told Revan, it becomes even more unbelievable. 'Tis possible this betrothal was arranged and she wasna told about it. 'Tis also possible that it was settled only after she left with Revan. Even if all else they charge Revan with is disbelieved, they can still hold that against him. It canna be proved or disproved, yet it gives them the right to pursue Revan, even kill him. Curse it, Revan should be told, but there is no way for me to reach him with this news."

"It doesna matter. He has enough threats against him. A new one willna make him any more wary than he is now. The moment he reaches Donnbraigh, it willna matter any longer. The Comyns and the Delgados would vigorously fight such a marriage. In truth, soon such a marriage will be impossible anyways. Douglas and all of his allies will be dead or fighting for their lives, if they arena running to cower in some hole."

Nairn sighed with relief. "Of course. Once treason taints the earl of Douglas and his followers, no betrothal will be honored. We must pray that Revan continues to elude those who are so eager to murder him."

"He will."

"He now has near to twenty men hunting him down."

"That lot couldna catch a blind deer that had two wooden legs." He grinned when Nairn laughed.

"True enough." He grew serious and then sighed. "So, all we need to worry about is whether Revan has the wit to hold fast to that wee brown lass ere he loses all chance to do so."

Chapter

✦15✦

THE SOUND OF REVAN CURSING FLUENTLY brought Tess out of her half-sleep. For two days they had ridden hard and fast, driven along by constant pursuit. At night they had slept huddled together, their passion killed by exhaustion and their stomachs nearly empty, for they had not dared to light even the smallest of fires. The hunt for them had been increased. The Douglas and Thurkettle had men everywhere. Now, within walking distance of Donnbraigh, they were encircled by their enemies. She had dismounted, sprawled on the ground, and left Revan to the chore of scouting out a possible approach to her kinsmen's keep. Sitting up, she frowned at him and found little encouragement in his black expression.

"The whoresons are everywhere I turn," he snapped as he sat down in front of her.

"I am surprised my uncle Silvio has allowed it."

"He is probably as undermanned as Nairn. I believe he hasna ignored them completely. They dinna act as boldly as they did at Nairn's. Your uncle may not have set any men after them, but I think he hasna let them run free, either."

"Even so, there are enough about to hinder us?"

"More than enough. I couldna find a single path to Donnbraigh that didna have someone watching it. I canna be

187

certain that waiting until nightfall will even help us this time.''

"Mayhaps we should just draw as near as we can and then bolt for the gates. I ken that isna the best of plans—''

"Nay, it isna, but 'tis the only one left to us.'' He smiled faintly. "I but pondered a way to tell you about it and make it sound both clever and safe.''

Tess laughed softly. "Even ye canna find words for that, sweet-tongued devil though ye are.'' She grew serious again. "Do we crouch here until it grows dark, then?''

"Aye, and pray that none of those curs sniff us out. 'Twill be dusk soon. The gates will close when darkness falls. We dinna want to be stuck outside. So as the sun begins to set, we will start on our way. We will move cautiously until we are seen, and then we will spur our mounts onward, straight for Donnbraigh's sturdy gates.''

"And pray that my kinsmen dinna mistake us for some foe and fill our poor mortal frames with arrows?''

Revan sidled closer, took off her cap, and began to unbraid her hair. "Ye shall leave this beautiful pelt flowing free so all who see you will ken that ye are a lass. That will stay their hands.''

"Are ye certain of that?''

"Aye. From all Nairn told me of these Comyns and Delgados, they willna harm a lass. Are ye not so sure?''

"Five years past I would have been.'' She leaned against him when he sat behind her to finger-comb her hair. "Now I am not certain of anything. The kinsmen I kenned back then would never have lifted a hand against any lass. But they are caught up firmly in these troubled times. Who can say how deeply mistrust may have settled in their hearts?''

"There is some truth in that, but I still dinna believe we need to fear them. Aye, they may well grab us the moment we enter their gates and hold us tightly until they are sure ye are Contessa, but they willna kill you. And that, my sweet Tess, makes you my shield.''

"'Tis only fair, sir. Ye have been mine for most of this thrice-cursed journey."

"This time we shall both have our backs to the enemy." He wrapped his arms around her, tugged her closer up against him, and kissed her on the top of her head. "Ye are to ride as low in the saddle as ye can, lass. If our enemies have any archers, ye dinna wish to give them too large a target."

"Aye, I understand." She glanced up at the sky. "Well, at least we dinna have to wait too long to start this mad game."

Tess grunted in protest when she was shaken awake. Straightening up, she blinked and realized that she had fallen asleep against Revan. The light of day was beginning to fade.

"I havena slept too long, have I?" She quickly stood up and brushed herself off.

"Nay, but we best not dally here any longer." Revan got to his feet, gave her a quick kiss, and took her by the hand. "Keep your eyes open. The moment we see one of the earl's or Thurkettle's men, we ride hard."

"Straight for the gates of Donnbraigh. Aye, I remember." She mounted her horse and, grimacing faintly, looked down at her outfit. "I wish now that I hadna tossed away that blue gown. 'Twas torn and stained, but it would have shocked my kinsmen far less than this travel-worn lad's attire."

Revan mounted, then smiled at her. "I believe that, after so many days of not kenning whether ye were alive or dead, or even where ye might be, your kinsmen will take little heed of your attire." He frowned when he noticed her glancing about and peeking into her saddle packs. "Have ye lost something?"

"My hat. I ken that 'tis worn and old, but 'twas my father's."

"I have it in my saddle packs. Ready?"

"As ready as one can ever be for such a mad venture."

He nodded and started toward Donnbraigh. Tess kept as close to him as she dared, letting her mare amble behind Revan's mount while she kept an eye out for their enemies. It was not long before the trees she and Revan had been sheltered in began to thin out and Donnbraigh came into view.

The tall, el-shaped tower house was a welcome sight. The high, thick wall surrounding it promised safety. There was little activity at the gates, and Tess knew those heavy iron-studded doors and the yett, that ominous gate of heavy interlaced iron bars, would soon be shut. She could remember from her youth how everyone returned to the keep or left it for their homes before dusk had truly settled. An hour or so would pass while the gates remained opened for the rare straggler. Then, just as the last gray light of dusk was fading into night, there would be the sound of those gates shutting tight. At first it had frightened her, but she had quickly grown to acquaint the sound with being safe. She had come to realize that those gates did not lock her in so much as they locked out all danger.

"To your left, Tessa," hissed Revan, yanking her free of her memories.

She barely had the chance to look at the man Revan had spotted. That man gave a cry of discovery just as Revan yelled at her to race for the gates. Tess crouched low in the saddle as he had told her to and spurred her mare into a gallop. She glanced behind to see Revan fitting an arrow to his bow. When she slowed a little, he gave her one sharp look, a clear order to continue on. Tess obeyed and an instant later she heard a man scream. She then heard the rapid approach of a horse and chanced a quick peek. Revan was right behind her. He had said she would be his shield this time, but he clearly meant to shield her as well.

Her concern about Revan was pushed aside as she espied riders converging upon them from three sides. The air was soon peppered with arrows. Tess prayed that her kinsmen

would decide to aid her and Revan simply because the
Douglas men were after them. Although none of the Comyn
men could possibly recognize her now, she hoped they
would decide to help two people hunted by so many and ask
the why of it all later.

The moment they were within arrow range of the walls of
Donnbraigh, Tess's fervent prayers were answered. She saw
one of the Douglas men thrown from his saddle by the force
of several arrows entering his chest and heard the screams
of others. Although she could not be exactly thankful that
men were dying, she was nevertheless relieved. She and
Revan now had a better chance of reaching the safety of
Donnbraigh alive.

Even after she passed through the outer gates, she did not
relax. The covered passage between the outer and inner
gates was not a welcoming one. It suddenly appeared to be
a long, dark, and dangerous tunnel. Glancing upward, she
caught the glint of arrowheads aimed down at her through
the murderholes in the roof. She tensed, waiting for those
arrows to strike her flesh. Until she was recognized, she
knew she would be seen as a possible enemy.

As soon as she cleared the inner gates and was within the
bailey, she reined her mare to a halt. The animal was startled
by such an abrupt stop and reared. It took her a moment to
calm the horse. The instant the mare was still, several armed
men encircled her, and one yanked her out of her saddle.
She saw Revan arrive and be roughly pulled from his saddle
as the loud slamming shut of the gates echoed throughout
the bailey. Afraid that Revan might be hurt by her kinsmen,
she began to struggle in her captor's hold.

"Be still, wench. Your companion will suffer no more
than a few wee bruises if he has the wit to surrender
peacefully."

That deep voice was familiar, and Tess turned her head to
look at her captor. It surprised her a little to see that it was
her cousin Tomas, for she would have expected him to be at
his own keep or with the king. She saw him frown and knew

he was beginning to recognize her. In the hope of hurrying along that recognition, she spoke to him in Spanish, praying that she had not forgotten too much over the last five years.

"Cousin, do you not remember me?" She saw surprise widen his brown eyes, then he scowled.

"I think I do," he replied in Spanish.

"Then think harder, you brainless fool," she snapped. "I am Contessa."

"Your tongue does carry her sting," he said. "Yet, this could be some trick. We have had a few played upon us by curs who thought to cheat us of the reward offered for your safe return."

"Has your wife, Meghan, learned of how you walk and talk in your sleep yet?" He paled slightly, and she knew she had strengthened her claim. Few outside of the immediate family knew about those habits.

Tomas turned her to face him, gripping her by the shoulders. She tolerated his searching gaze, smiling faintly as she waited for him to realize his eyes and his memory could be trusted. When he gave a glad cry and hugged her, she felt somewhat weak with relief. She did her best to answer his barrage of questions. It was several moments before she recalled that they were still speaking in Spanish and that Revan might be in need of some assistance.

Revan frowned, not able to understand one word of the rapid conversation Tess was having with the tall, very handsome man who so vigorously hugged and kissed her. He was nettled over how long it was taking her to remember him. The two men flanking him, each firmly holding one of his arms, were doing him no harm, but Tess had not really looked his way enough to know that. Watching the man handle her with such familiarity was also beginning to enrage him. He decided to remind Tess that she had not come to Donnbraigh alone.

"Tessa," he called, ignoring the way his guards frowned at him in open disapproval. "Now that they are assured that ye are a friend, do ye think ye could spare a moment to tell them that I am no enemy?''

Startled, Tess turned to look at Revan. After studying him quickly but carefully, she relaxed. He was not hurt, simply irritated. Probably doesna like being forgotten any more than I do, she thought and smiled. She was tempted to ignore him a little longer, but Tomas spoke up.

''Who is this man, Tess?'' Tomas asked in English, glaring at Revan.

''Sir Revan Halyard.'' She was shocked when Tomas stepped in front of her and drew his sword.

''So this is the low cur who kidnapped you.''

She grabbed Tomas's arm to halt his advance on Revan. ''Nay, ye canna hurt him. He is one of the king's knights.''

''I dinna care if he is the Pope's brother. *He* is the man who kidnapped you—aye?''

''Well, aye, but he never meant to hurt me, and he has saved my life.''

''After he put your life at risk.''

''My life was at risk ere he took me out of Thurkettle's hands.''

''I begin to think there are a great many twists and turns to this tale. Release him,'' he ordered the guards.

Tess hurried to Revan's side. ''Are ye hurt?'' she asked even though she could see no sign of a wound.

''Nay, I am fine.''

''We will go and join our uncle, Silvio, in the great hall,'' Tomas said, then ordered the men to see to Revan's and Tess's horses. ''Come.'' He signaled Tess and Revan to follow him into the keep.

When Revan took Tess by the hand and started after Tomas, she did not immediately fall into step with him. ''Is there something wrong?''

''Mayhaps this wasna such a good idea.'' Tess suddenly dreaded confronting her uncle Silvio.

''We need their help. These are your kinsmen, and 'tis clear to see that they welcome you.''

"Uncle Silvio will take one look at me, and he will ken all about us," she whispered, seeing that Tomas had stopped to watch them and not wanting her cousin to overhear what she was saying.

"He willna ken a thing."

"He will. I am certain of it."

"There is no brand upon your forehead, lass. 'Tis our secret."

She shook her head. "Uncle Silvio will ken it all with but one look. Tomas and his bride anticipated their wedding night. They never told Uncle Silvio, either, but the first time he looked at them, he kenned it all."

"Foolishness." Revan hoped he sounded more confident than he suddenly felt.

He started toward Tomas again. The man hesitated to be sure they were following him, then started toward the keep again. Revan ignored Tess's heavy sigh of resignation and the foreboding expression she wore, but both infected him. He did not want to believe that her uncle could guess they had become lovers simply by looking at them, but Revan had to admit to himself that he was beginning to feel a little bit worried.

As they stepped inside of the keep and walked toward the great hall, Revan saw the first signs of the Comyn-Delgado wealth. The alms table set near the door held a silver tray and was draped with fine embroidered linen. On the wall above it hung a beautifully woven tapestry. Beside the table was a heavy, elaborately carved chair. To use such expensive items for the alms table, used to set out offerings for the poor and the occasional traveling holy man, was something only a rich man could or would do.

That opinion was confirmed as Tomas showed them into the great hall. Here the signs of wealth were everywhere, from the tapestries hung upon the wall for warmth to the large number of candles burning. Chairs were as numerous as benches around the cloth-draped tables. It was not the display of a man eager to boast of his riches, however, but of one who used his money to better his surroundings, to achieve some comfort. Revan also suspected that the wealth was honestly earned, unlike that of far too many others he knew.

Revan turned his attention to Sir Silvio Comyn as they approached him. Silvio was a tall, lean man who possessed the same dark handsomeness Tomas did, although Silvio's was weathered by an added ten or more years. The man sat at the head of a large table at the far end of the hall in a high-backed chair, his foot bandaged and resting on another pillowed chair. When he, Tomas, and Tess finally stopped in front of Sir Silvio, Revan found the man's unwavering gaze unsettling. Silvio Comyn had the same dark, stirring eyes that Tess had. That steady gaze made Revan feel as if every little wrong he had ever committed was now exposed. It made Revan want to confess, and he knew that would be a very big mistake.

"These two were the ones who caused such a great row?" Silvio asked, glancing at Tomas.

"Aye. All of those slinking dogs we have had lurking about our lands were chasing them. 'Tis Contessa, Uncle Silvio." Tomas pointed at his cousin. "It took me a moment to recognize her."

Silvio studied Tess. "It has been five years."

Tess released Revan's hand and took one step closer to her uncle. "Dinna ye recognize me? I canna have changed so very much. Ye always called me the Wee Countess."

"Aye, the Wee Countess, though Your Ladyship is looking a wee bit bedraggled just now." He grinned and opened his arms. "Come and give your uncle a hug, lassie. We have been worried about you."

Although still a little nervous, Tess hurried over to hug him. The sight of him always brought her a touch of sadness along with the joy. He looked so much like her late father.

"What happened to your foot?" she asked after they had exchanged kisses and he held her by his chair with his arm about her waist.

"One of Tomas's useless horses trod upon it." He gave her a mock frown when she giggled. "'Tis better, but I coddle it because I wish to be fully able to fight for our king when the time comes." He looked at Revan. "And this must be Sir Revan Halyard."

"Aye, Uncle Silvio, but he isna guilty of all the black crimes Thurkettle and the Douglas claim he is."

"I felt certain those were all lies, which is why he wasna cut down the moment he rode into my bailey. Tomas, see that some food and drink are brought to us, then join us. There is a lot that must be discussed."

Tess did not like the sound of that but struggled to disguise her qualms. Silvio had her sit on his left and Revan on his right. When Tomas returned, he was seated on the other side of Revan. Tess decided her kinsmen looked a little too much like guards. Silvio might be willing to listen, but she suspected he was also prepared to condemn if the story he would demand was not to his satisfaction.

The moment the food and drink were brought and the four of them were alone again, Silvio pressed Revan for the whole story. Whenever Tess tried to add something, she was politely but firmly brushed aside. It began to annoy her.

"And ye agree with all he has said?" Silvio asked Tess when Revan was finished. "There is naught ye would change?"

"Nay," she replied. "In truth, he told it more harshly than I would have. The beginning of it all wasna as bad as he said."

"Oh? He didna kidnap you? Didna drag you from Thurkettle's keep whilst holding a knife at your throat?"

It was easy to see that that angered her kinsmen, and Tess sought to soothe that fury. "Aye, he did, but he never intended to hurt me. 'Twas but a ploy to escape Thurkettle, who believed it because he would probably cut his own mother's throat to save himself. It didna take long before I realized that Sir Revan had actually saved my life, not endangered it. Thurkettle wanted me dead. Still does."

"Ye call him Thurkettle now. Not uncle?"

"I do? Aye, I guess I do. Sometime between leaving Thurkettle's keep and getting here, I have ceased to think of him as a kinsman. He is the enemy, the man who wishes to kill me."

"And ye are certain that he tries to kill you?"

"Aye. 'Tisna just because I can help to expose him as a traitor, but also to get his greedy hands on my inheritance. When Revan suggested it, I fought to deny it, but I couldna. He has tried to murder me several other times, ere this race to the king even began. There were a few incidents I had fooled myself into thinking were accidents." She briefly related them to Silvio. "He has had his eye upon my inheritance since I went to live there."

"Sweet Mary." Silvio reached out to briefly clasp her hand. "God forgive us for sending you there."

"There is naught to forgive. Ye did as ye thought best. If I had told you about the trouble, I ken that ye would have sped to my aid. I didna ken it. And if I, who lived cheek to jowl with the man, didna ken his game, how could you have? There is no cause for guilt, Uncle Silvio."

"Mayhaps." He patted her hand. "I think that there is a great deal that ye havena told me, lassie, but it can wait." He glanced at Revan. "Did ye insist that she dress as a lad?"

"Nay," Tess answered before Revan could. "I was dressed this way because I was mucking about in the stables. 'Twas when I returned from there, through the tunnels, that I saw Revan."

"Tessa, tell him about the man ye saw. The one ye recognized but couldna name," Revan urged.

As carefully as she could, Tess described the man on the black, white-stockinged stallion. She watched Silvio's and Tomas's faces pale slightly, then flush as they went from shock to fury. She had hoped that she was wrong despite her own conviction, but their expressions killed that hope. They knew the man, knew him and shared her fears.

"That black-hearted traitor!" cried Tomas and hit the table with his fist. "'Tis MacKinnon. Angus MacKinnon."

"Aye," agreed Silvio, his rich voice thickened with anger. "He owes all he is and all he has to the king yet schemes to betray his liege lord. The Douglas wouldna work so hard or pay as dearly as he probably has just to gain one more soldier. He buys himself a murderer. The questions that must be answered are why and when does the Douglas want him to strike?"

"I believe the murder is to take place at the same time the battle does," said Revan. "If both James and his heir are gone, many a man will see no reason to keep on fighting. 'Tis their vow of allegiance that brings them to James's side more than any great love for the man. Aye, they swear loyalty to the king, but they dinna much care who is the king. And there are those who feel the Douglas has a righteous grievance even though they willna fight at his side. I suppose one could say that such men swear allegiance to the throne itself, being somewhat indifferent as to which man sits upon it or how he got there."

Silvio nodded. "Sadly true. This quarrel with the Douglases has taken up so much of James's short life that he hasna had the time to make many strong bonds amongst his people. Well, we shall send word to the court about the traitor in their midst. At least MacKinnon will cease to be a threat." He grimaced. "That just leaves the Douglas to deal with."

"'Tis more than enough," murmured Revan.

"Aye, and there is a great deal of planning that must be done. Though that can wait until the morrow. Now, I am certain, the two of you would like a bath and a soft bed. A good night's rest as well, eh?"

Revan nodded but said, "All of which will be welcome, but I am willing to stand watch or fight if ye have need of me."

"Against those curs outside of our walls?"

"Aye. They may be driven to attack."

"I think not. They fled the moment my men fired upon them. Once ye were within our gates, they disappeared."

"Could they not return with more men?"

" 'Tis possible and we will watch for them. But the Douglas couldna bring a strong force against Donnbraigh for at least a week, mayhaps longer. If ye are right and he plans to march against the king in a month's time, then he canna send a force here. He canna afford to bog down men and supplies in a fight with me. By the time he could take Donnbraigh and get his hands on the two of you, the need to silence you would have passed.

"However, ye must not think yourselves safe from all threat. 'Twould be best if you stay within these walls. I havena got the men to hunt down all of the Douglas's or Thurkettle's spies who will assuredly remain in the area, although I do intend to give it a good try."

Tess sighed, then grimaced. "They may have failed to kill me thus far, but they are doing a good job of keeping me a prisoner."

"It will soon end, dearling," Silvio assured her. "Now, Tomas, see that a chamber is readied for your cousin and her man."

Tomas was already out of the great hall, the door shutting behind him, before Tess realized what her uncle had just said. She choked slightly on the wine she was sipping and looked at Silvio. He turned from indulging in a staring match with Revan to look at her. She could see in his expression that, just as she had feared, he knew about her and Revan. Tess did not understand why Revan was not denying it—immediately and vehemently.

"Uncle Silvio, I believe ye meant to say *two* bedchambers," she finally said when both men just continued to watch her.

"Nay. I said one and I meant one. 'Tis foolish to part you two now. A bit like shutting the stable door after the horse has fled."

"Uncle Silvio, ye assume too much. Aye, ye come near

to insulting me. Mayhaps even Revan, too.'' She could see by her uncle's face that her pose of outraged innocence was not believed.

"Well done," he murmured, then quickly added, "Your honor is foremost in my mind, child. 'Tis why ye and this knight will be wed as soon as possible.''

Chapter

✦ 16 ✦

"WED? WE ARE TO BE WED?"

Tess was so surprised, she spoke in a whisper. She had feared that her uncle would guess her relationship with Revan, but she had not really expected the man to so calmly state that she and Revan would be married. The fact that Revan just sat there, silent and calm, also surprised her. For a brief moment she felt a tremor of delight, thinking that Revan's silence was indicative of acceptance and approval. She quickly smothered that feeling. Revan was silent because he had no argument. They had been lovers. Custom and honor demanded that he wed her if her family insisted upon it, as Silvio clearly intended to do so. Custom and honor were not what she wanted binding Revan to her side.

"Aye—wed. Do ye mean to tell me that ye havena been lovers?"

"Aye—I do." She could tell by Silvio's faint smile that her voice lacked conviction.

Silvio looked at Revan. "And you, Sir Halyard, do ye mean to tell me, on your honor as a king's knight, that ye and my lying niece havena been lovers?"

"Uncle," Tess protested before Revan could answer. "Is my word not good enough?"

"Ye didna give me your word." He stared at Revan. "Sir Halyard?"

Revan looked into the man's eyes and almost smiled, although he did not really feel amused. The man had the same kind of eyes that Tessa did. Silvio's dark eyes demanded the truth. It would be expedient to agree with Tessa's poor lie, but Revan knew he could not do it, not when Silvio called upon his honor and fixed those rich brown eyes on him.

"Aye, sir, we have been lovers, but ye were sure of that already, were ye not?"

"I was despite my niece's weak attempt to change my mind. So, ye will wed the lass."

"I will. As ye say, sir, honor demands it." When he looked at Tess, Revan decided that, true or not, it was not the wisest thing to say.

Hurt and fury battled within Tess, and she pushed fury to the forefront. It was easier to contend with while her uncle and Revan both watched her. They were settling her future for her, and she deeply resented it. Even if honor was not all Revan spoke of, even if he had declared some feeling and need for her, she knew she still would have resented it. Custom might well give the men of her family the right to marry her off as they pleased, but she had always considered that a stupid and oppressive custom. They could at least have done her the courtesy of asking her her opinion on the matter.

"Honor can go rot and the two of you can go with it," she snapped.

"Where would the world be without honor, lass?" Silvio idly drank his wine as he watched his niece.

"'Twould probably be a wee bit more peaceful. There is no need for this marriage ye are trying to ram down our throats."

"Nay? Ye and your man just admitted that fleeing your enemies wasna all the pair of you were up to whilst tramping over the borderlands for the last fortnight or so. If a man beds a lass, then he is obliged to wed her.''

''If that were so, then ye would have been wed a hundred times over.''

''Such pertness. None of those I bedded ere I was wed to Kirsten were virgin lasses. A bachelor is allowed his follies.''

''So a maid should be allowed hers!'' Tess was beginning to think that becoming involved with Revan had been a very big folly, indeed.

''Nay. A maid has a maidenhead and can get with child. Ye arena with child yet, are ye?''

''Of course not.''

Her conviction wavered almost as soon as the firm denial left her mouth. The Thurkettles were not particularly fertile, but the Comyns and Delgados were. If she took after her father's side in that aspect, Revan just had to look at her with a lustful glint in his eyes to set a babe growing inside of her. She quickly pushed aside all thoughts on that matter. It was too soon for her to know, and she could not afford the diversion at the moment.

''So, marriage isna needed,'' she continued. ''There is no bastard to fret about.''

''' Tis probably too soon for you to be certain of that.''

Tess felt strongly inclined to hit him for that insight. ''Well, if the need for a husband should arise, I can buy one.''

''Better to take a man of honor now than one of avarice later.''

''Where is Aunt Kirsten? She wouldna allow you to push me into this.''

''I wouldna be too sure of that, lass. And even if ye could win her to your side, ye canna. She isna here. I sent her and the children to stay with Tomas's wife and bairns. His keep is further from the reach of the Douglases, thus safer. She will be returned in time to see you wed.''

A soft cry of frustration escaped Tess as she got to her

feet. "Ye have no right to push me to the altar or force Revan to it."

"Tessa," began Revan, not sure what he could say, but hoping to stop the growing argument between her and Silvio.

"Just stay out of this, Revan. It is none of your business."

"Excuse my impertinence. I had thought that I was to be the bridegroom."

"And such a bridegroom—standing there with a Delgado blade between your shoulders."

"I havena even nudged the lad with my eating knife," murmured Silvio.

Revan ignored that. "'Tis honor that will set me before that altar. Your uncle has called upon it, as is his right."

Honor again, Tess thought and had to struggle against the urge to hurl her tankard at his head. She decided it was time for her to escape the great hall and the two men looking at her as if she was just some foolish child they needed to placate. She had no good argument, not one that would sway them. Neither could she expose the full reason their talk of marriage enraged her, of how much more she needed from Revan besides honor. Weariness sapped her wit. She needed rest and time to think. There was still hope of finding some way out of being married to a man who saw her only as a duty he must take on to appease his sense of honor.

"If ye fine gentlemen will pardon me, I believe I shall retire now." She started toward the door.

"Ye are just going to run away, then, are ye, lassie?" asked her uncle.

"Run away?" She paused after opening the heavy door to look back at Silvio and Revan. "Nay. Why should I? 'Tis just that my poor woman's heart is so aflutter from the heady romance of the moment that I really must go and lie down. I shouldna wish to embarrass my family by swooning from delight right here in the hall."

Tess shut the door behind her with extreme care. She then started up the narrow, winding stairs that led to the bedchambers. After a hot bath she would go to bed and try to think more clearly. When Revan joined her, she intended to have a few words with him—alone, unhindered by her uncle Silvio's talk of honor and duty.

AFTER staring at the closed door of the hall for a moment, Silvio turned to look at Revan. "Sorry, lad, but I fear ye must accept that wicked tongue of hers along with the rest of the lass. I am her kinsman. 'Twould be frowned on if I cut it out ere I set ye both before a priest."

Revan smiled faintly. "I have grown accustomed to it. In truth, most times I rather like it. Well, I had best follow and try to soothe this temper of hers."

"Nay. Set here a while longer." He refilled Revan's tankard with wine. "I realize she has changed some in the past five years, but I suspect her temper is still a short-lived thing. Let it cool. Mayhaps, if ye wait long enough, she will fall asleep, and ye need not worry yourself with it anyways."

"Not this night at least," Revan murmured.

"I sense a reluctance within you. Ye bedded the lass yet dinna wish to wed her?"

The question was asked calmly, but Revan knew Silvio was close to anger—very close. There was a lurking hardness in the man's fine eyes. Revan decided to speak the plain truth. If he judged Silvio correctly, the man would accept it even if he did not like it or agree with it.

"She is an heiress."

"Aye." Silvio frowned. "I had wondered if that was one reason ye seduced the lass."

"'Twas the best reason to leave the lass be. That proved impossible."

"'Tis no surprise. She is a pretty girl. Wee but bonnie. So, her being a lass of fortune and land troubles you?"

"I have my pride, sir." Revan could see that Silvio

would be no more understanding than Simon or Nairn had been.

"Pride willna feed your bairns or keep a roof over their heads. Nay, nor will it give them a future."

"'Tis why I had decided to remain unwed."

"Bedding virgins isna the way to hold to that decision."

"I ken it. I was holding firm to it until I met your niece. Sir, in my own defense, I swear I didna seduce Tess."

"She seduced you, did she?"

"Nay! I never meant to imply that. I—" Revan fumbled for the right words.

Silvio held his hand up. "Dinna fret yourself. I ken what happened. Two, young, hot-blooded people forced together day after day. 'Twas fated that ye should become lovers. I am not so old that I canna see that. 'Tis why ye have met with reason and not fury. That and the fact that ye will wed the lass as soon as the worst of these troubles with the Douglases are over."

"Aye, sir."

"Lad, ye do like the lass, do ye not?"

"Aye, sir."

"Then rein in your pride, dinna let it make ye act the fool. Ye like her, ye want her, and, with what she brings to the marriage, ye can make a fine life for yourselves. Many a man would fight tooth and nail to be in your boots. Do ye mean to waste all she brings to the marriage on a wastral's life?"

"Of course not."

"Then I dinna see what troubles you."

"Neither did my friend Simon or my brother Nairn."

"Which could be because ye are wrong. There is time yet for ye to cast aside such prideful nonsense. Now, go find that nephew of mine, Tomas, and he will show ye where to bathe. By the time ye join Tess, ye should find her more reasonable."

As the doors shut behind Revan, Silvio shook his head. He waited for Tomas to return, but several minutes passed before his nephew entered the hall. By then Silvio had decided to let matters stand. Revan and Tess had been lovers, and despite what troubles existed in their heads or hearts, marriage was now required.

"Neither the bride nor the bridegroom appeared joyful," Tomas remarked as he sprawled in a chair on Silvio's left. "Mayhaps it isna such a wise thing to force them to be married."

"The lass took the man to her bed, gave him her innocence. Honor demands marriage."

"True, but then, Tess is right in saying that she could buy a husband if and when she needed to."

"The lass thinks too much like a man. Aye, 'tis true. 'Twould also be a grave mistake. He is right for her. She said that clear enough when she allowed him to make love to her."

"I would have thought so and yet . . ." Tomas grimaced and shrugged. "They just dinna seem very happy."

"Nay. They both let pride rule them. Tessa wants him to speak of more than honor and duty, and Revan fears that, by wedding an heiress, he makes himself the basest sort of mercenary."

"Are ye certain that is all of it?"

"As certain as one can be about such a matter. Since she isna already swelling with child, there is time to let them sort themselves out. If Revan's information is right, we fight the Douglas's army in a month's time. Right after that those two will be married. Mayhaps by then they will see what I do when I look at them."

"And what is that?"

"That they are well suited. That they want each other. I but hope they can look around their pride and not let it ruin their future together."

Tess blinked and looked around, wondering what had woken her. She had not done much thinking. The hot bath had relaxed her so that she had crawled into bed and quickly gone to sleep.

When she spotted Revan walking toward the bed, she scowled. She suddenly remembered all she had wanted to think about, all that had happened with her uncle Silvio, and all she had wanted to say. As he paused to shed the robe and braies he wore, she tried to put some order into her sleep-scattered thoughts. She did not want to say anything that would expose her deep feelings for him. With all his talk of honor and duty, she was not sure he could be trusted with the truth of her emotions or that he would welcome any indication that he had won her heart.

Inwardly she grimaced. She, in the way that she behaved, had undoubtedly given him a multitude of hints about her feelings for him. However, she was determined not to give him the words that could give those hints the weight of fact.

"So, have ye and my uncle finished planning my life?" she asked as he climbed into bed beside her.

"I believe it was Silvio who did the planning. As ye did, I but complied."

"I didna comply."

"Ah, aye, 'tis true. I stand corrected."

"It would have been a wee bit more helpful if ye had stood firmly—against Uncle Silvio ordering us to the altar."

Revan sighed and ran a hand through his hair. He turned on his side to face her. Even in the dim light cast by the branch of candles on a table by the bed, he could read her expression. Her anger was still strong. Although it was strange for a young lass to fight the marriage plans her male relatives arranged for her, he could understand and sympathize. What puzzled him was that he was not sharing those feelings.

"Tessa, ye were a virgin. We are both wellborn. We both have families who see honor and duty as important. The moment we bedded down together, our fate was sealed. We just tried to ignore that truth and think ourselves free to break the rules. In truth, the moment ye passed one night in my company, our marriage was set.''

"I dinna see why it must be.''

He reached out to stroke her hair. ''Aye, ye do. We canna have our wellborn lasses running too free.''

"Just our wellborn lads.''

"As Silvio said—lads dinna have a maidenhead and canna get with child.''

"Nay, they can just leave bastards all about the country-side to haunt them later.''

"A good point and true enough—if they are foolish.'' He slid his hand down her side and rested it on her abdomen. ''I fear I was a wee bit foolish with you, lass. My bairn could already be stirring beneath this soft skin. Why not cease this bickering and just tell me what troubles you so about wedding me?''

Ye dinna love me, was what she ached to say, but she swallowed those words. She did not wish to hear him agree with that statement. It was hard enough to know that her love was not returned. To prompt him to put that knowledge into words would only make it hurt more.

"I dinna wish to have a husband who was brought to the altar at sword point.''

"There has been no threat of that.'' He kissed her cheek and edged close to her. ''Silvio but recalled me to my duty, to what my honor, and yours, demands of me.''

"Honor and duty.'' She spat the words out as if they were curses. ''They are cold things to bring to a marriage bed.''

"Tessa,'' he whispered as he pulled her into his arms and kissed her. ''Has any bed we shared ever been cold?'' He smoothed his hands down her back and felt her move against him involuntarily. '''Tis the fire we spark between us that has brought us to the point where we must confront matters of honor and duty.''

"And will this fire be able to survive, or will it be smothered into cold ashes by the weight of honor and duty?''

"Is that what worries you?" He brushed soft, light kisses over her face.

"'Tis something to consider." She tensed, trying to fight the pull of desire because there was so much they needed to discuss.

"Even such weighty things as those couldna dim the passion we share, lass. I had some firm rules concerning lasses of good family. They have held firm for many years. Yet, even they couldna still the hunger ye bred in me. Nor could all ye have been taught still your wanting. Nay, burdens though they can be, duty and honor willna cool this fire."

"Then why were ye reluctant? And ye were. I could see it in your face, feel it."

Revan grimaced. "Ye are an heiress, Tessa. I have naught—little coin and no lands. Although I can find few who dinna consider me a great fool for thinking so, I canna like wedding the land and money I havena gained by birth or skill."

"Ye mean it was your pride?" Tess found that alarming, for pride could be a strong and destructive thing.

"Aye, my pride. Tessa, I just didna like the thought that I needed to marry for such gain. It seemed to me to be the act of a whore. I have yet to find a man who agrees with that view. I begin to think I am the only man who holds it."

He smiled at her as he turned so that she was sprawled beneath him. "However, 'tis not gain that brings about the marriage but honor and duty. I will soothe my foolish pride with that. Come, Tessa, dinna frown so. We are well matched. Ye ken that as well as I do."

When he kissed her, she clung to him, fully returning the kiss. Although he had eased her concerns about honor and duty nudging him to the altar, he had given her a new one with his talk of pride. She grasped tightly at the passion his kiss stirred, needing it to wash all thought from her mind and replace the cold fear in her heart with the warmth of desire.

She eagerly matched his every kiss and caress. So

desperate was she to completely lose herself in the pleasures of the flesh, she grew more bold and more aggressive than she had ever been before. Revan's enthusiastic response to her tactics inspired her to go even further.

Tess nudged him onto his back and straddled him. After giving him a deep, fierce kiss, she began to kiss her way down his long, taut body, moistening and heating his skin with her lips and her tongue. She even used her own body to caress his, never missing a chance to rub against him. As she drew faint designs upon his stomach with her tongue, she curled her fingers around his erection and very slowly stroked him. The way he shifted beneath her and his hoarse murmurs of pleasure added to her own hunger.

While continuing the intimate play with her hand, she knelt between his strong legs. Revan whispered her name and looked at her. She smiled faintly and, holding his gaze, replaced the gentle caress of her hand with the warmer one of her tongue and her lips. He groaned, his hands tightening their grip in her hair, and, although his eyes grew increasingly heavy-lidded, he watched her. Tess boldly kept her gaze upon his face as she continued her intimate caress. It heightened her own desire to see how much she was pleasing him. She loved him slowly, retreating a little now and again when his control appeared close to breaking.

Finally he grasped her by the arms and tugged her up his body. Tess straddled him and eased their bodies together, trembling with pleasure as she felt him fill her. For a little while longer she held the reins, moving slowly and with care, to keep them on the edge of satisfaction for as long as she could. Then Revan suddenly took control. She gave a soft cry of surprise when he sat up, his strong arms around her so that she could not falter. The moment he leaned her away from his body and took the hard tip of her breast into his mouth, she lost what little restraint she had clung to.

Revan kept them lurking on the edge of release for a little while longer. He feasted upon her breasts as he gently moved her upon him. When her movements grew more frantic as her release shuddered through her, he let her draw him along. He held her tightly against him and kissed her, swallowing her cry and feeding her his, as the culmination of their hunger swept over them.

It was several moments before Revan felt inclined to separate their bodies. As soon as they had washed up and slid beneath the covers again, he pulled her back into his arms. He smiled faintly as she yawned and curled her body around his. Idly stroking her hair, he crooked one arm beneath his head and stared up at the ceiling.

"That, lass, was as far from cold and weighty honor and duty as anyone can get," he murmured.

"Aye, true enough. I suppose I must concede that ye were correct."

He chuckled. "Painful, is it?"

"Ye are far too arrogant now. It needs no boosting."

"Silvio apologized for being unable to bob that sharp tongue of yours ere he sees us married."

"Did he. Well, I shall see he pays for that insult." She smiled faintly when Revan laughed.

"Best ye get some sleep, then. 'Twill not be easy to bandy words with Silvio. Ye will need all your wits about you."

"Aye. Where do ye think I honed my sharp tongue?" She laughed softly along with Revan. "But, ye are right. Sleep is what I need. Even if I dinna squabble with Uncle Silvio, the Douglases and Thurkettle are still about."

"We shall be the victors in that fight, Tessa. Dinna worry on that."

She nodded and closed her eyes. The Douglases, Thurkettle, and all their treasonous plans did not really worry her that much any longer. Now that she and Revan were with her kinsmen, she felt safe, as safe as anyone could with a battle for the throne looming before her. All that concerned her about the battle between the Douglas and King James was that the king won and none of her loved ones were maimed or killed. That worry was one that would not really trouble her until the battle itself was at hand.

Revan concerned her now, he and their forthcoming marriage. Now that passion no longer held her fears at bay, they all rushed back into her heart. He had softened the threat of duty and honor, even given her the hope that he did feel more than passion for her when he spoke of their being well matched. Then he had ruined it all by talking of his pride, of how it would be sorely bruised by wedding an heiress.

Inwardly she cursed. Although she did not really feel that she had lied, she knew she had not told Revan the whole truth. She had spoken of a few thousand riders and made her land holdings sound somewhat meager. Tess dreaded to think of how he would react when he found out that a "few" was thirty thousand or more and that her land holdings were not only somewhat large but profitable. It was past time to tell him the whole truth, but she lacked the courage. It was going to be even worse if she gained all that Thurkettle now held. Most often a traitor's holdings were forfeited to the crown, but she knew, because of her role in bringing information against those traitors, that she could well inherit it all. If Revan thought his pride bruised now, when her full wealth was disclosed, he would surely feel it had been mortally wounded.

And she would be the cause of that shattered pride, she thought and cuddled closer to Revan. Considering how he felt about wedding an heiress when he was virtually penniless and landless, the truth of her riches would leave him with no pride at all. She shivered. That would be the death knell for any happiness they might find together. He would grow to hate her, the loss of his pride slowly eating away at any feeling he might have for her.

She felt like weeping but forced back the tears. It would solve nothing, and he would notice, then press for an explanation. She had about a month to find some solution, some way of salvaging a scrap of Revan's pride. If none presented itself, she knew what she would have to do—she would have to let him go, free him of the bonds of duty and honor. It would hurt, but she knew the pain would be greater if she had to see him stripped of his pride and watch that loss destroy them both.

Chapter

✦ 17 ✦

TESS YAWNED, THEN QUICKLY GLANCED AROUND
her to be sure no one had seen her. She hurried down the
stairs and into the great hall, embarrassed that, for the third
time in three days, she had slept through to the midday
meal. What troubled her a little was that she could go back
to bed and easily sleep for a few more hours. That had never
been her way, but she supposed the arduous travel with
Revan could have depleted her strength more than she had
supposed.

It also annoyed her to miss so much of the day. That
meant missing time she could spend with Revan. Although
the marriage was still being planned, she had not yet come
up with any way to salvage Revan's pride. Unless she did,
she would not allow the marriage to take place, and that
meant her time with Revan was limited. It was foolish to
waste it lying in bed like some pampered queen.

Entering the great hall, she admitted to herself that she
had another reason to want to be with Revan as much as
possible. She was dressed as a lady again, and she wanted to
impress that image upon his mind. If they were doomed to
part, she did not really want his strongest memories of her
to be those where she was dressed in the old, ill-fitting boy's
clothes.

"Ah, she lives." Silvio grinned as his niece blushed and hurried to her seat at the table next to Revan while the others in the hall chuckled. "I was about to send your man off to see if ye were still breathing."

As she helped herself to the wide array of food set out, Tess frowned at her teasing kinsmen. "Ye shouldna let me be so lazy. 'Tis a scandal."

"Ye have been hard-pressed since this rogue yanked you out of Thurkettle's grasp. Ye need rest. I but tease you, lass."

"I ken it. But, I believe I have 'rested' quite enough. I must not be left to lay about on the morrow. It becomes a habit too easily, I think." She smiled faintly when her uncle, Tomas, and Revan laughed.

"We sent out the third messenger this morning," Silvio reported.

"Three?" Tess was a little surprised at how full her plate was but started to eat, a little dismayed at how sure she was she could finish the hearty meal and a little more besides.

"Aye, Tess. Three. We want to be sure the king gets the information Revan and ye uncovered on his behalf."

"Why not send Revan?" Although she did not want Revan to leave, it was a reasonable question.

"Nay, we need the lad here. Besides, all of the Douglas's men, and Thurkettle's, ken his face and search for him."

A glance toward Revan revealed him smiling faintly. Revan did not believe Silvio told the whole truth, either. The reasons Silvio gave were sound ones, but she knew there was at least one other. Silvio wanted to keep Revan within reach until the wedding vows were exchanged. In a way Revan was a prisoner. Tess did not like it but made no complaint. There was little she could do to change it. Arguing with her uncle Silvio would certainly not help much.

"Any sign of their men? Do they still lurk in the area?" she asked.

"I fear so, although there arena so many. When my men

have the time, they set after the rogues. They consider it fine sport. We have culled a few men from the Douglas's traitorous army.'' He frowned as an uproar was heard from beyond the doors of the great hall. ''It canna be an attack,'' he murmured. ''No alarm was sounded.''

A moment later the heavy doors to the great hall were flung open. Two of Silvio's men entered dragging a man between them. He struggled in their hold, loudly cursing them. The rumpled state of his clothes and the trickle of blood from his mouth revealed that he had put up a fight from the start. Tess mused that Silvio's men had probably tried to shut the man's mouth as well and reached for another thick slab of bread. Suddenly she froze as the man looked their way. It was the man on the black stallion with the white stockings. Her uncle's men had captured Angus MacKinnon, the traitor. She shivered when the man's cold gaze rested on her for a moment before fixing on Silvio.

''Ah, lads, here is a fine catch,'' her uncle said.

''I demand to ken the meaning of this outrage, Delgado,'' the man said, uselessly trying to tidy his clothes as Silvio's men loosened their grip on him.

''Actually, the name is Comyn.''

The man gave a soft scornful laugh. ''Your family changes names as others do their shirts. Why have I been dragged here?''

''For the blackest of crimes, MacKinnon. We will take you to the king to answer for it.''

''Crimes? What crimes are ye babbling about? I was on my way to the king when these curs grabbed me. If we speak on crimes, ye had best consider the one ye commit—halting a king's man in his mission. I was taking an important message to the king.''

''Aye, a dagger in his heart. A message from the traitor Douglas.''

''Ye are mad, Delgado.''

Tess had to admire the man, if only slightly and fleetingly. His poise was awe-inspiring. There was no question of his guilt, yet he barely faltered when told that his crimes were now known. Only the faintest loss of color gave away the fear he had to be feeling, and one had to look very closely to see even that.

"Nay, but I think ye may be, MacKinnon. What could ye hope to gain with such a black betrayal? How can ye turn against the king, a man who has given you nearly all ye can lay claim to? Is this how ye repay our liege? With treason?"

"Ye have no cause to spit on my honor like this, Delgado."

"Honor? Ye have no honor, traitor. As for proof, for cause, may I present my niece—Contessa Comyn Delgado." Silvio smiled coldly when MacKinnon's eyes widened slightly, revealing his shock. "And her betrothed—Sir Revan Halyard."

"Ye call me traitor and treat me like some outlaw yet house these two as guests? Have ye heard nothing of the crimes they are charged with? Halyard is a kidnapper and a rapist. Your niece, Delgado, is suspected of aiding the man in betraying the king. Aye, and she is already betrothed—to a nephew of the Douglas who plots to steal the throne."

"I am betrothed?" Tess could barely speak above a whisper she was so shocked. "I canna be."

MacKinnon gave her a cool glance. "Aye, to one of the Douglas's nephews. 'Twas announced."

"Not to me."

"Dinna fret, Contessa," Silvio said. "'Tis but a ploy they use to try to strengthen their cause. If nothing else they tried to accuse ye with was accepted, the fact that Revan took a man's betrothed probably would be."

"And it would allow them to do just what they have been trying to do—kill him, or us." Tess was relieved to see that Revan was nodding in agreement. "My saying I wasna betrothed to this Douglas cur would carry no weight."

"None at all, darling."

"Ye can visit with the wench later, Delgado," drawled

MacKinnon, his tone arrogant and sneering. "I am a busy man."

"Ye will have a long rest soon, MacKinnon, though reaching your final rest may well be a very painful journey. The death of a traitor isna a pretty one."

"I am no traitor, Delgado. Ye toss about empty charges. I will see that ye pay dearly for the insult."

"The charges arena empty. Ye were seen, fool. Your conspiring with the Douglas traitors was witnessed."

"What are you saying?"

"Remember riding with your treasonous companions one afternoon and chasing down a couple caught watching you?" Silvio nodded when the man grew visibly pale. "The chase was ended. Ye thought them but peasants who wouldna ken the value of what they had seen. Well, ye erred badly, MacKinnon, and we thank ye for it. Here sit those witnesses." Silvio indicated Revan and Tess with an idle wave of his hand. "My niece recognized you, remembered seeing you at Tomas's wedding. She got a very good look at you, as did Sir Halyard."

"Her word willna hold firm against mine."

"Hers and Sir Halyard's. Once she pointed you out, he took a closer look. They can both swear to having seen ye riding with the traitorous Douglas's men, riding toward the Douglas lands. Now ye return to the king. James will be very eager to hear why. 'Tis a shame the two she saw riding with you werena caught as well."

"They were caught, sir," said one of the men guarding MacKinnon. "Well, one of them was. The other was killed. The one we hold is wounded. Old Alice cares for him and says he will live."

"Live to talk, eh, MacKinnon? I think ye will soon regret that ye didna stand more firmly against my men, thus forcing them to kill you. Death at their hands would have been a great deal more merciful than what ye face now."

The man cursed, then jerked free of his guards. Tess expected him to race for the doors despite the guards standing there. She gave a soft cry of surprise when he started toward her instead. Revan scrambled to his feet, putting himself between her and MacKinnon, but the guards grabbed the man before he could reach them. There was a brief, fierce struggle before they got a firm grip on the man. When MacKinnon was on his feet again, he glared at Tess. Although she knew it was somewhat cowardly, she tried to avoid that murderous look by hiding behind Revan.

"Ye will regret this, Delgado," MacKinnon told Silvio, only briefly diverting his glare from Tess.

"Regret serving my liege lord—King James? I think not. Secure him, men. I mean to deliver this traitor to our king—alive."

"Ye will all pay for this!" MacKinnon yelled as he was dragged away. "Especially you," he spat at Tess. "Fergus was a fool. He should have killed you years ago. I willna be so careless. Ye are a dead woman, bitch. A dead woman!" he screamed just as he was yanked out of the hall and the doors were slammed shut behind him.

Revan sat down, his gaze fixed upon Tess. She looked pale, and her hands shook faintly as she picked up her goblet of wine. He reached out and took one of her hands in his. Since she had just spent over a fortnight running from people who wanted to kill her, he was not sure what it was about MacKinnon's threats that bothered her so.

"'Twas just words, Tessa," he said. "Just words. The man hurls empty threats. He just wants to scare you."

"Aye. I ken it." She took a slow, deep drink of wine to steady herself. "He wants someone to share the fear that is eating away at him now. And by now I should be quite accustomed to people wishing to kill me. At times it seemed as if half of Scotland were trying to put me in the ground." She gave Revan and Silvio a weak smile, then sighed.

"I sometimes thought the same." He kissed her hand. "Ye didna quail then, lass."

"'Twas dark in that cave. Ye couldna see me that well, 'tis all."

"Tessa." He knew she was being evasive and was determined not to allow it. "Why were this fool's threats different?"

"'Tis foolish, but I suppose 'tis because he spoke them aloud. No one really has before. This also seems more personal. He doesna want me dead so that he can have my money or to save himself. He is already doomed. Nay. He wants *me* dead. There was such hate behind his words," she whispered. "Such fury aimed at me. Most everyone else after us has done only what they had been ordered to do. This man *wants* to see me dead. 'Twill take some getting used to."

"Ye willna have to get used to it, dearling," Silvio said. "The man is well secured now. His next journey will be to the gallows."

"I ken it, Uncle Silvio. I will shake the chill he has left me with. It but takes a bit of time, is all."

Revan and Silvio nodded and returned to discussing the battle they felt was certain to come. Tess was glad that she had soothed their concern. She wished she could soothe hers so easily. After all she had been through, she knew it was foolish to be so frightened by one person threatening to kill her, yet she could not shake that fear. Although she could not really explain it, even to herself, there was something different about MacKinnon's threat. Inwardly she shook her head. It was undoubtedly just his looks, that hawkish, predatory face, and the emotion he had embued his words with. She would put the man and his threats from her mind. He was locked up now, and no one from Donnbraigh would help him.

TESS paused in brushing her hair to look at Revan as he entered their bedchamber and walked by the bed she sat on. She was beginning to think that getting up earlier in the day would not buy her much more time with Revan. Immediately after the noon meal, he had left with the other men and had not returned until it was time to eat again. Even her uncle had hobbled off. She had spent the rest of the day helping what few women remained at Donnbraigh do their chores.

"The mighty huntsman has returned to his lair for the night, has he?" She faintly regretted her sarcasm. She was not really angry with him, but he was at hand.

Revan cast her a wary glance before undressing to his braies. "Looking for an argument, are we?"

"Mayhaps." She grimaced and set her hairbrush on the table by the bed. "'Twould be more interesting than hearing about Janie's bairn and how he is teething now or Maura's aching bones or the weather."

"Spent the day with the women, eh? It canna be so strange. Ye must have done that back at Thurkettle's keep."

"I didna do it much. I helped with the chores, did my part and all. Spending much time with the women often meant meeting up with your beloved, Brenda." She tensed, as the mention of Brenda brought on a sudden, clear memory that left her stunned.

Finished with his washing up, Revan rubbed himself dry as he turned to face Tess. The somewhat cross reply he was prepared to make to her reference to Brenda stuck in his throat. Tess looked strange, as if someone had struck her, but she had forgotten to fall down. He hurried over to the bed, grasped her by the arm, and lightly shook her.

"Tessa, are ye ill? Tessa?"

"I just realized how I could recognize MacKinnon's horse." She turned her head and stared at Revan, who frowned and slowly sat down beside her.

"Ye recognized MacKinnon," he said, his voice revealing the confusion he felt.

"Aye, but 'twas his horse that first caught my eye. I thought that was just because it was a fine stallion but then got distracted by the man himself, by the certainty that I had seen him. But now I realize I had also seen that horse before, that it was the horse that had first stirred a memory."

"Ye probably saw it at the same place—your cousin's wedding."

"Nay, I didna see the people come and go, didna pay any heed to that at all."

"So how did ye recognize his horse? Where else would ye have seen it?"

"At Thurkettle's keep."

"MacKinnon met with Thurkettle?"

"Well, he might have, but I never saw him. I just saw the horse. And 'twas *that* horse. I am certain of it. Several times I saw it tethered outside of Brenda's cottage."

"*Brenda* has a cottage? Why would she need one?"

"To tryst with her lovers, of course. Surely ye must have gone there a time or two." She studied him, wondering why he wore such a cross expression.

"Nay, I never went to her trysting cottage," he growled, irritated at this further proof of how thoroughly Brenda had fooled him.

"How odd, since she eventually takes all her lovers there."

"Then it isna odd at all, is it? For I was never the wench's lover."

Tess stared at him. He looked both annoyed and insulted. She tried very hard not to laugh, but several things conspired against her. It was a joyful relief to know for sure, at last, that he and Brenda had never been lovers. Revan also looked very much like a sulky child who had discovered that, even though the sweets had been given out freely and often, he had come up empty-handed. She clamped a hand over her mouth, but it failed to completely smother her giggles. When Revan scowled at her, she started to laugh even more.

"Ye find that amusing, do ye?" Revan was not quite sure what Tess found to laugh about and if he should be insulted by it or not.

"Aye. Pardon." She struggled somewhat vainly to stop laughing. "She had you thoroughly fooled. It fair stings your vanity, doesna it?'' Tess started to giggle again. '' 'Tis clear she guessed your game from the start.''

"Aye, 'twould appear that she did.'' He eyed her curiously. "Why do ye find this so amusing now? Ye learned it long ago.''

"Well, I did guess that she had fooled you, played a game with you. I just hadna realized how completely she had deceived you. Sweet Mary, Brenda spent more time out of her clothes than in them, yet ye thought her innocent?''

"Not innocent exactly, but''—he frowned—"surely ye saw that before now. Ye kenned we werena lovers.''

"I wasna sure.''

"I *told* ye we werena.''

"Ye didna state it quite so firmly then. Mostly ye just denied drooling over her or pining after her or—''

"Enough. Of course I denied all that. I didna drool, pine, sniff, or whisper poetry.''

"Well, 'tis no wonder ye didna get an invite to her trysting cottage.''

She laughed as he gave a growl of false anger and wrestled her down onto the bed. Once he got her pinned beneath him, he kissed her. Although their passion was there, easily stirred to life, Revan's kiss was one of affection, not demand. Tess found it painfully sweet. It was the forerunner of the love she sought, of the love she needed. It was the hint of what she was beginning to believe she could never have. She would have to set it aside or watch it wither beneath the chilling effects of his ravished pride. Pushing aside those mournful thoughts, she smiled at him when he ended the kiss.

"Poor Sir Revan,'' she teased. "He worked so hard and gained naught.''

"I wouldna say *naught*. 'Tis true that my vanity is sorely pinched to think she gave out her favors so freely yet not to me. But, I believe I hold the best the Thurkettle family had to offer a man.'' He grinned down at her when she blushed, then grew serious. "I am also very glad I didna share her bed so soon before I was destined to share yours."

"Destined, were ye?" She smoothed her hands up and down his arms.

"Aye, 'twas fate." He brushed the few strands of hair from her face with his hand.

"Fate could have given us less trouble to deal with whilst she interfered with our lives."

"It will soon be over. I am pleased to see that ye have shed your fears over MacKinnon's hot words."

"More or less. The threats still haunt me some, but I keep reminding myself that he is now a prisoner. Donnbraigh has some very secure dungeons and no traitors to help him. Soon I will forget about the man completely."

"Good." He brushed his lips over hers. "And I believe I have a way to help you do that more quickly."

Tess smiled as she wrapped her limbs around his lean frame. "Do ye, now. Best get started, then. I believe I feel a twinge of fear coming over me."

She laughed along with Revan, then accepted and returned his kiss. For a while his lovemaking would make her forget her lingering fear of MacKinnon, and she intended to take full advantage of that. However, she knew she would not be completely free of the man and the chill of his threats until he was gone. Although she hated to wish the horrible death meted out to traitors upon any man, she knew it was the only thing that would put an end to her fear.

"Ye can seek your bed now, Jamie." The new guard in the dungeons sat down in the chair the old guard had just left.

"I am right pleased about that, Dermott, m'lad." Jamie scratched his chest as he scowled at MacKinnon. "Silvio badly wants this cur to be sure to meet his fate. We dinna usually have to watch a prisoner so closely."

"Mayhaps Silvio fears someone would aid him."

"A traitor in Donnbraigh?" Jamie laughed and shook his

head. "Nay, not here," he said as he started up the narrow stone steps leading out of the dungeons.

"Fool," Dermott muttered as soon as the man was gone, then leaned forward in his chair to look more intently at MacKinnon. "Ye have gotten yourself into a fine muddle."

"This is an insult and an outrage. Delgado will pay dearly for it."

"I would give up that game, my friend. Ye showed your true colors when ye threatened the man's niece."

"'Twas but a moment of unthinking passion, of rage. It meant nothing and proves less."

"Ah, ye are clever with words, but I doubt 'tis skill enough to save your neck. I fear that must be left to me. 'Tisna the reason the Douglas set me here, but I ken it will serve. My job is nearly at an end anyways."

MacKinnon slowly stood up, staring at the guard in surprise. "Ye are a Douglas man?" he asked as he walked to the bars.

"Aye, though I begin to question the wisdom of my choice. But I made it and I will stay with it. That means setting you free. Once I do, I have ended my usefulness here. They will ken who let ye go, so I must go with you." He stood up and took the keys from the nail on the wall. "We will hie for the Douglas's keep. By the time they realize ye are gone, we should be a safe distance away."

"I willna leave here without that cursed wench." MacKinnon stepped back from the bars.

"Are ye mad? I canna get her now. She doesna sleep alone, for one thing. That Sir Revan is tucked up with her."

"Then we will wait until we *can* get her and take her with us."

"Ye dinna have much time left, my friend. Old Silvio plans to ride and join the king in a fortnight's time. If ye are still here, ye ride with him, straight to death at the king's hand. Aye, and it willna be a gentle death ye face."

"I ken it. I dinna mean to stay here until I am dragged off like a sheep to slaughter. But I would like to take that wench with me. Ye said we have a fortnight. There is some time left to us. Mayhaps I can yet have both my freedom and my vengeance on that wench for betraying me. There has to be some time when she is alone.''

''Aye, a time or two, but we could wait until Michaelmas before it coincides with my guarding you.''

''Then ye will have to take care of the guard who is here.''

''Ye are a bit too eager to put my life in danger. Your neck might be on the chopping block already, but I dinna mean to have mine there, too, just to satisfy your need for revenge.''

''Then maybe ye will be more willing to take a risk to collect the reward offered for the wench.''

''There was talk of a reward, a bounty price,'' Dermott murmured. ''I thought it but rumor.''

''Nay, not rumor. How long have ye been here? Ye werena sent here to try to stop her and Halyard?''

Dermott shook his head. ''I eased my way in here months ago because old Silvio and most of his kinsmen are close to the king and his court. They hear a lot, ken a lot. The Douglas wanted that information.''

''He wants the girl and Halyard, too.''

''There is no way to get our hands on Halyard, not secretly, not without rousing Donnbraigh. He is never alone.'' He rubbed his chin with his hand. ''But we could take a few days to see if we could get the lass.''

''A week.''

''A week, then, but then we leave. We will take the girl to Thurkettle.''

''The Douglas is closer.''

''Not by many miles. I want Thurkettle to have her. He will be far less swift and tidy in the killing of her. And he will pay a richer bounty, for he gains more by her death. Thurkettle gains her silence *and* her fortune.''

''She will be taken to Thurkettle, then. One week,'' Dermott said as he put the keys back on their hook. '' 'Tis all I will allow, all I can allow. Then ye must leave Donnbraigh—or die.'' He sat down and smiled faintly. ''The Douglas doesna want ye speaking to the king any more than he wants Halyard or the Delgado wench to talk. When the week is up, I will leave it to you to decide which ye find the sweeter—life or revenge.''

''I intend to have both.''

Chapter

◇ 18 ◇

"SIR REVAN THOUGHT YE MIGHT ENJOY A ride," Dermott said.

Tess frowned. "Aye, I would, but why didna he come for me himself?"

"He needed to finish his hunting, mistress, but he will meet us at a spot he himself has chosen."

She stood up and brushed herself off, looking down at the small herb garden she had been weeding. It was just one of the many chores she had busied herself with in the last week. Although she felt a little guilty, she knew she would not mind leaving the tedious work to spend some time with Revan. It puzzled her that she was still somewhat hesitant.

A small frown curved her lips as she covertly glanced at Dermott. She did not know the man. He was new at Donnbraigh. For reasons she could not name, he made her uneasy. The fact that everyone else at Donnbraigh appeared to accept the man did not help cure her of her wariness.

The sudden invitation from Revan also bothered her. He had insisted, as strongly as Silvio had, that she remain safely within the high walls of Donnbraigh. Then she recalled something Revan had said only the night before. He had claimed that all of the Douglas's and Thurkettle's men had been slain or chased off of Donnbraigh lands. She had thought it just something to soothe her lingering fears. This invitation indicated that it had been the truth. Tess felt relieved and a little lighthearted. She smiled at Dermott.

"Just give me a moment or two to wash this dirt off." She started toward the keep but paused to look back at Dermott. "'Tis just ye and I who shall ride out to meet Revan?"

"Nay. The curs sniffing around Donnbraigh may have been run to ground, but 'tis still not safe for ye to go beyond these walls so lightly guarded. Another man waits with the horses."

She nodded and hurried toward the keep. A small part of her still pressed for caution, but she forced it aside. To spend some time with Revan was a temptation too strong to resist, and she was sure he would not have sent for her unless he felt it was safe.

"WHERE is she?" MacKinnon hissed when Dermott walked over to where he stood with three saddled horses.

"She needed to tidy herself. She will be along in a few moments." Dermott glanced around to be sure that no one was near enough to overhear anything he and MacKinnon said.

"A few moments? Curse ye for a witless fool. She is a woman. They canna *tidy* themselves in but a moment or two. We shall be standing here for hours."

"Nay, for if she doesna appear soon, I shall go and fetch her. I can tell her that her man will worry if she isna there soon or some such thing as that. She willna be long. She isna one to spend long hours on her gown or her hair. Dinna be so fretful. 'Twill draw attention to us, and this isna the cleverest ploy ever devised."

"Did someone doubt it?"

"Nay, for they are all feeling secure now. This would be a very costly place to attack, and most of our compatriots are now gone—dead or returned to the Douglas or Thurkettle.''

''I hadna considered that. We will have no allies in our flight.''

''Our greatest ally will be time. We will be hours ahead of them if all goes well. Then there is the lass herself. They will tread warily in their pursuit, for they will fear for her. I hope your friend Thurkettle can harbor us as safely as I ken the Douglas would. There is where I foresee the greatest risk.''

''There is little, but if ye worry on it, ye can take your reward and leave. No one will stop you.''

''Except, mayhaps, the ones who will be after the lass,'' Dermott murmured. ''Here she comes. Mount and say nothing.''

Tess frowned as she walked up to Dermott, and he immediately helped her mount her mare. Try as she would, she could not fully conquer her sense of uneasiness. The other man, his helmet hiding his features, said nothing nor did he glance at her. That seemed a little odd to her, but she shrugged and turned to Dermott, who had just finished mounting.

''Must we ride very far?'' she asked him as they started out of Donnbraigh.

''Nay, ye willna be riding far.''

A tingle of wariness slipped down Tess's spine, but she fought to ignore it. She began to think that she was becoming a foolish woman frightened of empty shadows. Such unsubstantiated fear was not something she wanted to suffer from. She forced herself to concentrate only on the beautiful late spring day and how nice it was going to be to share it with Revan.

They rode in silence, which she did not really mind but did find a little strange, for the men of Donnbraigh tended to be a garrulous lot. Donnbraigh faded from sight soon after they entered the forest. Tess began to wonder just where Revan had chosen for them to meet. She turned to ask

Dermott where they were headed and gasped as he suddenly rode up close beside her and yanked the reins from her hands. He brought them all to an abrupt halt.

Tess cursed herself for a fool. She should never have ignored her own inner alarms. Before she could act to save herself, however, the other man had a tight hold on her wrists and was looping a rope securely around them. There were traitors within Donnbraigh. Tess found that almost impossible to believe despite being a captive.

"Why are ye doing this?" she demanded.

"For revenge," said the guard, who had remained silent until now.

When the man took off his helmet, Tess felt momentarily light-headed. The familiarity of that cold voice had warned her, but she was still stunned to see MacKinnon at her side. Fear caused a bitter taste in her mouth. This man wanted her dead, and she could foresee no immediate hope of rescue. It would be hours before the people of Donnbraigh realized the danger she was in. She opened her mouth to scream in the weak hope that someone was near enough to hear her, thus come to her aid, but Dermott was quick to gag her. She glared at both men in a fury born of her helplessness and fear.

"We intend to take you to Thurkettle," MacKinnon continued. "Dermott will gather the bounty offered for you, and I shall have the pleasure of watching you die. The Douglas is closer, though not by very much, but I believe Thurkettle will more satisfactorily appease my hunger for revenge. He is a man inspired to cruelty and excess when he is angered."

A cold shiver rippled through Tess. The man was correct in his judgment of her uncle Fergus. Thurkettle was well known and rightfully feared for his vicious furies. She had thwarted the man too often to believe that he would feel any kindness toward her or exhibit any mercy. Kinship meant little to him. By managing to stay alive and keep her fortune out of his hands, she had earned Thurkettle's enmity, and that could well mean a very painful death.

"MacKinnon," snapped Dermott. "Enough of this talk. Ye can play your foolish games with the lass another time. We had best be on our way."

"There is time. Hours yet."

"Hours we will need to outdistance Delgado and the lass's lover. And ye canna be sure that we will have hours. The guard could be found or Delgado and Halyard could return to Donnbraigh earlier than expected. Come on."

Tess was roughly jerked in the saddle when Dermott, still holding her reins, spurred his gelding onward. She grabbed the saddle horn to keep from falling. Only briefly did she consider tumbling from her saddle. It was no means of escape. She would probably injure herself and her captors would simply halt and put her back in the saddle, securing her more firmly and, undoubtedly, more painfully. She would have to wait and pray for some other, better, opportunity.

As they rode, she glanced, once, back at Donnbraigh. If the guard Dermott had subdued had only just taken up his post, then it could be hours before MacKinnon's escape was discovered. It would be at least as long before her uncle Silvio and Revan rode back into Donnbraigh. Her captors could easily put enough distance between her and Donnbraigh to make rescue extremely difficult if not impossible. She could not simply wait to be saved.

The problem of rescuing herself was not going to be an easy one to solve. She was bound and gagged, there were two men who would be keeping a very close watch on her, she had no weapons, and she had an appallingly poor sense of direction. As they made their swift, precarious way through the thickening forest, Tess tried not to give into hopelessness.

REVAN frowned, his good humor fading as he entered the bailey of Donnbraigh with the Comyns. Tess was always right there to meet him, yet today she was nowhere to be seen. Then he noticed the agitation of the people who were waiting in the bailey. He felt the pinch of alarm as he nudged his mount closer to Silvio's, hoping to overhear what his men hurried over to report.

"MacKinnon has fled," reported Silvio's sergeant-at-arms, Calum. "Dermott helped him. He must be a Douglas man. The traitorous cur has been slinking about here for months. I dare not consider all he might have learned."

"How could MacKinnon have escaped?" Silvio demanded as, with Tomas's help, he dismounted.

"Dermott let him out. He killed poor Seumus, who was on guard. We didna discover it until 'twas time to change the guard. Young Norman went down. He didna see Seumus but thought that MacKinnon was still secure, for there was a body on the cot. It took Norman a few moments to grow suspicious and go into the cell. 'Twas poor Seumus on the cot, his throat slit and the blanket pulled about him to hide his features."

"That tells me how MacKinnon got out of his cell, but how did the bastard escape from Donnbraigh itself?"

"By a very clever ruse. Dermott told us that Sir Halyard had sent him to fetch the lass, that Sir Halyard wished a wee tryst with her. Since the Douglas men in the area are now all dead or gone, we didna question it."

"Ye let them leave with Tessa?" Revan cried as he dismounted and grabbed Calum by the arm.

"We had no reason not to," protested Calum. "Dermott has been here, one of us, for months. There were a few doubters, but 'twas mostly ye yourself whom they wondered on." Calum gave Revan an apologetic look. "They thought your request a wee bit strange and suspicious. We dinna ken who ye are. We *thought* we kenned Dermott and could trust him."

"When was all this discovered?" Silvio asked.

"But a few moments ago," Calum replied. "We were just about to send someone out to find you and another to try and pick up their trail, if he could. I fear they have been gone for four hours, mayhaps a wee bit longer.''

"Sweet Mary, there are miles ahead of us already.'' Revan stared at the open gates, fear for Tess making it difficult for him to think of any plan. "Even if we rode at full gallop, we could never hope to catch them before they reached the Douglas.'' He suddenly recalled the threats MacKinnon had made as he had been dragged from the great hall of Donnbraigh. "If she isna killed before then. MacKinnon wants her dead.''

"Aye,'' agreed Silvio. "He can have that done without bloodying his own hands if he has taken her to the Douglas. He can also collect the bounty offered for her. I believe he will keep her alive and hand her over to that traitor.''

"And once she is in that man's hands, we have no hope of getting her back.''

"Probably not, but I am a stubborn man. I dinna mean to give up. Calum, we need fresh mounts and some supplies,'' he ordered, then turned to another man. "Martin, ye get out there and find us their trail.''

Revan, calmed a little by the action being taken, looked up at the dusk-clouded sky. "We have but an hour, mayhaps a wee bit longer, ere nightfall hinders us.''

"All we need to ken is *where* they are going. Once we are sure of that, darkness will slow us down, but it need not stop us. Also, there will be a nearly full moon tonight. 'Twill help.''

"'Twill help them as well,'' murmured Revan.

"I ken it, but mayhaps luck will be with us and 'twill slow them more than it does us or, better, stop them.''

It was on the tip of Revan's tongue to say that luck had not followed him and Tess too closely since they had fled from Thurkettle, but he bit back the words. He was sure that Silvio knew that and that the man knew how heavily the odds were weighted against them. The man would not appreciate being reminded of that fact. Revan wished he could borrow some of Silvio's stubborn optimism. He was chilled by fear and concerned that it would hold him back or steal his wits just when he needed them the most.

Only a few moments passed before they had fresh horses, some supplies, and weapons and were riding out of Donn-braigh. Revan wondered how well he would hold himself in check if such a small passage of time could feel like an eternity. He needed to regain his stern discipline, the alert calm he had always valued as a knight. The thought of what was happening to Tess or what might happen to her was making that control difficult to grasp. He struggled to set his mind on one thing and one thing only—the job of finding Tess.

"Is this fellow—Martin—good at finding a trail?" he asked Silvio as he edged his horse up next to the man's.

"Aye. Very good. We sometimes jest that we should be rid of our hounds and just keep Martin. He doesna eat as much, and we dinna have to clean up after him as often." Silvio's smile was a little weak.

"Do ye think they would have even left a trail?"

"The chance of it is good. Aye, better than good. Their greatest concern will have been to put as many miles between us and them as is possible. They wouldna use that precious time to be careful or to pause to try and hide their trail. They would also ken that we would guess where they were hieing to anyway."

"Then why do we waste time even hunting for a trail? Why not just set out after them?"

Silvio shrugged. "There are a few different ways they could go. The Douglas has several keeps. I fear I am not very sure which one he might be in. Also, there is ever the slim chance that they arena headed where we think they are. I just feel that 'tis to our benefit to learn as much as we can ere we charge off across the countryside."

Revan nodded, agreeing with Silvio yet hating to lose any time. "I pray a trail is all we will find."

"'Tis my prayer as well, Revan. I believe, truly believe, that she is still alive. MacKinnon has betrayed the king for gain, turned his back on a man who has done him naught but good because someone offered him more—more land, more coin. Who can say? That hints at a deep greed. He will want that bounty. If not him, then Dermott will.'' He turned to Tomas, who rode on the other side of him. ''Call for Martin. He needs to let us ken where he is.''

When Tomas lifted a hunting horn to his lips and blew on it twice, Revan inwardly shook his head. Tess's kinsmen had a rather odd sense of humor. Then he tensed as the faint reply of another hunting horn broke the expectant silence.

''Does that mean he has found something?'' he asked Silvio.

''Quite possibly. When Martin goes searching for a trail he is often deaf and blind to all else until he has found it. The fact that he has answered our call is nearly a confirmation of a find. Ah, and there is another call. He marks his place for us. Let us not leave him waiting for too long.''

Silvio spurred his mount into a gallop, and Revan quickly did the same. He paid little heed to the dozen or so other men riding with them except to note that they followed. His sole interest was in finding out which way MacKinnon had taken Tess and getting after the pair.

Martin stood at the spot where the forest began to grow more densely and calmly waited as Revan, Silvio, and Tomas reined in, then dismounted and joined him. ''Three riders went this way,'' he reported to Silvio.

''This veers farther to the east than I would have guessed it to go,'' murmured Silvio as he studied the trail Martin pointed out to him. ''Have ye followed it past this point?''

''Aye and it continues in this direction. I was on my way back to tell you.'' He ran a hand through his thick black hair and scowled at the tracks he had uncovered. ''They go far out of their way. 'Twill add many miles to their flight to the Douglas.''

''But none at all to a journey toward Thurkettle's keep,'' said Revan.

''I was just thinking the same,'' muttered Silvio.

"But why?" asked Tomas. "The Douglas is closer by several miles, and he is also offering a bounty for Tess."

"Thurkettle may be offering a bigger one. Tess's death can gain him two things—her silence and her fortune." Silvio grimaced. "MacKinnon has chosen Thurkettle to be Tess's executioner. I believe I ken the why of that choice."

"Because Thurkettle willna kill her quickly or cleanly," Revan said, fear tightening its grip on his heart.

"Aye, I fear so. Thurkettle has the reputation of being vicious when he is angry, and he must be very angry at our wee countess by now. His cruelty when enraged was one reason I hesitated to send her to live with him."

"Yet ye did send her." Revan's fear turned to anger, and he directed it at Silvio, blaming the man for placing Tess within Thurkettle's reach to begin with. "Even if he hadna been trying to kill her for five years, he was still a poor choice."

"He was her mother's choice. I think she believed it would be good for Tess to grow up with Brenda, a lass her own age. Eileen might not have liked her brother, but she had no reason to believe he would ever try to harm the lass. There was also the matter of Tess's inheritance. Thurkettle held control of that. If he had decided to push the matter, the courts and the king would have decided in his favor anyway. We were but the reluctant tools of the law."

"I ask your pardon." Revan sighed and rubbed the back of his neck. "I but ache to blame someone for all of this, and ye were close at hand."

"No need to apologize. I, too, ache to blame someone, but I was never too fond of chastising myself." He looked at Martin. "I ken how ye hate long rides, Martin, but we need you to join us. This is too important a hunt."

"I ken it. I dinna mind riding along, not if it will help the wee lass." He shook his head as he moved toward his horse. "I just wish I could have taught the lass how to find her way. It might have helped her now."

"Ye were doomed to failure in that, Martin. That lass was

born lost,'' Silvio said as he hurried to remount. "Come on, we need to cover as many miles as we can ere darkness slows our pace." He looked at Revan. "We will get her back. 'Tis not a pleasant thought, but Thurkettle's taste for cruelty could work for us."

"How could it possibly be in our favor?"

"Because he willna kill her immediately. He will want to savor what he thinks is his victory. And he will want to plan the best way to make her pay for the trouble she has caused him. That will take time, and time is what we need."

Revan did not really wish to think about what Tess would suffer at Thurkettle's hands. "Then let us ride, Silvio, and waste no more of that precious time here." He spurred his mount to a gallop straight toward Thurkettle's keep, straight back to the place he and Tess had so narrowly escaped once before.

"Now, there will be no screaming, wench, or the gag will be stuffed back in your mouth, and ye willna taste a drop of this water." Dermott cautiously eased the gag from Tess's mouth.

Tess made no attempt to scream. Her mouth and throat were so dry she doubted she could have made much noise even if she had wanted to. For the moment the water Dermott was clumsily tipping into her mouth was far more important than making some undoubtedly vain attempt to call for help.

When he moved away, she glanced around. The moon had risen, but the trees were so thick around them its pale light only reached the ground in scattered spots. They had stopped to water the horses and let the poor beasts rest for a moment. She sat on the ground, sore and exhausted, and tried to think of some way to get free. Glancing down at the rope binding her wrists, she slowly began to lift the knotted hempen shackles toward her mouth.

"If ye think to gnaw your way free of your bonds, I shouldna trouble yourself." MacKinnon crouched beside her. "Ye will be firmly set in your uncle's hands ere ye get through even one of these thick coils."

Inwardly she cursed the man, then glared at him. It had been foolish to think she could chew her way to freedom, but she deeply resented his knowing of her plans and exactly how fruitless they were. He was gloating over her dire predicament, and she hated him for that.

"I have but one uncle in Scotland—Silvio Comyn."

"Come now, Thurkettle is your mother's brother."

"He is no kinsman to me. He is a traitor, a murderer, a thief, and a liar. He could be your kin. Ye are so very much alike." She bit back a cry of pain when he slapped her across the face. "Beating me canna change the truth. Nay, nor will my death alter your fate. Ye are a dead man. It would be wise for you to see to your prayers. Aye, pray that the king ye seek to betray feels merciful and doesna make ye pay as dearly for your treachery as the ones who murdered his father did." She saw the brief look of fear that passed over his thin face before he could hide it, and it gave her a small amount of satisfaction.

"'Tis not I who is the dead man but James the Second. The Douglas will soon be king—although ye willna be alive to see it. Thurkettle is said to be in a rage, and the angrier he is, the deeper his cruelty. Ye will be a long time in dying."

There was no denying that. The thought of it had kept Tess terrified since her capture, and that terror was becoming harder and harder to fight. She prayed she would have the strength to die bravely, thus depriving Thurkettle and MacKinnon of their vicious sport. If she could not escape her fate, she desperately wanted to face it without any sign of cowardice.

She tried to think of some cutting reply and looked at MacKinnon only to tense. He was no longer staring at her face but at her legs. Tess cursed silently when she followed his gaze. Her dress was badly torn, her legs exposed up past her knee. The expression forming upon MacKinnon's dark face told her that he was thinking of yet another way to hurt and humiliate her. She stiffened with revulsion when he ran his hand up her calf.

"I can see ye have guessed my thoughts," he murmured. "A little pleasure ere we continue on toward the scaffold that waits for you."

"Pleasure? From a traitor like you? I think not."

"And I think ye will find me more of a man than that pale lackey ye have been rutting with."

"More man? Ye flatter yourself." She braced for his blow when he raised his hand, but Dermott grabbed him by the wrist, halting his attack.

"Leave her be, MacKinnon," Dermott ordered. "There isna any time for that."

"We are at least four hours ahead of any pursuit. Come, my friend, ye can have a turn as well. Ye canna tell me ye wouldna fancy plowing this field."

"I would. She is a fair wee lass and clean. But, I have never kenned a ride that was worth risking my life for. That is what I would be doing if I paused for a quick rutting now."

"Ye worry like an old woman," MacKinnon snapped as he got to his feet.

"Do I? Better that than not worrying at all when there is good cause for it. 'Tisna only wasting precious time, which we have far too little of. There is something else ye would do well to consider—that we might lose this race."

"What do ye mean? With such a lead, how can we lose?"

Dermott shrugged. "I dinna ken, but there is always that chance. Until we reach Thurkettle, we arena safe. Now, I ask ye, if we do fail and are caught by her kinsmen and her lover, do ye really want them to find her bruised and raped?" He nodded when MacKinnon frowned, concern etched upon his hawkish features. "Nay, I thought not."

"Rein in that lust." Dermott grabbed Tess by the arm and hefted her to her feet. "If ye want the lass badly, ask Thurkettle for her. He will owe ye for bringing her to him.

He will probably let ye have a time or two ere he kills her.''

"Aye, he will.'' MacKinnon briefly stroked Tess's cheek. "I fear our moment of delight must wait, my Spanish harlot.''

Tess was about to spit at MacKinnon as he started to walk away, but Dermott gagged her. She winced as he roughly tossed her into the saddle. They would have to ride more slowly now because of the dark. Although the voice of common sense told her it would be foolish to do so, she prayed for some miracle. She was becoming certain that only some divine intervention could save her from the painful fate MacKinnon was taking her to.

Chapter

✧ 19 ✧

FERGUS THURKETTLE SMILED BROADLY AS HE walked around Tess for the third time. She tried to stand tall but was not sure she succeeded. After riding almost without stopping for a day and a half, she was exhausted. Her legs trembled from the effort of keeping her upright. She was almost too tired to be afraid. That was a blessing of sorts, she supposed.

"Ye have done well, MacKinnon." Fergus turned toward the man who sprawled in a chair, Dermott doing likewise at his side. "As ye have, Dermott. I am certain the Douglas will reward ye well."

"I rather thought ye would reward me, sir." Dermott took a hearty drink of wine from an ornate silver goblet. "She is a greater prize for you than she is for the Douglas. 'Tis why we rode her although the distance was a wee bit greater."

After tightly grabbing Tess by the arm, Fergus dragged her over to a chair and roughly shoved her into it. He then sat down at the head of the table. His great hall was empty except for the four of them, and he regretted that decision now. If his men had been at hand, he could have ordered Dermott and MacKinnon killed, thus saving himself some coin. Once they were paid, they would be more wary and getting his coin back would be difficult.

"And what makes ye believe she is of more value to me than to the Douglas? In truth, with the final battle so near at hand, her silence isna of such great importance any longer."

Dermott shook his head. "Although I pray for victory as vigorously as any man, there is always the chance that the battle might not go in our favor. A loss would make her silence even more important. She could be a strong witness against you."

Tess met Thurkettle's gaze with an outward calm. Whether Dermott got his blood money or not, she knew she would be killed. She had no intention of giving Thurkettle the pleasure of seeing her fear.

"And mayhaps the lass will finally recall her blood ties and stand silent through a sense of family loyalty," Thurkettle said.

"And mayhaps she willna," Tess answered.

"Ye would betray your own kinsman, your mother's only brother?"

"Aye, just as she would if she were here in my place. Treason is a crime that severs all blood ties. My loyalty is to our king. Even if ye werena the low, slinking adder that ye are, I would stand loyal to him over you."

"Ye cut your own throat with those words."

"I am not such a fool as to believe that swearing silence will win me a pardon. Ye want me dead for more reasons than what I ken about you. I willna go to God with a lie still staining my tongue."

"Ye were always too cursed proud for a mongrel." Thurkettle poured himself some wine, took a sip, then looked at Dermott. "Ye didna bring me Halyard, so the bounty will be halved. After all, he can still speak against me."

Dermott gave Thurkettle a hard glance. "I will have the full bounty and mayhaps a wee bit more besides. If ye willna give it to me, I shall take her to the Douglas."

"He will pay ye no more than I will. Why should he?"

"To gain the fortune he doesna ken she has. Betrothing her to his nephew was but a ruse to ensure that ye had the right to hunt her and her lover down. The Douglas didna want a wedding, just her death. But, once he is told about her fortune, methinks there will be a very hasty wedding ere she is put to the sword. He and his nephew will hold all those riches ye so hunger for. Aye, and he willna be too pleased with the deception ye have practiced on him."

Thurkettle clutched his goblet until his knuckles whitened. "Ye talk very boldly, mayhaps foolishly, for a man who sits within my grasp. I could have your throat cut. I but need to call out to my men."

"Call them. Then ye can explain to the Douglas how it is that one of his kinsmen died in your keep."

Tess watched Fergus very closely. He was afraid, and that only added to his rage. It interested her to see that her traitorous uncle feared the Douglas. She was not sure what good it would do her, but she did know that it never hurt to be aware of an enemy's weaknesses.

"Although I find it very interesting to listen to traitors argue amongst themselves, do ye think I might be allowed something to drink?" Tess asked, meeting the glares of the men with a sweet smile. "I will need my wrists untied as well."

"I dinna think ye understand the danger ye are in, lass," Fergus said as he took his knife and cut her bonds.

Tess rubbed her bruised wrists, wincing as the feeling returned to them. "I understand perfectly. I am to die at your hands. The only uncertainty is how ye plan to do it." She picked up a goblet. "Wine, please?"

As he poured the wine, Thurkettle studied her. "Either ye have more stomach than many a man or ye are fool enough to believe that ye might yet be rescued. Even if those foreign dogs ye call your kinsmen and that young stallion come hunting for you, ye will be dead ere they pass through my gates. Once ye were returned here, ye were as good as dead, lass.''

"Ever the gracious host. One always feels so comforted in the arms of one's own family.''

''That sharp tongue of yours will soon be blessedly still.''

Before Tess could reply to that, Brenda entered the great hall. As always, Tess felt placed in the shade by the elegant, beautiful Brenda. As her cousin walked over to the table, Tess covertly watched Dermott and MacKinnon watch Brenda. Both men had greedy, lustful expressions on their faces, their eyes somewhat glazed with appreciation. She wondered how they could be such fools. Brenda was beautiful, but she was also ruthless. Tess knew her cousin could probably bed a man one night and calmly cut his throat the next morning if it suited her purpose to do so. It was not a characteristic that should be ignored, yet every man who saw Brenda seemed to do just that.

While Fergus introduced his daughter to Dermott, Tess turned her attention to the woman herself. It surprised her to catch Brenda giving Dermott an inviting glance. There was nothing about the man to draw Brenda's interest. He was plain, broadly built, and very ordinary. Tess decided that her cousin simply liked men—any man. She tensed when Brenda finally rested her gaze upon her. The gleeful triumph she could read in that look made Tess uneasy.

''So ye have finally succeeded in catching the ungrateful child,'' Brenda murmured as she sat down at the table.

''Aye.'' Fergus relaxed in his seat. ''MacKinnon brought her to me.''

Brenda smiled at MacKinnon, but her words were directed toward her father. ''I hope ye plan to reward him. Mayhaps I can be of some help to you in that, Father.''

MacKinnon nodded at Brenda. '''Tis an honor to await your pleasure, Mistress Brenda.''

''Ye willna have a very long wait,'' Tess said. ''Brenda's pleasure is given very readily and often.''

"I suppose these pathetic wee insults make ye feel brave, Cousin."

"Insults? I but spoke the truth. Mayhaps ye canna recognize it anymore?"

"Such wit." Brenda looked at her father. "Why does she sit at our table sipping our wine as if she were some guest? Considering how she has eluded you and your men for so long, I should have thought that ye would be eager to secure her." She pulled a delicate, lacy handkerchief from her sleeve and held it near her nose. "If naught else, ye should give a thought to our health. She is remarkably filthy."

"I beg your pardon, Cousin. Riding without stop for nearly two days can make one a wee bit untidy." She looked down at herself and gave a mournful sigh. "Ye are quite right. I am a sad mess. 'Tis odd that Sir MacKinnon didna notice when he attempted to inflict his lusts upon me, but 'tis clear that he isna too particular in his tastes." She glanced at Brenda and saw by the flush upon her cousin's face that the woman had understood the subtle slur.

It amused her a little when Brenda then glared at MacKinnon. Tess knew her cousin well enough to understand what it was that made Brenda angry. The woman did not like to share, especially not with her "mongrel" cousin. MacKinnon would not find Brenda too welcoming for a while. Stirring up a little discord between the pair was not much repayment for the death they intended to deal out to her, but Tess gained a faint sense of satisfaction.

"I believe we have had enough of your games, Contessa," Fergus said. "Dermott, fetch the guards." He smiled faintly at Tess. "Ye can stay in your lover's old cell. Mayhaps he will soon be joining ye there."

"She will be dead by then," Brenda said with clear anticipation. "I hope ye arena fool enough to think he can save you this time, Cousin."

"Your father and I already had this discussion," Tess said, but Brenda ignored her.

"MacKinnon and Dermott are Douglas men," Brenda

said. ''Those who might think to aid you will hie to one of the Douglas keeps. By the time the fools realize their error, the worms will be gnawing through your winding sheets.''

Those words were particularly cruel ones, Tess decided, even as two burly guards arrived to take her to the dungeons. She had not really given much thought of how difficult it would be for Revan and her kinsmen to find out where she had been taken. Brenda was right. They would assume she had been taken to the earl of Douglas. That error would steal whatever small chance she might have to be rescued. It was not easy to keep her stance erect and proud as the guards led her to the dungeons.

''WHY are we halting?'' demanded Revan when Silvio ordered everyone to rein in just out of sight of Thurkettle's keep. ''Our goal lies just ahead.''

''Aye, and he will be watching for us. The snake hasna stayed alive for so long by being stupid.'' Silvio scowled in the direction of Thurkettle's tower house. ''We need to take him by surprise, and that willna be easy.''

Revan shifted in his saddle and reluctantly nodded. He knew Silvio was right, and if he had had his wits about him, Revan knew he would have thought of that himself. It was hard to be sensible, however, when Tess was so close and so desperately in need of help. Even now, despite nearly killing their horses by riding them so hard for so long, it could be too late to save her.

He forced that chilling thought aside. Tess was still alive. He had to believe that. And, he mused as he glanced toward Thurkettle's keep, he would make Thurkettle and his pack of curs pay dearly for every hurt she may have suffered and every moment of fear she had to endure.

''Tomas, I think 'tis time we see if our coin has been well spent,'' Silvio said.

''What do ye mean?'' Revan asked the man.

''We have a man within Thurkettle's keep. At least, we paid well to have one.''

''For the whole time Tess had to stay there?''

''Nay, and ye need not tell me that that was a mistake. I can see it was. I dinna think the lass has told me even a small part of what she had to endure in that place.''

''She hasna told me much, either. What little I have learned hasna been good.'' Revan watched Tomas dismount and start toward Thurkettle's keep. ''How can he reach the man? Thurkettle will have secured the place the moment Tess rode through the gates. No one will be able to get in or out.''

''This man claimed he could aid us in just such an event as this. He should be ready for our arrival, as he would ken that we would come after our Tess. But, I have my doubts about him now. He didna tell us that Thurkettle tried to kill Tess, and he has been in our pay long enough to have learned about it, even been there to witness the last little 'accident' Thurkettle planned.''

''He may not have realized what game Thurkettle was playing. Tess didna see it herself until forced to. When Thurkettle made it so clear that he wanted her dead, she recognized those strange accidents for what they really were.''

'' 'Tis pure God-given luck that she isna dead already. 'Tis certainly not because of me or mine. My brother must be cursing me from his grave. I set his only bairn in the hands of a murderer.''

''Ye did as ye were asked. Aye, and as ye said, 'twas something ye would have been forced to do. Since Thurkettle was ward of her fortune, then he had the right to claim her as well. 'Tis no use to belabor what was. She has been lucky. I but pray she continues to be so. I fear we havena seen much good fortune since we fled Thurkettle's hold.''

Silvio smiled and shook his head. ''Aye, ye have had more of it than most can claim in a lifetime. God's sweet tears, Revan, ye have had nearly every man in the borderlands searching for you. Ye had Thurkettle's and the Douglas's hounds sniffing your trail, as well as every rogue and cur who had learned of the bounty, yet the pair of you made it to Donnbraigh unscathed." Silvio laughed. "Sweet Mary, ye and Tess have had the Devil's own luck. Dinna doubt that, laddie."

Revan slowly smiled as he thought about Silvio's opinion and saw the truth in it. "Aye, I guess we have been fortunate. It would seem that God doesna mean to take the lass yet. 'Twould be nice if He didna make her go through so many trials ere He let her ken she was safe."

"I should be a wee bit wary of criticizing the Lord and His ways at the moment," Silvio drawled. "We are in need of all the help we can muster."

After Revan whispered a quick prayer of apology for his impudence, he fell silent. There was nothing left to do but wait for Tomas to return. He hated the delay but struggled to remain patient. Some gallant but ill-planned gesture born of his fears for Tess would hurt him more than he wished to think about.

When Tomas finally returned, Revan nearly screamed at the man to hurry. He gritted his teeth and clenched his fists as he fought to sit quietly while Tomas ambled over to them. Revan calmed himself a little with the knowledge that Tomas would not be so calm himself if he had met with failure.

"Our man was there?" Silvio asked as Tomas reached him.

"Aye, he was waiting. He was a wee bit worried that we might have ridden to the Douglas."

"And our Tess is there?"

"Aye, brought in but two hours ago, so we did gain on the rogues."

"Can he get us inside?"

"He can and will, but we must wait until dark." Tomas mounted. "We need to work our way around to the western wall. It seems there is a wee door cut into that side."

"A door in the wall?" That made no sense to Revan. "Why would they weaken their own defenses so?"

"I dinna think old Fergus kens it is there, Revan," replied Tomas. "'Tis Brenda's door. She uses it to sneak in her lovers. Fergus may allow her to be very free with her lovers, but he obviously likes to forbid her some men. 'Tis well disguised. Our man, Matthew, says we willna see it until he opens it. Brenda and her whorish appetites have worked to serve us well."

Revan maneuvered his horse so that he was close beside Silvio and could hear everything that was being planned. "The man could be pulling us into a trap."

"'Twas something I worried about," Tomas said, then shrugged. "I dinna think so."

"'Tis not always wise to trust a man that can be bought."

"That adage may be too sweeping, Revan. Matthew says he wants no part of the treachery Thurkettle is planning." Tomas smiled briefly. "He says he doesna care a corbie's arse about the king himself, but James *is* our king, and he will have no hand in tossing him off the throne."

"Yet he demands payment. If he truly feels that way, he would help us simply because honor demands it."

"Honor doesna put much food in a man's belly, m'friend. Matthew is a poor man. As he said, we can afford to give him a wee bit of compensation for the risks he is taking. A very practical man, our Matthew."

"Did he say where Tessa was or how she fares?"

"He isna placed high enough to ken that sort of thing so soon after she has arrived," Silvio answered. "'Tis why I didna ask."

"Well, our Matthew has proved cleverer than we thought," Tomas said. "He does ken where Tess is. He says he is sure she hasna been harmed yet. She looked sadly weary and tattered when she arrived, but he saw no wounds or bruises, and she held herself proud. She has been put in the dungeons to await Thurkettle's decision as to the method of her death."

"Aye." Silvio cursed. "Thurkettle will want to think on the matter for a while, plan something he can truly savor.

Does Matthew ken whether or not Thurkettle expects us, is
ready for us?''

"Thurkettle expects us to race for the Douglas's keep, but
he is also ready for us. He is but watchful. There is no great
increase in defense. That matters little really. Matthew feels
certain that many will slip away or surrender if given but
half a chance. He has also gathered many an ally. Thurkettle
inspires more fear than loyalty. We capture or kill Thurkettle, and his defenses will crumble like dry bread.''

"So speaks Matthew?'' Revan was not sure the trust put
in Matthew was warranted, but saw no other choice.

"Aye. I am not too fond of depending so heavily upon
one man either. Yet, I do feel he can be trusted. There is
something else to be considered—'tis Tess we come to save.
Even amongst Thurkettle's pack of dogs there will be ones
who will want no part in the cruel murder of a wee lass.
Also, Tess lived here for five years. She may not have been
well treated by her kin, but she was well thought of by the
poorer folk in that keep.''

Revan thought about that for a moment, then nodded.
"Aye, she would be. The cold cruelty of Thurkettle and
Brenda would have helped that. Tess must have been a rare
touch of kindness for many of them.''

"There is the wall. Matthew spoke the truth. I can see no
door.''

"Ye are certain this is the right wall?'' Silvio asked, a
hint of derision in his rich voice.

Tomas replied with a sarcastic reference to Silvio's aging
eyes. Revan listened in faint wonder as the pair continued to
quietly, and amiably, bicker. Their kinsmen, who made up
the majority of the more than twenty men with them, were
quick to add their wry opinions. Revan recognized the tart
humor that came so easily to Tess. He heartily wished he
could share in their apparent confidence. His insides were
too tight with worry. While Silvio and his men thought of
victory, all Revan could think of was all that could go
wrong.

It was not a problem he had ever suffered from before, and he knew it was because Tess's life was at stake. Revan did not doubt the concern Tess's kinsmen felt, yet they would have anticipated such emotion, prepared for it, and compensated for it. It came as an unsettling surprise to Revan. That surprise combined with his new and tumultuous emotions had made it nearly impossible to calm himself, to remember only his training and how to use it to help her.

"I see something," hissed Tomas.

Yanked from his thoughts, Revan stared at the wall. It was a moment before he saw what Tomas did. The smoothness of the wall was now broken in one place. Slowly a line of faint light appeared. Matthew had spoken the truth about the door. Now all that remained was to see if they were all being invited into a trap.

"Dismount," ordered Silvio. "We must stay low as we run to the doorway. Stay low and go one at a time. Be sure the guard on the wall has passed by before ye race cross the clearing. We dinna want to alert our enemy too early. I will go first," he said to Tomas as he dismounted and crouched near the edge of the trees. "Tomas, ye and Revan come along after I get there and slip inside."

Crouched by Tomas, Revan watched Silvio make his way to the wall. Silvio was dressed in dark clothes, as they all were, and it was not easy to keep him in view the whole way. There was a brief clear sight of Tess's uncle when he finally reached the partly opened door and paused by a shadowy figure positioned there. The moment Silvio slipped inside the walls, Tomas started across the open space, and Revan quickly moved to stay beside him.

No one stood beside the door when he and Tomas finally reached it. That caused Revan to hesitate briefly, fearing some trap. Tomas went inside and yanked him along. Revan was relieved when he saw Silvio sitting with three other men against the rear wall of the smokehouse. He followed Tomas in hurrying to join the small group and was quickly introduced to the square, graying Matthew and the two other men.

"Nothing has changed," reported Silvio as they sat down near him. "Tessa is still in the dungeons, and that bastard Thurkettle dines and drinks with those two traitors, MacKinnon and Dermott."

"Can we get to any of them?" Revan asked. "What about the tunnel leading from the stables to the dungeons?"

"Sealed."

"Sealed?" Revan was not really surprised, but his disappointment cut deeply.

"Aye," replied Matthew. "Old Fergus had it blocked up shortly after ye and the lass escaped. He feared it could now be used for an attack instead of as a way to escape."

"I would have done the same, but I had the small hope that Thurkettle wouldna have the wit or the time."

"The man can be very clever when he scents a danger."

"So what is our plan?" Revan kept a partial watch on Silvio's men as they continued to slip inside the walls unnoticed by the guards who passed by on the walls with an easily judged regularity.

"We wait until most of our men are gathered," replied Silvio. "Matthew will then give a signal. The ones he has on his side have a diversion planned—a rousing argument and a fight. Most of the guards will be drawn to watch it. Half of my men will go up onto the walls whilst the rest of us get inside of the keep to get Tess and Thurkettle."

"What are the odds against us? I mean to say, how many men does Thurkettle have?"

"There could be two to every one of you," replied Matthew. "He has a dozen hard-eyed mercenaries who will fight until Thurkettle is clearly caught or dead. They are past worrying about being part of a crime, even one as black as treason. They are all past due for a hanging. Thurkettle has five men who will stand firm guard over him. Ye will have to cut them down to get to him. Most of his other men-at-arms could easily surrender. Their loyalty to that cur isna strong, and many are troubled by what he drags them into. The others willna fight.''

"How many guard Tessa?"

"None. 'Twas thought it wasna needed, and there really arena the men to spare. Old Fergus couldna fully stop the Douglas from taking men, and there are still some out looking for ye and the lassie.''

"There, lad." Silvio lightly slapped Revan on the back. "Good news. Luck is with us tonight. We shall have Tess free in but a short while and will rid the king of one low traitor as well.''

"I fear I willna believe it until 'tis done. I have tried to share your hopes, but I find it impossible.''

"Aye, I have noticed that. Ye are very black-spirited for a man who speaks of marriage only in terms of duty done and honor served.''

Revan silently cursed as he fought to meet Silvio's intent gaze with calm. "Duty and honor mean a great deal to me.''

"I can see that."

Silvio's grin was a smug one, and Revan tried to ignore it. He suspected that he had revealed a great deal of his inner turmoil to the man, and it annoyed him. What he was feeling was not something he wished to discuss or have known, yet he was sure that Tess's kinsmen had guessed it all.

The last of Silvio's men arrived, and Matthew gave his signal. As Revan joined Tomas and Silvio in creeping toward the keep, he promised himself that he would find the time to reconsider his betrothal to Tess. He did not like the feelings tearing at him. They stole his skill. Marriage to Tess could cause him to lose the one thing he could feel true pride in—his skill as a king's knight.

Chapter

◈ 20 ◈

"HOW DO YE LIKE YOUR ACCOMMODATIONS, dear Cousin?"

Tess eyed her beautiful cousin with disdain. "They could benefit from a wee cleaning."

When Brenda smiled, Tess wished she were free so that she could hit her. It did not surprise her to see Brenda. Her cousin liked to watch people suffer. Tess had noticed that shortly after she had come to live with the woman. Taunting someone chained to a wall and condemned to death would be exactly the thing to draw Brenda's interest. She swore to herself that she would not allow anything that Brenda said or did to touch her, that she would not give the woman that pleasure.

"'Tis a wee bit dark down here." Brenda leaned against the bars. "They say 'tis best to ponder the error of one's ways in the dark. It can lead to a cleansing of the soul."

"Ye would require a full year of nights for that, dear Cousin."

"Your wit can grow very tedious. Men dinna appreciate such a sharp tongue. A lass like you canna afford to have too many faults. 'Tis difficult enough for ye to gain and hold a man."

"I havena done so poorly." Tess inwardly cursed,

wishing she had left the subject alone, for Brenda would now pursue it, and Tess dreaded that. She did not have the confidence to bear up well if Brenda taunted her about Revan.

"One man in eighteen years?" Brenda laughed softly.

"Most women would consider one enough. Most women would consider your greed the mark of a whore." She could see that she had angered Brenda and knew that was not particularly wise but could not feel overly concerned about it. "Most men as well."

"Is that so? Sir Revan didna find me so unappealing."

"Men are notorious for taking whatever is offered. Their loins ofttimes rule their minds."

"A woman can conquer any man through his loins—just as I conquered Revan. If my father hadna threatened his life, Revan would still be in my bed. He must find ye a very poor replacement, but, as ye say, men will take whatever is offered."

Tess fought the sting of those words. Revan had said he had never been Brenda's lover. Revan's word was far more trustworthy than Brenda's, and Tess struggled to keep believing him. She would not let Brenda sabotage her faith in Revan. It would not be easy, however. Her confidence in her ability to hold the attention of a man like Revan was weak—very weak. The lack of any words of love from Revan only made that worse. Tess was sure Brenda had sensed that weakness.

"If ye intend to discuss each man who has shared your bed, Brenda, ye had best tell your father he will have to delay murdering me—for at least a year or two."

"Ye do think yourself amusing. 'Tis very possible ye are jealous. If ye and Revan hadna been forced together, away from everyone else, he never would have turned to you. Any time we are placed side by side, Cousin, the men will always choose me." She smoothed her hands down her sides. "Men like a wee bit of flesh upon their women."

"Your vanity is truly overwhelming. It leaves me quite speechless."

"Very little has ever succeeded in doing that. However, ye will soon be silenced forever. 'Twill be interesting to see how my father decides to end your poor life. He can be very clever. I have often been left astounded at how long he can keep his prisoner alive all the while inflicting great pain and injury. 'Twill be fascinating to see what ye can endure."

"I shall be pleased to provide you with as much diversion as I am able to. 'Twould sorely grieve me if ye grew bored."

"Very kind of you, Cousin. I sensed that ye wouldna be a disappointment to me. Now, I dinna believe Revan will long survive you, but, be assured, I will see that his last hours are pleasurable. Revan and I shall again savor the passion we indulged so often before his foolish loyalties forced him to flee."

"To be loyal to one's king is hardly the act of a fool, Brenda."

"Oh, aye, it is when that king gives out so little reward."

"Revan has his honor. Ye and your treacherous father canna say the same."

"Treacherous mayhaps, but alive and soon to be very powerful. There is ever the chance that, when Revan sees that his cause is a lost one, he will give that loyalty of his to my father. Then I could enjoy his skill as a lover for more than a few hours. 'Twould be a great shame to lose such a fine lover, to see that lean, strong body given over to the worms."

"I believe Revan would prefer the worms to a low, murderous traitor and his whore of a daughter."

Tess smiled faintly when Brenda abruptly stood straight, gripping the iron bars of the cell door so tightly that the knuckles of her hands grew bone white. Brenda clearly could not shrug off too many slurs. Tess briefly wondered if she should be wooing her cousin instead of insulting her, then inwardly shook her head. There was no mercy to be found in Brenda, and to plead for it would only give the woman pleasure.

"Mayhaps my father will decide to let ye just rot in those chains," Brenda hissed. "A slow death with an occasional taste of water to ensure that ye last a long time. I shall enjoy watching that, seeing ye die bit by bit as ye hang there in your own filth." Brenda turned and stalked away.

It was difficult for Tess not to call after her cousin. The images Brenda had left her with were horrifying ones. Tess trembled, and a chilling sweat broke out on her skin. She prayed that Thurkettle did not have the time to indulge in that style of execution, that he would want to be sure she was dead before he got caught up in the war against the king.

REVAN was the first to break into the keep itself. He felt a surge of exhilaration when he found MacKinnon there with Brenda, the pair clearly attempting to flee. He ached to fight MacKinnon and was pleased when the man drew his sword, proving that he would choose battle over surrender. Revan moved to face MacKinnon squarely and out of the way of his allies, who were still coming in and rushing to meet the threat of Thurkettle's personal guard.

"Kill him, fool," Brenda ordered MacKinnon as she got out of the men's way. "Kill him and ye can have me."

"'Tis no grand reward," Revan said, directing his words at Brenda but keeping his gaze fixed upon MacKinnon. "Near every man in Scotland has tasted that sweet."

"Kill him!" she screamed. "Cut him down, MacKinnon, ye coward."

"Shut up, ye shrewish whore." MacKinnon glared at Revan. "Ye willna take me alive, Halyard. I willna let ye turn me over to the king's rage. We will settle the matter here. Ye will have to kill me or set me free."

"I will have no difficulty in killing you. Ye will pay dearly for your part in trying to kill Tessa."

"Such heat for that bone-thin, sharp-tongued wench. Well, ye are welcome to what is left of her."

Revan felt the cold grip of fear. "If ye have killed her . . ."

"Killed her? Nay. I was leaving that chore to her loving kinsman—Thurkettle. He can be so ingenious in such matters. But, 'twas a long ride here, Halyard. I felt a need to taste what ye have protected so well, and it was sweet." He smiled coldly. "So sweet that I had myself many a taste ere I dumped her at Thurkettle's feet."

It was almost impossible to control the blinding rage that seized him, but Revan knew he had to. If he gave in to it, he could make a fatal mistake, and he knew that that was what MacKinnon wanted. It was an old game the man played, taunting an adversary until he made some blind, reckless move, and Revan was determined not to let the man win.

"If ye have hurt that lass—" Revan began.

"Let us just say that your slut's harbor isna so snug now. I have widened it a wee bit." MacKinnon lunged.

A harsh cry of fury escaped Revan as he parried that thrust. He knew his rage added strength to his blow, but he strained to keep it reined in, to stop it from clouding his mind. As he fought, he ignored Brenda's cries for his blood and prayed that MacKinnon was lying about what he had done to Tess.

Revan soon began to fear that he and MacKinnon were too evenly matched, that they would fight on until they both collapsed from exhaustion. It was as that concern entered his mind that his break came. MacKinnon's next swing was awkward. Revan blocked it as he pushed the man hard up against the stone wall. As MacKinnon fought to free himself, Revan drew his dagger and buried it in the man's throat.

He stepped back, allowing MacKinnon's body to slide to the floor. The death rattle had just sounded in the man's throat when the rustle of skirts caught Revan's attention. He whirled around in time to see Brenda rushing toward him with a dagger in her hand. As she tried to plunge it into his heart, he caught her by the wrist and twisted until the knife slipped from her fingers. He ignored her curses and threats as he dragged her toward the great hall.

Inside of the great hall Silvio, Tomas, and some of their kinsmen were swiftly culling the guards who tried to keep a swearing Thurkettle out of their reach. Revan shoved Brenda toward a youth who stood guard over those who had surrendered or were too wounded to fight, then plunged into the battle. He intended to reach Thurkettle first.

TESS frowned as her concentration on her prayers was broken a moment later. There was something going on in the keep, she was certain of it. The sounds were indistinct, and it was impossible to guess at their cause, but before there had been only silence. The fact that she was hearing anything at all was worthy of attention. It would require a great deal of noise to reach her deep in the bowels of the keep.

Suddenly for one brief moment, the sounds were clearer. There was the clash of swords, men shouting, and a scream of pain. An instant later a heavy thud echoed through the dungeons, and the noise was muffled again, the clatter of footsteps on the stone stairs further disguising them. Tess gasped when a wild-eyed, disheveled Brenda appeared, a bloodied sword in her hand.

"What is happening?" she demanded, trying not to let her hope of rescue rise too high.

Brenda just glared at her and ran past. Tess tried to lean forward but winced as her shackles held her in place. It was possible Brenda was headed for the tunnel. A moment later Tess had that suspicion confirmed as Brenda's screech of fury ripped through the stone caverns.

"That fool! That thrice-cursed and damned idiot. He has sealed it."

Tess watched as her cousin raced back and grabbed the keys from the wall. She tensed when Brenda tossed the sword on the ground and frantically scrambled to unlock the cell door, trying key after key. Something had filled Brenda with fear and a need to escape. Neither boded well for Tess, for a Brenda driven to survive could be a very dangerous animal. If it was an attempt to save her that was causing the uproar, Tess could find rescue near at hand. And Brenda, she mused, as she watched her cousin pick up the sword and enter the cell, could easily steal all hope just as it was in reach.

"Your father has chosen ye as my executioner?" She eyed Brenda warily as the woman stood in front of her.

"Nay, but I may yet have that pleasure."

"Someone has arrived to clear out this nest of traitors."

"Aye, your mongrel kinsmen and Revan. Those idiots my father hired are either surrendering or dying. 'Tis all gone—all chance of escape, all hope of a high place within the Douglas's court. I could have been so rich, so powerful. Now 'tis all gone. Even all my careful plans to get free of my father's plots canna work now. And 'tis all your fault."

There was the sharp edge of hysteria to Brenda's voice, and Tess knew that could make her cousin even more dangerous. "I didna draw your father, and ye, into the Douglas's plots."

"Since ye and that stupid king's knight ran off, nothing has gone as planned. Nothing. Well, I have a fine new plan now."

"Using me to buy your freedom?"

"Nay. I have no hope of freedom. None of those gallant knights"—she spat—"will allow me to escape punishment. Nay, I am for dying, and I mean to take ye with me."

"Ye could throw yourself upon the king's mercy." Tess tried to suck in her stomach, pull it back from the sharp sting of the sword point Brenda had pressed there.

"The mercy of the king? The same mercy his mother the queen showed those who plotted against his father? The same mercy his regents showed those two young Douglas earls when they dragged them out into the gardens and beheaded them? The same mercy James himself showed yet another Douglas earl as he stabbed him to death over dinner? I think I shall choose my own death, thank ye very much.''

''And go to your Lord with the stain of murder upon your soul?''

Brenda laughed, a high unsettling sound. ''He will never see that one amongst all the others. I am fated for Hell, and we both ken it, dearest Cousin. But, I shall have one last moment of pleasure ere I leave this earthly cesspit. They will be coming for you soon. Just as they do, just as soon as ye taste the sweet chance of freedom, I will kill you before the eyes of the men risking so much for your sake.''

Tess felt a little sick. She looked past Brenda to the steps leading out of the dungeons, then down at the sword scratching her belly. It would require a great deal of luck to break free of this tangle.

REVAN yanked his sword free of the man he had just fought and killed. He turned and found himself face to face with a sweating Fergus Thurkettle. The man had used his hirelings as shields, pushing them between him and his enemies. There were none left now. Revan smiled. It might not be an easy fight, but he was confident that he would win it. Thurkettle had let others do his fighting for him for too long. Even the man's fear and will to live could not replace the skills he had let rot over the years.

''Ye have the chance to surrender now, Thurkettle,'' Revan said, his sense of honor forcing him to make the offer.

''Surrender and face a crueler death at the hands of James himself? That is no choice at all.''

'' 'Tis the only one ye will get.''

''Then I will die or leave where I stand.''

''Ye will die.''

Thurkettle's first swing was easily blocked. Revan was not surprised, however, when the man's skill quickly grew less abrupt and ill thought out. Thurkettle had to have been a good swordsman once, or he would not have lived so many years. It was not long, though, before the man began to sweat badly and breathe heavily. Thurkettle was not in fighting trim anymore, and that would quickly prove to be fatal. Revan swallowed the savage urge to play with the man.

The end came a moment later. Thurkettle stumbled badly as he tried to avoid Revan's sword thrust. Revan's sword cut deeply into the man's soft stomach. It was not until Thurkettle collapsed, his hand clutching at his gaping wound, that Revan realized Silvio, Tomas, and the others were standing around watching him. He was grateful they had stood back and left Thurkettle to him. Glancing at the small knot of prisoners, Revan frowned. One was missing.

"Where is Brenda? The woman?" he demanded.

"Havena seen her since ye and this bastard began to fight," answered Tomas.

"She was here only a moment ago. I could hear her screeching."

"Does it matter?"

"It could. She is no better than her father."

"Ye think she has gone after Tess?" Silvio asked, a little anxiously.

"I feel sure that she has—either to use her to bargain with or to seek revenge. Wait," he called when Tomas and Silvio both bolted toward the door. "Brenda will be expecting us to rush down there. She probably *wants* us to."

"And what do ye suggest we do? Wait until she tires of the game?"

"Nay, we must play it out, but it need not be by her rules."

Revan strode over to a wall where a number of weapons were hung in grim decoration. He took down a savage-looking hunting crossbow. Grimly he fitted a bolt into the weapon.

"What do ye need this for?" Tomas asked. "Ye have a sword."

"I doubt Brenda will allow me near enough to put that weapon to use. I need something that will allow me to cut her down from a distance if she forces my hand."

"Ye can throw your dagger."

"My aim with a dagger isna true, I fear. This is better. Much better. If it can bring down a deer, it can bring down Brenda Thurkettle. I just pray she doesna force me to it. I have no stomach for killing a woman—even that traitorous whore."

"Ye mean to go alone," said Silvio.

"Aye. It might give some chance of surprise. I just believe that one man going to face the woman is the only way to do it, the safest. If a lot of us rush down there . . ."

"She could act hastily," Silvio finished. "Go and God be with you."

As he hurried toward the narrow stairway that led to the dungeons, Revan prayed that God was with him. He felt in need of such divine aid. Brenda was cornered. The woman had to know that escape was now impossible and that her chances of being excused from the charge of treason were slim. That made the woman especially dangerous. He prayed that he was not rushing to Tess's rescue only to watch her die.

"SOMEONE'S coming." Brenda tensed and peered toward the darkened stairs.

"Ye are letting your fear make ye hear things," Tess lied, for she had heard the soft scrape of a boot against stone.

"I dinna think so. 'Tis quiet now, which means that the battle is over. Someone is coming to find you." Brenda smiled briefly at Tess and pressed her sword point a little harder against Tess's stomach. "I shall make this victory a very sour one, indeed."

Tess winced as the cold stone wall scraped the skin on her back when she tried to pull back some more. She tensed when Revan stepped out of the shadows holding a hunting crossbow. Although fear for her own life still held her tightly in its grip, she felt joyous relief at seeing him alive and unhurt. She prayed it would not be her last sight of him.

"Step away from her, Brenda," Revan ordered, struggling to keep his voice soft and calm.

"Nay, I think not."

"Ye can gain nothing from hurting Tess now. Your father has lost. He is dead, most of his followers dead or captured. This will buy ye neither time nor mercy. 'Twill only add murder to your crimes."

"A person can only be hanged once. But then, a traitor isna hanged. He is gutted like a pig for market." She drew her sword point across Tess's quivering stomach. "Contessa betrayed us. I should execute her as a traitor."

As he raised the crossbow to aim it directly at Brenda, Revan hoped Tess still had the wit to try and help herself. Despite her bonds, Tess still had some ability to move. She could twist her body out of the way. Brenda still might be able to stab her, but if Tess moved at the right moment, the wound did not need to be fatal. He could not tell Tess what to do, however, without alerting Brenda. A trickle of cold sweat wended its way down his spine, and he shivered.

"Put the sword down, Brenda, or your well-used body will be sheltering this arrow."

"Ye would kill a woman? The great gallant Sir Halyard? Nay, ye havena the stomach for it."

Brenda laughed, and Halyard could not believe his luck. The woman relaxed ever so slightly as she mocked him, easing the press of her sword against Tess. He fired, nearly cheering with relief when Tessa twisted her body away from Brenda's weapon, but winced as his arrow found its mark in the woman's body.

Tess cried out softly as Brenda thrust the sword toward her. She contorted her body to avoid having that steel blade bury itself in her stomach, but she felt it cut into her side. Brenda screamed as Revan's arrow plunged through her chest so swiftly and deeply the point protruded out of her back. For one brief instant Tess held Brenda's gaze and trembled. In her cousin's eyes there was no sign of fear or regret, only fury and hatred. Tess sagged in her chains when Brenda collapsed onto the floor, her sightless gaze fixed upon the mildewed ceiling.

Revan threw aside his crossbow and yanked the keys from the lock in the door. He hurried over to Tess and pushed Brenda's body out of the way. The moment he freed Tess from the chains that had once held him, she fell into his arms. He cursed as he caught her and felt the blood from the wound on her side.

"How bad is it?" he asked, unable to see anything in the dim, insufficient light cast by a few torches.

"A flesh wound," she answered as he picked her up in his arms. "Her sword but tried to make my waist a wee bit smaller." She looked down at Brenda's body. "She *is* dead?"

"Aye. I am sorry."

"There is no need to be. She chose her path. She would have killed me just as she had threatened to. Aye, and ye as well if ye had continued to hesitate. She was her father's daughter."

After gently holding Tess close for a moment, Revan touched a kiss to her bruised mouth. "They have treated ye poorly. Do ye have any other wounds?" Although Tess did not act or look as if she had been raped, Revan could still hear MacKinnon's vile words. He needed Tess to reassure him that the man had lied.

"Nay, a wee bit bruised and saddle sore, but aside from this nicking Brenda just gave me, naught else."

"Ye werena mishandled on the journey here?"

"Ah, ye fear I have been abused. Nay, MacKinnon talked of rape, but Dermott told him to wait, that there wasna time for it. He also feared how much it might cost them if ye or my kinsmen caught them. He convinced MacKinnon it was wiser to rein in his lusts until I was in Thurkettle's hands.''

He kissed her again, relief adding a hint of ferocity to the kiss, then started toward the stairs. "We will have this wound seen to."

"The battle is won, then?"

"Aye, and with little cost to ourselves. Not many of Thurkettle's men felt inclined to die for him."

"What of the ones who took me before—Thomas and the others?"

"Dead. As is MacKinnon, Dermott, and Thurkettle. They chose to die with a sword in their hand rather than face the gibbet or worse. They chose us to be their executioners."

"I think that was what Brenda was doing as well. She had no intention of surrendering or being taken prisoner."

Holding her close against his chest, Revan nodded. "Their ending was more merciful than they deserved."

The moment they emerged from the dungeons, Tess found herself submerged in the care of her relatives. They all sought assurances that she was all right even as they tended to the wound in her side. It was decided that they would spend the rest of the night where they were and leave for Donnbraigh in the morning. Despite being separated from Revan, Tess was relieved when she was taken to her bedchamber. It was nice to be fussed over, but she was tired.

She was barely settled into the bed when Revan strode into the room. With exhaustion weighting her eyelids, she watched as he prepared for bed. His armor was gone and his hair was wet. It was obvious that he had taken a bath while she was being cleaned and dressed. When he slid into bed beside her, she cautiously curled up in his arms, needing to be near him, but not wishing to antagonize her wound.

"Will this make it hard for ye to reach the king in time to fight at his side?" she asked.

"Nay." Revan smoothed his hand up and down her arm,

aching to make love to her yet knowing it would have to wait. "However, it will be a close-run race."

"Ye will win it—the race and the battle. Ye will fight at the king's side and defeat the traitors."

"Aye. I feel we will. And when that is done, I ride back to marry you."

"Aye. To marry me." She closed her eyes and held him a little closer, for she knew now that the only right thing to do, the only thing she could do because she loved him so much, was to set him free.

Chapter

✦ 21 ✦

"COME AWAY FROM THAT WINDOW, CHILD."

Tess sighed and turned to smile at her aunt Kirsten. Silvio's wife watched her closely while kneading the bread dough. Cousin Isabella's little house was filled to the brim with the wives of the Delgado-Comyn men. Tess loved them all, but she was also heartily sick of the constant company.

After leaving Thurkettle's keep, it had taken them three days to get back to Donnbraigh. Tess would have felt guilty except that she had not been the only wounded one they had had to move slowly for. Then there had been a week of recovery at Donnbraigh amidst frantic preparations for battle. Messages flew back and forth between Donnbraigh and the King's supporters, including the assurance that Simon had spoken to the King, relaying all of his information and successfully convincing their leige of Revan's innocence. Her wound healed enough for them to travel to her cousin Isabella's—ten miles north of Arkinholm, where the opposing armies gathered. After a day of rest her wound had been healed enough for her and Revan to make love, but there had been no opportunity for privacy.

She had wanted to spend one long night making love with Revan before he rode off to war. Instead, they had to settle for a hurried coupling in Isabella's small orchard. While it had been gloriously fevered and frantic, it had not been the long romantic interlude she had craved. She had to smile, though, when she recalled how nearly every other woman waving at her man as he had ridden off to battle had looked as flushed and rumpled as she had.

"Your staring out that window hour after hour willna bring him home any sooner, lass," Meghan, Tomas's very pregnant wife, said as she tucked a loose curl of red hair back under her kerchief.

"I ken it." Tess walked over to the table and joined in the kneading of the bread dough. "'Tis just that they have been gone nearly a week. I keep thinking I might see or hear something."

"From ten miles away?" Kirsten shook her head, then smiled, her green eyes soft with understanding. "'Tis clear ye have lived a blessed life, child, and havena learned how it is when your man rides off to fight."

"There must have been some battle during my eighteen years upon this earth."

"Mayhaps not since ye were of an age to remember," Kirsten said. "Ye can never ken how long they will be gone, dearling. Nay, nor how much fighting they may have to do or how long the battle might last."

"A wee bit of common sense should have told me that. It does sometimes. Then I think that it must be over and wonder where they all are. I fear I also thought that all this cooking was because ye expected them to return."

"Well, aye, we do a wee bit," Kirsten said. "'Tis also a way to keep busy, which one must do at such times. If they do return we shall have a very fine feast waiting for them. If not, we will send it to their camp."

Meghan laughed. "Which we have done several times. Tomas said there are always men trying to join them simply because they are always so well provisioned. Soldiers always have more stomach than food to fill it."

"Oh. Do ye think I should send something to Revan, then?"

"Ye will be," replied Kirsten. "He is in the Delgado-Comyn camp."

"But his family fights for the king. Surely he would be with them." She saw the way the women looked at her and realized why—her uncle Silvio would keep Revan close at hand, as he had done since their arrival at Donnbraigh. "Humph. And they say they arena holding a sword in his back."

"They arena holding one, simply ensuring that he doesna get too shy or nervous and bolt," said Meghan.

"Revan wouldna ken what shy is if it leapt up and bit his nose clean off. I have never seen him nervous, either."

"Ye will see it when he kneels at the altar," said Isabella. Tess looked at her aging cousin, who peeled apples brought out of storage, apples as wrinkled as her still nimble hands. "Nay, what I will see is that cursed honor and duty he holds so dear."

"Ye canna fault a man for holding such virtues." Isabella neatly chopped up the apple she had just peeled and, after tossing the pieces in a large pot, got another wizened apple out of the basket at her feet.

"Child, what troubles you?" asked Kirsten. "The way ye act toward your young knight tells me ye want him for your husband, yet ye talk about the forthcoming wedding as if it were some curse, not a blessing."

"I fear it could well be a curse and a fatal one—at least to my heart and mayhaps my soul."

Tess glanced toward the other women sharing the large main room of the house. They were intent upon their stitchery and gossip as they sat in a compact circle near the fireplace. She then looked at the three women sharing the table with her. It was risky to tell them what she thought— but she needed to talk the matter over with someone. Here were three women—young, middle-aged, and old—who were all sensible and willing to listen. The temptation was too much to resist.

"Can ye all keep a confidence?" All three quickly

nodded, and Tess sighed. "I will understand if ye feel pressed to break this one. In truth, 'twould be unfair to swear you to silence ere I told you this, and I willna pain us all by begging for secrecy afterward."

"I believe I speak for all of us when I swear I willna break the confidence without much thought and consideration for you," Kirsten said, and Isabella and Meghan nodded.

"Thank ye. 'Tis about my forthcoming marriage."

"Phew, there is a surprise," murmured Isabella.

"I am glad, in a way, that Revan has been forced to spend so much time in the company of my kinsmen." Tess eyed her elder cousin with fond annoyance. "It has allowed him to see that my tongue isna born of perversity and a dislike for him, but is my birthright. Might I say what I wish to now?"

"Do continue, lassie."

"How kind." She grew serious again, frowning at the dough she worked with her hands. "I think it would be a grave error to go through with this marriage."

"Then ye shouldna have let the lad lift your skirts," snapped Isabella. "What is the matter? Doesna he do the job well enough to suit you?"

Although she could feel the heat of a blush upon her cheeks, Tess scowled at her white-haired cousin. "He does the job very well, thank ye kindly. In truth, I suspect he does the job better than most, although I couldna judge that as well as ye might, ye old corbie."

"Aye, I would be able to judge. I have had my share of fine stalwart lads. Why, I recall—"

"Oh, hush up, Isabella," said Kirsten. "We dinna need to hear about your scandalous past now. Tess wishes to speak of important matters. Go on, Tessa. If she interrupts again, we shall stuff one of her own apples into her toothless mouth."

It took Tess a moment to subdue the urge to smile. Things had changed in the last five years, yet they had remained the same. Isabella still snapped at everyone and tried to tell anyone who would sit still a moment about her licentious youth, while everyone else still snapped back at the woman. It all sounded so contentious to an outsider, but there was no disrespect and there was an abundance of love. She knew she could unburden herself to these women without fear.

"Why would it be such a grave error, dearling?" Kirsten pressed.

"Because I am an heiress and he is a poor knight with naught but honor and a good sword arm."

"The Halyards are a good family. I never heard that they were particularly poor, either."

"They arena. Revan is. He has no coin and no land and no hope of gaining any through his family. 'Tis the same problem many a younger son wrestles with."

"Then he should be well pleased with your dowry. I dinna accuse him of bedding you to gain it, but we ken that 'tis more than he could have gained in the usual way of things. A lass with your fortune would have been kept well out of his reach. Ye dinna fear that he weds you to gain that fortune, do ye?"

"Nay. The truth of the matter is that he *didna* want to wed me *because* of my fortune."

"I fear I dinna understand."

"It took me a while. Revan has what most would consider a very odd opinion. He sees wedding a lass for gain as naught but the act of a whore. He swore he wouldna gain his land or the coin in his pocket through marriage. If he canna get such things with his own wits and skill, then he will live without them."

"A very noble attitude," murmured Kirsten.

"Aye, but still odd. Dinna deny it. I could hear the confusion in your voice. Men dinna understand him, either. 'Tis a point of pride with him, Aunt. He admitted as much to me, for I sensed his reluctance when Uncle Silvio first said we were to be married and I pressed him for the reason for it. It sorely stings his pride to be seen as one who profits through marriage, to have both land and coin brought to the marriage by the wife whilst he brings naught. I suppose he feels—well—bought.''

"Foolishness. He will put that aside, child. Dinna worry on it.''

"Aye,'' agreed Isabella. "No man has died from having his pride pinched a wee bit.''

Tess sighed. "I ken that. 'Twill be far more than a pinch, I fear. He doesna ken the whole truth. When we first escaped Thurkettle and were hiding in that cave, he and I pondered the reasons why Thurkettle should want to kill me. Besides the need to silence me there was the chance of gain. That would explain the attempts made upon my life whilst I was living with Thurkettle. So, Revan asked if I had any fortune, and I said I did, but I lied about how much.''

"Oh, Tessa.'' Kirsten reached across the table to pat Tessa's hand, raising a tiny cloud of flour dust. "What did ye tell him?''

"That I had a few thousand riders and a little land here and in Spain.'' She grimaced when all three women just stared at her. "At that time I didna ken him well and didna want him to ken what I was worth. 'Tis hard to explain. It isna that I feared he would do me any harm or the like. I just didna want to tell him then.''

"And ye havena told him since then?''

"Nay, Aunt. The matter was never discussed again.''

"Silvio didna tell him?''

"I think he believes that Revan kens it all already. Revan was the first one to mention my fortune. He told uncle of how Thurkettle had tried to kill me before there was a need to stop me from telling what I learned. It wasna discussed after that. 'Twas also shortly after that that I learned of his feelings concerning wedding an heiress. I couldna tell him then.''

"Nay, I can well understand that. Unfortunately, ye must tell him sometime. He has to be told.''

"Have ye made any plans, Tess?'' Meghan asked.

"Well, first I tried to think of some solution to the problem, of some way to soothe his pride."

"There is none," muttered Isabella. "Not unless ye make yourself as poor as he is."

"I did think about that, but I canna do it. 'Tis not really my choice to make. The land and the money is for those yet to come as well. And such a gesture would bring its own problems. Revan would always wonder if I regretted it, if I resented him for all I had to give up. And if the children were to discover what I had done, they could resent it. Aye, especially if we remained poor. I myself might even grow to resent it for many reasons—when there wasna enough to eat or no pretty gowns for my daughter." She shrugged. "'Tis so hard to explain, but I feel certain that it wouldna solve the problem. It would just change it.

"However, if I keep my fortune and wed Revan, there will also be problems. 'Twill shatter his pride when he discovers just how much of a dowry I have, a dowry so large he couldna hope to match it. Stripped of his pride, he will grow to hate me. That will kill me. Little by little, as I watch him turn against me, I will die inside."

"Ye love him a great deal," Kirsten murmured.

"More than is probably wise. 'Tis what prods me to the decision I have finally made. I must set him free."

"But the family willna allow that," Meghan said.

"If I can get him away from this vast family, I feel that, in time, I can convince Uncle Silvio that it was for the best. Revan would need to stay out of their reach for only a wee while. I feel certain 'tis the only way either Revan or I can be at least content. Well, he will be. I must release him. Do ye understand what I am trying to say?"

"Aye," said Isabella. "Ye must let the lad go. Ye are right about that."

"Isabella!" cried Kirsten, then hastily lowered her voice when the other women glanced their way. "She has bedded the man."

"So? That willna ruin her for all time. Wedding a man

whom she loves, but who will slowly turn on her, will do just what she says it will do—kill her inside. Ye can steal a lot from a man and it willna matter very much, just cause a few wee times of anger and hurt. However, ye canna strip a man of all of his pride and expect him to still care for you. That lad will grow to hate her just as she says he will.''

"Mayhaps it isna as bad as ye say," said Meghan. "The size of your fortune may not matter at all."

"It will, Meghan. He is uncomfortable with what he thinks I have. But, he can see the chance of matching it or at least coming near to matching it. The true amount is a goal he will see as far beyond his reach. Aye, and if the king grants me all that Thurkettle has left, 'twill be even worse. I dinna think it would help if he loved me, either.''

Tess smiled sadly at the three women. "Now ye ken it all and ken why I didna want to force ye to swear to silence."

"Aye, but we didna help you very much," Kirsten said and sighed.

"Aye, ye did. The looks upon your faces, the concern behind your words, told me that I am justified in what I fear would happen if I marry Revan. I felt sure of my decision, yet there lingered a small part of me that feared I was throwing away any chance of happiness. Talking with you has finally silenced that wee contradictory voice."

"But how will ye do it? Revan is kept under a very close watch, friendly as that guard is."

"Aye," agreed Meghan. "It might well grow even tighter when the time for the wedding draws near."

"I shall have to watch closely for a chance. If worst comes to worst, then there could be a scene at the altar. I just pray that I have a wee bit of luck and that a chance to set him free does come in time."

"It has best be soon, then," mumbled Isabella, staring out the window. "The men have returned."

The next few hours were hectic. Tess met Revan's father, Thane Halyard, and his eldest brother, Colin. Nairn and Simon also joined the group. She suspected that her uncle

Silvio had given the men little choice. It was not until they sat at the table, finishing a hearty meal, that she was able to learn very much about the battle or what was to happen next.

"I ken that the battle went in your favor, but ye havena told us much else," she said as she refilled hers and Revan's wine goblets. "It must have been a stunning victory if the king has let ye return home so quickly afterward."

"There was hardly a battle at all, lass," explained Silvio. "Sir James Hamilton deserted the earl of Douglas just before the battle. That prompted a very large desertion within the traitor's army. Douglas camped that night with nearly forty thousand men only to wake in the morning to a sadly emptied camp."

"So there was no battle at all?"

"Well, a wee one. Ere the Douglas bedded down for the night, his army and King James's were nearly equal. The odds tipped heavily against Douglas when Hamilton joined the king. There was some fighting on the Esk near Langholm. Douglas's brother Moray was killed. His other brother, Ormond, was caught and executed."

"What of the earl of Douglas himself?"

"He fled to England with Lord Balvanie."

"He deserted his own brothers?" Tess could not believe it.

"Aye. Ran to save his own traitorous hide," muttered Tomas. "Well, he has saved little else. 'Tis all forfeited to the crown now."

Tess looked at Raven. "All that trouble and it ends so swiftly, so ignominiously."

Revan laughed. "Aye. I felt a wee bit cheated myself."

"Is that why the king let ye leave the army? Because it was so easy?" asked Meghan.

Silvio grimaced. "We have a fortnight. I fear Revan's kin dinna even have that. They must return on the morrow. The king is intent upon cleaning out all of the Douglas's allies.

If he is still punishing the traitors in a fortnight's time, he wishes us to rejoin the army.''

There was a moment of silence before the conversation was renewed. Tess shared the dismay and disappointment of the other women. She might never call Revan husband, but she suspected she would always worry about him. No matter how skilled the knight, he still faced death each time he drew his sword in battle.

Kirsten nodded to her, and with a sigh Tess rose to help the women clear the table. She doubted she would have an opportunity to be alone with Revan. That saddened her, but she told herself it was probably for the best. It was time to begin distancing herself from him. She prayed that that would help ease her pain a little when she had to send him away.

"A bonnie wee lass, Revan," Thane Halyard murmured as he joined his sons and Simon in the stable hayloft for the night.

"Aye, she is bonnie." Revan frowned when no one else climbed up the rough wooden ladder to join them. "No Delgado or Comyn? Am I to be allowed a night without the charming companionship of one of their number?"

As he spread his blanket over the hay, Thane smiled at Revan. "Two are bedded down at the foot of the ladder. Another at each door of the stable. I think there are a few outside as well."

With a soft curse Revan sprawled on his back on his blanket. "I gave my word. It should be enough."

"'Tis not enough in this matter, lad. Aye, they trust ye, but they will still watch ye closely until the vows are said. Even the finest of men can take it into his head to bolt as the day of his marriage draws near." Lying down next to Revan, Thane crossed his arms beneath his head and looked at his son. "Ye probably arena hiding your reluctance as well as ye think ye are."

"Well, no man likes to be prodded to the altar," Revan muttered, a little dismayed that he could be so easily read.

"Then ye should have kept your braies laced tighter, m'lad."

Revan cursed again as his family and Simon chuckled softly. "I can see that I will get no sympathy from you."

"Sympathy? Why should ye expect any sympathy? 'Tis evident that ye find the lass a delight beneath the blankets. She is a pretty lassie, too, with the finest pair of eyes I have ever had the pleasure of looking into. For all she is a wee thing, 'tis clear that she is strong. Proved that well enough in the fortnight ye spent racing about the borders. She has wit. Ye will be glad of that when the passion cools, as it will do over the years. And she has the land and coin I havena been able to give you," he added in a quiet voice.

"I dinna fault ye for that," Revan said in an equally soft voice.

"I ken it, lad. I regret it nonetheless. 'Tis why I was pleased when ye grew up to be such a bonnie lad. I hoped that face would help ye gain all I couldna give you."

"Ye mean ye hoped it would make some wealthy lass wish to buy me for her husband."

"Lad, ye have some very odd ideas. Ye expect sympathy for marrying a fine, wee lass many a man would want and then complain about the dowry that will come your way because of it. Get some rest, lad. 'Tis clear that weariness has dimmed your wits." Thane shook his head, then closed his eyes. "I am sorry that none of your own kin will be attending your wedding, but as soon as there is peace, we will have a celebration for ye and the lass."

A grunt was all that Revan could manage in reply. He was feeling very much put upon. His family had not made even the smallest of protests over how the Delgado-Comyns were keeping him a virtual prisoner. There were no chains binding him and no swords pointed his way, but he could not even walk to the privy without one of Tessa's amiable kinsmen at his side. It seemed to him that his family ought to take some umbrage over his treatment. Instead, they acted as if the Delgado-Comyns were already family.

He sighed and got more comfortable on his rough bed. It was childish to concern himself with such petty matters. Even though he knew he would not back out of his word to marry Tess, her kinsmen had every right to act as they were. In fact, they were being far more gracious than many another family would be. He was just suffering from a natural resentment over being forced to do something, of having no real choices. Revan swore that he would rid himself of that feeling, for Tessa was certain to sense it and that would hurt her.

As he closed his eyes, Revan made another promise to himself. He would, somehow, gain both coin and land on his own merit. One day, and he prayed that it would be soon, he would have a fortune equal to Tessa's. Then no one could accuse him of living off his wife's largesse.

TESS eased her body out from beneath her blanket. Hardly breathing at all, she began to creep toward the door. If she could speak to Revan, tell him that he was freed of his promise to wed her, then his family and Simon could help him get away. As she edged around the people sleeping on the floor, she silently practiced her speech for Revan. When a bony hand suddenly clamped down on her arm she barely stopped herself from screeching.

"Just where do ye think ye are creeping away to, lassie?" whispered her captor.

"Isabella?" Tess peered at the person gripping her arm. "Is that you?"

"Well, it isna King James, ye great idiot."

Lying down next to the old woman so that she could speak even more softly, Tess whispered, "Let me go. I think ye can guess what I am trying to do."

"Well, for a moment there I thought ye might be sneaking away to have a quick rut with your man."

"Cousin Isabella!"

"But I then recalled that talk we had just before the men returned. Sorry, lassie, but tonight isna the chance ye are looking for."

"His kinsmen are here. They could help him get away."

"Tessa, I doubt that ye would even make it out the door. Your kinsmen nearly cover this floor. There are more outside, in the stables, and even in the cow byre. We are knee-deep in Comyns and Delgados. One of them is certain to catch you or that pretty lad of yours. And ye can be sure that they will lock ye and him up very tightly after that. Ye will have to wait, lass."

"Aye. I suppose ye are right."

"I am. Ye would have to crawl through Silvio to get out the door."

"Uncle is sleeping by the door?"

"Right in front of it."

It was hard, but Tess had to accept defeat. She got back up on her hands and knees to return to her pallet. Tess had barely begun to inch along the floor when Isabella hissed her name.

"What is it?" she asked, now anxious to return to her bed before she was seen.

"If ye ever need anything, lassie, anything at all, ye come to me."

"Thank ye, Cousin. That is a comfort. Good sleep to you."

"And to you, Contessa."

When Tess finally reached her pallet, she crawled beneath her blanket and sighed. She was disappointed that the ordeal of sending Revan away was still ahead of her yet relieved that he would still be near at hand. She hoped that she would be able to conquer her contradictory emotions. If they lingered after Revan was gone, she feared she would never be able to overcome the pain of losing him.

Chapter

✦ 22 ✦

"WHAT EXACTLY DID HE CALL THIS PLACE?" Revan asked as they rode into the bailey of Thurkettle's keep.

Tess grimaced as Revan dismounted, then moved to help her down from her horse. Just as she had feared, the king had granted her Thurkettle's lands and money. Revan had not taken the news very well. His mood had been faintly surly for the whole journey. She knew he was now making an effort to be conciliatory, but after four days of enduring his moods, she was not sure she felt particularly interested in his effort. Inwardly she sighed and looked at him, stung by the hint of anger still clouding his blue-gray eyes.

"Simply Thurkettle's Tower." She shrugged when he scowled with distaste. "Ye can change it."

"'Tis yours. 'Tis your place to rename." His tone was less harsh when he added, "As ye well know, I canna even think of a name for my horse. Ye were going to think of one, remember?"

"Aye, I remember, and I finally thought of one as we traveled here, but I didna think ye were in the mood to discuss it."

"Nay. Mayhaps not." He knew he ought to apologize, that he had treated her badly, but he could not get the words

283

past the knot of resentment clogging his throat. "What name did ye decide on then?"

She moved closer to his gelding and stroked the horse's nose. "I thought of two actually. Ye can decide which one of them ye favor. Amigo or Compadre."

"I like the sounds of the words. Spanish?"

"Aye."

"What do they mean?"

"*Amigo* means 'friend' and *compadre* means 'companion.' 'Friend,' too, I think. Canna be certain. My Spanish has been sadly weakened by not speaking it for five years. Thurkettle wouldna allow it. It enraged him."

"A great deal enraged that man. I suspect when he awoke to find his toes roasting over Satan's coals, he was a wee bit enraged." He smiled faintly when Tess giggled, then lightly swatted him on the arm.

"Hush. Ye shouldna jest about the dead. Ye wouldna want old Fergus coming back to haunt ye."

"God have mercy on us."

Silvio and Tomas walked up at that moment, and Tess nearly cursed. That was the first reasonably pleasant conversation she and Revan had had in the last four days. She was annoyed to have her kinsmen put an end to it.

All concern over talking to Revan fled her mind when Silvio and Tomas each grabbed Revan by an arm and hurried him toward the keep. "What are ye doing?" she asked as she ran after them.

"Since your wedding is on the morrow," replied Silvio, "we feel it best if your lad is very well secured. Ye dinna mind, do ye, Revan?"

"I dinna suppose it would matter much if I did," Revan murmured.

"Nay, I fear not."

Tess cursed as she followed them into the keep and toward the steps that led down to the dungeons. "Are ye just going to toss him into a cell for the night, drag him out come the morning, and then wed us?"

"Aye. I ken it isna the best of ceremonies, lass, but we havena got the time for anything fancy or even for your aunts and female cousins to come here. We wouldna even have traveled this far except that there is a priest in the village. The one at Donnbraigh died about a year past. 'Twas just as easy to come here where we ken one is than to run hither and yon trying to find one."

"That wasna what I was meaning, and well ye ken it," she snapped as she stumbled after them, down the narrow, shadowed steps into the dungeons. "I mean that ye canna lock a man up on the eve of his wedding."

"Hold the lad, Tomas." Silvio got the keys and unlocked the cell door. "If ye are worried over his mood on the wedding night, lass, I shouldna be. A man can forgive most anything when he finds himself abed with a pretty lass."

"I wasna worried about the wedding night. Revan, why dinna ye hit them or something?" she demanded even as Silvio nudged Revan into the cell and locked the door.

"I dinna think that would be the proper way to treat one's future kinsmen, Tessa." Revan found it curious that he was not angry, did in fact have difficulty not laughing.

"These future kinsmen ought to be hanged. Give me those keys." She tried to snatch them from her uncle's hand, but he hung them back on the hook, which was out of her reach. "Will ye let him out of there?"

"Nay. Canna do it, lass. Now, the two of you have been very accepting of this marriage we have demanded. But 'tis the eve of saying your vows to each other. 'Tis the time when ye can grow very resentful, get nervous, and think of bolting, and when ye start to have doubts. Now, be honest, Contessa, I suspect ye have a doubt or two."

"Oh, aye, I have a doubt or two—about your sanity. Now, cease this mad game and set him free."

"'Tis no game, my Wee Countess, but common sense."

Tess gave a soft screech of surprise when Silvio suddenly picked her up and tossed her over his shoulder. "Put me down!"

"I will as soon as we get ye into your chamber." He started toward the stairs, ignoring the way she pounded on his back with her small fists. "We will send ye down a hot bath, lad," he called back to Revan. "Aye, and a hearty meal and clean clothes for your wedding day. If ye think ye are in need of clean linen for that bed, just ask the lad who brings ye down your bath."

"I believe I will be fine."

The moment Tess and her kinsmen were gone, Revan sat down on the narrow cot and laughed. He knew he ought to be enraged, but he was not, and that struck him as being funny as well. After a moment he sighed and sprawled on his back on the bed, idly noticing that it was new and not the rat-chewed cot that had been in the cell before. He was full of contradictory emotions concerning his approaching marriage. A little more time to sort himself and his feelings out would probably be for the best, but there was no time left. He prayed he would not hurt Tessa too much as he battled his own vagaries and confusion.

TESS laid on her back on the bed, exactly where she had been tossed by Silvio before he had run out of the bedchamber, locking the door behind him. She found it all very hard to believe. While she and Revan had been virtual prisoners since they had sought refuge with her uncle Silvio, it had been a captivity easily ignored. This was not. She did not understand why Revan had not been as enraged as she was. In fact, he had looked amused by the whole business.

She was still nursing her anger and puzzling over Revan's curious attitude when the servants arrived with a hot meal and a hot bath. It was very tempting to make a bid for freedom, if only to prove a point, but she resisted the urge. Instead, she sat on the bed silently glaring at them. They hurried through their chores and fled the room. She hoped they went straight to her kinsmen and reported on her fury, then cursed. Silvio would probably find her bad temper a source of great amusement.

After indulging in a long, hot bath and feasting upon her meal, she felt sleepy but fought the temptation to lie down and close her eyes. She could not go to sleep now. It was far too risky. She could easily sleep straight through until morning and lose all chance of giving Revan his freedom. The way he had acted when she had been awarded all Thurkettle had forfeited only made her more certain of the need to let him go.

The second time she caught herself dosing, Tess knew she could wait no longer to act. Since she was in Brenda's old bedchamber, she did not need to worry about the door her kinsmen had locked. She walked over to the huge wardrobe against the wall, pushed Brenda's many gowns out of the way, stepped inside, and opened the door at the back. It let her into the next bedchamber, the one Brenda had always put the handsomest male guests in.

Cautiously Tess eased into the hall. Although careful to keep an eye out for anyone who might sound an alarm, she hurried outside. There were a few things she needed to do before she could go to Revan.

"She has put our guard to sleep and tied up the stable lad."

Silvio stared at the grinning Tomas for a moment, then laughed. "She is her father's daughter. No question of it. I wonder how she put the guard to sleep."

"She tipped some small vial of liquid into the water bucket just before the lad took it round to give each man a drink. A sleep draft. Probably Brenda's. As for the poor stable lad, she just tiptoed up behind him, tapped him with a lump of wood, then tied and gagged him."

"Has she finally made her way to that lover of hers?"

"Aye, she went in through the tunnel. Mayhaps ye shouldna have had it cleared. Made it too cursed easy for her." Tomas moved to the large bed in the center of Silvio's bedchamber and lay down on it. "Are ye still certain we should let her do this? She will be no maid yet no wife."

"I ken it." Silvio lightly drummed his fingers on the arm of the chair he sat in. "I dinna like the thought of that at all. But, Kirsten swears to me that this is the right thing to do. Didna your Meghan say the same?"

"Aye, she did."

"And they are both right, as is that old corbie, Isabella, who fair bent my ear ere we left to come here. Ye saw how the lad acted when she got word that she now owned all of this as well. When she tells him about her fortune, he willna be able to live with it. I canna believe the women fully understand how deep a man's pride runs, how much a part of him it is, but they do ken what can happen if ye strip a man of that pride."

Tomas grimaced and nodded. "He isna a cruel man, but he could easily destroy our Tess. She loves him."

"Aye," Silvio agreed in a soft voice. "More than I had guessed. It takes a very deep love to do what she is doing. She is going to let go of the one she values most in this world because she canna bear to chance that the marriage could destroy him."

"I canna understand how the man can be so blind. He cares for her. I am certain of it."

"Oh, aye, he does, the young idiot. The man was half-mad with worry when she was in Thurkettle's hands."

"Yet he will leave her."

"Sometimes, lad, a man has to be faced with losing something ere he realizes how much it means to him."

For a moment Tomas stared at his uncle, then his eyes widened, and he started to laugh. "Ye are a sly one. Ye dinna believe he will go very far at all, do ye."

"Nay. Not more than a mile or two. Come on, lad. We had best take up the watch upon the walls until our men wake up." Silvio stood up and started out of the door, Tomas quickly falling in behind him. "Just dinna let either of those young idiots catch sight of you. If they think I have stuck my spoon into the pot, they could become very bullheaded."

* * *

REVAN frowned as a light drew nearer to his cell. He sat up in bed when he saw Tess. She smiled faintly, set her lamp on the table, then tugged the stool over and set it beneath the hook the keys dangled from. Revan tugged on his braies and reached the cell door just as she started to unlock it.

"Thought ye had your own set." He crossed his arms over his chest and leaned against the cool iron bars.

"I lost them when we first fled from this place." She opened the cell door and looked at him. "We have to talk."

"Now? In the middle of the night?"

"Aye. Now. Tomorrow will be too late, much too late."

She went and sat on his bed after placing her lamp on the small table next to it. Revan hesitantly moved to sit beside her. She was looking so serious, so grave, it began to worry him. He took her hand in his. When he met her gaze, he felt a flicker of alarm. Even in the dim light he could read the sadness in her eyes.

"Tessa, what is wrong? Is it Silvio? Tomas?"

"Nay. They are fine. 'Tis me, Revan. I need to tell ye something about me that I dinna think ye will like to hear."

He smiled, relieved, for he was sure that there was little Tess could tell him about herself that was as bad as she seemed to think it was. "What about you, Tessa?"

As she stared down at their entwined fingers, she said, "I lied to you." She glanced up and noticed that the look of indulgent amusement had left his face. "Well, I didna tell ye the full truth."

"The full truth about what?"

"My fortune."

Revan tensed, not liking the turn the conversation had just taken. "What about your fortune?"

Simply mentioning her inheritance had him tense and wary, anger lurking just below the surface. Tess wanted to weep but fought to maintain her calm. Her money and her lands, things that should be a source of comfort, were going to cost her the one thing she really needed to be truly happy.

"Do ye remember when we were trying to decide what other reason Thurkettle could have to want to kill me, and ye asked me if I had some money, some fortune, or land?"

"Aye. Ye said ye had a bit of land here, in Scotland, and a bit in Spain, as well as a few thousand riders. Ye dinna have these things?"

There was the hint of hope in his voice, and she sighed. "Aye, I have them. Mayhaps I should tell ye about my bit of land." In a flat voice she described her large, profitable estates in Scotland and in Spain, watching him pale a little more with each detail.

"And the few thousand riders?" he asked in a tight voice as he released his grip on her hand and stood up.

She folded her hands in her lap. "Thirty thousand at last counting."

"Sweet Mary." He ran a hand through his hair as he paced once around the cell. "That accounting doesna include all that Thurkettle has left behind, does it?"

"Nay. There has been no time to tally that yet."

Tess watched him pace for a moment. She could not be sure if it was a sign of agitation or if he sought some solution. Then she decided that it did not really matter. The look of utter horror on his face said all that needed to be said. There was no way that he could live with her fortune, and she knew that giving it all up would not help them, either.

"Get dressed, Revan," she said as she stood up.

"What?" He turned sharply to face her.

"Get dressed."

Still stunned by what she had told him, he simply obeyed her, moving to tug on his clothes. "Are we going somewhere?"

"*Ye* are. Ye are leaving here. Ye dinna have to wed me in the morning." She held up her hand to silence him when he started to speak. "Nay. Dinna tell me about duty and honor. They are very fine sentiments, but we both ken that few people will judge ye poorly if ye dinna hold to them now. There will probably be many a man who will think ye are admirably clever.''

''Mayhaps. However, although ye have opened the cell door for me, how am I to escape?''

''Through the tunnel, just as ye did before. Uncle had it cleared. But this time I regret to say that ye canna do it with your knife at my throat.''

He ignored that. ''And once I step outside of that tunnel, I shall be swiftly taken up by your kinsmen.''

''Nay. The way is clear. Ye need but saddle your horse and ride away.''

''No one is in the stables?''

''The stable lad is tied and gagged.''

''The men standing watch upon the walls?''

''Asleep. Brenda sometimes took a potion to make her sleep. I poured some into the water bucket just before the lad took it around and gave each man there a drink.''

''Ye gave this a lot of thought.''

''More than ye will ever ken,'' she murmured. ''Ye had best go.''

''Your kinsmen will only hunt me down,'' he said as he tugged on his boots.

''Well, I may not be able to stop them at first, but ye need hide out for only a few days. By then I shall have convinced them to let bygones be bygones.'' When he just stood there staring at her, she demanded, ''Well? Ye shouldna waste time. I canna be sure how long the guard will be asleep. And ye shall want to have as large a start on my kinsmen as ye can get.''

''I canna help but think 'tis wrong to sneak away like a thief in the night. I said I would marry you.''

''Aye, ere ye kenned what I was really worth. Ye canna live with it, Revan. I saw the look upon your face just now. I saw how ye acted and felt when I was given this keep and whatever comes with it. Ye only grew accepting when ye decided that ye might still be able to match that. I dinna think ye could ever make yourself believe that ye could match what I have now.''

''The king himself would have trouble matching what ye have,'' he snapped, then sighed and ran a hand through his hair. ''I am sorry. 'Tisna you I am angry with, Tessa.''

''I ken it. But it will be. One day it will be. Little by little that anger ye hold will poison our marriage, poison us. 'Tis best if ye just leave now, Revan. 'Tis really the only solution.''

He knew she was right, yet he felt oddly hurt. '''Tis strange. I had come to believe that ye cared for me, yet ye are merrily sending me on my way.''

''Merrily?'' She laughed shakily. ''Ye can be such an idiot.'' She cupped his face in her hands and kissed him. ''Aye, I care for you.'' She traced the shape of his face with her fingertips. ''At times I think I may care for you too much. 'Tis why I must let ye go.'' She got behind him and gave him a little push. ''Leave.''

Revan hesitated only long enough to realize that he could think of nothing to say. With one last look at her he headed for the tunnel. There were a lot of good reasons to do exactly as she said. He had thought of several himself. It did not make sense to feel so reluctant. Annoyed at himself for his uncharacteristic hesitation, he moved faster. Within moments he was mounted and riding out of the keep.

For a while he just rode blindly, unable to form one single coherent thought. It took him a moment to realize that his horse had finally halted. He suspected he had not given the animal any direction. Revan looked back toward Thurkettle's keep, but he had already entered the forest, and the trees combined with the night's shadows to obscure the keep from view. It was a place he should be glad to get far away from, yet glad was the very last thing he felt.

''There should be a sense of freedom, the feeling that a burden has been lifted from my shoulders,'' he muttered as he patted his horse's neck. ''There is none of that, Amigo.'' He spoke the name carefully and smiled faintly when the animal whinnied. "Aye. It suits you. She chose well. I wonder what she will name that lump of stone she now holds."

He cursed and shook his head. That was no longer any of his concern. Tessa herself was no longer any of his concern, no longer to be a part of his life. He was riding away a free man. Tessa had released him from all promises and obligations.

It hurt and that briefly annoyed him. There should only be a small sense of regret. Everything was just as he had thought he wanted it to be. His pride intact, he could return to being a knight in King James's service, a knight with no entanglements to interfere with his skills or the execution of his duties. Ever since he had first looked into Tessa's huge brown eyes, he had been sure that this was just what he wanted.

Memories of Tessa crowded into his mind. He remembered how she laughed, how black her eyes grew when she was caught in passion's grip, and how brave and uncomplaining she had been throughout their life-threatening ordeal. Revan frowned as he clearly recalled how she had looked as she had set him free—her pretty face pale and her big eyes clouded with sadness. It hurt to remember that look, for he knew he was the cause of it. She did not want him gone. She was doing what she thought was necessary for his happiness.

"But, curse it, I am *not* happy." He scowled at Amigo when the horse snorted. "I am not happy and she is not happy, so how can this be the only solution, the right thing to do? If it is, 'tis the worst one I have every heard of."

Revan knew what the solution was—conquering his pig-headed pride. That was at the heart of their problems—he was too proud to accept that Tessa had wealth and he did not. He frowned. When put that way, it sounded more like envy than pride.

He weighed it up in his mind again and again—wincing as he listed what Tessa had and sighing as he listed what he could contribute. There was always the chance that he could yet gain some land and wealth if he continued to ride in King James's service. It would be a salve for his pride but gaining it would leave Tessa alone a great deal, alone to manage and defend all her holdings as well as any family they might be blessed with. He knew she had the wit to do it alone, but she should not have to.

There was one reason for his hesitancy and confusion that he had avoided considering, but suddenly he faced it squarely. He loved her. Matters were not as simple as they should be because of that emotional bond, and he knew it was foolish to keep trying to ignore it. He loved her. Revan found it a little exhilarating to finally accept it.

And because he loved her, he would always know in his heart that he had not married her for her wealth, he thought as he sat up straighter in his saddle and looked back toward the tower house. Tessa would know it as well. Most people would consider him simply a lucky man to have won such a well-dowered bride. The few who sheltered less charitable thoughts did not matter. It was exactly what everyone had been telling him, but he had refused to listen, had held firm to his own view, and had stubbornly refused to be swayed. Now, faced with the choice of living without Tess at his side or living with her wealth, he could see it. He was also sure that, with some time to consider the matter, he and Tess could find ways to further placate his pride. They could put some of her wealth in trust for their children just as the wealth she now held had been put aside for her when she had come of age.

Laughing softly, he turned Amigo back toward the tower house. The way he felt was further confirmation of the rightness of his action. Faced with leaving, he had been confused and miserable. Now that he was going back, now that he had made the decision to stay with her, he felt lighthearted and eager. He urged Amigo into a slightly faster pace, hoping to get back to his cell as secretly as he had left it. It would be fun to see Tessa's face when she found him still there. He would pause only long enough to untie the poor stable boy.

"HERE he comes."

Silvio tugged Tomas back down behind the wall. "Dinna let him see you."

"They are going to realize that we ken the whole of it. If naught else, the guards will wonder why they all went to sleep at the same time. It would be reported."

"'Twill be a while ere they recall that." He grinned and winked at Tomas. "'Twill be fun to see how the lass plays this in the morning." He laughed along with Tomas.

Chapter

⬥ 23 ⬥

A HEAVY SIGH ESCAPED TESS AS SHE STUDIED
herself in the mirror. The gown she wore was of the finest gold
silk. Her hair was loose and festooned with gold ribbons. She
was sure she looked as lovely as she ever could, and it was all
for nothing. Very soon she was going to be facing her angry
kinsmen and trying to talk them out of hunting Revan down
and dragging him back. It was not something she looked
forward to. For a little while after she had set Revan free, she
had considered running away herself. Only the knowledge that
it would solve nothing had stopped her.

There was a rap at her door, and her uncle called, "Are
ye ready, lass?"

"Aye, Uncle Silvio," she answered as she moved to open
the door. "Quite ready." She managed a small smile.

"Ah, lassie, ye do look bonnie. Very bonnie, indeed." He
kissed her cheek, then took her by the arm. "Ye will have
your laddie so beset he will have trouble saying his vows."

"More trouble than ye ken," she muttered as he escorted
her down the stairs.

"What was that, dearling?"

"Nothing. Has the priest been found, then?"

"Aye. Tomas brought him from the village nearly an
hour ago. He waits in the great hall. Once ye are there, we
shall fetch your groom."

Tess looked away and winced. It should have been such a happy day for her, but it was turning into the worst day of her life. What she wanted to do was curl up somewhere and weep out her pain, but she was going to have to deal with what could be a very emotional confrontation. She was surprised that Revan's escape had not already been discovered. The men must have been too embarrassed to report what she had done to them. It had given Revan plenty of time to get away, but she did wish the discovery of his flight could have come a little earlier.

When they entered the great hall, Tess covertly watched the men gathered there as Silvio escorted her over to the priest. She recognized a few of the guards who had been on the walls the night before. Each of them smiled courteously and gave a slight nodding bow. Not one of them gave even the slightest sign that they knew they had been given a sleeping potion and by whom. That did not seem reasonable to her, but before she could think about it much, Silvio introduced her to the priest.

"Ye stay here with the good father, Tess," Silvio said and winked. "He will tell ye all about the duties of a good wife while I help Tomas fetch your young man. Best to listen well to the father. I think ye are in need of it."

Before she could make any reply, Silvio strode away. The priest took what her uncle said as a serious command and immediately began to lecture her on the proper behavior of a wife. Tess found it both painful and tedious. It hurt to listen to the priest because she so wanted to be a wife—Revan's wife—and that future was now lost to her. After the priest mentioned duty for the fourth time and stressed obedience for the third time, she began to ignore him. She nervously watched the heavy iron-studded doors to the great hall, tensely awaiting the outcry that would soon come.

SILVIO smiled as he stepped up to Revan's cell, the keys dangling from his fingers. "Your bride awaits you."

"I am ready." Revan idly brushed his hand over the rich blue doublet he wore.

After testing the cell door to see if it was open, Silvio murmured, "Locked." He used the key.

"Ye locked it yourself." As soon as Silvio unlocked the door, Revan stepped out of the cell.

"Aye, that I did—the first time."

Revan slowly turned to look at Tomas and Silvio. Both men wore faint smiles and watched him closely. Their dark eyes were alive with amusement. They knew everything. Revan was certain of it.

"How fares my bride?" he asked as he started up the steep narrow stairs, determined not to be the first to mention his near escape.

"Very pretty and taut as a bowstring," Silvio replied as he followed Revan.

That was not hard for Revan to imagine. Poor Tess had to feel as if she were walking on broken glass as she waited for his disappearance to be discovered. Her wits must be sadly scattered if she had not yet guessed that her kinsmen knew everything or that he must still be at the keep. He hoped he did not offset her too much with his unexpected return.

At the top of the stairs he hesitated, struck by a sudden bout of knee-trembling uncertainty. What if he was wrong about how she felt about him? She had sent him away. Her reasons for that might not have been as noble and self-sacrificing as he had thought. Tess might simply not want to marry him.

Inwardly he shook his head, banishing that fear. She did care for him. No one could look at a person as she had when she had set him free and not care. It might not be the love that he now knew he craved from her, but the seeds of that emotion were definitely rooted in her heart.

"Ye have had your chance, lad," Silvio said quietly. "Ye have made your choice."

"I ken it." He started on his way again. "Just a brief attack of uncertainty."

"The lass might be grateful if ye would keep walking when that happens. I left her with the priest. He is instructing her on the virtues of a good and dutiful wife." Silvio just smiled when Revan glanced his way.

"Cruel. Punishment, is it?"

"The lass could use a wee bit of instruction on duty and obedience."

"I can see that I must hie to her rescue yet again." Revan increased his pace, Tess's chuckling kinsmen quickly matching it.

Revan stepped into the great hall a moment later and halted when he saw Tess. She was as beautiful as he had ever seen her, the rich gold of her gown suiting her coloring perfectly. Or it would do if she were not as pale as parchment. He hurried over to her, a little worried that she was about to faint for the first time since he had met her.

Tess wondered if her lack of sleep, her pain, and the several lapses into heavy weeping during the long night had disordered her mind. It was not until Revan reached her side and took her hand in his, his warm and very solid hand enclosing her suddenly cold one, that she knew she was not seeing things. Revan really was there, dressed for his wedding and watching her with concern.

"Revan," she said, her voice little more than a hoarse whisper. "Ye are here."

"And where else would he be?" asked her uncle Silvio.

She was about to reply, "About fifty miles away and riding hard," when Silvio ordered the priest to begin the ceremony. Tess had a hundred questions she burned to ask but could not utter even one of them as she and Revan knelt before the priest. She saw no sign upon Revan that he had been forcibly dragged back and his expression was one of serious calm. Unable to think clearly, not knowing what to do or say, Tess simply went along with the ceremony.

"A toast to the bride and groom," bellowed Silvio as he stood up, his wine goblet raised high.

Tess quickly grabbed her wine as Revan stood up and pulled her to her feet. She was only just beginning to think clearly again. The wedding ceremony and the feast that had followed it seemed more like faint memories instead of things she had just done. For the first time since Revan had walked through the doors of the great hall, she was not feeling as if she were locked into some strange dream.

She smiled at the men gathered around the table and started to lift her goblet to her lips. It suddenly came to her notice that several men were clearly waiting for her to drink first. Since it was a toast in her honor, that was somewhat odd. She frowned as she realized the ones who hesitated were men who had stood guard the night before, men she had given the sleeping potion to. It took a moment, as her memories of the past few hours were very confused, but she realized that these same men had hesitated in the same way with each and every drink of wine.

They knew. The knowledge shook her, and she took a deep drink to try and steady herself. They immediately drank their wine as well, confident that she would never take a dose of her own poison. As they all sat down again, she thought the matter through several times, and her shock began to change to annoyance. If the guards knew they had been dosed and that she had done it, then her kinsmen knew as well. Her attempt to free Revan had been no secret. She would not be surprised if it had been watched from the moment she had slipped out of her bedchamber. She had suffered through hours of fear and nervousness for nothing. Tess glared at Silvio.

"Ye kenned it all from the start, didna ye?" she snapped at her uncle. "Ye have been playing your own game, not mine."

Revan quickly stood up, grabbed Tess by the hand, and pulled her to her feet. "I believe my sweet bride and I shall retire to the marriage chamber now."

"Now? 'Tisna even sunset. And I havena finished talking to my conniving uncle."

"Aye. Ye have."

Tess screeched softly in surprise when Revan picked her up and tossed her over his shoulder. Many a ribald remark was bellowed after them as he strode out of the great hall. She relieved her embarrassment a little by pounding vigorously upon his broad back.

"Put me down, ye great idiot."

"Is that any way for a blushing bride to speak to her husband? I thought the priest had instructed ye on the correct manner of a wife."

"The priest belched out a great deal of nonsense I paid no heed to. Now, put me down."

"When we get to our bedchamber."

She cursed him and got a light slap on her backside in reply. When he entered the bedchamber they were to share and tossed her onto the huge curtained bed, she quickly sat up to glare at him. The need to push her tousled hair off of her face before she could give him the full force of her glare only added to her annoyance.

In fact, she was not quite sure why she was angry with Revan. His taking her away from a hearty argument with her uncle was a small offense. She decided that it was simply because Revan was there. She had spent a hellish night, torn up inside over his leaving, and worrying about the consequences of setting him free, only to find that it was a needless self-inflicted agony.

"Did they find ye and drag ye back here?" she asked, noticing that he had started to undress.

"Nay. I rode but a few miles and then turned back."

"But I gave ye what ye wanted." She tried to keep her mind on the important discussion she was trying to have, but when he took off his fine linen shirt, she could only think about what a beautiful chest he had.

"Aye, and I really thought that I wanted it." Stripped to his braies, he walked over to the bed and ran his hand over her hair.

She got up onto her knees so that she could look him in the eye. "And just what do ye want?"

Revan slipped his hand beneath her heavy skirts and stroked her thigh. "I want you, Tessa—right now."

His touch already had her breathing fast, and she fruitlessly tried to fight her weakness for him. She put her hands on his chest, intending to push him away, but was distracted by the feel of his warm taut skin beneath her hands and by how fast his heart was beating. When he began to undo her gown and brushed his lips over hers, she sighed and gave in. Nothing seemed quite as vital to her at the moment as the need to know his touch again.

After he removed her gown, he gently pushed her down onto the bed and covered her body with his. Tess clung to him, occasionally easing her grip only enough to allow him to finish undressing her. When their flesh finally met, she trembled. She was starved for him, the night she had spent believing him gone forever only adding to her hunger.

Tess greedily welcomed his every caress, his every kiss, and did her best to return each one in kind. She could not seem to get enough of the feel of him, of the taste of him. For as long as she could, she fought to restrain her body's screaming need for completion. She wanted the pleasure, the sweet closeness, to last forever.

When Revan finally united their fevered bodies, she cried out with a mixture of heady delight and faint disappointment that the lovemaking would soon end. She clung to him, returning his fierce kiss, and tried to pull him as deeply within her as she could. Her release forced the words she had kept locked in her heart out of her mouth in a passion-thickened cry. She paid no heed to that compulsive confession, hearing only Revan hoarsely calling her name as she sank into the blind abyss of need. Tess held him close, her limbs curled around his lean body, when he slumped against her.

She watched him carefully when he finally eased the intimacy of their embrace and moved to wash up. Even when he gently performed that intimate service for her, she could not stop looking at him. She told herself not to be such a fool, but a part of her was still afraid that he was not real, that he was simply a vision produced by her exhausted mind.

Revan returned to bed and started to tug the covers down. Tess moved to slip beneath the lavender-scented sheets and felt something crinkle beneath her backside. She frowned at the letter she tugged out from beneath her as she joined Revan beneath the covers. Someone had left it on the top of the bedcovers, but they had missed it in their need to make love. Her eyes widened when she saw Revan's name scrawled on it, as well as the king's seal.

"'Tis for you." She handed it to him and saw by his expression that he was as surprised as she.

"Mayhaps 'tis just some orders," he murmured as he tore it open and, slipping his arm about her shoulders, held her close while he read it. His amusement over how hard she tried not to read his letter faded as he discovered what the king had written to him.

"I have been given all that MacKinnon owned," he said, his voice soft with shock. "A fine piece of property and what coin and goods there might be to tally up."

"Oh, Revan, 'tis wondrous news. 'Tis well past time that he gave ye some reward for your loyalty."

Tess impulsively kissed him, then snuggled closer to his side. She was happy for him but knew that her happiness was prompted by more than Revan finally getting some of the reward he so richly deserved. Now he had land and coin in his purse. Now they were just a little more equal. She glanced up at him and frowned. He was looking at her a little oddly.

"Is something wrong?" she asked. "Must ye leave on the morrow or something?"

"Nay. Tessa? When ye were told that ye were granted Thurkettle's lands and money, were ye told anything else?"

"Well, Uncle Silvio did say that there were a few curious conditions, but he said discussing them could wait."

"The rogue," Revan muttered, then laughed and shook his head.

"What is it?"

"Your uncle has been aware of your decision to set me free for quite a while, I think."

"Well, there is the chance that he was told ere we left Isabella's. Why?"

"Because we have been playing his game. 'Tis the only reason he didna tell ye, or me, what those curious conditions were. Aye, Thurkettle's fortune is yours. However, 'tis now half mine. It seems the king gifted it to you *if* ye didna become my wife by *my* choice. In other words, if I ended the betrothal, ye got all of this. But if we did wed as planned, then it was to be yours and mine equally."

She snatched the letter from Revan as she sat up straighter, then read it—twice. "Can he do that?"

"He is the king." Revan kissed her cheek. "He can do whatever he pleases. Are ye angry?"

"Nay," she said, then shook her head. "Uncle Silvio has been toying with us. If he had told ye about this—"

"I might have stayed? He probably thought it would be a poor reason for me to do so, and he was right. He wanted me to come back to you because I had discovered that it was what I wanted, not because the king graciously made us more equal. Your uncle wanted me to win over my own choking pride *before* I wed you."

"Is that what ye did, Revan?" she asked in a soft voice.

He held her close, resting his cheek against her hair. "Aye. Mayhaps I just needed to be faced with losing you." He shrugged. "I also discovered that, when I eyed my pride squarely and honestly, it carried the taint of envy."

"Envy? Why? I did naught to earn all of this. Ye have

earned everything ye have, even when it was but a few riders in your purse. I got what I have through other people dying.''

Revan chuckled, then pulled back a little to meet her gaze. "Ye earned this place, lass."

"Aye." She smiled, feeling a small tingle of pride. "I suppose I did in a way."

He gently brushed a few strands of hair from her face. "I rode away thinking that ye were right. And, aye, ye were, but only because I had not taken the time to look at myself closely. Everyone had told me that I was the only one who viewed marrying an heiress in the way I did. They told me that it didna matter what ye had if I kenned in my heart and mind that I wasna marrying for gain. Aye, and that ye kenned it, too."

"I never thought ye were after my fortune, Revan. Not even when we were in that cave and I lied about how much I had. I canna explain why I did that, but I swear it wasna because I thought ye would want it."

"Maybe ye already sensed what a thickheaded fool I could be." He smiled when she shook her head. "Aye, I was. I was willing to toss away our happiness, hurt both of us, simply because I didna want a few people to speak ill of me. When I rode away, I was reluctant, confused, and miserable. When I made the decision to return, all of that faded. That was even more proof of how great a mistake I had nearly made. For the sake of my overwhelming pride, I was walking away from what I really wanted, deserting and hurting a wee brown lass who loved me more than I deserved."

His words made her feel wonderful, but she tensed slightly over the last few. "I never said that," she was compelled to say, and she lowered her gaze so that he could not look into her eyes.

"Aye. Ye did." He grinned as he cupped her chin in his hand and forced her to meet his gaze. "Ye fairly screamed it not long ago. I was—'' He laughed when she quickly put her hand over his mouth.

'' 'Twas but the heat of the moment,'' she muttered as she recalled the particular moment he referred to.

Revan studied her for a little while, then asked in a soft voice, ''Have I made ye afraid to love me, Tessa?''

''Nay! I just—'' She bit her lip, not sure what she could say without confirming what she had just tried to deny.

''Ah, 'tis pride, then.'' He pushed her down onto her back and lightly pinned her there with his body.

''Everyone has a little,'' she mumbled.

''Aye, and we should see more clearly than most just how dangerous it can be if we let it rule us.''

''I am not letting it rule me,'' she protested. It was pure cowardice, a fear of opening her heart to him and not getting all that she hungered for in return, but she was not going to confess that to him.

''Then look me in the eye and tell me that ye dinna love me.''

Tess glared at him. He was playing the game unfairly. She had to be the poorest liar in all of Scotland, and they both knew it. The words might come from her lips smoothly enough, but her eyes would reveal the truth.

''Oh, why dinna ye go and do something besides tormenting me? Thrashing Uncle Silvio would be nice.''

Revan laughed and kissed her neck before looking into her eyes again. ''Say it. Ye canna spit out the lie, can ye?''

''Oh, all right then, curse your hide. I love you. Happy now?'' She started with surprise when he gave her a hearty kiss.

''So sweetly spoken,'' he murmured, laughter in his voice. ''Ye do ken how to woo a man, lass.'' He laughed when she lightly punched him on the chest. ''Come, Tessa, where is the harm in our loving each other? Why do ye fear it?''

''Loving each other?'' she repeated his words in a nervous whisper. ''Ye love me?''

"What do ye think brought me back here?"

"Duty. Honor. Your horse."

He ignored that last muttered nonsense. "Neither duty nor honor was strong enough to cure me of my destructive pride. I love you." He wrapped his arms around her when she suddenly clung to him, pressing her face against his chest. "'Twas what made me realize that returning was the only thing to do, the right thing."

"When did ye ken that ye loved me?"

"Well, 'tis rather hard to say. I didna want to, did I? My pride ruled me, and I kenned that loving you was the surest way to make me act against that pride. 'Twas there but I tried to ignore it. Even when ye fell into Thurkettle's hands and I was half-mad with fear for you, I tried very hard not to admit why that should be. When did ye ken that ye loved me?" He rubbed his cheek against her soft hair as he waited for her reply.

"In the cave. That night that ye went out to lead Thurkettle's men astray. When ye returned unhurt, I kenned it then. Well, I admitted it to myself then."

"Aye. I am sure, now, that that is when I began to love you, if I hadna begun already."

For a long time she held him close, silent as she savored the knowledge that he loved her. She needed a while to control herself, suffering from an absurd urge to weep. Revan would never understand that the tears would be ones of joy, of release from all her fears. Men saw tears as a sign of something wrong, and she knew that now was not a good time to try and teach Revan otherwise.

"Will everything be all right now, Revan?" she finally asked, needing assurance that he had truly conquered his pride, that it and the bitter anger it could stir would not return to haunt them.

"Aye, my wee brown love. Everything will be all right. I will save my pride for more worthy things, such as my pretty brown-eyed wife and all the bonnie bairns we shall have together. That trouble is behind us. 'Twas left to rot in the forest where I sat for so long and wrestled with my own heart and mind.''

She closed her eyes and sighed with relief. Love could have merely overshadowed his pride, leaving it to stir to life later. His words convinced her that she did not need to fear that. That threat to her happiness was truly gone.

''Are ye at ease then, Tessa?''

''Aye.''

''No more fears?''

''Well . . . I wouldna say that.'' She smiled against his skin when he laughed. ''Marriage is a very grave matter. I wish to do it right, to have such a good one.''

''Ye will, lass.'' He tipped her face up toward his and touched a kiss to her mouth. ''Just love me as I love you, and our marriage can only be good.''

''I believe I can do that. 'Twill be very easy.'' She ran her foot up and down his calf. ''Did ye decide on which name ye wished for your horse?''

''Aye—Amigo. I dinna suppose ye gave any thought to what ye might call this place?'' He began to nibble her ear.

''Aye. Casa de Halyard. And—Revan?'' She smoothed her hands over his broad back.

''What?'' Moving his gentle kisses to her throat, he began to lose interest in the conversation.

''*I* will name all of our children.'' She grinned when he briefly glanced her way, then laughed. ''I shudder to think of our wee bairns spending their early years as 'Boy' or 'Girl.' ''

He cupped her face in his hands. ''And we shall have the bonniest bairns in all of Scotland.''

''Aye, with fine blue-gray eyes and fair hair.''

''I was thinking of deep brown eyes and coal-black hair.''

''Is this the first disagreement of our marriage?'' she asked with a faint smile.

Revan smiled back at her. '' 'Twould be nice if they were all so small. Just never forget that, no matter how angry I might become or how foolish I might act at times, I do love you, Contessa Comyn Delgado Halyard.''

"Ah, aye, and I love you," she whispered. "So very much. And I shall love you—until the last day of forever."

"'Twill do for a start," he murmured and kissed her.